Between Two

Dreams

S. LEE FISHER

THE WOMEN OF CAMPBELL COUNTY BOOK 4

Copyright © 2023 by S. Lee Fisher and RNS Publishing

All rights reserved. No part of this publication may be reproduced, distributed, or transmitted in any form or by any means, including photocopying, recording, or other electronic or mechanical methods, without the prior written permission of the publisher, except in the case of brief quotations embodied in critical reviews and specific other non-commercial uses permitted by law.

All characters and events depicted in this novel are entirely fictitious. Any similarity to actual events or persons, living or dead, is purely coincidental.

Warning: the unauthorized reproduction or distribution of this copyrighted work is illegal. Criminal copyright infringement, including infringement without monetary gain, is investigated by the FBI and is punishable by up to five years in prison and a fine of $250,000.

For more information, email: sleefisher@sleefisher.com

Beta Readers: Nola Li Barr, Inghild Okland
Editing: Wandering Words Media
Cover Design: Best Page Forward

*Dedicated to Ralph with love, my biggest fan.
You are my one and my only dream come true.*

1

NASH RAMBLER

CAMPBELLSVILLE, PA, AUGUST 1953

Twenty-three-year-old Harriett Bailey Kepler parked her stately, light green Buick Roadmaster sedan at the end of the driveway. The path to the garage was blocked by a tomato-red Nash Rambler convertible and a smiling, wavy-haired, blond, muscular man wearing a white T-shirt and a pair of chino trousers. She rolled her eyes.

"Isn't she pretty!" Eddy, Harriett's estranged husband, proudly waved his hand at the vehicle.

Harriett closed the car door. Smoothing her skirt, she chuckled. "It is cute. Did they forget to make half the car?"

Eddy blushed as he jumped into the driver's seat without opening the door. "She's what they call 'compact.'"

"Well, I agree with that statement. It's at least three feet shorter than my sedan. I think they forgot to add a trunk!"

Eddy turned the ignition, firing a sputtering six-cylinder engine. "I have all the room I need. Move that boat of yours, and I'll take you for a ride."

She grabbed her briefcase from the passenger seat. Walking up the long flight of stone steps leading to the most prominent house in Campbellsville, she turned and said,

"Not tonight, Eddy. I have a ton of paperwork to review before my board meeting in the morning." Tossing him her keys, she added, "Park mine in the garage. Move yours to the street!"

Eddy pouted. "Since I got back from Korea, all you do is work. How am I supposed to win you back if you never have any fun?"

Her head snapped to attention. "Korea? You mean Italy, don't you?"

"Ah, yeah. Italy. I only say 'Korea' because, you know, that was the bigger war." He turned to hide his wide eyes. *Oops!*

Before entering the double outer door to the red brick estate, she asked, "By some miracle, did you make supper? I mean, you're here, bothering me."

Eddy frowned and slowly exited the Rambler, hesitating before admitting, "Ah...no." He bound up the steps two at a time until he was beside Harriett. He reached for her shoulder as she opened the door. "I was car shopping today."

She exhaled a deep sigh. "Did you even go to work? Even if you are Alice's brother-in-law, Mr. Lupinetti won't tolerate unreliability. And if you don't work, how will you pay for your new toy?" She pointed to the convertible, then added, "As far as winning me back, I spelled that out very clearly."

The recently reunited couple was separated three years ago after only a few months of marriage. A drafted Eddy was shipped off to Trieste, Italy while Harriett remained stateside, living with her parents. She completed secretarial school, then college, before entering the fast lane for promotion, first to lead secretary, then on to General Manager, before finally landing an executive role with Dugan and Co. For reasons unknown to Harriett, Eddy failed to communicate with her while abroad. Now, discharged and back home, he naively assumed nothing had changed. To his surprise, rather than a welcome home with open arms,

Harriett presented him with a list of criteria to be met before she'd even consider reuniting, the biggest of which was tending to her mother, Olive Bailey. Eddy conveniently ignored the list.

Harriett closed the door in Eddy's face, threw her attaché in her office, and trudged out to the kitchen to begin evening meal preparation. The petite college graduate, known for exceptional intelligence, physical strength, and mastery of baking, fell short in cooking skills. Kitchen adeptness eluded the otherwise talented brunette. Harriett simply could not cook, even to save her eternal soul.

She flung open the refrigerator door and stared into space. *What is wrong with that man?* Her arm automatically reached for the egg tray to make her signature dish, egg salad sandwiches. She slapped her hand. "Stop. Geez Louise, pick something else."

Grape jelly, made from the vines planted by her father, sat next to the eggs. Her second favorite food. Her shoulder dropped at the thought of Tobias Bailey, Papa. It had been ten months. She wondered how long she would feel the raw pain of his death. Perhaps forever.

Harriett untied the plastic bag of Wonder Bread, grabbed two slices and the jar of Skippy peanut butter, and placed them on the yellow chrome kitchen table beside her sister Alice's homemade jelly. Sandwich assembled, she carried her plate along with a glass of milk into her office, closed the door, and sat down at her desk.

Three file folders of equal importance needed the attention of Dugan and Co.'s first female CFO. She knew she was in for a long evening, but willingly attacked her chores, realizing her scheduling demands would increase with the start of the fall semester's classes for her master's degree next month.

No sooner did Harriett open the first file when Eddy

barged into the room, out of breath. "Harriett, I'm sorry, don't be mad."

She slowly lifted her head from her papers. "Eddy, why all the drama? I thought the army would have drilled that out of you. What are you talking about?"

Eddy bit his lower lip. Hanging his head, he said, "I accidentally backed into the telephone pole."

"Backed—what? My Buick! Are you kidding me?" Harriett jumped to her feet, bolting out the door to survey any damage. The sleek, curved chrome back bumper was dented, dead center. "Geez Louise, Eddy! How did you not see the pole?"

"I'm sorry, Harriett, I really am."

"All you had to do was back mine onto the street, pull yours out of the way, then drive mine in. Was that too much to ask?" In an unsuccessful effort, she licked her finger and rubbed; trying to buff out a black streak. "Give me the keys. I'll pull it in myself."

Harriett snatched the chain from Eddy and easily pulled the two-ton vehicle into the garage.

Eddy ran to open her door. "It's so big compared to mine. I didn't think I was that far back."

"Eddy, I'm not going to question you again. But in the two months since your return home, you have not succeeded in fulfilling even half of my list. You only got a part-time job. You refuse to admit why you didn't write those three years. You're supposed to help me around the house. And I must constantly remind you to check on Mother." Her hands flew to her hips. "I expect more of you, and I expect it now. This weekend, we talk. Do you understand?"

His head bobbed up and down. "Yes, Mrs. Boss. I understand. Don't wait up for me. I'm going to the club!" He jumped into the Rambler.

"Get it through your thick head. You don't live here, Eddy! Not until you meet my demands."

Ignoring her reply, Eddy threw the car in gear and sped off to the veteran's club for a night of gossip and beer.

∞ ∞ ∞

Earl Kepler was sitting at the bar drinking a beer when Eddy sauntered in, looking tanned and smug.

"Hey, Earl, fancy meeting you here. Isn't Mom cooking tonight?" Eddy laughed at his own comment, knowing Abigail Kepler possessed less cooking skill than Harriett.

"It's Thursday night; Mom has Bible study. After living there all these years, you really can't remember?" Earl shook his head in disgust. Eddy returned home in late May, and already Earl was tired of his brother's immature actions, especially when it came to Harriett. "I eat here every Thursday evening."

Eddy waved him off. "Yeah, yeah. I remember now." Abandoning Earl, Eddy crossed the room to join two high school buddies. "Keith, Bobby, how goes it?"

Bobby watched Eddy approach. Turning to Keith, he whispered, "Crap, here comes Kepler. He's such a worthless piece of..."

The blast of a siren halted his comment and Eddy's advance. Two shorts followed by two long bursts signaled all Campbellsville volunteer firemen to assemble quickly.

Keith grabbed his hat and suit jacket. Running toward the door, he muttered, "It had to be on a day when I wore my best suit. My wife will kill me if I get this dirty."

Eddy watched as half the room bolted toward the exit and the fire station. Like many rural communities, Campbellsville did not pay full-time employees as firefighters. Instead, they relied on its citizenship to voluntarily supply disaster protection. A simple signaling siren system alerted firemen and the general population to the type of emergency. One long repeating blast indicated a structure fire, repeating short blows was a forest fire, while two shorts followed by two longs warned of a vehicular crash.

Eddy and Earl quickly finished their beers; Earl grabbed his food "to go," and they headed home as the siren continued to call Campbellsville to action. No fun was to be found at the Vet's club that evening.

The brothers sat in the living room, watching *The Jack Benny Program* on television. Earl glanced at his watch as he turned the knob from the Pittsburgh CBS station to WIIC, noting that Abigail was long overdue home.

"Hey, switch channels to WMAC. I like the local Madison News."

Eddy's command was interrupted by Abigail opening the front door. She dabbed her swollen red eyes with her handkerchief.

"Mom, what's the matter? Why are you so late? Are you okay?" Earl rushed to his mother's side.

"Oh, it's been just the most wretched night." She paused to blow her nose. "Do you remember Mrs. Eddington?" She looked directly at Earl. "I believe she was in your class at school?"

Earl guided Abigail to a chair before answering. "You mean Debra Garland? Yes, she graduated a year ahead of me. Her sister Karen was in my class."

"She's a member of our Bible study group. Nice woman, a little flighty, brings cookies and brownies all the time."

Eddy raised his eyebrows at his capricious mother, labeling someone else as flighty.

Abigail continued. "Her son, Tommy. Such a good boy! Eddy, you know who I mean, don't you?"

Eddy shook his head. "Mom, get on with your story."

"Tommy is the boy that bought your old car. I tell you, that boy looked up to you, Eddy. He nearly broke your high school football records. Tried to copy you every way possible."

Earl rubbed his mother's back. "Mom, what are you getting at?"

"That child, Tommy, was going to Penn State on a football scholarship." Abigail began sobbing. "He was to leave next week to begin practice." She pointed and waved her index finger directly at Eddy. "You could have done the same thing, son!"

"Take a couple of deep breaths, Mom. What happened to Tommy Eddington?"

"Earl, he crashed. Was killed in a head-on collision." Abigail wiped her eyes on her sleeve. "Mrs. Eddington won't be baking brownies anymore."

The weight of Abigail's announcement hit Eddy directly in the stomach. He caught his breath as the color drained from his face. To steady his trembling hands, he grabbed the arms of his chair. "Mom, you said he's dead?"

"Yes, Eddy. Gosh, he tried to be just like you. All Debra talked about was how Tommy idolized you. Eddy this and Eddy that. That kid worshiped you."

Eddy felt a chill throughout his body. His stomach churned, acid burning his throat and mouth. He gagged. "I think I'm going to be sick." Covering his mouth with his hand, he darted out of the room.

Earl handed his mother a glass of water. "Here, Mom, drink this. Calm yourself."

She swallowed, then asked, "What's with Eddy? That was a strange reaction."

No sooner had she posed the question when the TV anchorman reported. "Now we have breaking news from Campbellsville. Eighteen-year-old Tommy Eddington, high school football star and upcoming Penn State freshman player, was fatally injured in tonight's head-on car crash. It happened on state route 58, what the locals call 'Creek Road,' just after six this evening. Eddington was returning home from his summer job when a pick-up truck driven by Pittsburgh resident Rodney Smith crossed over on a curve into Eddington's lane. Both drivers were killed immediately."

Eddy returned in time to see a picture of his old car, folded like an accordion, being towed from the scene. Any remaining stomach contents were spewed onto the floor.

2

THE MORNING AFTER

The following day, Eddy washed his face and brushed his teeth. The mirror reflected puffy red eyes circled in dark bags of drooping skin, resulting from a night of sleepless tossing to and fro. Eddy finished shaving, then dressed in his best shirt and trousers. He sat at the kitchen table, rubbing his eyes as the clock at the town hall chimed six times.

Earl yawned as he took the chair opposite Eddy. "Little brother, why are you up so early?"

Eddy frowned before answering. "That accident last night got to me, Earl."

"I hope not just because the 'infamous Eddy Kepler car' is squashed. Please tell me there is more to you than that!"

"Cut the sarcasm. I'm serious. What kind of role model was I to that kid? Or to any other kid? Mom says he idolized me."

"I'll not disagree. You are a piece of trash!"

"So much for brotherly love! I mean it, that kid was going to Penn State on a football scholarship to play for Rip Engle.

That could have been me! Should have been me, if I wasn't such a screw-up."

"Again, no argument here."

"Earl, don't you get it? It's time for me to grow up." Eddy sipped a cup of coffee, choked, then added creamer. "God, she can't even brew a decent cup of Joe."

"So you're finally growing up, Peter Pan?" Earl tossed Eddy a warm slice of buttered toast.

"I'm going to Madison to get my old job back at the mill. Then I'm going to look in on that despicable Olive Bailey. Maybe Harriett will take me seriously next time, when I ask her out again."

Earl scratched his head. "I heard her prerequisites. Are you going to tell her why you were silent for three years? Come completely clean?"

Eddy tilted his head to the side. "I have to if I want her back. So, yes, I am."

Earl contemplated the conversation. He leaned toward his brother before speaking. "Eddy, you better damn well be genuine with her. She deserves the truth of Rosa and Joey and your antics in Italy. Be sure to tell her about Korea too." He stood, walking to his brother; he clasped Eddy's shoulders and squeezed tightly.

"Ouch. Easy there!" Eddy swiped at the air, missing his target.

"You don't merit that good woman. She's truly amazing." Earl tightened his grip again. "Treat her right, brother, or you'll have to answer to me."

∞ ∞ ∞

Dante Lupinetti answered the knock at the front door. "Eddy, you're not scheduled to work today. What can I do for you?"

Eddy lowered his head. "Mr. Lupinetti, sir, I probably need to resign."

"Why only probably?" The grocer chuckled at his part-time butcher's remark.

"Well, if I get my old job back at the mill, then yes, I need to quit. But, if I don't, then…I need more hours."

"Good luck, son. I hope you get the job, because, truthfully, I can't afford more hours. I only hired you because you are our dear Alice's brother-in-law and because you worked here in high school. I'm already fully staffed."

Eddy relaxed. He grabbed Mr. Lupinetti's hand and pumped. "Thank you, sir. I'll let you know this afternoon."

Eddy parked the Rambler in the parking lot outside the Madison steel mill. He looked skyward at the cloud of ash hanging in the air. *This car will disintegrate within a year from all this crap. If I'm hired, I better ride the bus*, he thought.

A smartly dressed blonde sat at the reception desk in the lobby of mill headquarters. Eddy smiled, his eyes twinkling, as he greeted her.

"Hi. I'm Eddy Kepler." He extended his hand. "I was hoping to be hired." He blurted the words.

"Hello, Eddy Kepler. If you have a seat over there, I'll call my head of hiring." She smiled back and pointed to a row of straight-backed wooden chairs. She watched, admiring his body and the whisp of hair that curled on his forehead, as he walked to the other side of the room.

Eddy stared at the hands of the wall clock as they moved from quarter past the hour to quarter till the hour. His leg bounced up and down when the girl called out, "Eddy Kepler, Mr. Mack will see you now. Please follow me."

Eddy walked down the hallway to the sound of the girl's heels clicking on the tile floor. She motioned toward an open door; Eddy entered.

A man of about 40 years of age, hair graying at the temples, extended his hand as Eddy removed his hat.

"Have a seat, son. Did I hear Miss Donahue correctly? Your name is Kepler?"

Eddy shook his hand in return. "Yes, sir, Eddy Kepler."

"You wouldn't happen to be related to Harriett Kepler, would you? Now that is one talented little woman!"

Eddy inhaled at the mention of Harriett. "She's my wife."

Mr. Mack slapped Eddy on his back. "You don't say! Well, what brings you here today, son? How may I help you?"

Exhaling, Eddy replied, "I'm looking for work. I just returned from Korea, sir, and I...well, I need a job. Can't let my wife support me." He added, with bravado.

"No, you cannot! Although, she is capable of supporting even more than herself and her husband." Mack chuckled. "Where did you graduate from college? Are you a metallurgist?"

Eddy blushed. "Sorry, sir. I don't have a college degree. You see, I was drafted and never finished school."

"Thank you for your service, son. What skills do you own? What job did you have in the service?"

"I was in property procurement. I worked in supply."

"Splendid. I think I have just the job for you." It was Mack's turn to blush. "But Kepler, I'm terribly sorry—this is an entry-level position, and I'm sure it's well below your skill level. Hell, if you have half the talent of your wife, you'll be running the entire department before long." Mack paused. "I'll tell you what I'll do. I'll move you in as an apprentice, with the promise of promotion within six months. I can squeeze a little more for you in salary too, considering Harriett—I mean, Mrs. Kepler."

Eddy smirked, smiling the infamous Eddy Kepler grin. *Damn*, he thought. *Harriett, you really are an asset!* "You have a deal, Mr. Mack. I'm humbled. I don't mind working my way up the ladder. It's only fair."

Mack reached for Eddy's hand. "Splendid. Can you start Monday? Provided that meets Harriett's schedule."

"Monday it is, Mr. Mack. I'll see you bright and early, say nine a.m.?"

Mack blushed the second time that day, "Perhaps eight-thirty, if it's not an imposition?"

"You got it!" Eddy swaggered as he retreated down the hall toward the exit. "I'll be damned!"

∞ ∞ ∞

He drove directly to the grocery store to inform Mr. Lupinetti that his resignation was, indeed, a request for termination of employment. Olive entered the store as Eddy was leaving.

"Olive, my luck today is on a roll!" Eddy blocked her from entering.

"Who are you? Move, you twit. You're blocking my way," she said, sneering. Recognition crossed her brow as her lips turned up at the corners. "I'll be damned. It's my delinquent son-in-law. Precious Harriett's pet project. Do you mind stepping aside?"

"Olive, let me help you, please. I'll wait for you to finish shopping, then I'll drive you home or take you to your next destination. I gather Friday is errand day?"

"You gather correctly. What's all this sugar and honey about?" She cocked her head. "Oh, I get it! Trying to get to Harriett through me. Well, you're dumber than I remember. That girl is dead to me. I want nothing to do with her and she of me. So go sniffing around some other tree to get in with her good graces. You're wasting your time here."

Olive pushed him aside. Barging into the store, she

handed a grinning Lupinetti her list. "This afternoon will do!" Then spinning on her heel, she charged out.

"Olive, Mrs. Bailey, wait." Eddy rushed after her. "I mean it. Let me take you home." He pointed to the Nash Rambler. "My car's over there."

Olive snickered. "Well, it's better than that last hunk of junk you owned, but not by much!" She waited for Eddy to open the door.

Flashbacks to his days courting Harriett washed over him. A chill ran through his body, despite the hot August sun.

"Allow me," he said as he held the passenger door.

To himself, he thought, *at least she and I are on the same page.*

Eddy parked the Rambler on Maple Street. Walking Olive to her door, he reached for her arm as she approached the two steps to the back porch.

Olive jerked away. "Don't touch me! What the hell is the matter with you? Leave me alone."

Eddy sucked in a long deep breath. Harriett is a clever girl. This is not an easy assignment. It will take every last nerve to deal with this witch. No wonder she wanted to be rid of Olive.

"Olive, seriously, I only want to help. Do you have any chores that need to be done? Gardening, repairs, anything?" He glanced around the yard at the weed-infested beds and immediately regretted his question.

Olive unlocked the door. She returned within a minute, throwing a hoe at him, she said, "Have fun, Pretty Boy!"

∞ ∞ ∞

Eddy dragged his feet up Keplers' porch step and into the house after brushing dirt from his trousers. Why did I offer to work when I'm dressed in my good clothes? he thought. Hope Mom can get out the grass stains!

The Kepler homestead was a modest shingle house with a small, rarely used kitchen. The dining room was filled with a large, round, pedestal oak table surrounded by eight mismatched chairs. A crowded living room held a large, upright, out-of-tune piano that Abigail pounded relentlessly, several upholstered chairs, and a sofa, all popping at the seams. Two full-sized bedrooms and two dormer bedrooms completed the second floor. Abigail and Edgar Sr. occupied the largest room, with all the boys piling into the other large bedroom, now in Earl's possession. Eddy, happy not to be sharing, had taken the most generous of the two tiny dormer rooms. All shared one bath.

Eddy plopped into a stuffed living room chair, too tired to walk to the dining room.

In the kitchen with Abigail, Earl was heating soup while she assembled sandwiches. "Eddy, is that you? Not like you to be late for dinner. Come help carry."

She was answered with a grunt followed by the sound of snoring. Earl wandered into the living room to find his disheveled brother spread over the chair, arms dangling at his side, head back, mouth open, making ungodly snorting sounds.

Earl kicked his foot. "Eddy, wake up. Time to eat."

"Huh?" Eddy, rubbing his face, smeared dirt from chin to forehead. He opened his lids to see Abigail and Earl standing over him, both laughing.

"Looks like my son put in his first decent day's work since coming home." She turned to leave. "I'll get you a wet cloth to clean up."

"Mom, stop coddling him. He's a grown man. He can walk to the bathroom." Earl shook his head, then returned to the dining room. "Come on, Mom. Let's eat while the soup is hot."

Fifteen minutes later, Eddy hauled himself to the dining

room with a clean face and hands. "Mom, I'm sorry to make a mess of my clothes, but do you think you can get the grime out?"

"I'll try, Son. How did you get them so dirty?" Abigail asked as she crunched a garden radish.

"I helped Harriett's mother today with some yard work." Eddy slurped his soup hungrily.

Earl and Abigail glanced at each other; eyebrows raised. "What did you do for her? Clean the coal shoot?" Earl chuckled. "You're a mess."

"I know. I know. I should have changed clothes first." Eddy bit into his sandwich, adding as he chewed, "I want to make this right with Harriett. Oh, and I almost forgot—I got a real job today."

"Congratulations, Eddy! At the mill?"

"Yeah, it turns out having Harriett as a wife is a real advantage. I'm working in the office in supply, not on the mill floor." Eddy managed a wide grin.

Earl puckered his lips and nose. "Did you take advantage of her position and hard work?"

"Of course! But, it was easy. Seems she has quite the reputation in Madison." Eddy's fingers flew into the air. "I didn't have to stretch the truth—at least, not much."

Earl stood, pushing his chair back. He leaned toward his brother. "You watch yourself. I'm keeping tabs on you, and you don't have room for error."

"Geez, Earl. You're awfully protective of my wife." Eddy closed his fingers into a fist. "I think I'm the one that should be warning you." He raised his arm. "Stay away from my wife!"

Earl rolled his eyes. "She's my dear sister-in-law, that's all."

Eddy ate a second sandwich as Abigail scurried, cleaning

up the kitchen. Washing his food down with a can of beer, he belched before finally leaving the table.

"Eddy, I've been waiting ten minutes for your plate so I can finish in here. Did you just walk away and leave it on the table?" Abigail stood hands on hips, staring at the lone crumb-filled plate. "Did you leave your manners overseas?"

∞ ∞ ∞

Harriett unlocked the front door to the sound of ringing. She ran to her office and grabbed the receiver, hoping she made it in time. "Harriett Bailey Kepler, speaking."

"Harriett. Hi, it's Eddy." He waited for the voice to answer.

Clicking her tongue, Harriett inhaled to catch her breath. "Hi, Eddy. I just walked in the door. How may I help you?"

"So formal? I called to tell you that I'm serious about working on your list."

She dropped her briefcase onto the floor, then slid a swivel chair away from the desk. "It's about time. Just what are you doing?"

"To start, this morning I got a job at the mill, but not as a laborer. It seems my Army skills have paid off. I'll be working in supply. Got me a regular desk job!"

Harriett looked at her wristwatch before speaking. "Good for you. Ah, Eddy, sorry, but I have an appointment. I hate to cut this short, but I must run."

"Wait, don't hang up. I saw your mom today. Can you spare me a few seconds to tell you?"

She pursed her lips. Her ruse failed. "Fine, I'll talk a bit." She sank into the chair in surrender as evening shadows filled the room.

"Thanks, kiddo. I worked all afternoon in her garden. I was thinking; maybe we could go to a movie tomorrow night? You used to enjoy them. What do you say?" He crossed his fingers behind his back.

"This is my last free weekend before the fall semester starts. I've enrolled in two weeknights and one Saturday class again, so I'm extremely busy." She exhaled a long deep sigh. "But...okay, why not? Make it the early show, and you can tell me all about your job and Mother. Now, I really must go." She cradled the receiver.

Eddy smiled, fist-pumping the air as he listened to the dial tone. "I got it made in the shade!"

3

PICTURE SHOW

Harriett glanced at the clock as she labored through her stack of paperwork. *Yikes*, she thought. *This day is flying by*. Picking up the phone, she requested C-A-one-seven-five, crossed her fingers, then waited for her call to be answered.

"Hello," said the baritone voice.

"Earl, good. I was hoping you'd answer." Unaware that she was holding her breath, Harriett exhaled. "Any chance you can visit tomorrow afternoon? It's been a while since we chatted, and this is my last free weekend."

"Sure, Harriett. What time? I hear you're finally going out with Eddy tonight."

"Did he mention our date?" She frowned, unaware of the flutter going up and down Earl's body.

"It's all he can talk about. He's been bragging all day." The tingling dissipated as the realization set in that Harriett and Eddy would most likely get back together, despite Eddy's transgressions.

"We're just going to the movies. It's not like he's moving in." Immediately she regretted her harsh words to Earl and that she accepted the date with Eddy. "He wants to tell me about Olive and his new job."

"He finally came to his senses, understands just how special you are." Earl started pacing around the phone stand. "From my viewpoint, it's long overdue." Earl paused before adding, "Harriett, I'll be over tomorrow afternoon, but…be careful tonight, please."

Harriett cocked her head to the side. "I shall Earl, but that's a strange thing to say, isn't it? He's my husband. He wouldn't hurt me, would he?"

"Not physically, not physically." Earl rolled his eyes, knowing Eddy's secret and the pain it already inflicted on Harriett.

Harriett replaced the receiver, collected her paperwork, straightened the bottom edges, and placed it in her leather attaché. The attaché, monogrammed "HBK,' was given to her by Earl when she graduated with her bachelor's degree. Only 15 months ago, though it seemed like years. She had already completed six courses toward her master's degree when her incommunicado soldier husband wrote to say he was coming home—coming home! Three years he went without writing, leaving Harriett in the lurch, wondering why. Was he sick, or wounded, or did he just not care?

When Eddy returned in May, he demanded refuge in Hill House, *Harriett's* house, which she purchased with her diligently earned money. Harriett refused, giving him a list of prerequisites to meet before she would consider accepting him as her husband again. To obtain redemption, he must find a job, contribute financially toward household expenses, sleep in a separate bedroom, confess the circumstances of his silence, and most of all, assume responsibility for Harriett's contrary mother, Olive Bailey.

Three months passed without Eddy making a concerted attempt to restore his status as a husband, then, out of the blue, he called yesterday saying he found a job and worked at Olive's. Harriett deliberated her decision for a moment, then headed upstairs to bathe and dress for her date.

∞ ∞ ∞

The doorbell rang promptly at 6:45. Harriett grabbed her purse from the entryway credenza. Locking both sets of doors, she turned to see Eddy standing on the front stoop, a bouquet of daisies in his hand.

"Wait, Harriett. Put these in water before we go." He thrust the flowers in her face.

"Thank you. Achoo!" She sneezed, took the flowers, unlocked the door, and ran to the kitchen. She grabbed her only vase, an exquisitely cut crystal antique circa the Civil War, from the dining room. She shoved the flowers in then filled the vessel with water. "Okay, let's go. I don't want to miss the previews."

Eddy held the passenger door for her, remembering their first date when she forced him to remember his manners.

"Thank you," she said as she took her seat in the Rambler. She fingered the faux woodgrain dash. "Nice car. Tiny, but nice."

"Just like you." The Infamous Kepler grin filled his face. He quickly slipped into a parking spot one block from the theater. "You don't mind walking, do you? This is opening night, and I'm afraid the show will be packed."

"No, I enjoy the exercise," the athletic woman replied. "What's playing? I didn't bother looking, since I so rarely go out."

"Campbellsville went all out this week with a number one, grade-A release: *From Here to Eternity*. I'm shocked they paid to bring it here so soon, but happy they did."

Harriett whistled. "Wow. They were talking about that

movie at the office." She rubbed her hands together and quickened her pace. "Come on, Eddy, let's get good seats."

Scurrying down the center aisle, she found two seats, literally in the middle of the left side of the theater.

"Excuse me," she said as she began her climb over four patrons on the aisle.

"Harriett, surprise seeing you here." The voice belonged to Bobby Renner. "Lynette, Keith, move over so Harriett doesn't have to scale the likes of us to find a seat."

"Thanks, Bobby." She waited for the foursome to slide in before sitting.

"My pleasure." Bobby smiled, hoping to take advantage of his viewing partner to increase his standing in the community and his place of business. His wife, Lynette, punched him in the side as if to say, *well done.*

Leaning over Bobby, she capitalized, "Harriett, we are having guests over next weekend, for Labor Day. Please join us? It's just a cookout. You know, barbeque, salads, cake, nothing fancy. But we sure would love it if you could attend." Lynette smiled at her shrewd invitation as Eddy took his seat.

"Wow, Harriett! How'd you find seats on the aisle?" Eddy handed her a Coca-Cola and a small tub of buttered popcorn.

The corners of both Lynette and Bobby's mouths turned down. "Eddy, are you two…ah, back together?"

Eddy flashed the Kepler smile. "I sure hope so. Hey Bobby, hi Keith. How goes it?"

Lynette interjected, "Of course, Harriett, Eddy is welcome to the BBQ; please bring him along."

It was Harriett's turn to frown.

Keith whispered to his wife, "I guess dealing with that bore is worth the price of getting in good with Harriett."

She replied with a kick to the shin.

"I haven't accepted yet. Please don't add two to your

guest list until I have the chance to check my work and class schedule. May I let you know if I can attend on Wednesday?"

"Of course." Lynette and Bobby answered in unison.

The lights began flickering and the heavy velvet curtains pulled aside as previews came into focus. The crowd quieted. The only sound was an occasional cough and the crunch of popcorn or Cracker Jack.

Eddy broke the silence by whispering in Harriett's ear. "Do you remember our first date?"

Harriett stared at him for a moment before answering. "Yes, all your buddies ridiculed you for dating Plain Jane Bailey."

"No, I mean that cute, little, blue-and-white dotted dress you wore. Do you still own it?"

Harriett held her breath in disbelief. "You remember what I wore on our first date?"

"Of course, I do. That was the night you stole my heart, Harriett…"

The conversation was interrupted by a cacophony of "Shhh," coming from the audience.

Harriett found Eddy's hand and wrapped hers inside. He squeezed it gently as they sat watching the movie. Tears streamed down her face, some created by the big screen, some for her self-chastisement for still loving this man, and some for the joy of being in love.

The audience applauded during the final credits. Many remained in their seats to read the fine print and listen to the music. Periodically a woman sniffled or blew her nose. Eddy and Harriett walked arm-in-arm back to the car.

"What do you say, Harriett? How about a banana split? They're your favorite." He leaned down to nuzzle her neck.

She pushed his face away. "Not in public, Eddy."

"Why not? You're my wife!" Eddy threw his hands to his hips, feigning indignance.

Harriett's face softened slightly; her eyes twinkled as her brow relaxed. "Sure, I didn't eat dinner. Popcorn didn't quite fill me. Ice cream sounds good."

The bell on the door of Teddy's Apothecary tinkled as the couple entered. The usual crowd turned to see who entered.

"Harriett!" Teddy called from the pharmacy. "What brings you in?" He stopped short when he spotted Eddy behind her. "Oh."

"Hi, Teddy. How are the girls and Alice?" Harriett sat down at a table; all the booths were occupied. A chubby, awkward high school girl brought them each a glass of water and menus. "Thanks, Darcie—two banana splits, please," said Harriett. "Do you intend to work after school starts?"

"I sure do, Mrs. Kepler. If Doc can be flexible with my schedule." The girls glanced toward Teddy. "Maybe put a good word in for me? I'll be back in a jiffy with your order." She scooped up the menus again and rushed away to tend to the busy Saturday night crowd.

Eddy reached for Harriett's hands across the table. "Does everyone in this town think you're the cat's meow?" He scrunched his face. "From what I see, you call the shots, Harriett; you're top dog."

She chuckled out loud. "I don't know about being the pinnacle of society; however, I play an active role in the town, the company, and my life. A lot has happened in three years, Eddy."

"Hmmm." Eddy gazed at Harriett but was deep in thought, reminiscing his time in Italy. "Yeah, lots changed."

Darcie placed two banana splits and extra napkins on the table in front of two eager faces. "Enjoy." She hurried away.

Eddy slurped a spoon of whipped cream. "You didn't answer my question."

"Which question?" Harriett felt her shoulders tense.

"Do you still own that cute, blue-and-white dotted

dress?" Eddy reached across the table to wipe the corner of her mouth.

"Oh, that question. Actually, yes, I still own that dress; I'd rather buy quality items, classics, and keep them longer than buy cheap and throw away."

"Hmmm, so my concept of buying quantity over quality doesn't fly with you?" Eddy chortled.

"Not really. I'd rather do without, wait, and save until I can purchase quality. I guess everyone is different."

Eddy's face glowed. "Yep. I want it all, and I want it now."

"I think you have it *all* on the front of your shirt!" Harriett giggled, pointing to a stream of ice cream sundae sliding down Eddy's chest.

"Oh crap! Mom will kill me." He hurried to wipe the mess. "Ah, screw it." Throwing his napkin onto the table, he leaned over and planted a deep passionate kiss on an unsuspecting Harriett.

A few snickering teenagers interrupted the kiss, saying, "That's the infamous Eddy Kepler at work!"

Color crept up Harriett's neck until her cheeks glowed red. She pulled away. "Eddy, I had a nice evening, but I have work to do. Do you want to talk about Olive and your job? If not, please take me home now."

Eddy stood, sulking. "Harriett, let's go."

He walked her up the stairs to the front door, then placed an arm on either side of her, preventing her from unlocking the door. She was trapped in his arms, an easy target for another kiss—this one was gentle and tender. His tongue traced her lips, then probed into her mouth.

Harriett wiggled her arm in front of her body, her mind spinning in confusion. She found his chest and pushed backward. "Eddy, please stop. Don't ruin tonight. I enjoyed myself, but I have work to finish. I must go in."

Eddy brushed her neck with his tongue. "Okay, darling.

Can I see you tomorrow? I do need to tell you about my job. I just didn't want to ruin tonight with…boring details."

"I consider them *important* details. I'm sorry, but that will have to wait until next weekend. You should have told me at the apothecary." She opened her purse to retrieve her key.

"Then, you'll see me again?"

She bit her lip as she considered the request. "Yes, Eddy, I'll see you again." She managed to twist around to unlock the door. Slipping through quickly, she turned the latch, leaving Eddy wanting and panting standing on the front stoop.

4

BEST MAN

The next morning, Eddy and Earl sat at the breakfast table drinking coffee.

"How was your date last night?" Earl asked, then adjusted his necktie. Before Eddy answered, the clock chimed a quarter till the hour. "Mom, get a move on; we're going to be late."

"It was the living end, Earl. What a woman. She has the whole town eating out of her hand. Man, oh man, I hit *paydirt* when I picked Harriett." Eddy poured himself another cup. "Want more?"

"Thanks, but no, we gotta go. Mom!" Earl turned away from Eddy to hide his displeasure. He secretly hoped that Eddy had botched the date and that Harriett would be crying on his shoulder this afternoon.

"Hey, Earl, care to go cruising with me today?" Eddy asked as Abigail descended the stairs.

"Sorry, no can do. I'm busy today."

"Fine. I'll see you after church." He strolled through the living room.

Abigail frowned at her youngest. "Edgar, it wouldn't hurt

you to go to Sunday services. Pay some respect to the Lord. Maybe some good will rub off on you!"

"Not this week, Mom," he called, already halfway to his room. Muttering to himself, he added, "Or any other week, for that matter."

The front door closed as Eddy climbed into the shower. The warm water streamed over his body in waves of emancipation and optimism. *She'll take me back,* he thought. *I'll make it up to her. I'll forget the past and start a wonderful life with my spunky little prodigy. We'll make beautiful, brilliant, blonde babies and be the envy of the town. Eddy and Harriett, Campbellsville's own version of Ozzie and Harriet.*

Eddy finished shaving, splashed on a generous slathering of Aqua Velva, then slipped into a new Izod shirt. His bulging biceps stretched the arm cuffs. Harriett's brother Albert, a meteorologist, and brother-in-law Teddy, town pharmacist, frequently wore the "crocodile" shirts. Not much into clothing status, Eddy figured if the shirts were good enough for Albert and Teddy, then he, too, would buy at least one, to impress Harriett. Whistling as he strutted out of the house, he jumped into his Rambler, heading north, no destination in mind.

An hour later, Abigail and Earl returned home from church services at Saint Mark Lutheran Church. Abigail unpinned her hat and sank into a living room chair.

"Earl, if you don't mind, I'm going to take a nap. I'm feeling tired today."

Earl touched his mother's forehead. "You don't feel warm. Is your stomach sick?"

Abigail smiled. "Such a good son you are. I'm just tired, Earl. Do you mind eating out?"

Earl chuckled at her request to do the daily norm. He leaned down and kissed her forehead. "I'll bring you back a tasty surprise."

"Thank you, dear." Her eyes closed as she fell into a deep sleep.

Earl checked his watch—only one o'clock. He was an hour early for his appointment with Harriett. *What the heck*, he thought. *Maybe she hasn't eaten. It's worth a try.* Jumping into his Bel Air, he drove across the river and up to Hill House.

Harriett jumped at the sound of the doorbell. She ran a comb quickly through her wavy brown locks before opening the door.

"Earl! I wasn't expecting you just yet," she said as she glanced at the grandfather's clock in the foyer. "Come in, please. I was finishing some paperwork." She motioned toward her office. "Please, have a seat."

"Did you eat?" Earl asked without moving.

Harriett tilted her head. "Ah…" Her stomach growled. "I guess not." She laughed.

"Then come on. I'm taking you out to Sunday brunch." Earl placed his arm around her shoulder and urged her forward.

Harriett looked down at her red-and-white striped trousers and red, sleeveless blouse. "I'm not dressed to go out, Earl."

"Harriett, you look beautiful." He blushed.

She pretended not to hear. "I need to wear at least a skirt to Sunday brunch. Will you give me fifteen minutes to change and do my face?"

"Harriett, you may have all the time in the world."

Taking advantage of an escape from the awkward moment, Harriett rushed up the stairs, away from her brother-in-law. She stared at her reflection in the mirror as she penciled in her eyebrows. *Oh, Harriett, watch yourself! He was the best man at your wedding, not the groom.*

"Hah, 'best man' is right!" she said aloud. "Drats."

She slipped a multicolored, floral, gathered skirt over her

head, re-smoothed her hair, cinched a wide belt around her waist, and slipped into a pair of red, Ferragamo, wedge heel shoes, accented with a bow. "This will have to do. It is too hot for nylons."

Earl caught his breath as she walked down the steps. "Goodness, you look stunning."

Harriett giggled. "Earl, this outfit is far from stunning." She twirled. "Summer casual." Her radiating smile betrayed her. She was far more excited about this impromptu lunch than she was over last night's movie and ice cream. "Where to?"

Earl bit his lip. "Madison's steak house?"

"Geez, Louise. Sounds good to me." She linked her arm through Earl's, allowing him to escort her to his Chevy.

∞ ∞ ∞

Eddy drove aimlessly for several hours, euphorically enjoying the illusion of last night's conquest. The warm late-August sun beat on his windshield, blinding his westward trek. A tanned arm hung over the edge of the open window as the breeze blew his regrown blonde locks. The time approached the three o'clock hour as the old swimming hole came into sight. He stopped the car and sat watching children and families splash in the water. His mind wandered back to the day he saved Harriett from a rattlesnake on the far bank after a fun day of swimming and frolicking.

"I'm going over to visit!" he said aloud to himself. "Dammit, I'm her husband. I can visit her if I please."

Within 15 minutes, Eddy threw the Rambler in gear and parked in front of Harriett's house. He climbed the front stairs and knocked on the door. No answer. Descending back to street level, he peeked through the garage window. Her Buick was there. *Odd*, he thought. Back up the stairs—he knocked again, then circled the house and sat on one of the cushioned patio chairs to wait.

Forty-five minutes later, Eddy heard a car door close. He snuck to the terrace outside her office and watched as Harriett and Earl walked arm in arm to the front door.

Enraged, Eddy clambered over the bushes to meet the pair. "You son-of-a-bitch!"

Ambushing an unsuspecting Earl, he pushed him backward. Harriett, still linked, stumbled, twisting her ankle; she fell to her knee and dropped her handbag.

"Eddy, you hurt me!" She glared at her red-faced husband.

"I thought you were too busy to see me today! But you're not too busy for Earl."

Earl regained his balance. Helping Harriett to her feet, he brushed debris from her skirt. "Are you okay?" He peered into her eyes, then turned to his brother. "Eddy, that was uncalled for!"

Harriett seethed, inhaling through her teeth. "Eddy, what are you doing here? I told you I had a full day."

Eddy faced Earl; their noses almost touched. "I want to know what he's doing here."

Earl leaned forward, making facial contact. "I was invited." Spittle bounced off Eddy's cheek.

"Both of you, stop! Right now!" Harriett crammed her body between the two men. "Grow up! Both of you start acting like adults."

Earl felt the blood rushing up his neck. He backed away from his brother, then hung his head. "I'm sorry, Harriett."

"Well, I don't like being told what I can and cannot do by a woman." Eddy scowled at the pair.

"Really?" Harriett laughed aloud. "If you intend to move back into this house, you better get used to a female in charge. Otherwise, walk away right now."

The brothers looked in silence at Harriett, both dumbfounded that the petite girl commanded their compliance.

After a moment, Eddy mumbled. "The world is changing too quickly for my blood. But, my dear wife, I must admit that you are a force to be reckoned with."

Harriett retrieved her purse from the ground. "Glad we have that settled. Now both of you leave. I have work to do!" Opening the front door, she entered her house and locked the door behind her. She wilted into her desk chair, swiveled around, and poured herself a stiff drink, neat.

∞ ∞ ∞

Back home, both brooding brothers sulked side by side as Earl fished for his keys on the porch.

"You started it by taking her to lunch," Eddy complained as they walked through the front door.

"Stop it, Eddy. You sound like a spoiled—"

Earl stopped speaking. He looked at his mother, still asleep on the couch. One arm hung dangling over the side. Her face was pasty white.

Earl rushed to her side. Shaking her gently, he said, "Mom. Mom, wake up." There was no response.

Eddy stood in disbelief, mouth hanging low.

"Eddy, call the ambulance. Right now." Earl touched Abigail's cold forehead, then searched for a pulse. He found none. "Eddy, I think she's gone."

Eddy picked up the receiver, then waited for the operator to ask, "Number please."

"Madison hospital ambulance, and hurry." Eddy rushed to his mother's side and picked up her drooping arm. Squeezing her hand, he pleaded. "Mom, don't leave me. I'm not ready to be on my own. I still need you, Mom." The limp appendage did not respond.

The tears began to flow freely down Eddy's face. He sank to the floor. Resting his head on his mother's chest, he wept uncontrollably until he heard the sirens of the ambulance.

"Earl, what happens now?"

Earl embraced his brother. "We just have to wait and see. We'll get through this together, brother."

5

THE END OF AN ERA

Three days blurred by. Harriett remained faithfully at Eddy's side as the town paid their respects to Abigail. Eddy's usually rosy cheeks were ashen, his hands shook visibly, and he wept openly. His knees buckled as the casket was lowered into the ground. Holding his hand, Harriett willed her strength to Eddy. Earl, a solitary figure, stood directly behind the headstone, envious of the support offered to Eddy.

Abigail Kepler was laid beside her husband, Edgar Sr., in the Lutheran cemetery. Individual church denominations and families within Campbellsville maintained their own burial grounds, resulting in at least a dozen different humble cemeteries. The dates on the headstone read *"born 1886 died 1953."* Abigail was 67 years old.

Eddy, Earl, their brothers George and Roy, and their wives, children, cousins, and friends gathered at the veteran's club after saying goodbye to the benevolent woman. Earl arranged for roast beef and pasta to be served as entree selections. The crowd chattered as they reminisced Abigail's generosity, ability to forgive, and sometimes ditsy personality.

As the assembly dwindled, Harriett leaned close to Eddy. "Eddy," she whispered into his ear. "Are you okay to be by yourself? I need to visit the ladies' room."

Eddy numbly nodded his head. Rather than taking the direct path, Harriett detoured her route to the washroom. She approached Earl from behind and touched him on the shoulder. He jumped as a tingling sensation spread throughout his body. He knew that Harriett was behind him.

"Earl, tonight is not the time to be alone in your house. I think you should stay with me. Eddy is also staying. I have the guest rooms ready for use." She waited for a response. "Earl?"

His face betrayed him, displaying the depth of his pain. Although only 39 years old, the wrinkles around his eyes and graying temples made him look older. He covered his face with his hands, rubbed his eyes, then acquiesced.

"Sure, Harriett, you know best." His smile failed to materialize.

Harriett stood on tiptoes to brush his cheek with a kiss. "Good. I'll stay here with both of you until everyone is gone."

Earl watched her walk away before turning to look at his despondent youngest brother. *Luckiest SOB on earth*, he thought.

∞ ∞ ∞

The heat of the day lingered into the evening hours as Eddy, Earl, and Harriett trekked up to Hill House with Harriett after riding in the hearse all day. The brothers exited the Buick before she pulled into the garage.

Once inside, Harriett ushered the men up the main staircase. "Eddy, this is your room. Earl, you're over there. Do you mind sharing a bath?" She indicated the appropriate space. "I'm changing out of these dark clothes." Her heels echoed on the hallway floor as she called over her shoulder. "Help yourself to a drink, then meet me on the terrace."

Eddy fumbled with the wooden hanger. His trousers slipped to the floor several times before he unlatched the slacks-rod. His new suit jacket lay crumpled on the bed; his striped tie hung half-over a chair. The sound escaping his mouth was that of a trapped animal lamenting the loss of existence. Harriett ran into the room to find Eddy clad in only his boxers and dress shirt, kneeling on the floor, moaning in agony. He clutched his torso as he rocked to and fro.

Sitting on the floor beside him, she embraced his shoulders. Eddy grasped her, enfolding her in his arms. Burying his head in her chest, he wailed.

"It's okay, Eddy. Everything will be okay," she said as her hand gently circled his back. The familiar ripple of muscles, apparent through the shirt, stirred dormant feelings for Harriett. Whatever his excuse, she realized at that moment that she must give him another chance.

"I know how hard this is. When Papa died…" She stopped to catch her breath. "Eddy, I'm here, darling. Just let it all out." She squeezed him tightly. "I still love you, Eddy."

They glanced up as the silhouette in the doorway gasped. Earl's face drained all color, his mouth went dry. He coughed to clear his throat. "Harriett, I'll make us each a drink," he said, then turned to leave.

"Earl!" Her eyes pleaded as they filled with tears of regret and hope.

"No need, Harriett. He's your husband." Earl walked away, leaving the couple entwined.

∞ ∞ ∞

Fifteen minutes later, Eddy and Harriett joined Earl on the back patio. Sinking together into the settee, they held hands as Earl handed them each a glass.

"It's no longer 'on the rocks.'" Earl frowned as he refreshed his drink with ice and bourbon from a nearby cart.

"Anyone hungry?" Harriett asked. "I have several casseroles in the fridge. Alice and Laurie sent them over."

Eddy rubbed his stomach. "I was too emotional earlier, but I think I can eat now."

"Earl?" Harriett kissed Eddy's hand before releasing it and standing.

"I guess so. May I help you?"

"No. You two have plenty to discuss. Sit, talk. I'll make us each a plate of food."

Earl waited for the door to close before speaking. "So, are you moving back in?"

Eddy ran his fingers through his hair. "I don't really know. I hope so, but Mom's death is too raw to think about that." He gulped his drink. "What should we do with the house? If I move in here, will you continue to live there?"

"I guess we make that decision after you know what you're doing. Can't sell the house if you're not moving out, now, can we?" Earl's dark, lifeless eyes reflected his mood. His pulsing temple veins were visible. He tried hiding his grief; however, his head throbbed. His life was spinning out of control, losing two women he loved at once.

"Earl, will you help me with Harriett? I think it will be easier for me to explain my story if you're here to help buffer."

Stomach bile burned Earl's throat. He gagged, then swallowed. "What can I possibly do to help?"

"She respects you." Eddy's eye latched onto his brother's.

Earl coughed. "I earned any respect coming my way."

"Please, Earl! I want to work this out. Losing Mom hit hard. I can't lose Harriett too."

"Mom's death is a blow for both of us." Earl exhaled what little air filled his lungs. His heartbeat echoed in his ears. I'll help you with Harriett. If you patch things here, I guess I'll move back to Pittsburgh. Nothing left for me in Campbellsville." Earl turned his head as water seeped from the corner of his eyes. He dabbed with the back of his hand. "Let's get things in order here, and then we can put the house up for sale, okay?"

"Thanks, Earl, you're the best brother ever." Eddy hugged him around the neck.

"Sure, sure. Whatever you say."

6

A NEW INNING

Harriett returned with a tray of plates, utensils, napkins, and accoutrement. "Will you boys set the table? I'm going back for the food."

Eddy jumped to his feet, took the tray, and headed to the outdoor eating area. A large, rectangular, metal filigree table was surrounded by eight oversized chairs, each dressed with a thick, comfy, fabric cushion. He brushed a stray leaf from the tabletop, a clue that fall was quickly approaching, before laying each place. Earl opened the French doors leading to the kitchen as Harriett came out.

"Let me take that," he offered.

"I got it. Easier to put it directly down than transfer and risk dropping," she said, securely carrying the heavy load. "Hope you're hungry."

Menu offerings included fresh garden salad topped with plump, juicy, vine-ripened tomatoes, a chicken-and-broccoli casserole, and chocolate cake for dessert.

Eddy's stomach growled at the sight of food. "Boy, this looks good. I see you learned how to cook."

Both Earl and Harriett burst out laughing. "No, Eddy. I

did not." She looked at Earl, "Do you remember the night we almost burned down your house?"

"How could I forget? Those pork chops were harder than shoe leather, and the potatoes were charred pebbles."

He continued laughing as Eddy's head swiveled back and forth from his wife to his brother.

"I guess I missed some stuff."

"Yes, Eddy, you did." She looked directly into his eyes. "Care to make up for it?"

Earl cleared his throat. "Do you want me to leave?"

"No! Please stay." Eddy made the request. "I want to get some things off my chest. Tell you what really happened. Okay with you, Harriett?"

"I've waited three years. If this is not a good time, I can wait a couple more weeks."

"No, I need to do this now." Eddy reached over to grab Harriett's hand. "Harriett, I do have a new job. I was to start Monday, but, well…"

"You are delayed because of the funeral. Yes, I understand." She waited a moment before asking. "With whom?"

"With whom what? Oh, you mean the job. At the mill, but not on the production floor. I have a white-collar job working in supply. Not a huge salary, like yours, but better than a mill grunt." The infamous Kepler grin spread across Eddy's face, for the first time in four days. He waited for her to indicate her approval. "Plus, I told you I was over helping Olive. That yard of hers is starting to look pretty good."

Harriett dropped her head; looking at her food, she raised her eyes to meet Eddy's gaze. "Both positive. I assume you are fine with my financial requirements?"

Earl chewed his casserole. Finding it hard to swallow, he excused himself and went inside.

"Yes, Harriett. And…" Eddy stopped. Harriett allowed

silence to ensue. "I want to tell you why I didn't write. Do you want to hear it?"

He continued talking, with Harriett intent on every word. He only stopped when Earl returned fifteen minutes later.

"So, you see now why I didn't write?" Eddy asked.

Harriett stood, leaned over, and kissed his lips. Earl stared, bewildered.

"Harriett, you're okay with his behavior?" Earl tilted his head to the side questioningly.

"Oh yes, Earl. Gambling is an addiction. I'm so proud of Eddy for kicking the habit, all on his own." She kissed Eddy again.

All three flinched, startled by a ringing phone. Harriett smiled. Jumping up, she ran to answer it.

"Gambling?" Earl muttered after she left, fully aware of Eddy's transgressions with Rosa. "What are you talking about?"

Eddy interrupted before Earl said more, in case Harriett could hear them from inside. "I told her, Earl. I was ashamed of gambling away my paycheck every week. I had no money to send home, and I was in debt. I was afraid that if I wrote, I would be tempted to ask for money." Eddy kicked Earl under the table. "And that's just not fair to Harriett. It was easier to pay off my debts and break the nasty habit alone. And that's just what I did!"

Earl choked. The heat rose in his neck. "Oh, is that what you did! Great story, Eddy."

Earl stood as Harriett returned.

"Wrong number!" Her grin stretched from ear to ear.

"Harriett," Earl's sad eyes locked onto hers, "I don't think I can stay here tonight, even though I know I should, but not for the reasons you think. I'm going home." He glared at Eddy. "You are unbelievable! It's high time you grow up, little brother."

A look of confusion crossed Harriett's face. "Earl?"

Eddy grabbed Harriett's hand. "Let him go. We all suffer from grief differently." He squeezed her hand until Earl was out of sight.

∞ ∞ ∞

Eddy helped Harriett wash and dry the dishes. "Where did we get all of this stuff?" he asked, observing kitchen cabinets filled with a cadre of items.

"We?" she laughed, then reached for his hand. "Some were wedding gifts, but most of these things I bought. I wanted to wait to supply our house together, but my girlfriends at work assured me that men don't care about dishes and furniture as long as they are fed and have a comfortable place to watch TV."

"Smart friends. So, you have a television?"

"Yes, in the living room. If you watch, do you mind keeping the volume down? I have work to finish in my office, especially since I took the last three days off for bereavement."

"You got it, honey." He hung his dish towel over the oven door then grabbed a beer bottle from the refrigerator.

"Eddy, we still need to take this slowly. Do you understand?" She bit her lower lip to steady her trembling nerves.

"Yeah, babe, whatever you say!" Smiling, he strutted to the front of the house, turned on the TV, and plopped onto the couch.

Harriett's head was spinning. *That seemed too easy a transition*, she thought. *Please, don't make the same mistake twice, Harriett.*

7

DECISIONS

*E*arl dragged his legs up the two front porch steps, unlocked the door, and flipped on a light. The single 40-watt bulb cast shadows throughout the empty room. He collapsed into one of the stuffed chairs only to have a runaway spring jab him in the backside.

"Ouch!" He stood, rubbing his butt. "I should probably burn this old house and everything in it to the ground," he mumbled.

He wandered into the kitchen. Mindlessly opening the refrigerator door, he searched through the collection of casseroles and food items contributed by caring friends and neighbors. The small, close-knit town of Campbellsville supported each other in times of need, supplying those in mourning with plenty of food for themselves and visitors.

This will do, he thought as he removed a Pyrex baking dish. A layer of sliced potatoes topped with cubes of Spam and canned green peas was drizzled with what looked to be condensed soup. He scooped two large spoonfuls into a saucepan, ignited the gas burner, and stirred. Minutes later, he was standing at the stove eating the concoction out of the pan.

After one taste, he spewed the contents of his mouth.

"That's disgusting!"

As he looked at the mess, he began to sob. The tears flowed freely, morphing into gut-wrenching moans. He grabbed his hair with both hands, pulling it upwards, hoping the physical pain would alleviate his emotional grief.

How can I possibly lose both of them in one day? Is there any justice in this world? He lumbered into the dining room then flung the pan into the table. He slumped into a chair, arms dangling at his sides, head tossed back, allowing his tears to fill his ear before hitting the floor.

Through his anguish, Earl prayed. "Why God? Eddy does not deserve that wonderful woman. I thought you were loving?"

His neck creaked as he laid his head on the table, sobbing himself to sleep.

∞ ∞ ∞

Earl awoke the following day with dried potatoes covering his face. Wiping his cheek with his hand, he stumbled to the kitchen to make coffee then removed the phone receiver from its cradle.

"Number, please," said the operator.

"Hi, Mr. Logan, our main office, please." Earl waited for the girl to exhale and connect him to the phone company's corporate headquarters.

"Logan here." The vice president in charge of lines and supply answered his phone.

"Mr. Logan, Earl Kepler. Any chance I can continue my bereavement by taking a vacation day today?" Earl held his breath.

"Kepler, yes, of course. It was your mother, is that correct? So sorry for your loss."

"Yes, sir. Thank you." Earl sighed. "I'll be in tomorrow. I have a few details to attend to today." Earl hesitated. "Thank you, Mr. Logan."

"Kepler, before you go—are you considering moving back to corporate?"

"I don't know, sir. That's one of my details. May I answer tomorrow?"

"Yes, yes. Goodbye, Kepler." The phone went dead.

Returning to the kitchen, Earl cleaned last night's mess from the table, tossed the unsavory casserole into the trash, then searched the refrigerator for a breakfast option. He settled on frying himself an egg.

After washing his dishes, Earl braved entering Abigail's room carrying a cardboard box. He sniffed. The floral scent of Arpege lingered in the bedroom. Her generous splash for Sunday services hung in the stagnant air of the closed room. Earl lifted the bottle of cologne, last year's Christmas gift, as tears filled his eyes.

Abigail's closet door hung open; several dresses were strewn about as discarded burial choices. Earl folded her clothing, piece by piece, placing them in the box until full. The only items on the shelves were several handbags and a dozen hats. The red feathers and head of a bird circling the crown of a black netted hat caused Earl to chuckle. He remembered when Abigail purchased the hat. She strutted through the house, hands on her hips as if she were a Paris fashion model.

He finished boxing his mother's items, placed the containers into the trunk of his car, and drove to St. Mark's Lutheran Church, where he deposited Abigail's most precious belongings into their charity box.

"Goodbye, dear Mother," Earl said before leaving. "You are with the saints in heaven while Dad is burning in Hell."

∞ ∞ ∞

Eddy's first day in the new job was relatively uneventful. He arrived home to find Earl already eating his evening meal.

"What are you doing here?" Earl, munching a piece of fried chicken, looked up to greet his brother. "I thought you'd be with Harriett."

"Got any more of that?" Eddy asked as he took a chair across the table. "So did I, but Harriett doesn't want to rush things. She has a sweet setup! TV, a beautiful big house, lots of money. I'd be a fool to let this opportunity slip by."

"Huh! It wouldn't be the first time." Earl pulled a bag of chicken from the refrigerator and threw it at Eddy. "Get your own plate. If you intend to live here, you'll share responsibility."

"No problem, Earl. It will be good practice for when I move in with Harriett." Eddy snapped the cap off a bottle of beer. "So, I guess you decided not to sell?"

"What? And give you free rein over Harriett? No way in hell. Someone has to look out for her when you drop the ball, and I intend that to be me."

"Coveting another man's wife is a sin, Big Brother." Eddy sneered.

"So is adultery and lying. Don't be so quick to judge." Earl carried his plate to the sink, washed and dried it, then placed it in the cabinet. "Clean up after yourself. No taking turns here. You use it; you clean it. Understood?"

"Yes, sir!" Eddy jumped to attention and saluted.

"Asshole." Earl left Eddy standing alone.

∞ ∞ ∞

Earl's car automatically crossed the bridge to the older side of Campbellsville and started up the hill. When it reached the top, it turned right, stopping in front of the sizable red-brick structure, the largest home in Campbellsville proper. Before climbing the front staircase, Earl peeked through the garage window. The green Buick was inside, its dented rear bumper repaired.

Harriett answered the knock at the door, still holding the pale blue, round-toed heels that matched the sleek, three-quarter-sleeved, pencil dress. Double-breasted rows of fabric-covered buttons highlighted a centered bow-topped belt that snapped in the front. Her matching blue hat and gloves lay on an entry table.

"Earl! I didn't expect company tonight. I just got home from the office."

Earl caught his breath. "You look stunning." He shook his head as if clearing his mind before continuing. "May I come in? I'll only stay a few minutes."

"Sure, Earl. Make yourself comfortable." Calling back, she added, "Let's sit in the office."

Before sitting, Earl filled the ice bucket with cubes, then poured two drinks.

"Ahh, that's nice," Harriett said as she took the glass. She scanned the stack of papers on her desk as Earl sipped his drink. "What's on your mind?"

"I want you to know that I am staying in town."

She looked up from a file. "Oh. I thought you may be tempted to return to Pittsburgh."

Earl blew air, sputtering his lips. "I considered it for a brief moment. But to be honest, I want to remain close to you."

Harriett pursed her lips. Her eyes narrowed. "I'm going to give Eddy another chance."

"I know. But I'll not leave you alone with him. Harriett…"

He stood. Walking to the desk, he stopped directly in front of her. "Harriett, I've only just admitted this to myself, but…"

The couple stared into each other's eyes for the briefest of moments before Harriett interrupted.

"Don't say it, Earl. I don't want to hear it." She frowned. "If you don't say it, then it isn't so."

Earl raised his drink. "Then here's to conscientious denial."

She clicked her glass against his. The sound of leaded crystal echoed throughout the room. "Cheers. May we two remain scrupulous as long as I am still Eddy's wife."

8

GROUND RULES

Sunlight leaked through the window blind, hitting Eddy's eyes. He rolled over and grabbed his pillow. The double bed in Harriett's guest room offered much more comfort than his single bed tucked into a dormer at his mother's home. The bright September morning rendered sleep impossible. Eddy grabbed his work trousers and a tee-shirt, carrying them to the guest bathroom, as Harriett exited her bedroom.

Startled by a half-naked male physique, she blurted. "Eddy, please wear clothing in the common areas of the house."

"Don't be a prude. It's not like you haven't seen it before." Eddy moved toward the bath.

"Eddy, my house, my rules. And it's been three years." Harriett called back as she descended the stairs to the kitchen. "We need to set some ground rules. This morning!"

"Fine, sweetie. Whatever you say."

Harriett heard the toilet flush directly above her as she sat at the table buttering her toast. *Need to insulate the floorboards,* she thought. Ten minutes later, Eddy sat across the table with a big mug of coffee and a wide grin on his face.

"Sleep well, my wife?"

Harriett frowned. "Not really, but that's not what I want to discuss."

"What? Having me so close, yet so far away makes you uncomfortable? We can fix that; I'll move into your room." The infamous Kepler grin spread from cheek to cheek.

"Slow down, soldier. I want to reiterate the stipulations of moving in and reestablish some guidelines. Maybe you should take some notes?"

"Nah. I'll remember."

"Fine, I typed them up for you. Sign your contract here." Harriett placed a two-page, typewritten document on the table.

Eddy watched cautiously. "You're kidding, right? A contract?"

"No, Eddy, I'm not. I've learned how to navigate this world. Verbal is not binding enough for me in my current position. I prefer written and signed. Understood?" Her steady but cold eyes met his. He shuddered at her resolve.

"Get on with it, then."

"The first condition was for you to explain your three-year silence, which you did by telling me about your gambling. Is that the entire story?"

Eddy coughed, then swallowed some coffee. "Yes. That's the entire story."

"Fine, but I'm warning you. If I find out otherwise, the deal is off."

Eddy rose. Walking to Harriett, he leaned over her chair and kissed her neck. She flinched, regretting that her body responded to his touch.

"Harriett," he purred in her ear. "I kicked a nasty habit. Let's leave it at that."

She paused long enough for Eddy to sit down. "Second was the job, to which you complied. How was your first day?"

Eddy scowled. "It was fine. I have a desk, I don't get dirty, I make decent money, and it's at the steel mill. Nothing more to say. I'll contribute to house expenses. You tell me how much, and I'll just hand it over to you to use as you please."

"So, do I take it you don't want an active role in paying bills?"

"You got that right. You're the financial whiz. This is yours."

"You buy your clothes, alcohol, and entertainment on your own. I pay for my schooling and such."

"Agreed."

"Now, to the tricky part. I am serious about you staying in your own bedroom. No conjugal exchange at this point. But you must keep your marriage vows." She placed her hands, palms down, on the paper. Gazing at Eddy, she waited for his response.

Eddy gritted his teeth, then snarled. "This really is torture. You know, you are an attractive woman. It's hard to stay away from you!"

Harriett pursed her lips. "You managed for three years; just continue on a little longer." She waited a moment. "That brings us to Olive. Are you ready to take over?"

Eddy stood, his hand waving up and down his body. "I'm already dressed and on my way. I'm working on garden clean-up this week. I got her."

"Then I won't hold you up. Review and we'll sign tonight." She collected her papers. "Eddy, I do want this to work, but as a partnership based on open communication, truth, and trust. A marriage takes two to be successful, both husband and wife."

"I'm on the same page, Harriett. I want this, too." Eddy blew her a kiss, then walked out the door.

∞ ∞ ∞

Olive Bailey clomped down the porch step to greet her visitor. "Eddy Kepler. Twice in one week. She has you henpecked, doesn't she?" Her hands flew to her hips, chuckling as Eddy squirmed. "Oh, and I'm sorry to hear about Abigail."

"Thanks." Eddy turned toward the old chicken coop and storage area. "I thought I'd finish cleaning up your vegetable garden today. Is that okay?"

"Suit yourself. I'll not complain about free help. Can you pick the rest of the grape crop? I already got most of them and already made juice. I want to work on jelly next week."

Eddy cocked his head. "I thought you gave up jelly-making? That Alice did it now."

"Well, you thought wrong. They are my grapes, and if I want to make jelly, then I'll damn well make jelly. Besides, I can actually do it right this year, without Tabs getting in my way." Olive spit the words.

Eddy cringed. *Yikes*, he thought. *She really is a cold-hearted bitch.* "I am so sorry that your dear husband is no longer with us. He was a good man."

"And how would you know?" She quipped her reply. "Get to work if that's your intention. Half the day is already over." She spun on her heel and stomped back into the house.

Eddy worked for a full hour before knocking on the door.

Olive stared directly as she stood behind the screen. "What do you want?"

Eddy hesitated, his shoulders slouching. "Could I bother you for a glass of water?"

"Use the hose on the side of the house!" She turned and slammed the door in his face.

Eddy broke into roaring laughter. "Clever girl, Harriett. Clever girl!" He turned on the water, pinched the hose to retard flow, and gulped.

∞ ∞ ∞

Three hours later, Eddy gathered weeds, tools, and a basket of grapes. He placed the grapes on the porch, then, after rapping on the door, headed to stow the tools in the coop. Olive opened the door, grabbed the grapes, and turned the lock, shutting out Eddy and the rest of the world.

He whistled his way home as he walked down the alley between Maple Street and Hill Street. He entered the house from the garage level. After stripping out of his soiled clothing, he placed them on top of Harriett's laundry basket in the basement and walked up the steps in his boxer shorts.

"Harriett," he called. "Where do I put my dirty clothes?" He peeked into the office to find her working at her oversized mahogany desk.

"Geez, Louise. Is nakedness going to be the norm? Please, Eddy." She bit her lip then wiped her hands on her slacks. *Is he doing this to wear me down deliberately? Be strong, Harriett!* "As for laundry, you do it yourself. Partnership, remember? I'm not your slave."

"What? I don't know how to use those machines."

"No problem. I'll teach you. And be prepared to take notes this time." She returned to her work, avoiding looking in the direction of his firm butt and muscular thighs. "Oh," she added. "Dinner preparation is per rotating weekly schedule. I'll finish out this week; you get next week. But I'm not much of a cook, so be forewarned."

"I can't cook either, but I'm willing to learn. We may shed a few pounds. But there is always a restaurant. Do I need to buy groceries for my week?"

"Only if you want something to prepare. Now, please, I must work." Her eyes remained on her desk. "Oh—Eddy, with all the activities this week I forgot to mention. I accepted Renner's BBQ invitation. Monday is Labor Day. Are you coming along?

"Of course. I'm your husband, and we need to be seen together as a couple." He grinned. "I'm taking a shower before dinner."

Eddy strutted out of the room, hoping Harriett was admiring his backside.

She was.

9

GOSSIP

CAMPBELLSVILLE, SEPTEMBER 1953

The morning sun grew higher in the autumn sky. Harriett sat on Alice's front porch steps watching the Labor Day parade with two-and-a-half-year-old Polly on her knee. Eight-month-old Maggie squirmed in her mother's arms.

"Maggie!" Alice whispered in the infant's ear. "Please sit still. You're hurting Mommy."

Harriett glanced at her sister's glowing face then at her waist. "Alice, for goodness' sake, are you pregnant again?"

Alice moaned, "I think so. I've only missed my courses once, but I'm pretty sure. I'll go see Doc Paulson if I miss this month."

"Maggie, come to Aunt Harriett." She reached for the child. "Polly, will you sit on the stair in front of me, sweetie?" Harriett steadied the toddler as she stepped down by grasping the back of her pinafore.

"You'll be a great mother, Harriett. Some day." Alice blushed as she spoke. "How's it going with Eddy? Can you resist him?" She giggled.

"Geez, Louise, Alice." Harriett lowered her voice. "This is

not about S. E. X. He's my husband, after all." She paused. "I let him sleep in this morning. He was pretty shaken up by Abigail's passing. I think he's growing up, finally."

A drum cadence echoed off the hillside, interrupting their conversation. Polly jumped up and down as the marching band approached. The women clapped and cheered.

"We're going to a BBQ today. It's our first social invitation as husband and wife. Can you believe it?" Harriett touched her sister's hand. "He confessed to his silence. He was gambling and broke, and embarrassed to admit it." Tears filled Harriett's eyes. "Oh, Alice. I still love him."

"Give it time, Harriett. If he truly has matured, you'll work things out."

∞ ∞ ∞

Harriett brushed her thick brown curls as Eddy climbed the back staircase.

"Harriett, I'm home. When are we expected at Bobbie's?" he asked as he ran into the guest bathroom.

"In forty minutes. I'll meet you in the kitchen."

Harriett smiled as she listened to the water running in the shower. She retrieved a bottle of wine from the pantry, then wrapped a dozen freshly baked cinnamon rolls in waxed paper. She remained an enigma—she could expertly concoct light, delicate sweets using flour, sugar, butter, and cream, but change the components to meat, potatoes, vegetables, and oil and the results were inedible. How was she capable of baking such delightful treats, yet remain unable to cook supper? A recipe was a recipe; what was the difference? Regardless, the talented Harriett possessed an Achilles heel.

The sound of footsteps bounced down the staircase. "Eddy, will you grab the wine?" she asked, her back facing the staircase.

"Why are you all dressed up? I thought this was a casual cookout?" Eddy asked. He gasped when Harriett turned to face him. "Wow! You look stunning. Like a movie star."

"This is casual attire," she said, with a grin, although her blushing face betrayed her.

She wore an emerald green-and-white striped dress, cinched at the waist with a large, buckled belt. Buttons along the front of the dress were fastened mid-thigh, exposing slim, muscular legs and a pair of shorts in a matching green-and-white dot. Short sleeves encircling taunt biceps were cuffed in the same dotted material as the shorts. Finishing her ensemble was a green canvas shoe.

She donned a wide-brimmed straw hat and oversized pair of sunglasses as Eddy grabbed the wine.

Eddy whistled. "When did you grow up?" He reached for the door. "I'll drive."

Harriett smiled then took Eddy's hand. "I had three years." She placed the cinnamon rolls in a crocheted tote. "Let's walk, instead. I don't want to waste such a beautiful day."

Ten minutes later, the couple rounded the side of the Renner house leading to the backyard. Several picnic and card tables crammed the flat, grassy space. Harriett sneezed at the freshly mown lawn that sloped between Maple and Pine Streets. Tiki torches flanked the property perimeter, awaiting dusk lighting.

"Harriett, thank you for coming." Lynette rushed to greet the newcomers. "What a gorgeous outfit."

Her round, postpartum body stretched the yarn of her sweater. Clam-digger slacks pulled tight over her full thighs. A silk scarf tied around her neck was the only remnant of her once trim youth. His old conquest paled in comparison to Harriett's elegance.

Eddy's eyes grew round. "Hey, Lynette. Thanks for the invite."

"Hi, Eddy." She took Harriett's arm. "Bobby and Harry are waiting for you," she said as she tugged in the men's direction.

"These are for you." Harriett offered the cinnamon rolls.

Lynette's eyes sparkled. "Oh, thank you! I was hoping you'd bring these. Don't tell anyone. I'm saving them just for Bobby and me. Now, here are the boys."

Eddy watched as Bobby Renner and Harry Boring surrounded Harriett, welcoming her into their community clique. He scanned the crowd looking for other classmates and friends; however, all the men were with Harriett. Only the women remained.

Eddy intercepted Lynette, offering her the wine. "This is for tonight."

"What kind is it?" she asked as she removed it from the paper bag.

"No clue. Harriett picked it."

Lynette grinned. "My goodness! French. *Chateauneuf du Pape!* That sounds expensive." She mispronounced the name, then shared the label with the other women, who giggled in response. "Eddy, did you visit there when you were in the army?"

"I was in Italy, Lynette. Not France."

"Aren't they almost the same?" The women chuckled as Eddy rolled his eyes. "Eddy, the only geography I studied in high school was that of the male physique. You, of all people, should remember."

Eddy scoffed then looked at the intensity of Harriett's engagement. "Ladies," he said and smiled the infamous Eddy Kepler grin. "Please excuse me. I believe there is an important conversation going on across the room."

The men barely noticed him join. All were listening to

Harriett, who was explaining the difference between portfolio investment and investment funds.

"Investment management is a huge advantage, especially considering municipal funds." She handed Harry her business card. "I'm a CFO, not a financial manager, but call me, Harry, and I'll recommend you to a reputable firm in Madison. Campbellsville will be in good hands."

"Thanks, Harriett." Bobby and Harry shook her hand, while the others queued to follow suit.

"You're welcome. This is my home, too. I want to see the town prosper." She spotted Eddy on the outskirts of the group. "Eddy," she said as she extended her hand to him. "Glad you joined us."

Eddy beamed at Harriett. "Hey, guys. Bobby, Harry. Was the little woman helpful?"

Harriett pinched Eddy's hand and frowned. Eddy mentally filed his mistake.

Trying to recover, he asked, "Anything I can do for the town? I have a new job in supply procurement."

Bobby kicked Harry on the leg then answered. "Ah, no, Eddy. We're good. Please pardon me, I have hot dogs to grill."

Harriett stood on her tiptoes then kissed Eddy's cheek. "I'm glad you came over. Gosh, they had a ton of questions. I'm happy to help, but…" She giggled. "They need more than me. Sometimes I think they skipped high school."

"Most of them did. You're talking to all the sports jocks, Harriett." Eddy ticked his tongue on the roof of his mouth. "The only important thing to them in high school was winning the next game and finding the next date."

"It seems so long ago, doesn't it?" Harriett sighed. Her hand reached for Eddy's. "Come, let's get something to eat. I'm starving."

The couple found seats on the edge of a picnic table.

Harriett easily slid into the middle, allowing Eddy's big frame a spot on the end.

"I'll get us each a plate. Harriett, will you get our drinks?" Eddy pointed to a washtub filled with ice and bottles.

"Sure."

As she approached, she overheard a hushed conversation coming from the side of the house.

"...don't know what she sees in him."

"I heard he left her high and dry. For three whole years."

"I heard the same. He didn't write. Just left her in the dark."

"She's too good for him. I never understood the attraction to start with."

Harriett waited silently for the conversation to end. Three or four distinct voices, one belonging to Harry, continued.

"Truthfully though, I wouldn't have dated her back then. Would you?"

"Nah. She was pretty plain. But, God, look what she's blossomed into! Who knew?"

"Eddy, obviously. That son-of-a-bitch always was lucky. Hedged all his bets on a scrawny little nothing."

Harriett thrust her hand into the tub. Clinking bottles together, she grabbed a coke and a beer before turning the corner to confront the men.

Faces reddened and conversation stopped as Harriett stood staring, hands on her hips. "You should be ashamed of yourselves! Eddy was your friend." The words sputtered from her lips. "Or don't you remember that all your old glory was due to his talent? None of you would be high school stars if it wasn't for him."

Harry tried to stammer a reply.

Harriett cut him short. "Shut up, Harry Boring. Suddenly I'm in your good graces, now that I have a pretty face and free advice to offer. But I still remember the day you ousted me from playing baseball. Just because I was good at it. Hurt your male pride. All of you are pathetic."

Harriett spun around, dropped the drinks back into the tub, and sprinted over to the picnic table. "Eddy, come on. We're leaving."

Eddy cocked his head. "I thought you were hungry."

"I am. But I'm not eating with these people. Come. I'll fill you in on the way home."

Lynette rushed over. "You're not leaving, are you?" She looked desperately at Bobby, who was busy grilling hotdogs and hamburgers. "Honey, hurry. Harriett and Eddy are leaving."

Bobby dropped his spatula; the grill flamed as he rushed over to his wife. "What's wrong? Why are you going?"

Harriett bit her lip. "I suggest you ask Harry Boring and his cohorts that question. Funny, I thought we all outgrew all the pettiness of school. I remember being teased, even bullied, but I overlooked it as childhood foolishness." She shook her head. "I forgave and forgot. Seems like I'm the only one to do so."

Eddy's head swiveled from Harriett, Bobby, Lynette, then back to Harriett.

Harry Boring hurried over to join them. He grabbed Harriett's arm. "I'm sorry. Don't leave, please."

Her eyes narrowed and latched onto Harry's round pleading orbs.

"Harry, what the hell happened?" Bobby questioned, with upturned palms.

"Don't bother." Harriett pulled free. "You'll have plenty of time to gossip after we're gone. Eddy, I have no time for malicious minds. I think it's time we join Madison Country Club, mingle with some of *my* friends."

Eddy gazed over his shoulder at his old teammates and friends as Harriett dragged him by the hand. He fell into step as they walked down Pine Street. "Harriett, tell me what happened, please."

She linked her arm in his, recanting the details of the overheard conversation.

Eddy stopped mid-step. "What the hell? I thought they were my friends!"

Blocking Harriett's path, he enfolded his wife in his arms.

"You defended me?" he whispered.

"Yes, Eddy. What they said was shallow and simple-minded." She leaned her head into his chest. "I tolerated their teasing as a kid; I will not do the same as an adult."

Eddy gently pushed her away. His mouth widened into a broad smile. Gazing into her eyes, he asked, "Are we really joining the Country Club?"

Harriett laughed. "Yes, Eddy. I would have joined last year, but they base membership on men, not women. More arrogant fools. I need you to apply for us."

"With pleasure."

He tilted his head toward her mouth. His kiss was a mere brush of lips, but sparks shot throughout her body, tingling fingers, toes, and every nerve in between.

"Come on. Let's go get something to eat!"

10

ANNIVERSARY

OCTOBER 1953

September wasted into October as Eddy and Harriett adjusted to living together alone for the first time in married life. The three months they had lived together at Olive's, before Eddy was drafted, seemed like a different lifetime.

Harriett worked long hours at Dugan and Co., then attended classes every Tuesday and Thursday night and Saturday morning. Surprised to enjoy his job, Eddy extended his workday, beginning at eight and ending at five-thirty. Cohabitation was a cinch when neither occupant was home.

Sunday morning, October 11th, Eddy rolled over, pulling a light blanket over his head to block the sun. *It must be late*, he thought. Yawning and stretching, he wandered down to find Harriett in her usual spot, behind her desk.

"I thought you'd be up early," he said, showing a full set of teeth, as he rubbed his eyes and yawned. "Any coffee?"

Harriett kneaded her neck as she looked up from her work. "Good morning, or is it afternoon?"

"Hey, it's only ten."

"Is that all?" She smiled. "I've gone for a five-mile run,

finished all my classwork, and now I'm working for my job." She motioned to a coffee mug before continuing. "I made my first two cups with the press, but I'll drink more. Why don't you perk a pot?"

Eddy leaned down to kiss her forehead. "Sure thing, Peanut."

"Peanut? Where did that come from?"

"You were always just like a tiny nut encased in a shell, waiting to be cracked open. I think the peanut shell is gone."

Harriett shook her head. "Eddy, that's the strangest thing you've ever said."

"Okay, maybe I need caffeine. Be back in a jiffy."

Eddy returned, carrying two mugs of black coffee. He handed one to Harriett, then sat down in Teddy's old chair.

"Harriett, I was thinking."

"Oh no. Did you burn too many brain cells?" She giggled.

His tongue ticked, "Be nice. Our anniversary is coming up. I want to take you out for a nice dinner. Do you think you can work me into your schedule?"

She gazed at her husband. "You remembered?"

"Of course. It was the luckiest day of my life." The infamous Kepler grin spread across his face. "How about it? Let's do up the town, all proper like!"

"I'd love that." She looked at her calendar. "Saturday night? Class is over at noon. I'll be home at one." She tapped the edges of her papers together. "What do you have in mind?"

"You let me worry about that. You just get all dolled up." He gulped the rest of his coffee. "Want more?"

"No, I better stop."

"Suit yourself. I'm off to see your mother." He spun on his heel, blew a kiss then trotted off.

She waited to hear the back door close before dialing. "Hello," the voice said.

"Hi, Earl."

A moment passed before he spoke. "Hi, Harriett. How are you doing?"

"I'm well, thank you." She bit her lower lip. "Earl, did you remind Eddy of our anniversary?"

More silence. "No."

"Really?"

She heard a rush of air inhaling through his teeth. "No, Harriett. I didn't mention anything." He paused. "Eddy is on his own. I'm not going to help him succeed with the woman I…"

Harriett lay the receiver on the desk, not wanting to hear the end of his sentence. She sat staring at the phone for several minutes, then picked it up. It was dead.

∞ ∞ ∞

Olive's gardens, dilapidated after Tabs' death, were now edged, weeded, cleaned of all debris, and ready for a long winter, thanks to Eddy's hard work. Hearing the snip, snip of trimmers, Olive peeked out the kitchen window to find Eddy pruning the hedgerow next to the alley. Her lips turned up, into an unfamiliar smile. *That boy is determined,* she thought. *Reminds me of a love-sick Tabs.*

After brewing a third cup of tea with the same teabag, she slipped into the back parlor, her private sanctuary, to read. Harriett, her siblings, and her father were prohibited from entering Olive's room. On the rare occasional invitation, the Bailey offspring gaped in awe at Olive's collection of photos. Framed pictures dating back to the early 1900s cluttered every flat surface. One particular photo of Olive standing with a young West Point cadet garnered a place of honor. Despite the prevalence of dust throughout the room, the polished silver West Point frame glistened, void of fingerprints, tarnish, or dirt.

Although washing her hands of her mother, Harriett continued to supply Olive with reading material from the college library. Olive sank into the stuffed chair, set down her cup, then felt for her bookmark. She opened C. S. Lewis's *The Lion, the Witch, and the Wardrobe* and continued reading about Edmund, Peter, Susan, and Lucy's adventures in Narnia. Two hours later, she rested her head on the chair back, closed the book, and sighed.

Olive wrapped an old sweater around her house dress. Carrying the book, she walked to the top of the yard to find Eddy munching on a sandwich.

"Will you give this to Harriett?" She thrust the book in Eddy's face without greeting him first.

Eddy ducked to avoid Olive's hand. "Sure. Did you like it?"

Olive took a camping stool from the shed, opened it, and sat down beside him. "I did. It was delightful."

Eddy's eyes widened. He did a double-take of the cover. "Want me to ask for similar books?"

Olive thought for a moment. "Nah. That was enough fluff for one season. Maybe a mystery or thriller next time."

Eddy swallowed hard, clearing his throat of the dry sandwich as he waited for his mother-in-law to speak.

"So, Eddy Kepler, are you and my daughter back together?" She smirked watching Eddy gulp.

"Ah, yes. We are back together." He paused. "Well, almost. We still sleep in different bedrooms." His face reddened. *Why did I volunteer that piece of information?*

"Nothing wrong with separate bedrooms. Tabs and I had them most of our married life."

Eddy coughed. "We're working out some petty details right now. Things will be back to normal soon." He motioned to the yard, "Looks ready for fall. Is there anything in particular that you want me to do?"

Olive considered the condition of the property. "The grass needs cutting a couple more times, and there's snow to shovel in the winter."

Eddy sucked on his lower lip. "Do you mind if I limit my visits to maintenance? At least until spring?"

Olive stood. Refolding the stool, she said, "I have a couple small chores inside. Maybe next week you can tackle them. I assume you can use a hammer. But otherwise, I grant you amnesty!" She chuckled and walked back to the house before calling over her shoulder. "By the way...thanks, Eddy Kepler."

Eddy's mouth dropped. Did Olive Westchester Bailey just *thank* him? Maybe he should listen to his dear, departed mother and attend church services. The universe must be unbalanced!

11

CÔTE-D'OR

CAMPBELLSVILLE, OCTOBER 1953

The week flew by. Harriett hurried into the house after her Saturday lecture. She tossed her attaché into the office and stopped at the powder room before heading to the kitchen. There, she halted mid-stride. Her antique crystal vase contained a dozen long-stem red roses and was sitting in the middle of the kitchen table. An envelope addressed "Harriett" rested in front.

"Wow."

She slowly opened the envelope, removed the card, and read, "To my darling wife on our anniversary. Love, Eddy."

"That's a nice surprise," she said.

"Glad you feel that way." The voice came from the corner. Harriett jumped. "Eddy! I didn't see you."

A low, guttural laugh answered. "I guess not."

Eddy stepped into the sunlight with his hands held behind his back. "I have another surprise." He placed a wrapped box on the table beside the roses.

Harriett sat in one of the chrome chairs. Her infectious smile prompted Eddy to chuckle.

"Don't look so shocked. Open it." Eddy pushed it closer.

"Eddy, this is a complete turnaround from you. I'm flabbergasted…in a good way." She ripped the floral wrapping paper away from a box of liquid-centered, chocolate-covered cherries. "Yum. These are so much better than the creams!" Her hand flew to her hips. "Did you remember how much I like these? Come on, tell me."

Eddy leaned in to kiss her cheek. "Well, I confess I asked Alice about the candy, but everything else was my own doing." His face glowed like a boy waiting for praise from his father.

Harriett broke the seal and gobbled a cherry. "Geez, I'm starving."

"Don't eat too many. I have a special evening planned for you." Eddy reached to move the box away from her.

"Hey, give those back. Just one more!"

"Only if you share."

The couple chewed their chocolates in silence before Harriett added, "I almost forgot. I have our wedding cake top in the refrigerator. Esther had it in her freezer all these years. I hope it's still good."

"Doesn't matter. Cake is cake. I'll eat it." Eddy rubbed his belly, then walked to the back stairs. "Now let's get ready for tonight."

∞ ∞ ∞

The Nash Rambler pulled into the Madison Steak House promptly at six o'clock. Eddy jumped out, running to hold the door. Harriett's slim leg poked out of the car. The point of her red stiletto touched the pavement, followed by the three-inch heel. Eddy extended his hand to steady her. He whistled as she stood beside him. She wore a tea-length, red, satin dress. The rounded boat neckline was trimmed in black-dotted piping that matched two black-and-white dotted gussets. A red headband sporting a petite bow adorned her head. Red, leather, wrist gloves nearly met the three-quarter length, coordinating bolero jacket.

Eddy slipped his arm through hers. They walked to the awaiting doorman; her full petticoat swished back and forth.

"Welcome back to the Madison Steak House, Mrs. Kepler. You look lovely, as usual."

"He knows you?"

Harriett grinned. "This is my favorite restaurant. I come here often." Turning to the doorman, she said, "George, this is my husband, Edgar Kepler, Jr."

George pumped Eddy's arm. "Pleasure to finally meet you, Mr. Kepler. Your wife is one of Madison's most distinguished businessmen." He blushed. "I mean businesswomen."

Eddy forcefully withdrew his hand. "Well, George. Hopefully, you'll be seeing much more of *both* of us."

"Mr. and Mrs. Kepler, your table is waiting. This way, please." George opened the door, then handed them over to the Maître d'.

The waitstaff smiled as Harriett and Eddy strolled past. Some spoke, others nodded acknowledgment.

"They all know you." Eddy tilted his head as he waited for Harriett to be seated.

"Eddy, Earl brought me here last year when I graduated from college. That was my first visit. Since then, I have been promoted. You already know I can't cook; I must eat somewhere." She accepted the napkin and placed it on her knee.

"Aren't these prices steep for weeknights? Just how much money *do* you make?"

"Enough, Eddy." She closed her menu to look directly at her husband. "Don't worry. I eat here twice a month, max. Usually, I go to Howard Johnson's or grab something at

Teddy's. When we join MCC, we'll eat in one of their dining rooms."

Eddy glanced up from his menu. "What is MCC?"

"MCC. Madison Country Club. Both Tom and Vincent belong and are willing to sponsor us."

Eddy chuckled. "You have this all planned, don't you?"

"I do. MCC has a formal dining room, a grill, and a pub room, used mostly by men. That's where all the business gets done. Well, there and on the course," she rambled, running her words together. "They have tennis courts, a swimming pool, croquet courts, and a beautiful eighteen-hole golf course. Geez, Louise, listen to me. I think I'm excited."

"Do they allow women in the pub?"

"It's not forbidden, although it's frowned upon. It took four visits—and Tom and Vincent complaining—for the men to finally relax when I'm there." She shook her head. "Men can be so stupid!"

Eddy sighed. "It's always been that way, Harriett. We are taught to act like that. You'll change their minds, you'll see. You certainly changed mine. Now, what should I eat?"

Unaware of being agitated, Harriett's shoulders dropped at Eddy's compliment as the waiter approached to begin their order. "I get the petite filet, medium," she told him. "You'll want a full-sized or oversized one."

"Mrs. Kepler, what are you drinking tonight?"

"Hi, Timmy. I'll have a Manhattan, on the rocks, please."

"Hmm," said Eddy. "I took you for a pink squirrel, gin fizz kind of gal."

Harriett twisted her lips into a frown. "Eddy, I am a woman competing in a man's world. I must be smarter, work harder, and invest more time than the men do, just to earn my place. And I must drink like a man, too, if I'm to be respected."

Eddy's eyes widened. "Pardon me." He threw his hands in the air, fingers spread.

Timothy waited silently, turning his head to hide his grin. When the conversation paused, he asked, "And for the gentleman?"

"The gentleman is Mr. Kepler, and I'll have a whiskey, neat."

"Do you have a preference?"

Harriett spoke, cutting off Eddy. "Give him OS, bonded eight, bourbon. Thanks, Timmy."

Eddy stopped the waiter from leaving. "Timothy, is it? Make it a seven and seven. I prefer having taste buds for my steak."

"You got it, Mr. Kepler. Coming right up."

Harriett hung her head. "I am sorry, Eddy. I should not assume it's okay to order for you. Now back to food. The asparagus tips and sauteed spinach are excellent."

Eddy reached for her hand. "Too many vegetables. I'm here to eat cow, darling."

∞ ∞ ∞

Eddy gaped as the waiter rubbed the large wooden bowl with garlic, tossed romaine lettuce, then cracked a coddled egg topped with freshly squeezed lemon into the center.

"We're eating raw egg?" He pointed to the sideshow, then sipped his drink.

"If you want an authentic Caesar, then yes." Harriett's eyes twinkled.

"Okay, I'll trust you. Like I said, I'm here for meat, not grass. I'll at least taste the greens." He stood, glancing toward the bar.

"Sir, the men's room is straight ahead, around the corner, then on your left."

"Thanks, Timothy." He wiped his mouth, placing his napkin on the table. When he returned, it was refolded, standing upright beside his salad plate.

"Swanky place." Noticing the waiter waiting for the signal to serve, Eddy nodded his head. Timothy piled salad onto their plates, checked their drinks for refills, then left the couple alone to eat.

Harriett allowed Eddy several bites before asking. "Well? Do you like it?"

"Actually, yes. What are these salty slimy things?"

Harriett covered her mouth just in time to catch her spraying drink. "Anchovies. I thought you were an experienced man of the world."

"I am worldly in some subjects. Not fine dining." He scratched his head. "And where did you get your education?"

"Watching and absorbing. There is so much out there beyond Campbellsville. Sometimes I simply observe and say nothing." Harriett wiped her mouth with her napkin, folded her hands on the table, and sat quietly as Timothy cleared their salad plates.

The low buzz of chatter floated over the table as weekend diners packed the restaurant. Eddy fidgeted at the lull in their conversation by adjusting his tie. He gazed at his wife, admiring her red lips, the flow of her hair off her forehead, her tiny upturned nose, and the curve of her neck, bare of jewelry.

"Hmm," Eddy mumbled aloud.

"Hmm?" Harriett tipped her head to the side. "What are you thinking?"

"Thinking about baubles, that's all." The Kepler grin spread across his face. "I think our dinners are here."

Eddy nodded to his left as Timothy arrived with two sizzling platters.

"Madame, your petite filet, medium. And sir, your jumbo

ribeye, medium rare. May I bring you anything else at this time?"

Harriett handed him her empty cocktail glass. "Eddy, may we share a bottle of wine? I don't usually drink much, but this steak smells like it's lonely."

"Sure, Harriett. Do you have a favorite?"

Harriett dipped her head in acknowledgment. "Yes, Timmy, a bottle of Burgundy. Do you have anything from Beaune, Côte-d'Or?"

"I'll check, but I believe we do. Thank you, Mrs. Kepler." The waiter bowed, hurrying to retrieve the requested bottle.

"Eat, Eddy, don't wait for the wine." Harriett cut her bright green asparagus, glistening with butter sauce, and took a bite. "Best vegetable ever."

Eddy scooped a large forkful of a twice-baked potato. Golden gooey cheese hung in strings as he lifted it to his mouth. "Nope. This is."

Timothy returned with a bottle labeled "La Maréchaude, Aloxe-Corton Premiers Crus." He removed the cork, presented it to Eddy, then poured about an ounce into a ballooned goblet. Eddy took the cork and stared blankly at Harriett.

"Timmy, I'll taste, if you don't mind." She reached for the cork, inspected it for signs of mold, sniffed it, then swirled her stem. "Nice legs."

"Sure are!" Eddy smiled.

"The wine, silly." Harriett sipped then sloshed the wine around her tongue. "Lovely finish. You may pour, thanks, Timmy."

Glasses filled and waiter gone, Eddy gapped at Harriett. "You *are* a woman of the world. You surprise me every day, Harriett Bailey Kepler."

Harriett blushed. "Eat Eddy. Your meat is getting cold."

The couple ate, talking minimally as they savored the

combination of the juice from the meat, combined with the tannins of the wine. Harriett, stomach filled with spinach and asparagus, offered Eddy the last several pieces of her filet. He took them hungrily.

"You don't want this? It's delicious. I see why you come here so often." Eddy shoved another bite into his mouth and washed it down with wine.

Timothy, stealthily waiting in the sides, swooped in to refill their wine glasses, offering Harriett the remaining drops.

"No." She covered her goblet with her hand. "Give it to Mr. Kepler, please. I've had more than enough."

Eagerly accepting the wine, Eddy finished chewing. "Dessert?"

"Our wedding cake top is waiting for us at home. This was a lovely evening, but I'm ready to leave."

"Anything you say, Peanut." His hand flew into the air motioning for the check. Eddy tried not to gulp as he read the total. "No wonder that wine tasted so good…"

"Ahh, sorry, Eddy. But it was a special evening, wasn't it?" Harriett cocked her head, grinning coquettishly. "I believe after three years of being ignored, I'm worth it."

Eddy chewed on his lower lip. "This one dinner may compensate for all three years," he mumbled under his breath. "Harriett, how much do I tip?"

"Ten to fifteen percent. Please excuse me while I powder my nose."

Eddy watched as she walked away. *I nearly flunked math… how do I calculate ten percent?* Then, in a stroke of brilliance, he remembered. Move the decimal point two places. He stashed bills into the leather folder, then looked at his diminished wallet and sighed. *This is one expensive broad*, he thought. *But she's all mine…and downright impressive.*

12

THE PEARLS

Harriett sat close to Eddy on the drive home, pressing her head against his arm. After parking the car on the street, Eddy nudged his sleeping wife.

"Harriett." He caressed her face. "Harriett, we're home."

She opened, then shielded her eyes from the streetlight. "Oh, I must have dozed off."

Eddy chuckled softly. "You slept most of the way home." He leaned over to kiss her. "Let's eat cake."

"Sure thing, Marie Antoinette." Harriett giggled.

"Huh?"

"Never mind."

Eddy rushed to open the car door. After steadying her, they walked arm in arm up the grand, terraced staircase. Eddy unlocked the front door before scooping Harriett into his arms.

"I never had the honor of carrying my wife over the threshold. Better late than never." His arms encircled her, lifting the tiny woman, and twirling her around. He stepped into the outer entryway, and Harriett giggled, tossing her head back as she clung to Eddy's neck.

"Allow me." She opened the second set of doors.

Not stopping at the living room or office, Eddy mounted the stairs before gently dropping Harriett onto her bed.

"Change, darling. You look stunning in red, but I imagine you would like to get out of this get-up before dessert. I'll be waiting with drinks."

"Oh Eddy, I've had enough alcohol for one night."

"Just one more?" He blew her a kiss, then turned his back on her.

∞ ∞ ∞

Eddy stood in Harriett's office, clinking ice cubes one at a time into crystal rocks tumblers. He added whiskey, then topped it with Seven-Up. The clank of heels hitting the back staircase hastened him into the living room. He removed his suit jacket, loosened his tie, then unbuttoned his cuff links in time to see Harriett enter the room. She wore a flowing, brightly colored, floral, floor-length chemise. Puffy pink pom-poms adorned kitten heel mule slippers.

Eddy gasped. "Again, you look amazing." He handed her a drink. "Where did you get that?"

"It's called a Mumu. Albert and Laurie brought one back for everyone after they honeymooned in Hawaii." She spun around. "Pretty, isn't it?"

"It is on you." Eddy extended his arms. "Come here. Let's sit on the couch," he said as he pulled her to the sofa.

"I thought you wanted cake?" A revealing glint crossed her eyes as her lips puckered.

Eddy seized her waist. "You're all the sugar I need tonight." Leaning over, his lips grazed hers as he drew her near.

Harriett reached to move his jacket as she nestled into his

arm. Her hand struck something solid in his suit pocket. She fumbled inside.

"What is this?" she asked as she removed a strand of pearls. Her eyes widened. "Oh, Eddy!" Harriett jumped onto her knees. Bending forward, she kissed his mouth. "This evening is more than I hoped for. You do love me!"

Eddy held his breath, his eyes widening as he stared at his gift to Rosa. *Oh my God. Where did they come from?*

After latching the necklace around her neck, she fingered each of the tiny orbs. "I don't have any real jewelry." Tears began to form in her eyes. "I buy clothing and other items for the house, but in my mind, jewelry is for a husband to give to his wife."

Eddy sagged. Arms flaccid. The color drained from his face. *No. No. Not the pearls.*

"Say something, Eddy." She paused. "Oh, did I ruin your surprise? Well, I couldn't be more delighted." She raved, slurring her words together, as she smothered his face in smooches.

Buzzing filled his ears. After several minutes, he regained command of his senses.

"Happy anniversary, dear." Reverberating the low guttural tiding, he slouched back. Eddy raised his glass in a toast. "To many more?"

The emotions of the previous three years, coupled with one too many drinks, overwhelmed the unsuspecting Harriett. She grasped the sides of her face. With water streaming from her eyes, she sobbed. "I love you so much, Eddy Kepler. Besides our wedding day, this is the happiest day of my life."

Eddy stood on wobbling legs. His head spun with thoughts of Rosa and Joey, heart aching from what he was about to gain at the expense of such loss. Lifting Harriett, he carried her up the staircase for the second time within 30 minutes. Gently placing her on her bed, he sat astride her body.

"Will you be Mrs. Kepler tonight?"

She purred. "I have been waiting three years to be Mrs. Kepler." She unbuttoned his shirt, lingering after each button to stroke his chest. His shirt fell to the bed. Trembling, she caressed his shoulders and biceps.

He reached for her hand, placing a finger in his mouth. "I like the taste of these tiny digits." After each finger received equal attention, he focused on nuzzling her neck.

Harriett moaned. "No marks, please Eddy."

"I thought you liked this?"

"Oh, I do," she murmured. "But I can't have marks."

Eddy's nibbling moved further down her body.

Harriett tingled. Butterflies, compounded by three years of abstinence fluttered through her body. She engulfed his mouth with hers. The sound of his belt clanking as his trousers hit the floor intensified their anticipation.

Eddy straddled her, whispering, "Mrs. Kepler, I'm home."

Harriett groaned into a climax as the office clock chimed ten.

∞ ∞ ∞

A panting Eddy rolled onto his side. Not since he was 15 had he endured five months of celibacy. Three hours of lovemaking left him sweating and spent. Drifting into sleep, he mumbled, "Love you, Rosa."

"What?" Harriett asked drowsily.

"Goodnight, darling."

"Goodnight." Spooning him, she wrapped her arms around his broad shoulders, immediately falling asleep to his soft rhythmic snoring.

13

THANK YOU

Albert Bailey, Teddy Jenson, Darrell, and Toby Cline smoothed the wet concrete. The back half of Olive Bailey's basement floor was finished while waiting on Eddy. Around noon, Eddy clanged down the outside entrance.

"Hi, guys. Sorry, I'm late." He grinned. "Exhausting night."

Albert glared. "If it was with my sister, I don't want to know. Keep it to yourself, Kepler."

Eddy scoffed. "Let's just say that we are once again happily married."

"Son of a bitch!" Albert said, throwing him a rake. "Spend some of that pent-up energy spreading cement."

The beeping sound of a truck in reverse floated down the coal shoot.

Teddy glanced toward the swishing sound of wet concrete flowing down the trough. "Here we go. Grab your tools and start moving."

Eddy rolled up the sleeves of his T-shirt, tied a bandana handkerchief around his head, then pulled on a pair of leather gloves. Stepping through the rebar supports, he guided the heavy mixture forward for Darrell and Toby to distribute into the corners, while Albert and Teddy smoothed the surface.

Three hours later, five men stood crowded together on the staircase. Sweat, dripping from their noses and temples, splattered onto the gray floor.

Eddy leaned against the stone wall and swiped away a cobweb. "Oh my God! That was hard work." He exhaled before swatting a dangling spider.

Darrell sunk onto a step. "I'm too old for this kind of work."

"I told you that Lloly and I would take your place, Dad." Toby examined his father's face for signs of physical distress.

Darrell laughed. "Toby, you're as kind as your namesake, but I'm not 40 yet! I'm slightly out of shape, that's all." Reaching for Toby's shoulder, he added. "Besides, Lloly is only 11. He's not strong enough to do a man's work."

Eddy laughed. "You mean Harriett's champion, the kid that tried to run me off, isn't in high school?" He shook his head. "Brave little soldier. I think I like that boy!"

Their conversation was interrupted when the first-floor door opened. Olive called down, "What's all the chatter? Shut up and finish. I want you out of here!"

Albert clenched his teeth. Looking at Eddy, he said, "At least I give my sister credit, having you tend to that bitch. Saves us the hassle."

"I actually don't mind her." Eddy hesitated. "At least, not as much as I used to."

"Well, take off your boots, and let's get out of her hair."

The men climbed the stairs to a waiting Olive. She greeted and thanked them with, "Don't track up my kitchen!"

Escaping quickly, they sat on the porch step, relacing

boots when the door opened. Olive poked her head out. "Eddy Kepler, do you mind staying a minute?"

"Sure, Olive."

A grinning Teddy waited for the sound of the door to latch. "I think she has a crush on him."

∞ ∞ ∞

Eddy twisted the nozzle of the hose, then sprayed his cement-caked boots with water. Stomping them dry as he walked, he collapsed into one of the Adirondack chairs sheltered by the grapevines. While he was exhausted, arms dangling at his side, the chilly October air was refreshing. He watched fluffy white clouds move from west to east while he daydreamed of the previous night's conquest. *Success. She is once again my wife.* The squeak and slam of the screen door jarred his musing. The woman, wrapped in a shawl, carried a tray.

"I brought you a cup of tea." Olive handed him a teacup and saucer. Three cookies surrounded the cup. "Figured you'd be hungry."

"Thanks, Olive. I only ate a piece of toast this morning." He hungrily scarfed down all three cookies before sipping his tea. "That was kind of you."

Olive blew air through rolled lips. "I don't think I've ever been called 'kind.'"

"Then how about 'thoughtful?'"

"Nope. That neither." She smiled. "Doesn't my daughter feed you?"

"I let her sleep in this morning. She works hard, never takes any downtime. I couldn't wake her; she was sleeping so soundly."

"Hmm." Olive pondered. Pulling a book out of her apron

pocket, she asked, "Will you give this to Harriett and thank her? I'm ready for another one."

"Sure. Olive." Eddy paused before continuing. "What happened between you and Harriett? Why is she so angry with you?"

Olive pursed her lips. Staring into Eddy's eyes, she contemplated. "She blames me for Tabs' death."

Eddy tilted his head to the side. "Does she have reason to do so?"

"Yes." She bit her lip. "I don't want to talk about it. It truly was an accident." Olive placed her teacup on the arm of the chair before grabbing Eddy's hands. "I miss him, Eddy Kepler. I really miss him."

She turned her head to hide the tears welling in her eyes. Pulling a handkerchief from up her sleeve, she blew her nose. "I need to get inside. Thanks for all your work."

14

MOVING DAY

*H*arriett reached across the bed. Feeling nothing, she rolled onto her side. *I know I didn't dream last night.* A quick glance around the room confirmed last evening's pleasure. Trousers, shirt, Mumu, bra, and panties were strewn around the room, draping the vanity, and hanging from the mirror. The angle of the sunshine beating through the window sparked unease. The hands of her alarm confirmed her suspicion. One o'clock in the afternoon!

Harriett jumped out of bed. She quickly gathered discarded clothing, then turned the faucet knobs. Warm water luxuriated over her body, removing all tension. She scrubbed her hair, then massaged her scalp. Streaming tears followed the suds down the drain. Although she had waited three years for such bliss, she was overwhelmed by the emotion of feeling whole.

"You must learn to cook," she exclaimed aloud. "You're a wife." She dried her body and stepped onto the scale which read one hundred-one pounds. Throwing on a sweater and pair of trousers, she bounded down the back stairs and into the kitchen. Assembling canisters, bowls, and other ingredients together, Harriett opened her recipe box and read. Within 10 minutes she was kneading dough. Punch, fold, punch, fold, she continued until the yeasty blob was a smooth, pliable mound. *I can't cook, but I can bake.*

She placed a large glass bowl on top. Leaving her creation to rise, she walked back to her bedroom. The act of moving Eddy's clothes from the guest room to the master was completed subconsciously. Eddy, standing in the doorway to his room interrupted her back-and-forth path.

"Harriett." He reached to steady her as she bounced off his chest. "What are you doing?

She stood on tip-toes, answering with a kiss. "Moving you back where you belong."

"Are you sure that's what you want?"

"Oh yes, Eddy. After last night, I am positive." She bit her lip as she caressed his cheek. "Is it okay with you?"

Eddy lifted Harriett, swung her in circles, then set her gently on top of the bed. "It's more than fine by me, Mrs. Kepler. Now we can get on with making a future together."

Harriett glanced at Eddy's soiled clothing. "What have you been doing? You're a mess." She pulled at his belt buckle. "Take these nasty things off. I don't want you getting dirt on the bedspread."

Eddy stripped out of his tee-shirt. Chuckling, he asked, "Are you sure that's the only reason for me to change?" He dropped his trousers, sat on the edge of the bed, then removed his socks.

"Now, what else would I have on my mind?" Harriett tossed the items in her arms at Eddy, who ducked. Clothing toppled to the floor, and Harriett jumped onto the bed. Pushing Eddy over, the couple lay wrapped in each other's arms. "Welcome home, Mr. Kepler. By the way, I love my pearls!" She fingered the strand around her neck. "I'm never taking them off."

Eddy hid his cringe. "I don't think you can bathe in them, darling. Now, where were we?" He leaned over, kissing his willing partner, before exhausting the afternoon and their energy.

∞ ∞ ∞

Harriett gently wiggled out of Eddy's arms. Stretching, she glanced at the clock. "Oh, Geez Louise. It's already nighttime." The streetlight shone through the front window, casting long shadows on the wall. She nudged her sleeping bedmate. "Eddy, wake up or you'll not sleep tonight."

"Hmm." He rolled onto his back. "Is it morning?"

Harriett giggled. "No, silly. But we need to eat supper and take our baths before we go to bed. Work in the morning."

Eddy reached for Harriett as she tried to leave. "You better get used to morning showers. I have an evening activity to add to your schedule." He slapped her across the butt. "We have two bathrooms. We'll both shower in the morning from now on."

Harriett guffawed. "Then we better go to bed at ten, because I need *some* sleep." She sighed, exhaling a long breath. "Shall we see what we can scrounge up to eat? I confess, I slept late this morning and skipped breakfast. I'm famished!"

Eddy sat upright, sliding one leg and then the second from under the sheet. Harriett smiled as she watched his firm quadriceps and the ball of his calf muscles flex. *You are gorgeous*, she thought. Aloud she asked, "Where were you today?"

"I was helping the boys at your mother's house. We poured a concrete floor in the basement." Eddy pulled on his boxers and trousers.

"Oh. I'd rather not ruin my mood by speaking of her." A frown crossed her face.

"She's been modernizing the place. Maybe we should consider doing updates here too. What do you think?"

"Hmm. I haven't thought about it. I spent the last year and a half cleaning up the gardens and buying furniture." She glanced around the bedroom. "Is this room too feminine for you? Is that why you're asking?"

The yellow-and-green floral print of the bedspread was repeated in the draperies. Glass perfume bottles along with a matching set of comb, brush, and mirror filled the vanity top. Delicately carved crystal lamps adorned both nightstands. The girly room, similar in style to one of the guest rooms, was certainly on the 'fluffy' side.

"Honey, I don't care what décor you put in a room. I was just thinking, maybe we should update the kitchen. It's a big space. I have a couple ideas. Come on, let's go downstairs. I'll show you."

∞ ∞ ∞

Dough seeped from under the bowl out onto the countertop. A stringy blob dangled over the side as it inched toward the linoleum floor. Both Eddy and Harriett gasped at the sight as the aroma of yeast bombarded their nostrils.

"Oh no! I forgot all about this. What a mess." She grabbed the hanging dough and plopped it into the sink, preventing a gooey second surface.

"What were you making?" Eddy smiled as he reached to prevent the lava-like spread of more dough.

"I intended to make maple rolls." She chuckled, then lifted the covering. The mound, minus restraints, gushed outward. "Goodness! Eddy, help me."

Eddy squished a clump of the would-be rolls through his

fingers. An impish grin crossed his face as his arm moved through the air, tossing the dough into Harriett's face.

She gasped as the soft mass stuck to her forehead before dropping. "What the heck?" Her wide eyes closed to slits as she scooped a glob into her arms. Raising up onto her toes, she dumped it over Eddy's head.

"That's disgusting!" He permitted gravity to take over. The dough splattered to the floor as he grabbed Harriett's waist pulling her on top of it.

"Stop. Eddy!' She giggled. "This mess will take hours to clean up." She pushed his chest as he tumbled the two of them around the floor.

"Don't worry, Mrs. Kepler," he said, as he nuzzled her neck. "You're not alone. I'm here to help."

∞∞∞

Delightful red, orange, and yellow leaves provided visual relief from the daily commute. The following evening, Harriett parked in the garage, then headed into the kitchen.

She stood in front of the refrigerator, staring into space. Hearing the door, Eddy ran up, grabbing her from behind. "What's so interesting in the icebox?"

"Nothing. That's the problem. I have no idea what to make to eat." She turned around to see him grinning.

"Distracted, are we?" Eddy chuckled aloud as a grin spread across his face.

"No. Well, maybe. But I hate cooking." She blushed. "You have any ideas?"

"Let me see." Eddy began pulling odds and ends from the refrigerator. He continued the process in the pantry. Before long, he was slicing, grating, sauteing, and whisking. Twenty minutes after starting, he served Harriett a beautiful omelet on a heated plate.

The aroma of fresh herbs and cheese made her salivate. "Where did you learn to cook?" She rubbed her growling belly. "Keep this up and you may have a permanent job."

"Fine by me. I actually don't mind cooking. I only dabble, but can learn." Eddy poured two glasses of a chilled French Rosé. "Eat up. No dessert tonight. No time." He smirked. "Especially since our maple buns from last night were over-inflated."

"Tell you what. I'll make you a bargain." Harriett pulled two frozen chocolate gobs, cream-filled individual chocolate cakes, from the freezer and placed them on a plate to thaw. "You cook and I'll bake. Do we have a deal?"

Eddy eyed the sweet chocolate cakes. "Totally acceptable. I can live with that. Now eat, before your eggs get cold, and I'll share my ideas about this kitchen."

Harriett bit into her omelet. "I almost forgot, since we went to bed hungry after that clean up." She tugged at a curly lock of his hair. "Tell me what that handsome head of yours is conjuring up."

Eddy stood and walked to the far corner of the expanse. "Look at all this waste of space. I was thinking that we should turn this into a laundry room. You know, move the washer and dryer up from the basement." He glanced at Harriett, hoping to see approval. "I don't mind walking up and down two flights of stairs, but…you're so busy. I thought it would be a great time saver."

Harriett nodded her head without speaking.

Eddy walked back to the table. Motioning to the sink, he continued. "If we install more cabinets, a wall oven, and some counter space, you could have a real baking center. And I could use this area for cooking." He motioned to the range. "Have you ever considered a professional stove?"

Harriett choked on her food. "Eddy, I barely boil water. Why would I want a different stove?"

"Point taken. But If I'm going to take over meal responsibility, I might like some updates. Bigger refrigerator, ovens, more burners, you know!"

"No, I don't, but it sounds good to me. Draw up some rough sketches and we can get some prices." Harriett sipped her wine. She marveled at her husband's animation. "Eddy," she hesitated. He seemed happy, at home, but she needed to be certain. "Are you sure you want this marriage?"

Eddy stood behind her chair. Leaning over, he brushed his fingers through her hair. "Harriett, I am so happy to be home with you."

15

LONELY

NOVEMBER 1953

*E*ddy placed the rake back into the shed before collecting the pile of leaves. He tossed them into the burning bin, lit a fire, and watched the flames shoot skyward. Olive Bailey's property was once again beautifully manicured, trimmed, and pruned, thanks to Eddy's efforts. As he guarded the fire, he admired his work. *Olive better be happy*, he thought. He spent every Saturday of every weekend since late summer puttering at the Bailey residence, in compliance with Harriett's stipulation.

Olive poked her head through the open, back screen door. "Eddy Kepler, do you have a minute?"

"Sure." To himself, he thought the question repetitive. Eddy crossed the threshold and removed his boots, gloves, and jacket before stepping into the kitchen. "Olive, I'm here. What do you need?"

A faint voice echoed from inside the bowels of the house. "In here."

Walking into the dining room, Eddy moved in front of the center staircase of the entryway and peeked into the front family parlor. Still no Olive.

"Are you coming?" The voice came from the inner sanctum of her private parlor. "I'm in here."

Eddy hesitated, remembering Harriett's stories of how Olive forbade entry to her cloister.

"You want me in there?"

"Yes. Now hurry, the tea is getting cold."

Eddy stepped through the door. The room was decorated in greens, whites, and browns. A green-and-white magnolia pattern covered a feathery, stuffed sofa and matching chair. A solid white club chair and footstool sat next to a floor reading lamp. Shelves filled with books and photographs lined one entire wall. Side tables were filled with more photos. A sparklingly polished silver-framed picture of a young woman and uniformed man occupied a place of distinction, front, and center.

Eddy leaned in for a closer look. "Who is that?" He scratched his head. "Looks like Alice."

Olive sighed. "It's me, with my brother Fred at his West Point graduation."

He gulped. "Wow! You were a real looker, Olive." He paused awkwardly before adding, "Not that you're not pretty now."

"Cut the crap, Eddy Kepler." Olive chuckled. "You don't have to sugarcoat for me. I prefer the truth. It's what I give and what I prefer to get."

He wiped his palms on his trousers. "Ah. Oh, well, you are still handsome for a woman your age."

"You better quit while you're ahead." She motioned to the green magnolia chair. "Have a seat. Want some tea?"

"Sure. I'd like that." He accepted the saucer from her outstretched hand. "What's on your mind?"

"Truthfully?"

"Well, yes! You just said you like it straight. So do I."

Olive pursed her lips. "I simply wanted to talk. I wanted some company." She offered him a sandwich before adding, "I get lonely sometimes."

Eddy bit the savory, then chewed. "Yep, I bet you do. Tell me about Fred, was that his name?"

Olive scowled. "Not today. Maybe someday. But not today, okay?"

Blowing air vibrated his lips. "Then, tell me about growing up on the farm. I understand it was quite the enterprise."

"Ah, Westchester Farm! That it was. You know, I began working for my father when I was only nine or ten years old…"

The two sat talking long into the afternoon. Eddy listened as Olive reminisced about life as a child, living in the opulent mansion of Westchester farm, losing her mother as a toddler, and working as an accountant for her father.

"I never knew you worked with numbers, just like Harriett." Eddy tried to scratch his chin using minimal motion, not wanting to break the mood.

"Hmmm," Olive pondered. "I think it's more like Harriett copied me rather than me imitating her."

Eddy cleared his throat. "I don't consider it copying at all. It's more about being passed down from mother to daughter."

Olive cocked her head, then paused several moments. "I suppose you're right. I always accused her of usurping my dreams. I guess it's possible that she inherited it from me through no fault of her own." Olive stood. Walking to a side table, she lifted a framed photo of a young woman in a wedding dress. Handing the picture to Eddy, she continued, "There's a lot to be said about family traits. This is me, but Alice looked just like me at this age. Polly seems to be following suit, and will probably be even more stunning than either her mother or me."

"Both you and Harriett are brilliant women, Olive. And if you pardon my bluntness, stubborn."

The house echoed with Olive's deep guttural laugh. "Eddy Kepler. I think you may be the first person on earth brave enough to call me stubborn."

The infamous Kepler grin crossed his face. "I'm not a chicken. Olive, tell me more about your siblings."

A darkness seemed to drape Olive's face. She dabbed the corners of her eyes with her handkerchief. "No. Like Fred, I prefer to forget my family today."

Eddy jumped to his feet. "I'm sorry. I'll leave then."

"No, don't. Please stay for a while longer." Olive looked around the room. Her eyes landed on a picture of herself sitting with twin babies. "Why don't I tell you the story of how my nephew, Sinclair, almost drowned the night I got kicked out of school?" She smirked. "That's a real doozy of a tale."

Eddy leaned back into the chair, listening intently to every word said until the clock chimed four times.

He jumped. "I'm sorry to cut this off, but I need to get home." He turned to leave, then, facing Olive, he added, "Olive, Harriett and I are hosting Thanksgiving dinner this year. Your whole family will be there. Why don't you join us?"

Olive choked. "Thanks, but I better not. I don't think Harriett's ready to forgive me yet."

"Why don't I speak to her?" Eddy tilted his head to the side.

"Not this year, Eddy Kepler. But thanks."

He placed his hands on his hips. "Are you sure I can't change your mind?"

"I'm sure." Olive turned her back to her son-in-law, then

stomped out of the room and up the stairs, switching off each light as she went, leaving him alone and in the dark.

Eddy waited until he heard a door slam shut above him, then he silently closed the kitchen door. Walking the five blocks home with labored steps, he mused at his conversation. *I must mention Olive's loneliness to my wife.*

16

GUESS WHO'S COMING TO DINNER

Harriett was sitting at her desk as streetlights began twinkling one at a time, shining through the large window. She glanced at her wrist. Six-thirty. Lifting the receiver from its cradle, she dialed.

"Hello," said the baritone voice.

"Earl. Hi, it's Harriett," she said, her voice strained and forced. "We are hosting Thanksgiving this year. Please plan on joining us."

She waited. For the past four weeks, she deliberately avoided her one-time champion, feeling too awkward after Eddy's return to her bed.

Finally, the voice spoke. "Hi, Harriett. How are you? It's been a while."

"Yes, Earl, a month. What do you say? Three o'clock?" She swallowed hard.

"I think I'll eat at home, this—"

"Please, Earl," Harriett interrupted. "It means a lot to me. Please come over."

His sigh sizzled in her ear as if he were frying an egg. "Okay. For you, I'll be over. What may I bring?"

She smiled as she exhaled. The usual lilt returned to her speech. "Good. Bring nothing. I'm baking pies. My sisters are bringing side dishes, and Eddy's making the turkey."

"Harriett?"

"Yes?" She bit her lip as she waited for what might follow. Acid bubbled in her stomach, pushing up to singe her throat.

"Are you doing okay, Harriett?" His voice was close to a whisper.

"Yes, Earl. I'm fine," she stuttered. "We're fine. Working things out."

"Then I'll see you Thursday at three. Thanks for the invitation." He dropped the phone and it clicked dead.

Harriett rolled her shoulders, then stretched her neck slowly from side to side. Feeling the knot on the right, just below her ear, she kneaded the soft tissue. *Yikes! That hurts.*

∞ ∞ ∞

The clock struck seven as Eddy heard the garage door closing and Harriett's heels on the staircase. Twisting the cap off the bottle, he poured twice.

"Hi, sweetie." He greeted her with a cocktail. "Dinner is ready. How was your day?"

Ice cubes clinked against each other as she sipped the bourbon. "Winding down for the holidays. It should be smooth sailing until the new year. How about you?" She stretched to kiss his cheek.

He tried unsuccessfully to prevent the corners of his mouth from turning up. "I had a great day." Bending down, he wrapped her waist, then kissed her mouth. "You are looking at the new manager of supply for the steel mill!"

Harriett squealed with delight. "The entire mill operation in Madison?"

"Yes, ma'am." He lifted her with one arm, then twirled

her in a circle. "It's a big promotion, Harriett. And this time, I got it all on my own! No help from you." His face beamed with pride.

"Oh Eddy, I'm so proud of you. But I didn't get you your job."

"I'm afraid you did." He puckered his lips. "I was hired on the spot when I mentioned you are my wife. But this…this was all me." He pulled a piece of paper from his pants pocket. "My salary." His grin grew bigger.

"Ah." She whistled. "Nice number."

His face changed to an impish child-like smile. "How close am I to you?"

Harriett placed her briefcase on the floor. Reaching up on tiptoes, she kissed his lips. "Over halfway. But it's not a competition."

"I've been a competitor my entire life."

"Well, then consider us part of the same team. When one player improves, the entire team improves; no need for individual assessment."

"I think team Kepler is ready for Madison Country Club."

Harriett swallowed another sip. "I'll get the appropriate paperwork tomorrow."

"I should do it. Especially now that I'm more qualified." His chest puffed out like a strutting rooster.

"Darling, of course, you are worthy of joining the club. But Mr. Roland and Mr. Vincent will be our sponsors. Please allow me to do it, this time. Okay?" She stroked his sleeve in appeasement. "Oh, by the way…Earl is coming to Thanksgiving dinner."

"Oh." Eddy's face dropped. "Hey, on that note, what do you think about inviting Olive?"

A stream of alcohol flew out of her mouth and across the hallway. "What? Why would you even think of asking that question?"

"She's your mother. You include my brother. She's your family after all. I think she gets lonely in that big house." Eddy pulled his handkerchief from his pocket and began wiping the mess off the floor.

Harriett creased her brows. "That's her own doing, not mine. I shall be giving thanks on Thursday. I am not thankful for her."

"Sorry. I'll drop it. At least for now." He motioned for her to follow him into the dining room. "Come on. I want to eat in here tonight, to celebrate."

The formal table was laid with a slightly rumpled cotton cloth, formal crystal and china, and garnished with paper napkins. A homemade centerpiece featuring yellow chrysanthemums and ivy toppling from a pickle jar, flanked by tapers shoved crookedly into Waterford candlesticks, decorated the middle of the table. The mismatched scene was almost cartoonish; she imagined clowns carefully tumbling down the Hall of Mirrors at Versailles.

"Ha!" The guffaw escaped her mouth before Harriett could suppress it.

Eddy pouted. "Are you laughing at me?" Brushing the tablecloth with his hand, he tried to smooth a wrinkle. "I'm not much for ironing."

"I see that. Eddy, this is perfect. Really." Her growling stomach changed the conversation. "What goes on my pretty plates?" She rubbed her tummy.

The smile returned to Eddy's face. "I made stuffed pork chops, mashed potatoes, gravy, and canned peas. Just like the night I proposed to you."

∞ ∞ ∞

Eddy held her chair, then easily pushed her up to the table as if she were on rollers.

"Wine?" he poured without waiting for an answer.

Harriett inhaled the earthy scent of rosemary and sage. "I must say, you're doing a great job cooking, Eddy." She raised her glass in a toast. "To your promotion! Salud."

"Bottoms up!" Eddy hungrily sawed into his meat. "How long will it take for our club approval? Any idea?" His lips smacked as he chewed and talked.

"With both Tom and Glen sponsoring us, it should be quick." She paused before placing a forkful of potatoes in her mouth, then washed it down with a sip of wine. "We should be full members for all the Christmas parties and, of course, long before golf season begins."

Eddy's leg bounced up and down. "I know what I'm asking Santa for." He grinned as he grabbed his hands together and slowly pulled his arms back and above his head. "And I know what to buy you!"

Harriett grinned. "I think I'll let you oversee equipment; that's right up your alley in supply. Sound okay to you?"

Eddy continued his swing forward. "Woosh!"

Crystal connected with his joined hands in front of his body. Wine flew across the table, soaking the cloth. The goblet bounced, spun, then crashed to the floor, leaving a puddle of red liquid on the carpet.

"Shit!" Eddy jumped to his feet. "Son of a bitch! Harriett, I'm sorry." His speed as a star high school football running back kicked in. Before Harriett's big round eyes could constrict back to normal size, Eddy jumped up, uprighted the glass, and tossed his paper napkin on the wine stain.

"I'll be right back with towels. At least the stem didn't break," he said, then sprinted through the butler's pantry to the kitchen.

Harriett added her napkin to the spill, but the volume of liquid soaked right through. She grabbed her empty bread dish, then tossed the saturated paper on top as wine dripped from the dissolving paper.

"Shit." Eddy returned with a dishtowel. Kneeling over, he began to scrub.

Harriett gently touched his arm to halt his movement. "Easy." She tugged on his elbow. "Allow the fabric to wick the wine from the rug. Don't scrub. You'll push the stain further into the carpet fibers." Her calm clear voice contrasted with Eddy's frantic amplitude.

Eddy met her eyes. She cupped his chin as he rested on his haunches. Moving forward, her lips met his in a passionate embrace.

The dishtowel was completely soaked by the time they parted.

"Wow." Eddy inhaled. "If I'd known I'd get that response, I'd have spilled wine in May!"

Harriett tilted her head. Her lips curled slightly. "It wouldn't have worked in May. I'm so proud of you Eddy." She kissed him again. "You have done a one-eighty since your return. Such a different person from the boy I married…still as handsome as ever—" Her lips brushed his cheek. "—but now, you are a mature, responsible man. I'm so happy you've changed."

∞ ∞ ∞

Harriett surveyed her dining room table. What a contrast to her first entertaining experience, only two years previous. She chuckled to herself, remembering using borrowed lawn chairs for furniture for Tabs' retirement party. Today, Thanksgiving 1953, her carved mahogany table was graced with fine linen, crystal, china, and a purchased floral arrangement. All plastic containers were sequestered to store leftovers. Old sawhorse and plywood tables were hidden in the garage.

Twelve matching, carved chairs encircled the table. The kitchen table, moved into the entryway to accommodate the children, was replaced with a card table to be used for food staging.

The kitchen countertop was filled with serving dishes, platters, silverware, and pies. Oh, the pies! Pecan, pumpkin, blueberry, apple, and peach. A 25-pound turkey roasted in the oven. The smells were intoxicating. *I've come a long way in two short years*, she thought.

Around 2:45, the doorbell rang.

"I got it." Eddy trotted down the polished center hallway. Opening the door, he greeted Esther and Darrell Kline, and their four children. "Come in. Welcome." He extended his hand to Darrell, who shook in return.

Lloly stopped mid-door, placed his hands on his hips, and stared at Eddy.

Toby pushed him from behind. "Lloly, move. Let us in."

"Not until this fella promises me he's being nice to Aunt Harriett." Lloly's gaze penetrated deep into Eddy's eyes.

Eddy chuckled. "Aren't you the little man!"

Lloly clenched his teeth. "I'm eleven. Old enough to take care of myself and my aunt." With his chest inches in front of Eddy, he stretched his adolescent frame. Inheriting stature from his father rather than his petite mother, Eddy still cast towering shadows over Lloly's pre-puberty height.

"Cool your heels, little guy. I'm on the straight and narrow." Eddy gently pulled the boy inside. "Truce?" Eddy grabbed the boy's hand and shook. "Let the rest of your family in. That good food belongs on the table."

Six-year-old Violet ran into the kitchen to envelop Harriett with her tiny arms. "Aunt Harriett, happy Thanksgiving."

"Hi, sweetie." Harriett kissed the child only to be blitzed by her siblings. "Goodness, it's good to see all of you."

Seventeen-year-old Toby, Tabs' namesake and oldest grandchild, sat a large casserole of candied yams on the card table. "Aunt Harriett, if you have time, can we talk a little bit about college? After dinner?"

Harriett smiled. "We can, and we may. Your question should be 'may we discuss,' not 'can we discuss.' Do you understand the difference?"

Toby tried not to roll his eyes. "Yes, ma'am. *May* we talk about college?"

Harriett ruffled the teen's hair behind the ears. "Yes, we may."

Red-faced, Toby excused himself to greet his cousins pouring through the door. Next to arrive was a pregnant Alice Jenson, carrying baby Maggie, followed by her pharmacist husband, Teddy, who was juggling multiple bowls. Toddler Polly wobbled behind them. Hearing the other children's voices, Polly toddled into the kitchen, then latched onto Harriett's leg with a bear hug.

"Goodness!" Harriett tossed the chubby child into the air. "It's good to see you, too. Oh my, you look more and more like your mommy every day."

The entire crew rushed to meet David, June, and Susie Ralston, visiting from Atlanta for the first time since Tabs' lamentable death. David's career as an airplane pilot blossomed as commercial air travel spread to include middle-class Americans.

Lloly blushed, then shied away from his eleven-year-old cousin, who, in their younger days, carried a crush on him. The tables had suddenly turned, as Lloly gazed upon Susie's lengthening torso, thinning waistline, and developing breasts.

Last to arrive were Albert and Laurie Bailey, directly followed by Earl, who was cradling four bottles of wine in his arms. Earl passed the bottles to Eddy while trying to avoid eye contact. "Here you go brother," Earl said, as he turned to disappear into the kitchen.

"Happy Thanksgiving!" Eddy tackled Earl's shoulders, preventing his escape. "Glad you made it, bro."

With everyone present, Laurie passed a tray of stuffed celery, while Albert assembled cocktails for the adults. To the children's delight, David offered alcohol-free Shirley Temple cocktails served in crystal martini stems.

"Don't clink each other in a toast," he warned. "Heaven forbid you chip those expensive glasses."

In contrast to the delicate etched Bavarian crystal of the 30s and 40s, Harriett's were a weighted lead. David held his hefty goblet high, watching light refract through the cut facets of the bowl.

"Harriett, what brand is this?" Dazzling rays spread across the ceiling.

"Waterford, from Ireland. Gimbels had a special last year." She flushed. "I bought the entire set, service for twelve."

Both Albert and David cringed at the thought of replacing the crystal.

"Don't worry about it! I bought it to share with all of you." She thrust her hand into the air. "Happy Thanksgiving to my dear family!"

The children mimicked by raising their drinks high.

Sentiments of "Happy Thanksgiving!" "To Aunt Harriett!" "Harriett hosts the best parties!" and, "It's always so elegant at Harriett's." followed.

Boisterous banter buzzed until a tiny voice asked, "Where's Grandma?"

The hush was immediate. Esther and June reached for each other's hands as Albert scowled and Alice shielded the tiny questioning child.

"Polly," Alice whispered in the girl's ear, "we talked about why Grandma can't come today."

"But she's family, she's Grandma?"

Harriett's face drained of all color; she swayed before sitting on the stairstep. "Come here, Polly." She beckoned with outstretched arms. Alice's face squared in a warning.

Polly shuffled to her aunt, then asked again, "Why isn't Grandma here?"

An intense draught filled Harriett's lungs. She paused. Flashes of Tabs' gentle kindness and Olive's callous mothering filled her thoughts. Exhaling, she said, "Grandma was a bad girl. She's not allowed to come today, sweetie."

"What did she do?" Polly settled down on the step beside Harriett, intent on learning of Olive's transgression. Teddy grabbed Alice by the elbow as she swooped in to protect Polly.

Harriett glared at her sister. "She told a lie, sweetie."

"Okay, thanks, Aunt Harriett." Polly jumped down from her perch to run to her mother. "Mommy," she tugged at Alice's skirt. "Grandma was a bad girl," she said giggling with glee.

The crowd collectively exhaled, as chatter once again echoed through the spacious house.

Minutes later a second hush ensued with the tinkling of a bell announcing dinner.

17

KIDDIES' TABLE

Toby unsuccessfully scanned the place cards on the kitchen table—the kids' table—for his seat. They read "Heddy," "Lloly," "Susie," "Polly," and a highchair for "Maggie." No Toby, Tobias, or Tabs Two. Shyly, he approached Harriett and pulled her aside.

"Aunt Harriett, did you forget me?" His face was ashen, distraught, muscles tight with the anxiety of being overlooked.

Harriett rubbed his back, then guided him into the dining room. "Darling, we have an open chair here." She pointed to his name. "You are graduating in six months and going off to college. That's an adult, in my book."

Toby's face beamed as he sat between his indicated dining partners, Earl and David. Several seconds passed before he began to frown again.

The teen waited anxiously for Earl to take his seat before he leaned over to whisper, "Earl, look at all this silverware. I am not sure what to use." He fumbled with the edge of his napkin, then mimicked Earl by placing it on his lap.

"Stay calm. Follow my lead." Earl smiled. "You're among friends and family. What better place to learn?"

Earl lifted his own napkin, folded it into a triangle then draped it across his legs. Toby followed his direction and refolded his.

Earl patted the boy's hand. "Your Aunt Harriett is a wise woman. This may be a family dinner, but for you, it's a learning experience."

Toby exhaled. "So much for a vacation from school."

"My dear boy, your education is only just beginning!"

∞ ∞ ∞

The family, children on laps, sat around the table until well into the evening, talking, joking, and reminiscing. Even little Polly remained, wiggle free, on her father's lap, playing with unused spoons. Maggie slept at Alice's side. The clock chiming six startled all back to reality.

Harriett reacted. "Geez Louise. We better get this food packed into the fridge before it spoils." She stood and carried a tray to the kitchen. Heddy, Susie, Esther, and June followed, each toting ample food, enough for another family meal.

While Harriett cleared the table of linens, Eddy slipped into the kitchen and piled mounds of turkey, potatoes, yams, green beans, and gravy on two plates. Large slices of pumpkin and pecan pie filled a third dish. He molded a layer of foil around the edges to prevent spillage as Esther re-entered.

"Shhh," Eddy whispered, finger in front of his lips. "This is for your mother."

Esther sucked on her lower lip. "You're taking a big risk smuggling food to Olive, especially with your newfound reinstatement as husband! Are you sure Mother is worth it?"

"Don't say a word. And yes, Olive deserves some holiday

company. I won't be long." He glanced around the room. "Cover for me?"

Esther quickly searched the pantry. She tossed a wicker pie keep at Eddy. "Here, this carries three pies on two trays. Use them to stack your plates. Hurry! Before Harriett finds you."

Heddy and Susie, carrying heaps of dirty china, interrupted the conversation. The girls ran water into the sink for washing without noticing Eddy slip silently out the back door.

∞ ∞ ∞

"Goodnight." Albert kissed Harriett. "Perfect, as usual. Thanks, Sis." Taking Laurie's hand, the couple bid her adieu.

Harriett watched the last of her family walk down the front stone steps. Sighing, she happily accepted the beginning of the long holiday weekend. Mounds of washed and stacked dishes cluttered the bare dining room table, waiting to be displayed in the glass-front, built-in cabinets. Before tackling the job at hand, she wandered into her office, pulled an LP from its jacket, and clicked on the hi-fi. The house filled with the sounds of Charlie Parker's wailing alto saxophone.

Dancing her way back to the dining room, she bounced off Earl's chest. "What are you still doing here?" she asked as he caught her, preventing her from falling.

Earl, arm around her waist, looked her in the eyes. "I'm here to help. By the way, where is that no-good brother of mine?"

Harriett eased away slowly. "Earl, be nice," she said, uncomfortable with the awkward closeness.

"Harriett, is he treating you as a gentleman should treat a lady? You can tell me if he doesn't."

Her eye twitched. "I know, Earl. But I can take care of myself." She dropped her head.

"There is no easy way to say this." Earl swallowed to wet his throat. "Hell, here goes. I'll just spit it out! All women should have a man worship her, sit her on a pedestal, a place of honor. And you, of all women...so accomplished and incredible...you deserve that, and more." He gently lifted her chin until their eyes met. "I want to be that man for you, Harriett."

"Earl, I can't. Please." Her eyes glistened. "If you truly feel that way, please allow me the opportunity to repair this marriage." She pulled out of his arm. "You and I...wrong place, wrong time, Earl. Let's leave it at that."

His shoulders slumped. Sad eyes met hers. "If that's what you really want...then, come on. Let's make quick work of this mess." He motioned to the dining room. "I'll hand things to you, and you fill the cabinets."

She managed a contrived smile. "Okay. I appreciate your help. And you're right, where is Eddy?" She glanced into the hallway searching for her delinquent husband. "Geez!" she said shaking her head. "Sometimes, I don't know what makes him tick!"

Harriett handed Earl the last item when Eddy opened the back door, carrying an empty pie keep.

Hearing the noise, Earl motioned for Harriett to hide while he investigated, catching Eddy in the act of washing three plates.

"Where the hell have you been?" Earl bumped Eddy's shoulder too aggressively, causing a temporary unbalance.

"What's it to you? God, Earl, you're not my warden." Eddy retaliated with a push. "Back off."

"No, Eddy, I'd like an answer to that question, also." Harriett entered the kitchen through the butler's pantry.

"You left me all alone with a ton of clean-up. Earl was good enough to stay and help."

Eddy scowled at his brother. "I'm sure Earl had ulterior, impure motives for staying. Didn't you, my big brother?" The disjointed accusation sounded like he searched for the words, as if English was his second language.

"That's enough. Eddy, please. Confess." Harriett approached, spreading her legs apart into a sporting stance. "You took food to Mother, didn't you?" she asked, pointing to the sink.

Earl touched Harriett's arm. "I'm leaving. Thanks for a delicious meal, but this is between the two of you."

"I'm thrilled you joined us. Goodnight, Earl." Harriett stretched to kiss his cheek. Turning, she faced Eddy again. "Now! Back to you. Why, Eddy? After I forbid it?"

Eddy hissed through clenched front teeth, which were visible between parted lips. "Who made you judge, jury, and executioner over Olive? You asked me to take care of her, and that's just what I'm doing!"

"Don't yell!"

"I'm not yelling. I'm defending your mother and my actions." He rinsed the plates before drying them.

"Well, I'm in charge because—just because!" She felt the heat rising in her neck.

"You're in charge because you made yourself the family dictator. Just because you're an executive at work doesn't automatically bestow the rank of Family Emperor on you." His nose jerked into a spasm. "Your siblings are more than capable of making responsible decisions, but you don't allow them." Eddy stomped into the office to pour himself a drink, with Harriett following close enough behind to be his shadow.

"How dare you?! I was forced to grow up and take control. At least I had Papa until that witch killed him!"

"That's a pretty strong allegation. Leaving yourself open to liability." Eddy gulped his drink, poured another, then sat in the leather chair, crossed his legs, and calmly stared at his wife.

His composure ruffled Harriett. "Rather pompous, aren't you? The no-good husband that deserted me! Abandoned me!" Both eyes twitched.

"We've been through this. I was embarrassed by my obsessions. End of story." He bared his teeth. "Are you going to throw that in my face every time we have a fight? Tell me now, because if so, maybe we should…"

"We should what?" This time, Harriett's voice echoed throughout the house. "What Eddy?"

"If you like, I'll move back in with Earl." He gave her a self-satisfied smirk.

Harriett burst into tears before collapsing into her desk chair. "No. That's not what I want. I'm mad at you, but you're still my husband." She gazed into Eddy's eyes. "We can't be threatening each other with separation every time we fight. I'm sure we'll have plenty of arguments."

Eddy wiped the smirk from his face. "You're right. Every relationship has strains and stresses. Differences in opinions. Tonight, I dispute your banishment of Olive. If you want me to look after her, then give me some flexibility to do it my way. Compromise. Okay?"

"Okay. I don't like it, but I'll agree—with one caveat. Don't hide your actions from me."

With a truce reached, the couple finished tidying the house before retiring. The one night when neither had to awaken early the next morning—thus permitting leisurely late-night activities—was the first night since their reunification that they both sought sleep immediately.

18

TREASURES OLD AND NEW

DECEMBER 1953

*H*arriett rummaged through the attic, looking in stacks of boxes four feet high abandoned by the Songer family. A cold December wind whistling through a back window sounded like an approaching train. Harriett rubbed her hand around the frame, searching for the breach. A whooshing chilly breeze entered a crack in the bottom left. Harriett marked the spot with a pencil for a later repair, then glanced out the window to spy Eddy traipsing through the woods carrying a bowsaw and hatchet.

She returned to her copious boxes. The heaviest were in the center of the room. She emptied them, finding photo albums, high school yearbooks, a complete set of encyclopedias, issues of *Good Housekeeping* and *Look* magazines, and a linguistic atlas. Three of the boxes contained every issue of *The National Geographic Magazine* from 1905 through 1950. A complete 45 years of history were preserved in the attic. She fingered through the treasures and pushed the encyclopedias and *National Geographics* over to the staircase to be relocated onto the abundant shelves in her office.

Moving deeper into the gigantic fourth floor, her gaze

landed on the area where her family of raccoons had sheltered. She laughed to herself, remembering Earl's bravado and late-night rescue shortly after she moved in. Remnants of claws scratching cardboard confirmed her memory. None of the five containers were taped shut; rather, the top flaps were interwoven for security. She flipped the first box open, then gasped. It was as if she were punched in the stomach; all air was expelled from her diaphragm. Her breath quickened as she removed an object. An electric, three-light, window candolier, one of the many that graced the stately home's windows with blue light during the holidays. She loved walking the streets at Christmas to view Campbellsville's light displays. None was more splendid than the blue lights on the hill. She recalled Olive admiring the lights, even as a child.

These fixtures must be ancient, thought Harriett. Rummaging deeper into the box, she discovered multiple broken bulbs labeled, "GE Mazda Made in the USA." She cradled several of the fixtures and ran down two flights of stairs.

"Eddy," she called out the back door. "Eddy, look what I found!" There was no sign of Eddy. Harriett deposited her find on a chair, then headed off into the backyard woods. "Eddy!"

After several moments, she heard a voice calling, "Over here."

Bowsaw in hand, Eddy dragged a blue spruce pine tree toward a startled Harriett.

"What are you up to?" She pointed to the tree. "Is that our Christmas tree? I thought we'd pick it together."

Eddy frowned. "Harriett, you don't need to be part of every decision of this family. I'm capable of choosing a suitable tree." He tugged on the nine-foot, perfectly shaped specimen. "Where do you want it?"

Harriett scrunched her lips as tears welled in her eyes. "I

didn't mean to be critical." She inhaled. "Eddy, I'm really trying, but it's hard for me. I've been on my own for three years, I had to do everything my—"

"Oh, here we go again!"

"Eddy!" She slumped to the ground and covered her face with her hands. "Please. I don't want to fight."

"I'm just on edge. I thought this would make you happy." He continued his trek to the house. "Now, where does this go?"

"If it's okay with you, I always put it in the front living room. In the big window." She stood and brushed dead leaves from her trousers. "I came out to tell you that I found the electric candoliers. The blue ones the Songers placed in every window. Do you remember?"

His mood lightened slightly as he recalled childhood memories of the blue light display on top of the hill. "Yes." He nodded. "Not a manly thing to say, but I thought it was pretty."

"I found the fixtures in the attic, but we need bulbs. Do you think you can run to the hardware store and try to match them? Of course, blue, if possible."

"Yeah. I'll do that. How many do we need?" The couple walked across the paved patio, tree in tow.

"I'll have to count. I'll do that next, so you can make it before they close today. Does that fit into your schedule?"

"Sure. I'll put this tree in some water, secure it upright, and wait on your count. Do you need me to help carry decoration boxes down?" His amicable comments were without enthusiasm.

"Yes, thank you. That would be most helpful. Eddy?" she reached for his arm. "Truce? I'm sorry I'm a control freak. I'll try harder."

His brow remained creased as he replied, "Yeah, sure. No

problem." He dropped the tree and went in search of a washtub.

∞ ∞ ∞

While Harriett inventoried the candle fixtures, counted the windows, and tallied bulbs needed for purchase, Eddy sulked up the back stairs. Settling in the stuffed club chair in the master bedroom, he brooded. His thoughts traveled across the ocean, back to the tiny Alpine cottage where he, Rosa, and Joey spent a blissful holiday together. This would be the second Christmas without them. Absentmindedly, he went to Harriett's vanity and pulled open the top drawer, the drawer that stored the strand of pearls. They were not Harriett's, although she mistakenly took them to be. Ironic. The pearls he skimped and saved to buy for Rosa prompted his reconciliation with Harriett.

Fingering the tiny orbs, Eddy removed them from the vanity. He scoured the basement for a small box, lovingly wrapped the necklace in fabric, then addressed the package to Sofia Romano, Trieste Italy, in hopes that she would deliver it to her daughter.

Harriett bounced down the steps, count in hand. "Wow, I didn't realize we had so many windows." She handed a fixture to Eddy, a 20-dollar bill, and her list containing bulb count and a few assorted other items. "This should cover it."

Eddy shoved the package and note into his pocket. "If not, I'll get it." He brushed her forehead with his lips and ambled out.

"Eddy!" Harriett called after him. "Why don't I make you a pie for dessert tonight?"

"Sure. Sounds good." The car door slammed.

∞ ∞ ∞

Harriett puttered in the kitchen, peeling apples and kneading dough. Before Eddy returned, the kitchen smelled of cinnamon and brown sugar. She was wiping down the countertops when Eddy climbed the cellar stairs, two large bags in hand.

"What did you get?" Harriett smiled as she tossed her dishcloth into a sink of soapy water.

"I bought you a present. I'm sorry I snapped at you." Eddy pulled a large box from the paper bag.

Harriett's eyes widened. "Oh. Let me see."

Eddy turned the box so a clear, cellophane-covered opening displayed a star Christmas treetop. "I'm not sure what you used in years past, but when I saw this, I thought it was perfect for your elegant tree in your elegant house. Like it?"

She tugged at the flap. Opening the box, she carefully removed the faceted glass star that was securely bound to sturdy cardboard.

She ran her fingers over the cuts, square, diamond, and triangle. "Oh, plug it in. I want to see all the light."

Eddy chuckled. "Let's take it out of the packaging first." He yanked at the tape, freeing the star. "It's not fine crystal, but I think it's very pretty." He moved to a wall outlet and inserted the prongs. Dazzling light bounced off the walls and ceiling.

Harriett gasped. "It's perfect. Thank you!" She hugged him tightly before turning to her oven. "I made French apple pie. I love that crumbly streusel topping."

Eddy smiled, then carted the star into the front room. "Save the box for packing?"

"Absolutely." Harriett gathered the carton and set it on the back staircase, waiting for her next trip up. "Eddy, I've been thinking…" There was no answer.

Harriett found Eddy sitting on the floor, staring blindly at the tree. He rubbed his eyes as she entered the room.

"You okay?" She sat down beside him, then looped her arm around his waist.

"Yeah, a little melancholy, that's all." He paused, giving himself time to concoct a retort. "I guess I'm missing Mom, that's all." His body tensed but his face masked the lie.

Harriett leaned her head on his shoulder. "I certainly understand. I still miss Papa. Sometimes the pain is fresh, raw, cutting too deeply, especially around the holidays. But cheer up; we'll tackle this together." She jumped at the sound of her timer. "Pie's done. I think we should start the kitchen remodel in January. Have you given it additional thought?"

"Some. I'll draw up some plans." He forced a grin. "Chicken okay for supper tonight?"

"Sounds wonderful. You're in charge, darling. I love everything you make."

19

BAKED GOODS

The Saturday before Christmas, Eddy rapped on Olive's back door. It was a bright, blue-skyed, cumulus cloud-filled, chilly December morning—the kind of day that made you love winter, even despite the cold.

Olive, dressed in a ratty, patched housecoat covered by an even more tattered apron, answered the door. "What are you doing here? And what's in your hand?" she grumbled but motioned for him to enter.

"I bought you a wreath for the front door." Eddy held the pine-and-holly circle high in the air. A whiff of fresh pine floated by. Long streamers from a puffy red-and-green plaid bow flowed in front. "Do you want me to cut a small tree for you, after I hang this?"

Olive cocked her head and stared at her visitor. "Why the hell would I want a messy tree in my house? Hang the wreath if you must, but no tree." She slammed the door in his face.

Eddy pounded the nail as quietly as possible. Slipping the wreath over its hook, he straightened the ribbon, then admired his work. *This will cheer up that crotchety old curmudgeon*, he thought. After stowing his hammer, he headed back home to complete a full list of pre-holiday "honey do's."

Harriett, busy in the kitchen, was baking a mountain of sweets. Cookies, pies, cakes, maple rolls, and fudge inundated the table and poured into the dining room.

"Eddy, glad you're back," she said as he bounded up the basement stairs. "Do you have time to hang the garland?"

Eddy scoured the kitchen. The aroma of spices, sugar, fruit, and dough attacked his nostrils. "Who the hell are you baking for? The entire United States Army?"

Harriett smiled. "I'm helping out Alice and Esther. They are so busy with the children. Alice is starting to show, but still suffers from morning sickness, so I decided to lend a hand." She motioned to the butler's pantry. "Besides, I'll give most of this to the staff. A small token of appreciation, but it's important that I recognize them. And, then there's Earl…"

"Well, thank goodness we don't have to eat all of this. We'd both be waddling instead of running." He paused. "Hey, do you think you can bake something for my staff too? I only have four reports."

"Of course. Tell me how many, and I'll have treats baked and wrapped for you to distribute on the 22nd."

He kissed her forehead. "You're too clever. I never thought of giving them a gift. Well, this is my first year, you know," he justified.

"Oh!" She rushed to the oven as her timer buzzed. Two trays of raisin-filled cookies were set to cool on the counter. "The best part. These—" she waved her hand over the baking sheets, "—are for us!"

∞ ∞ ∞

Harriett staged the last of her concoctions, all waiting for appropriate packaging, then headed up two flights of stairs to the attic. Tonight, she would reintroduce and light the window candles, haloing the house in a glowing ring of blue. She was shocked to find electric outlets conveniently installed under each windowsill. She marveled at the consideration taken when retrofitting the house with electricity. After all, it was built during the end of gaslights. But then, the window candles were the signature feature of the house. She smiled, knowing the tradition would continue.

At dusk, Harriett joined Eddy on the front terraces. Each window twinkled three blue spheres, an elevated center candle flanked on each side by shorter posts. Yards and yards of pine branch garlands draped the front double doors. Two gigantic wreaths hung from their centers.

Harriett gasped in awe, then, linking her arm in Eddy's, began crying.

"What's wrong? Don't you like it?"

She sniffled her reply. "Oh, Eddy, it's perfect. This is just perfect. Our first Christmas together. Finally!" She buried her head into his shoulder and sobbed. She never saw his frown.

∞ ∞ ∞

Eddy loaded his Rambler's front seat on Tuesday, December 22, with boxes of goodies, each individually wrapped in clear red cellophane, tied with a green ribbon, and garnished with a candy cane. Name tags were attached to the ribbons. A pumpkin pie for his secretary, a box of thumbprint cookies for his supply clerk, an iced red velvet cake for his assistant, a tin of chocolate fudge for the switchboard operator, and a tower of assorted, stacked, wrapped, and tied baked goods for his boss. The packages added a festive air to the usual plain, antiseptic office occupied by Eddy.

Harriett also loaded her car. The only difference was that she filled the back seat and trunk. She enlisted the mail clerk to bring a metal cart to be loaded, then rolled to her office, thrice. Every corner of her spacious room was filled with confections.

Kimberly Coil, Harriett's assistant, peeked into the room. "Good morning, Mrs. Kepler. It smells divine, in here!"

"Kimberly, good morning. I have something for you. Come, sit, before it gets crazy. I think I'll take off tomorrow, so no need to come in. We'll pick up on the 28th. Should be a quiet week, before the new year rush and preparations for fiscal year-end in January." Harriett pulled a large cake from her treasures and a gift box from behind her desk. "Kimberly, you're a Godsend. You know that don't you? This doesn't begin to show my appreciation, but..."

Kimberly held up her hand. "Wait. I need to get my gift for you."

The women exchanged packages. "Shall we open them now?"

Kimberly grinned, then attacked the wrapping paper. "Yes!"

Inside was a light blue, cashmere, long-sleeve sweater. Three decorative bows adorned the boat-neck garment in a centered, vertical row. Tiny pearl buttons trimmed the neckline and sleeve edges.

Kimberly gasped. "Mrs. Kepler! This is spectacular! Thank you so much." She rushed to Harriett's side and gave her neck a bear hug. "I love it."

Harriett chuckled. "Good. Now, shall I open mine?" She waited for an answer.

"Of course...but it's not..."

"Hush. This is not a competition. It's two people wishing each other Merry Christmas."

Inside the box was a pair of pink leather gloves that matched an old but favorite coat of Harriett's.

"I noticed that your old pair were discolored. I hope you like them." Blood rushed up Kimberly's neck, stopping at her chin.

Harriett returned the embrace. "They are beautiful. I actually placed those gloves in a pile to be donated to a winter clothing drive, but, I couldn't bear to part with the coat." She blushed. "So these are perfect."

A ringing phone interrupted the pleasantries. Kimberly rushed to her desk, while Harriett placed the cake beside the phone.

∞ ∞ ∞

On Wednesday, Harriett luxuriated in the off day to deliver the neighborhood and her family baked goods. Bundled in her favorite coat and new pink gloves, she slipped into a pair of ankle-length high-heel booties trimmed in fur. Most sidewalks were clean of snow, although a few delinquent citizens refused to shovel in front of their houses.

Campbellsville never used road salt. Their one plow pushed deep snow to the side, leaving tracks to freeze and refreeze on the streets. An occasional topping of cinders was added to provide extra traction. After the first snowfall, boots were a necessity to prevent wet feet and the annihilation of shoes.

Errands complete, she settled beside the tree for last-minute gift wrapping. The lights twinkled in the late afternoon haze of premature, daily, winter darkness. The front window offered no illumination from the still-dark street light, but Harriett didn't mind. She enjoyed the cozy, warm glow of the faceted treetop and window candles.

Teddy and Alice were hosting a mini-family Christmas

dinner, minus David, June, Susie Ralston, Albert, and Laurena Bailey. The Baileys were traveling to Rochester, New York to be with Laurie's family. Despite there being fewer adults, an obligatory kiddie table was required for half of the twelve attendants.

Harriett organized gifts by family, and she coordinated her use of wrapping paper accordingly. All the Kline gifts were covered in reindeer, while the Jensons' were in jolly Santa, for the younger children. The Ralston family's holly-wrapped packages were posted two weeks ago. Candy canes covered the Bailey stack that awaited their return. She presented each loved one with two packages: an article of clothing and a toy for each child, and an article of clothing and a tool for each adult. Female tools equated to kitchen gadgets or small appliances for cooking, while the male tools were more hobby, fun-themed.

She selected a shiny red foil covered in green and hollyberry wreaths for her final gift. Pleased with her choice, she laid the box on top of the foil and cut a corresponding rectangle. Lovingly and crisply folding in the edges, she camouflaged the cellophane tape. This box needed to be perfect. She finished with a plaid ribbon and bow, then tucked it under the tree beside four other foil-wrapped gifts.

Eddy arrived home from work early. He burst into the living room, carrying a paper bag. "Hi Peanut," he said, leaning down to kiss her. "Have a good day off?"

"I had a glorious day." Her face beamed. "I haven't been this happy in a long time, Eddy." She gathered her supplies into a pile before standing. "How about you?"

"Good. Good." He shifted the bag to his other hand. "Hey, can I use some of that paper? I need to wrap something."

She grinned as she handed him the roll of candy cane print. *No need to waste the beautiful foil for my gift*, she thought as she glanced at the bag. *Hmm. No department store shopping bag or fancy boutique logo, just a plain old, brown paper bag. I wonder what he bought?*

"I'll take the rest of this up to the attic and give you some privacy." She grinned when her tummy turned flip-flops. She felt like an anxious child, full of anticipation, and the temptation to turn around to sneak a peek.

Eddy made fast work of his wrapping. When Harriett returned, four additional gifts lay under the tree, two of the boxes identical.

"I put the roll on the back stairs," Eddy called from the kitchen. "I made a quick tuna casserole for tonight. Figured we'd have enough rich food this weekend. Raisin-filled cookies for dessert?" He pulled a clear Pyrex bowl from the refrigerator. "I have a surprise for you tomorrow night."

Harriett's stomach engaged in a tumbling routine again. "I'm so glad that it's just you and me tonight and tomorrow, alone, all by ourselves." She hesitated and sighed. "The past couple years have been lonely, especially after Papa…" She stiffened a sniffle. "No more! You're here."

She charged him from behind. The force of her attack almost knocked him off balance.

"Whoa. Easy there, little dynamo." He whirled around to scoop her into his arms.

∞ ∞ ∞

The oven timer and Eddy's voice interrupted Harriett's reading. She was snuggled into her office leather chair with her legs tucked under her; she inserted a bookmark, then stood. A blazing fire roared, sparks flickering then floating up the chimney. A warm halo of glowing light was cast onto the wood paneling and bookcases. The scent of fresh pine from the tree and charred wood enveloped the room.

Eddy arrived with two bowls. "Thought we'd eat in here."

Eddy inhaled, suddenly comforted by the memory of the tiny cottage he shared with Rosa. The office was equivalent in size to the entire Alpine cabin; decorated with its double bed, sink and pump handle, table, two chairs, rocker, and basket that served as Joey's bed.

Shaking his head to dispel painful memories, he forced himself back to the present. Sitting down on the chair still warm from Harriett, he motioned for her to join him. "Hey, let's visit Earl tomorrow afternoon."

Harriett frowned. "Is he spending the holiday alone? I hate the thought of that. Let me talk to Alice. I'm sure there is plenty of room for him to join us."

"Sounds good."

She took a bite of casserole. "Yummy. What's your secret?"

"Sour cream." He paused. "What were holidays like while I was gone?"

The joy drained from her face, leaving shock and remnants of pain. "Of course, they were lonely without you. Let's not go there. You're here now."

Eddy exhaled a deep sigh. "Yes, I am here."

Their silent, casual meal concluded with the requested cookies. Harriett washed up the few dirty dishes, then returned to the office. With a click of a lever, Perry Como began singing carols.

Eddy called from the living room. "Babe, *Amahl and the Night Visitors* is on NBC. Come in and watch it with me."

Harriett sighed but complied by turning off the hi-fi and walking to the front room. "We're missing that beautiful fire," she whispered into Eddy's ear as she snuggled into the crook of his arm.

Eddy continued watching the television without responding.

20

CHRISTMAS EVE

*H*arriett slept late. Reaching high into the air, she rolled her back, stretching like a cat. She smiled, tucking blankets around her ears, then glanced at the gently snoring body beside her. The clock chimed eight as she jumped out of bed and slipped into her shoes. Moments later, an aroma of percolating coffee floated upward. Two cookies and cup in hand, she headed for her desk. What a glorious feeling—nothing was on her calendar. Although finals were over for the semester, she opened a textbook to review and waited for Eddy to awaken.

Around 10:30, her thoughts were interrupted by the clatter of dishes. She gathered her sweater around her shoulders and sighed.

Fifteen minutes later, short-order duties complete, Eddy called out. "Harriett, breakfast."

"Good morning sleepyhead." Harriett exchanged a kiss for a plate of scrambled eggs and buttered toast. "Merry Christmas Eve." Her knees buckled as she spoke the words. Waves of flooding emotions filled her eyes with tears. "Goodness, Eddy. This is the first time that I can wish you Merry Christmas to your face."

Eddy backed away. "Don't get all weepy on me. More coffee?" The fluorescent overhead light fixture exaggerated the creases in his brow.

She wiped the back of her sleeve across her eyes. "Yep," she said, taking a deep breath and extending her cup. "What are you doing today?"

"I have to run out later this morning, but nothing after I return. Any big plans for us?"

Harriett daydreamed for a moment, then reached for Eddy's hand. "After supper, I thought we could go for a walk to look at all the Christmas lights."

Eddy nodded without meeting her gaze.

"Then…it's just us, the fire, and Bing Crosby."

"Okay." Eddy gobbled his breakfast, then deposited his plate in the sink. "Will you wash up? I gotta run." He zipped his jacket, wrapped a scarf around his neck, and sped out the back door, without disturbing the greeting cards taped around the frame.

Every archway in the kitchen, the butler's pantry, and the office was encased in Christmas cards tacked to the framework—greetings sent from clients, coworkers, friends, family, and Madison's corporate world. Harriett set about hanging those received yesterday around the fireplace. She opened and reread each card, making a mental note to accompany her written record of the over 200 senders. Many cards were imprinted with a signature and greeting. Harriett preferred more personal, handwritten salutations. She was not a fan of cards covered in glitter, either; they made a mess on the floor.

Capitalizing on Eddy's absence, Harriett scurried down to the garage. She unlocked the trunk of her Buick and removed a clanging collection of clubs—specifically, golf clubs; one of Eddy's gifts. She hoisted the shoulder strap around her neck and lugged the leather bag upstairs, puffing as she carried it into the living room. A large ribbon bow waiting on the staircase was placed on top of the driver; allowing streamers to cascade down the sides. After slipping a wrapped copy of Ben Hogan's *Power Golf* under the tree, she checked the bag's pockets for tees, balls, and gloves. Finding everything in place, Harriett finished by tying clusters of bells to the zipper of each compartment. It sounded like a miniature troika gliding on frozen tundra as she partially camouflaged the bag by sliding it behind the tree. Her first Christmas was staged and ready. All she needed was club admittance, which Tom Roland guaranteed—and for Eddy to return home.

She busied herself with a light dusting before unrolling Eddy's sketches for the kitchen renovation. A first-floor laundry room, carved out of the far corner, removed a large chunk of space. A washer, dryer, storage cabinets, sorting bins, ironing area, retractable clothesline, and folding counters were fed by the back staircase with easy second-floor access and closets above. The French doors leading to the paved patio now connected a breakfast eating area to the outdoor spaces. Two specialized work areas provided Harriett with an upscale baking complex complete with two wall ovens, and Eddy with a commercial-size cooktop oven–combination range, large enough for the biggest holiday turkey or goose. Multi-purpose, deep, double sinks, smack in the center of the room, divided the two areas. Harriett was unsure where Eddy got his ideas, but she approved. The newly designed rooms were efficient, organized, and industrial, but still cozy enough for a home.

A bowl of foil-wrapped pears, compliments of a client and Harry and David, caught Harriett's attention. She unwrapped and washed the fruit. Juices dripped down her chin and onto Eddy's drawings as she sank her teeth into the pear. *Goodness*, thought Harriett as she slurped the sweet liquid with no regard to the papers. *This is the best pear I've ever eaten.* Her snack was finished bending over the sink, savoring every drop. Core discarded, there was nothing left to do but wash her face and wait.

∞ ∞ ∞

Eddy hurried around the side of the Maple Street house as the wind whipped through his hair. It was not a white, snowy holiday, but it was cold. He should have worn a hat. Olive opened the door on the second knock. Although it was still morning, a single 40-watt bulb barely lit the kitchen.

"Eddy Kepler, what brings you out today?" Her permanent wrinkles and frown disguised her smile. "Come in. I was just making tea. Join me for a cup?"

"Absolutely." Eddy shivered before he removed his coat. "Brrr."

"Brrr, indeed." Olive steeped two cups of golden brew, adding sugar to both, then opened her cookie jar. "I baked. Like a cookie?"

"I'm always ready for a sweet." He reached into the jar and pulled out a Toll House cookie. "These look good. Did you eat the raisin-filled I snuck out last week?"

Olive snickered. "I have two left in the refrigerator. That's a damn good cookie. Made me hungry for more."

"Did Harriett learn to bake from you?"

Olive guffawed. "Eddy Kepler! I don't bake. I bought those cookies down the street."

Color washed over Eddy's face. "Could have fooled me. Well, you did fool me." He reached into his jacket pocket and pulled out a wrapped box. "Merry Christmas, Olive," he said as he handed her the gift.

Olive's eyes grew wide. "You brought me a gift? No one ever bothers with me—well, that's not true. Esther's kids sneak out every so often to visit. Toby stands guard." She laughed. "As if I'm going to hurt them. June brings Susie by when they're home. And—Harriett would kill Alice if she knew, but Alice brings Polly and Maggie once a week. But…" She stared at Eddy. "Why did you bring me a gift?"

Eddy chuckled. "And on my own accord, too! I did it because I wanted to. I even picked it out myself." He puffed out his chest. "Open it."

Olive tore the wrapping paper from the box and opened the top flap. Inside, she found a tin of tea and a silver strainer. Eddy grinned at her curious expression.

"It's a special English breakfast blend. Smell it. I got it at Gimbels." He handed her a second gift.

"What? Another present? Eddy Kepler, are you trying to score points with my daughter?"

Eddy choked and coughed. "Ha. Do you really think Harriett encouraged this? If she knew, she'd be furious." He immediately regretted his words as the blood rushed to his face. "I'm sorry, I mean…"

"I know exactly what you mean. Don't apologize for her. At least she feels the obligation to send you to look after me." Olive took the second gift from his hands and tugged at the wrappings.

"Actually, I'm caring for you voluntarily. Teddy, Darrell, and even Albert are more than willing to help out." He blushed. "But there's no need. I'm happy to do it."

Olive looked down. Avoiding his gaze, she focused on the box of chocolate-covered cherries in her hand. "Liquid centers?"

"They're the best kind."

After a moment, Olive stood and walked to the front entranceway. She returned, rifling through several sealed envelopes, then handed him one addressed "Eddy Kepler."

"Merry Christmas," she said.

"You anticipated me giving you a gift?"

"No, I didn't. I intended to give you this without your reciprocation." She motioned toward the card. "I have gifts for all of the grandchildren. Not my kids, only you, but..." She sat silently in thought. "I never knew my grandparents. Hell, I never knew my mother." She waved her hand in Eddy's face. "Open it."

As Eddy tore the top edge and removed a Christmas card, a fifty-dollar bill floated to the floor. "Goodness! That's a lot of money. I can't take that."

"Yes, you can, and you will. You do tons of work for me, and I appreciate it." She smirked. "Don't you dare tell my family I said so!"

Eddy retrieved the money. Opening the card, he read the inside signature: From *Harriett's mother*. He smiled at the quirky way Olive identified herself.

He gently kissed her cheek in thanks. Olive's body stiffened, while her arms hung limp at her sides. "Merry Christmas, Olive. Shall I bring you a plate of food?"

Happy to have the embrace ended, Olive sat down in her chair to resume drinking tea. "No. Alice will bring her little girls and a plate of food. She's a kind woman. Thoughtful, like her father."

They sat talking and laughing for half an hour until Olive suddenly stood and motioned to the door. "Time for you to leave." She pointed toward his coat. "Be off now."

Eddy cocked his head to the side, puzzled by her abrupt change of mood. "Okay, Olive. Merry Christmas." Her face, relaxed minutes prior, was tense, the muscles tightly drawn around her mouth.

He stepped onto the back porch to the sound of the door slamming and locking behind him. He thought he heard a whispered, "Merry Christmas, Eddy Kepler," and the sound of a sniffling nose.

∞ ∞ ∞

Harriett sat in her office, reading a novel. It was months since she had had time to read for pleasure. Her job and classwork demanded most of her time. She inserted a bookmark and closed the book when she heard footsteps. *Our first Christmas together!* she thought, giggling to herself as she smoothed her hair from her face. It was 3:15. Plenty of time for a long, relaxing bubble bath before dinner and a glorious first Christmas Eve together.

As she read, she heard the door open and close, then the movement of items, coming from the kitchen. It was Eddy stashing the fifty-dollar bill in his pants pocket and tossing the card on the counter.

The couple met in the hallway and hugged.

Harriett tickled his ear. "Merry Christmas, my husband. I was thinking of dressing for dinner. Shall we eat in the dining room?"

Eddy responded with a nuzzle. "Sounds perfect. I have some prep work to do in the kitchen. Why don't you bathe while I cook? Once supper is in the oven, I'll shower, and we can meet in the living room for a pre-dinner cocktail."

"Yum." She caressed his face before turning toward the staircase. "I'll plug in the window candles first. I love you, Mr. Kepler."

His mouth spread from ear to ear. "I love you too, Mrs. Kepler."

After 30 minutes of soaking in the tub, the steaming water had cooled to room temperature, leaving Harriett's skin cold and wrinkled. She dried, then wrapped her hair in a towel and her body in a thick, terry cloth robe. Taking large strands of hair, she rolled them around metal rollers, then snapped the clips and rubber edge to secure. Retrieving a box the size of a portable record player from the linen closet, she unpacked a plastic bonnet, slipped it over her head, turned the knob, and waited. Warm air blew through the tubing, filling the cap and exiting the perforated holes. She marveled at the modern invention. What used to take overnight was now accomplished in an hour. The lazy afternoon afforded Harriett time to luxuriate in moisturizing her body and face as she waited for her hair to dry.

The chime of the timer jarred her from a cat-nap. She jerked awake and giggled. After refolding the plastic tubing and replacing the case in the closet, she began unrolling her quick-dried hair. Her curls hung in soft mounds, awaiting a brush, while she clipped the top of her nylons to her garter belt. She straightened the back seams before sliding a slip over her head.

This night had occupied her daydreams every day of the past two weeks. She had planned exactly what she would wear, what she would say, and how she would feel. She had stared into her closet, trying to decide—red, black, or green and white? Each offered specific attributes—comfort, plunging neckline, or a sleek, fitted skirt.

She chose the new green-and-white silk with a fitted waist and skirt. The black dress, her favorite, with its plunging neckline, was more formal, better suited for cocktail hour at the club. The red dress was more comfortable, but it was the same dress she wore on their anniversary date. She wanted something new, memorable, just for this evening. As she dressed, she admired herself in the mirror. Despite her petiteness, Harriett was proud of her small, tight breasts, defined arms, and firm neck muscles. She maintained the body of an athlete, helped by taking the stairs instead of the elevator and always parking blocks from her destination.

She glanced at the nightstand: 5:30. Dinner was scheduled at six. All she had left to do was zip her dress, brush her hair, apply makeup, and complete the look with a few pieces of jewelry. She sat looking in the vanity mirror. Picking up her brush, she stroked her locks away from her face. Usually a quick-change artist, she took her time applying her makeup tonight, drawing perfect arches to her eyebrows, lining her lips before adding red color, and applying the perfect amount of rouge to her cheeks.

She smiled in approval, then opened the top vanity drawer. All that was needed was her necklace. She felt for the pearls, but her fingers found empty space. Her breath quickened as she rifled through all six drawers with no luck. She emptied the contents of each drawer onto the middle of the bed. Her fingers flew through the stack, picking up each item and placing it to the side one by one. Her pearl necklace had vanished.

Tears filled her eyes. Her brows creased as she fought to search her memory. *What did I do with them? Where could I have put them?* She opened each dresser drawer, repeating the search ritual until every item she owned was piled high onto the bed.

∞ ∞ ∞

At 5:45, Eddy exited the guest bath shower, zipped his trousers, and inserted cheap button cuffs links into his sleeves as the kitchen timer beeped. He rushed down the back stairs to remove the food from the oven, cuffs flapping like birds' wings in the air. After a brief stop in the office to turn on the hi-fi, he returned via the front steps to finish dressing. Hearing muffled sobs, he peeked into the master bedroom to find a rumpled Harriett sitting on the floor, head in her hands, crying.

"Harriett, darling, what's the matter?" Eddy sat beside her embracing her shoulders.

Harriett turned her face to his. Black streaks of mascara

smudged her cheeks. Red smears from her mouth stained her hands. Eddy chuckled at the sight. "Goodness, you look like a clown. What has you so distraught? Don't cry!" He cuddled her closer.

"Oh, Eddy! I don't know how to tell you." She choked as she gasped for air. "I...I lost my strand of pearls."

Eddy stiffened and backed away.

Feeling him tense Harriett burst into louder wails. "Oh—oh!" she wheezed. "I'm so sorry. I've spoiled today." She kneeled before him, begging. "Can you forgive me?" Her head fell to his lap. "I always put them in this top drawer, but they are gone. I don't know what could have happened..."

She rubbed her eyes, spreading black around the edges. She looked like one of the raccoons that had inhabited the attic.

Eddy held his breath. Minutes passed before he answered. "Don't worry about it, Harriett."

She gulped. "How can I not worry about it? It was the perfect necklace. The perfect anniversary gift, for the first anniversary we spent together." She moaned. "I love those pearls. Please, forgive me, Eddy."

Eddy's eye twitched. *I never should have stolen them, even if they don't belong to her*. He forced his body to relax, disguising his guilt. "Clean yourself up, Harriett. Why don't we eat in the kitchen, considering this evening's events?"

The color drained from Harriett's face. "Oh, Eddy. I am so sorry! I ruined it all."

Eddy stood, torn between his lost love and the woman he called wife. Slowly walking to the doorway, unable to confess to his crime, he said before leaving, "I'll hold dinner for 30 minutes."

∞ ∞ ∞

Harriett peeked into the dining room as she walked down the hallway. Her face was scrubbed clean, void of all chemical enhancements. She wore a pair of black, gabardine wool trousers. A pink, cashmere sweater was tucked in at the waist, cinched with a thin, black, leather belt. The outfit was finished with a silk scarf tied around her neck, a gift from her friend Katherine. Tears formed, but did not fall, as she viewed the empty dining room table. *So much for a perfect holiday!*

The kitchen table was set with everyday dishes, plastic placemats, and paper napkins. Instead of elegantly served courses, a bowl of salad, bottles of dressing, and the casserole pan occupied the center of the table. Harriett cringed when she noticed Eddy wearing a pair of chinos and a knit sweater, spoiling the effect of one of her gifts.

Harriett pushed her food with her fork as she stared at her plate. Eddy ate hungrily in silence.

He stood after 15 minutes of nothing. "Are you finished?" He reached for Harriett's full plate.

"Yes, I'm done. Eddy, I'm really..."

"Just drop it, Harriett. I don't want to discuss this anymore. What's done is done." He scraped the remnants of her meal into the trash, making grating noises, like nails on a chalkboard, as he dumped.

Harriett swallowed several times, but the lump remained lodged in her throat. *Dunce.* She approached him from behind, then slipped her arms around his waist. He flinched.

"Eddy? Maybe we'll feel better after we exchange gifts. What do you think?" She rested her head on the middle of his back. "Please?"

"Fine. I'll be in shortly." He answered without facing her.

Harriett moped into the living room. Sinking into a chair, she tucked her legs under her, assuming a sitting position as close to fetal as possible. Eddy followed and sat on the couch, his eyes focused on the rug.

Harriett waited for him to speak. Finally, she resigned. Walking to the tree she retrieved the smallest box and handed it to him. "I hope you like these."

Eddy reluctantly tugged at the paper. Flipping open what looked to be a box for jewelry, his face reddened as he viewed a pair of gold monogrammed cufflinks. He rubbed the engraved initial. "They're very nice."

Harriett's shoulders dropped. "Oh." She bit her lip. "I know your mother made your current pair. They are sweet." Her voice quivered. "But I wanted you to have something... a little more appropriate to wear to the club."

His expressionless face mouthed meaningless words. "They are lovely. Thank you."

She gulped for air as if punched in the stomach. Mustering all her strength for composure, she suggested, "Okay, my turn to open."

She examined the rectangular box handed to her by Eddy. It was too big to be jewelry, too small to be an appliance, and too light to be clothing. She turned it over, then tugged at the corner of the paper. Inside was a box of Brach's chocolate-covered cherries, liquid center. Biting her lip to hide her disappointment, she said, "Oh good. Liquid centers."

Harriett exhaled a deep sigh, placed the box back under the tree, then glanced at the set of partially hidden golf clubs. "Eddy, I have an idea. Why don't we wait to open the rest tomorrow night?" She fidgeted, pulling at her neck scarf. "We don't have any traditions. Let's start by opening one gift on Christmas Eve. Save the rest to open Christmas night. Sound okay?"

Eddy turned the knob and the television glowed. "Suits me just fine." He rested his head on the back of the sofa and stared at the TV.

Harriett's attempt to snuggle under his arm was met with complaints of soreness. The couple spent the rest of their first Christmas Eve on opposite ends of the sofa, mindlessly gazing at a variety show filmed in black and white. At eleven o'clock, the news weatherman reported sightings of an unknown sleigh flying high above the North Pole.

Harriett stood, collected the discarded wrapping paper, and excused herself. "Goodnight, Eddy."

There was no response.

21

SANTA'S STASH

The sound of giggling children met Harriett and Eddy as Teddy opened the front door. The Jensons' Victorian house combined old and new. The exterior gingerbread trim was in direct conflict with Alice's sleek, modern, minimal inside décor.

"Merry Christmas! Welcome, please, come in." He motioned at each of them, balancing a stack of wrapped gifts. "Goodness, did you buy out the store?"

Harriett blushed. "You know me. Everyone gets two packages!" she said as she stomped the snow from her boots before crossing the threshold.

Eddy just rolled his eyes and pushed his way inside.

The children squealed at the sight of more gifts. Polly and Maggie held hands and jumped up and down in circles.

Esther looked out from the kitchen to see why the decibel level increased. "Those two little ones are going to be as close as you and Albert."

Potato peels flew into the sink as Alice responded without looking up. "Or you and June."

"Fair enough. Merry Christmas!" Esther called to Harriett, then directed her attention to a turkey.

Earl was the last to arrive, also toting a stack of gifts.

Harriett greeted him at the door. "Oh, Earl. You're not obligated to buy everyone a gift."

He smiled as she took the top four boxes so he could more easily see where he was walking.

"Nonsense. You're my family now. Especially with Mom gone and the others living all over the country. Right, brother?" He turned to Eddy for help with the rest of his packages.

"Whatever you say. Merry Christmas." Eddy sat without helping.

Harriett set the gifts under the tree, then returned to help Earl. "What's with Eddy?" Earl asked.

Harriett frowned, shrugged her shoulders, then whispered, "I screwed up."

"Impossible." Earl took her by the arm. "Come, I'll get you a drink. Eddy, name your poison." Earl made his way to the drink cart in Teddy's office. The room was smaller than Harriett's spacious library/den, but adequately comfortable as a home workspace. An intermediate-sized blonde desk and chair, and a pair of sleek, light-colored, low-backed wooden chairs sat in front of metal bookshelves. The feel was modern, almost aseptic. The matching metal drink cart was just inside the door, located for easy access from the hallway.

He returned with three glasses in hand. "Alice, Teddy, thanks for the invitation. I hated the thought of eating alone."

Teddy extended his hand. "Nonsense. You're our brother. Don't you ever spend a holiday by yourself. Do you hear me?"

Earl smiled as he shook Teddy's hand. "With that said, may I help with anything?"

Eddy scoffed. "Earl, you're a man. Relax. Let the women do their jobs."

Earl roared with laughter. "Says the man who cooks dinner every night!"

"Touché." Eddy grinned, allowing his shoulders to ease. "Point taken. But sit down anyway. The girls have this. The men can help with cleanup."

Heddy placed a bowl of mashed potatoes on the table, then walked to the living room. "Everyone, dinner is ready. Aunt Alice asks that we all take our places. She has name cards on the main table."

Polly grabbed Maggie's hand and dragged her to the kitchen. "In here, Sissy. Mommy will lift you into your highchair."

Alice rubbed her expanding belly, then picked up Maggie. Kissing her on the top of her head, she slipped her legs on either side of the seat bar. "Merry second Christmas, little one. You were only a newborn last year." She smoothed the child's dress. "You're growing too fast."

She watched the ever-growing, independent Polly teeter as she climbed into her chair. "I do it, Mommy," was the child's response when Alice tried to help.

Earl found his place card and sat between Eddy and Harriett. Eddy grumbled under his breath as Earl held the chair for a blushing Harriett. The exchange of puzzled looks went unnoticed. Teddy presented a juicy, golden-browned turkey, then took the head of the table. Alice sat across from him at the end, closest to the kitchen and the children. Esther and Darrell filled the other side.

Alice crinkled her brow at the awkward seating. She motioned to Harriett and mouthed. "Did you move the place cards?"

Harriett shook her head and rolled her eyes.

Esther frowned, then sighed. "Lloly Cline. Get in here."

Lloly hung his head, hands behind his back, ready to be charged correctly. He volunteered before the accusation was made. "I did it. I moved the place cards."

"Why?" Esther steadied her breath, trying to hide a grin.

"Aah. Uncle Earl is nicer to Aunt Harriett…and I'd rather he sits beside her than Uncle E…"

Esther raised her hand. "Stop. Don't you dare say it! Especially not on Christmas."

"Okay, but it's true." Lloly grinned at Earl.

Earl stood and exchanged seats with Eddy. Then, winking at Lloly, he responded by raising his glass high in the air. "May I make a toast? To my extended family, Merry Christmas. I love you all!"

They answered, "Here, here." "Merry Christmas."

Lloly added, "Love you too."

"Thanks for making sure I was included."

∞ ∞ ∞

Giving the men a reprieve, Toby, Heddy, Lloly, and Violet washed the dishes and recapped all their gifts from Santa, as the women packaged and stored leftovers. With chores complete, the group moseyed back into the living room to find the men napping. Earl and Eddy shared opposite corners of the couch, knees touching, while Teddy and Darrell each slumbered, heads resting on the low backs of Alice's avant-garde chairs.

Esther kicked Darrell's foot. "Wake up, sleepyhead. There's a ton of gifts to attack before we call this day done."

Darrell yawned, coughed, then blew his nose. The noise was sufficient to awaken the others.

Harriett plopped on the floor with the children. Violet and Polly cuddled on either side. "I'll start." Crawling on hands and knees, she handed each person one gift. Everyone oohed and aahed at her choice of clothing. Next, she distributed the tool gift, then sat back to watch the wrapping paper fly through the air.

Earl waited with gifts on his lap, not wanting to open them.

"Earl, you too!" Harriett encouraged him with a kick to his foot. "Open your gift from Eddy and me."

"I was going to open it at home," Earl stammered.

Teddy tossed a wad of paper at his head. "No, you don't. You open with the rest of the family."

Color crept up his neck as he picked at the taped edges. He lifted the lid of the box to reveal red tissue paper sealed with a gold sticker, embossed with a knight on a jumping horse.

"Goodness, that's fancy," he said as he slipped his finger under the logo. Pulling back the tissue, he found a gabardine trench overcoat with a tan, black, white, and red plaid lining filling the box.

"It's waterproof," Harriett mumbled under her breath. "I hope I got the correct size. I can't return it."

Earl twisted his head toward Harriett. "Why can't you return it?"

"Because." Her face color matched the red in the lining.

"Because why?" Eddy asked, a little too loudly.

Harriett muffled her reply. "I bought it in London."

Eddy spit his drink across the room. "London! When the hell did you go to London?"

"Watch the language," said Alice.

Harriett jumped up from the floor. "Tom has one. He and his wife went to London this summer. Since I admired his coat, I asked him to buy one for Earl." She scowled at Eddy.

"This past summer?" Eddy growled. "Now I understand."

Earl swiveled his head from Eddy to Harriett, wondering

what underlying exchange he had missed. "I love it, Harriett." He looked for a size label. "Let me try it on."

Harriett smoothed the shoulders of the coat as Earl slipped in his arms. She had secretly measured Earl's favorite suit jacket, giving herself a greater than 80 percent chance of guessing the correct size. Her sleuthing paid off. The coat hung perfectly over his casual corduroy sports coat.

"Good." Harriett let out her breath in a long hiss. "It fits. It has a removable liner, for cold weather. You know, both Mallory and Shackleton wore the Burberry's brand on their exploration of Mount Everest and the South Pole."

"Who?" asked Lloly.

Esther and Alice screamed in unison. "Don't ask who!"

"We'll get a 20-minute dissertation on each of them from Harriett," Alice continued, smiling.

"Hey!" Harriett tossed a ribbon at her oldest sister. "Be nice. Nothing wrong with a little knowledge."

Alice answered, "*Little*, is the keyword. You never give *little* explanations."

The children giggled at the arguing adults.

"Well, Harriett, I love the coat. I'll allow you to tell me the history of the brand some other time." Earl removed the raincoat, refolded it, and gently placed it back in the box, before kissing Harriett's forehead. "Okay, my turn to play Santa."

Harriett took a seat on the couch beside Eddy as Earl distributed presents. Each child received a wrapped book with a paper bow stuck to the top. The men, including Eddy, each received a thin, rectangular, bowless box containing a new necktie. Alice and Esther were given matching packages tied in paper ribbons with similar silk scarves inside. Harriett's box was the only oddly shaped one of the bunch. Earl handed her a small, square package, about three inches by three inches, meticulously tied with a silk fabric ribbon.

She pulled the ends, undoing the bow, then removed the wrapping. A gasp circulated the room as she lifted the blue, hinged lid. Inside was an initial pin brooch. The silver-colored, script-style "H" sported three leaf-shaped green stones making the crossbar. Clear gemstones filled each post of the H.

Harriett's beet-red face turned toward Earl, then to Eddy. Eddy's face matched Harriett's in color. "Oh, Earl!" she cried. "It's absolutely stunning. Is it rhinestones set in silver?"

The question caused Earl's face color to match his brother's. "No." He lipped the response.

"Never mind. I shouldn't have asked." Harriett turned a deeper red. "It is a beautiful piece of costume jewelry. I love it."

Earl whispered in her ear. "It's not fake. It's emeralds and diamonds, set in platinum, from Tiffany's. Merry Christmas, Harriett." He reached for her hand, but she withdrew.

Harriett's face drained of all color, her eyes rolled back into her head, and her ears began to buzz. Limp muscles allowed gravity's influence. As if in slow motion, Harriett slid off the edge of the couch and into Earl's lap as the adults watched in shock.

Teddy reacted first. "Lower her head," he called as he raced to the bathroom. "I'll get smelling salts."

Eddy sat motionless, staring at his wife in his brother's arms, still clutching tightly to the brooch. "What the—"

Alice interrupted, "Language, Eddy."

Eddy glared at Alice, then at Earl. "You and I need to have a serious discussion, Brother. I'll save it for tomorrow."

Earl steadied Harriett's back. "Not now, Eddy. For God's sake, it's a harmless birthstone. How about helping your wife?"

Teddy waved a bottle under her nose. Her head jerked forward at the whiff of ammonia. All buzzing faded.

"What happened?" she asked as she looked around the room.

Alice applied a cold, damp cloth to her forehead. "You fainted, sweetie. Hold this to your head." Relieving Earl of all duties by supporting Harriett, she continued, "You're fine, now. How about sitting back on the couch?"

Eddy and Earl helped Harriett back onto the sofa. Wide-eyed children sat huddled in the corner, holding each other's hands.

Lloly moved closer. "Aunt Harriett, are you okay? If you tell your coat story, will you feel better?"

Harriett looked at her nieces and nephews. "Kiddos, come here. I'm so sorry if I frightened you. Come give me a hug!"

Toby looked at his mother for permission. Esther nodded her head. Moving forward, he dragged Heddy and Violet toward their aunt. Polly waited for her cousins to start before grabbing Maggie. The two babies reached Harriett first.

"You have a boo-boo, Aunt Harriett?" asked the curly-haired toddler, four months shy of her third birthday.

Harriett took her in her arms. "Only a little boo-boo. Almost all better." She kissed each of the children. "Goodness, I've made this a Christmas to remember, haven't I?'

Toby's deep, baritone voice mumbled, "Yes, ma'am."

∞ ∞ ∞

Harriett and Eddy rode the couple blocks home in silence. Eddy dropped his load of boxes onto the living room floor.

"Please, Eddy, be careful with those." Harriett gently placed her stack under the tree.

Eddy clenched his teeth. "We need to talk!"

"Please, Eddy. I just want to have a nice, quiet evening together, alone. Our first Christmas." Her lips quivered. "I don't want to fight."

"Hmm. You should have considered that before spending all that money on my brother." He growled the comment as he clomped down the steps to retrieve another load.

When he returned, Harriett met him with her hands on her hips. "You're mad about the coat? Is that your beef?" She spun on her heel. "If you're worried about not getting equal value, Eddy, come sit down." She pointed to the living room. "You still have gifts to open!"

Stunned, Eddy sat on a chair closest to the tree, silently watching Harriett.

She yanked the golf bag from behind the tree and pushed it in front of him, the bells jingling merrily. "Merry Christmas. Be sure to look in every pocket!" She plopped into the nearest chair to watch.

Eddy went pale. "Harriett? I thought we were going to be fitted at the country club."

"You *were* fitted. I scheduled a meeting with the pro. Provided him with all the requested measurements, waist to floor, in-seam, shoulder to hips, shoulder to foot." She sneered at him. "Be assured! They are custom-made, for you."

Eddy raised his eyebrows. "Aah. How did you manage that?"

"Very cleverly. Now look in the pockets." She crossed her arms in front of her body.

Eddy's mood mellowed slightly. "Wow. That's impressive." He stood, then said, "Why don't I make us both a drink before we continue?"

Harriett nodded, but her arms remained crossed.

Eddy handed her a glass, then slid open each zipped compartment. Contents included a pair of kiltie spiked shoes, extra spikes, tees, a silver MCC ball marker, a ball mark repair tool, a dozen loose balls, a bag towel embroidered with the Madison Country Club logo, and a copy of the *USGA Rules of Golf*.

Harriett sipped her drink, allowing her shoulders to relax as she watched Eddy explore each compartment.

"Harriett, I don't know what to say. Thank you for being so creative and clever." He moved the bag, then stood.

Harriett giggled at the sound of the ringing bells and finally relaxed. "I hope you like them. The shafts are steel, the woods are persimmon, and the putter shaft is wood." She handed him the box containing Ben Hogan's book to unwrap. "Here. Open one more. Then it's my turn."

Eddy gasped at the thought. "Aah, remember I said I had a surprise for you? Well, we were accepted as members at MCC. The letter came addressed to me, I guess because I'm the man." He opened the book. "Oh, thank you."

Harriett grinned. "Sorry to ruin your surprise, but I already knew. The head pro, the guy I worked with to buy your clubs, called me as soon as our membership went through. If you look deeper in the shoe pocket, there's the summer's lesson schedule."

Eddy frowned. "Well, I think I fell a little short..." He handed her a box.

Inside she discovered a dozen golf balls and a coupon confirming a subscription to *Golf Digest Magazine*.

Harriett reached for a small box hidden in the back of the tree. "You have one more to open."

Eddy waved his hands. "No, no. You've given me enough, already."

Harriett bit her bottom lip. "A minute ago, you were comparing your stash to Earl's. Now you don't want the rest of it?" She tossed him the box. "Think fast." He caught it mid-air.

Eddy ripped off the paper. The box was imprinted with the words "Tag Heuer." "Is this German? Why in hell would you buy a German product? I thought you were smarter than that, Harriett."

She clenched her teeth tightly. "It's Swiss." The words came out in a hiss. "The Maregraphe is their latest chronograph model. You can track the phases of the moon, tides, and a bunch of other stuff." Her arms crossed again. "*That*, I can return, if you don't want it."

Eddy hung his head as she continued, "If you have nothing else for me to open, then I agree. You fell short! I'm going to bed." She bent down, snatched the Tiffany box from under the tree, and walked toward the staircase. "I think you should sleep in the guest room tonight!"

"Harriett—" Eddy fumbled to think of anything that could salvage the night.

"Don't bother, Eddy. Merry Christmas and goodnight." She hesitated at the top of the stairs, listening for footsteps, then slammed her bedroom door shut.

Her fingers trembled as she fumbled with the zipper on the back of her dress. It was as if the tips refused to grip hold of the pull tab. Finally, on the third try, she managed to yank it down until it lodged on the fold of extra fabric at the waistline seam. That slight bit of resistance was her breaking point. Still fully dressed, she rolled into a ball, knees tucked under her chin, and wept. Around three in the morning, she managed to cry herself to sleep.

22

LIQUID CENTERS

The next morning, Eddy found Harriett sitting at the kitchen table with a mug in her hand and a cold compress over her eyes.

"Harriett, can we talk?" He poured a cup of coffee, then sat across the table from her.

She raised her hand, palm out. "I don't want to hear it. Just stop."

"I'm stupid. Yesterday was completely FUBAR."

"I don't know what that means. I'm assuming you mean a real mess?"

"You got the idea." He reached for her. "It's an army term—"

She jerked her hand away at his unexpected touch. "Just let it go."

He paused, then moved to the stove. "Hungry? I'll make breakfast."

"I already ate a bowl of Corn Flakes." She moved to the sink to rewet the compress before placing the cloth in the refrigerator to chill. Red puffy slits, the only remnants of her bright eyes, stared at Eddy. "When did we get a card from my mother?" She held the greeting in the air, above her head.

Eddy hesitated. "It came yesterday."

Harriett smiled. "I have just the place for this!" With tape attached, she added the card to the framework encasing the back stairs, next to the baseboard and touching the floor. "There we go. That's her spot of dishonor."

"Yikes. Harsh," said Eddy as he whisked three eggs with cream.

Without reply, Harriett walked out of the room and into her office, closing the door behind her.

∞ ∞ ∞

Around three in the afternoon, the phone rang. "Harriett, it's Alice. Why don't you and Eddy come over tonight for some leftovers?" She paused a moment before continuing, "We have more food than we can eat, and I have no room in the freezer."

"Alice, I'm not in the mood for company."

"I figured as much. And that's exactly why you need to join us." Alice spoke more sternly. "I won't take no for an answer. You know, I can be stubborn, too."

"Oh yes. You get that honestly from Mother!"

Alice bit her lip. "Speaking of Mother...I know you despise her, but it was really kind of you to send her a box of candy and special tea." She paused. "I took Polly and Maggie to see her this morning, and all Mother did was talk about your gift. Goodness, and Polly loves the cherries with liquid centers as much as you and Mother."

"Hmm. Is that so?" Harriett whispered through closed lips as she recalled the two like-sized gifts under the tree. Her mind seethed, realizing Eddy imprudently bought the same candy for both her and Olive.

"Oh, come on, Harriett. You know I take the girls to see her. Don't act so surprised!" Alice didn't wait for a response. "We'll see you at six."

"Here's what's going to happen," Harriett snapped before Alice could hang up. "Eddy will join you tonight, and you may send home a plate of food for me. It will be like old times, when I first moved into this house." She inhaled. "I am not coming."

"Looks like I'm not the only one to inherit the Westchester stubbornness. Suit yourself." The phone receiver slammed into the cradle.

Harriett rested her head on the back of her leather desk chair. *What a holiday disaster*, she thought. After spending the next 10 minutes pondering the consequences of her mood, she reconsidered her decision. Her position as CFO rendered her best friend—Katherine White, secretary to the CEO—an unlikely confidant. In the past, Harriett shared all matters of private thoughts and feelings with Katherine, until her confidence was broken the day Katherine unwittingly imparted secrets to her boss. Harriett needed the assurance of trust; her faith in Katherine was shaken.

"Geez," she sighed out loud. "I need Alice more than she needs me!"

Harriett picked up the phone and dialed Alice's number.

"Hello."

Heaving air from her diaphragm, Harriett spoke. "Alice, I'm sorry. You're right. I am just as stubborn as Mother. May I change my mind and come for dinner?"

"Six." Alice allowed Harriett to anguish several moments before adding, "Good girl! See you later."

Harriett moaned as she rubbed her temples. Wandering into the kitchen, she found Eddy sitting at the table, the contents of his golf bag organized, on display, and ready to be inventoried.

Eddy looked up. "Your eyes aren't puffy anymore."

Harriett shook her head. "That was a backhanded compliment."

"Hey, Harriett, you did a bang-up job with this purchase. I have everything I need. Only thing left out is learning to swing a club."

His smiling face was void of all tension from the previous day. Harriett marveled at how quickly he rebounded. But then, he had lots of practice, and had gotten lots of gifts, and she had neither.

"Glad you like it." Opening the refrigerator, she reached for the damp cloth wrapped in waxed paper. "We're going to Alice's for leftovers at six. You don't have to cook tonight."

Eddy's smile spread wider. "Great!"

"My head is throbbing. I think I'll take a nap. Will you wake me up at five?" She turned to walk away, but reconsidered. "Oh, and I know that you gave Mother a gift. Another lie. Or did you simply forget?"

Eddy gulped. His smile faded as he waited for her next move.

She spun around to face him again. With a deep sigh, she declared, "I'm calling a truce. Christmas is over. My disappointment is partly my own fault. I should have taken control, set up expectations instead of leaving things to chance." Slapping the cloth to her forehead, she moaned, and walked away, leaving a befuddled Eddy alone with his golf clubs.

23

MIXED DOUBLES

JULY 1954

*A*s spring turned to summer, what began as an uneasy truce between Harriett and Eddy soon dissipated into the status quo. The pain of the previous Christmas was forgotten, or at least shelved to the back of her memory. Harriett outfitted herself with golf equipment, and she and Eddy were already competing in mixed doubles club events.

The rolling hills of central Pennsylvania rendered a flat golf course impossible. However, they also provided exquisite views. Pinks of budding spring trees morphed into summertime's many shades of green, rivaling the shades of Ireland, delivering undulated beauty from each tee into the horizon. The course architect managed to incorporate as many flat stances as possible. The shot could be up or downhill, but if you landed in the fairway, players were 90 percent guaranteed a level ball.

Madison Country Club held a "couples" event over the Fourth of July holiday, offering three levels of participation: advanced, intermediate, and new golfers. Harriett and Eddy enrolled to compete with other beginners.

Eddy rubbed her shoulders as they waited at the first

hole. "I'm betting we're in the top three," he whispered in her ear.

She turned her head and grinned. "I'm not settling. I'm out to win!"

"Okay, then! We'll win!" He removed his driver, placed it behind his shoulders, and stretched by rotating at the hips.

"Don't forget what Beeno told us about keeping our elbows together on the follow-through." She grabbed his left arm. "You try to swing like a ball bat and always open up. You look like a chicken trying to fly."

Beeno Powers, a quirky, talented player, was Madison Country Club's golf professional. He wore knickers, argyle knee socks, and plaid sweaters daily. The Keplers scheduled individual private lessons and one joint session out on the course each week. Both natural athletes, Eddy and Harriett excelled. What Harriett lacked in fairway distance, she compensated with a delicate touch around the greens. Her chipping, pitching, and putting were usually spot on. Meanwhile, Eddy blasted his way to the pin, only to lose strokes once putting.

Every Sunday was spent at the club. Mornings, Eddy played golf while Harriett enjoyed a tennis match. They met for lunch at the grill. Harriett joined a women's nine-hole league that was permitted on the course after one in the afternoon. A standing dinner reservation at six, in the main dining room, allowed plenty of time for showers.

Harriett loved the women's locker room, with its varnished, wooden, floor-length lockers, bright green, blue, and yellow plaid carpeted floors, private showers, and well-lit vanities. It offered concealed bathing and a cheery atmosphere, without being too frilly.

Today's event was members-only, a best-ball, mixed-doubles scramble. The Keplers were the front runners in the "new golfer" division. Eddy adjusted the club in his hand and took a practice swing.

Harriett pointed to the gaping space in his arms. "There," she pointed to his elbows.

Eddy shook his arms, regripped, and swung again.

"Much better."

"It felt better, too." He smiled at Harriett's light blue, knee-length golf skirt and matching, collared, MCC-logo shirt. "You look darling."

"I'm not here for a fashion show. I'm here to play golf," she said as she whipped her club.

The starter announced, "On the first tee, we have the last pair from the beginner flight, Harriett and Eddy Kepler playing with the first group from the intermediate flight, Flip and Kitty Grant."

The four players shook hands, although not in direct competition. Wishing each other well, Eddy and Harriett watched in silence as Flip took the tee. Flip swung two practice shots, addressed the ball, and with a loud crack sent it flying down the fairway. At the last minute, it turned left, heading toward a cluster of trees.

"I think you're safe." Eddy pointed to the edge of the rough. "Over there."

Flip frowned. "First hole jitters." Flip turned to see how many of his friends witnessed it.

Eddy rolled his shoulders, took back the club, then let loose. His ball faded right, but managed to stay out of the fairway bunker.

"You're slicing because of your elbows," whispered Harriett, as Eddy grabbed the handle of his pull cart and headed toward the red tees.

MCC, like most courses, offered players different challenge levels and hole distances via the tee boxes. Professional, blue tees; men's, white tees; senior, green tees; and women's, red tees. The options offered varied hole difficulty and accommodated various skill levels. Eddy and Flip used the white while Harriett and Kitty used the red, giving women capable of hitting a long ball a distinct team advantage.

Kitty had the honors. Despite playing golf for over 10 years, she was always nervous when playing with new people. Her ball went straight, but only about 70 yards. The Grants would be using Flip's ball for their next shot.

Harriett bent over to stretch, addressed the ball, adjusted her grip, then swung. The petite woman connected squarely in the sweet spot. The ball took a low trajectory, down the fairway, outdistancing Eddy and Flip, to land right dab in the middle.

Every intermediate and advanced player waiting clapped. Several whispered to each other, "Yikes, better watch out for her," or, "How long has she been playing?"

Flip and Kitty walked to Flip's ball, which sat in the first cut. It was a good lie, but the wrong angle to approach the green. Kitty hit first, whiffing the ball forward about 10 yards.

"Kitty, calm down. Why are you so tense?" Flip asked as he selected his five wood.

Kitty moved from side to side. "She's a natural. I played tennis against her last year. Whipped me in three straight sets."

"Just take a deep breath. You're not competing against her, so it doesn't matter." He took back the club. The swing was fluid, but he dropped his shoulder; he hit the ball fat. It landed in a front sand trap. Kitty winced. "Don't fret," Flip said. "That's an easy up and down."

The Grants hung back until Eddy and Harriett hit. Harriett's three-iron was right on target; however, she needed more club, landing 20 yards short. Eddy's five-iron landed on the green in regulation.

Harriett whooped. "Nice shot, Kepler."

They marked their ball and waited for the Grants to hit out of the trap. Kitty's ball ran up the lip rolling back to her feet. She groaned. Flip tossed her ball out, spotting his in front of her indent. He picked it clean, too clean. The ball landed past the pin and skittered off the back of the green.

"Oh, Flip, I don't like the way this is going."

"Kitty, if you don't calm down, I'll never enter you in another tournament. You can stick to tennis!" He glared at his wife. "You're making me nervous."

Harriett waited for Flip's chip to stop rolling before removing the pin. She dropped it on the ground, then surveyed the undulations before heading back to Eddy's ball.

"Eddy, you putt first, give me a read. From the other side, I saw a left to right break, about one cup length." Harriett pointed to the place on the green before adding, "Don't overpower it; let me see the roll."

"Yes ma'am. No pressure!" Eddy feigned a grimace as he marked the ball. He muscled his stroke, pushing it to the right and past the break. Harriett snorted.

"Hey, sorry," Eddy said, smiling. "I got us here. It's your turn."

"Pardon me?" Harriett grinned at Eddy. "I think my drive helped!"

"Well, yeah." Eddy whacked her on her butt. "Go get 'em, tiger."

"I think I prefer 'tiger' as a nickname over 'peanut!'"

She lined up the ball logo with the hole, positioning it one cup to the left. Allowing herself one smooth practice swing, she stood over her putt. Her follow-through equaled her takeaway.

As Beeno explained, "It's like petting a cat. You pet the head, body, and tail. The whole cat, not half."

The ball came to a stop three inches from the cup. Eddy dropped the putt for a par.

"Nice start, Kepler!" Eddy said as he raised his hand for a high-five.

Harriett jumped to hit it. "You too, Kepler. That's what I call teamwork!"

∞ ∞ ∞

The day ended with the Keplers scoring six over par, 78. They beat everyone in the new golfer flight and the Grants by eight strokes.

The players milled outside the grill, on the terraced patio, waiting for the course to clear and watching the 18th green. Most of the metal tables and chairs and some of the wooden rockers on the covered porch were already filled. Kitty and Flip bade the Keplers goodbye to seek close friends and much-needed relaxation. The round ended in complete disaster for Kitty.

As each foursome finished, they joined the cocktail hour. Harriett, visiting with another new couple while Eddy went for drinks, overheard the first foursome of the advanced group talking to the pro: "For God's sake, Beeno, next time we play this format, don't send the newbies out first! Slows down the entire field."

His wife chimed in with, "Did you look at the score cards? The first group out took double par on number one. Double par! On a best ball!"

Beeno's face reddened. "Sorry, folks. That wasn't my idea. The club president arranged team times."

"Why the hell did he do that? I realize his term just began, but that was downright dumb."

Beeno shuffled his weight from one foot to the other. "He was afraid to alienate the newer golfers. If Advanced went off ahead, there'd be big gaps between holes. First off could be finished with dinner before the course cleared. He wanted the new people to feel included. I guess neither way is the best."

"Then intersperse us. Maybe the better players can keep the rummies moving!"

Eddy handed Harriett a drink. She tugged at his shirtsleeve and whispered, "Eddy, who's that guy with Beeno? He's bitching about slow play."

Eddy glanced in their direction. "Oh, that's George Anderson. He's an asshole."

Harriett giggled. "One in every crowd."

Beeno excused himself from the Andersons. Spotting the Keplers, he walked over, hand extended in congratulations. "You two had an excellent round! My best students of the year."

Eddy chuckled. "Considering some of the other posted scores, I'd say your best students of the past decade."

"I agree, Kepler! May I ask, was this a joint venture? Both of you contributing?" Beeno looked at Harriett for confirmation, knowing she executed as many worthwhile shots as Eddy. She stared past him, focusing on the group leaving the 18th hole. "Harriett, what's wrong? You look like you see a ghost."

"Oh my!" She reached for Eddy's arm. "Is that Stan Kirk?"

Beeno looked behind himself, then frowned. "Yes. Don't repeat this, but he's not my favorite member."

"I know. We are!" Eddy joked, without noticing his wife.

"Eddy, I despise that man. Take me home, now! Please!" Harriett sat her drink on the table and turned toward the locker room.

"We can't go yet! They have to hand out the trophies, and I want supper." Eddy finally looked at Harriett's face. "Good God, you're white! Sit down, Harriett."

"No, Eddy. I want to leave."

"Harriett, since when do you run away? From anyone?" Eddy gently pushed her into a chair. "What's the deal with Kirk?"

Her hand trembled as the memories of Stan Kirk's sabotage washed over her. "Did I ever tell you how he tried to get me fired?"

Eddy stared in disbelief. "Get you fired? When? How?"

"It's a long story. One Beeno doesn't need to hear."

"Oh, but I *want* to hear. I don't like the man." Beeno sat next to Harriett. "Go ahead, Mrs. Kepler. I won't tell."

She rolled her eyes, but it only took that little encouragement for Harriett to begin. "Short version…just after my promotion to general manager, Kirk forged my signature on a purchase order to supplement his girlfriend's business. He was fired, but it almost ruined my career." She sipped her cocktail. "He's a slime."

"Sure is, Mrs. Kepler. You don't have to worry about him. Most members have him pegged as a no-good schemer." Beeno looked to see who Kirk played with. "See that woman?" He pointed to Kirk's playing partner. "That's his business affiliate's wife. Rumor has it, they're having an affair."

Eddy smirked as Harriett's eyes grew wide. She made a mental note not to share any more information with Beeno.

"He's a low handicapper, but several members have complained that he cheats. I'm surprised he isn't kicked out of the club already. That group he's with are about the only members who will play with him."

Harriett's color returned. "Okay, Eddy…we can stay for the trophy presentation and dinner." She smiled. "It might be nice for him to witness us get the new golfer award, especially since we beat half of the intermediate flight too!" Revived, she stood, facing the pro. "Hey Beeno, will you announce our score?"

"Absolutely! I want everyone to know you're coming after them."

∞ ∞ ∞

Happy hour over, Harriett and Eddy headed to the locker room for showers and to dress for dinner. Members flooded the dining room, filling it with a cacophony of clinks, clangs, and chatter. The Keplers, seated at a table with several other new members, enjoyed a hole-by-hole replay of the day.

"God, Harriett. Are you good at everything?" asked Karen Donahue. "I can't win at tennis, now it looks like I won't win at golf either."

Harriett blushed. "I work at things."

"No she doesn't!" Eddy objected. "Everything comes easily to her. Even graduated high school a year early."

"Stop, Eddy. You're embarrassing me." Harriett blushed.

"Take the praise, Harriett," said Duffy Donahue, Karen's husband who was nicknamed after his golfing skill. "Pretty hard to come by, most times."

The waitstaff cleared the salad plates, readying the table for the entrée.

"I'm getting hungry." Eddy rubbed his belly as a plate of steak, asparagus, and potato Au gratin was set in front of him. "Yum, that smells wonderful."

The aroma penetrated their nostrils. Rich, buttery cheese sauce, buttery bearnaise, and melted butter vegetable bath.

Harriett gagged; her stomach turned somersaults. She voiced a quick excuse, then ran to the restroom. If she had waited a minute longer, she would have vomited in the hallway.

She returned to find her covered plate waiting for her and her companions half-finished with their meals.

"Eddy, I can't eat all this butter. It's making me sick." She pushed the dish away. "I'll eat bread," she said as she grabbed a dinner roll.

"Butter?" Karen automatically reached for the spread.

Harriett turned white, pursing her lips shut, she fought another round of nausea. She waved Karen off, waiting several moments before answering, "No thank you."

Dessert was a choice of either coconut cream or lemon meringue pie. To everyone's surprise, Harriett accepted both.

Karen, a middle-aged, full-figured redhead, scoffed. "Two desserts and she's still under 100 pounds. I weighed that in third grade!"

Harriett managed a smile. "But I didn't eat dinner." She passed on the coffee, ate all her pie, then sat back, awaiting the award ceremony.

Club president Patrick Johnson took the podium. His wife, Beth, looked on, beaming with pride at their newfound status. Pat cleared his throat. "Good evening, ladies, and gentlemen. I hope you had a fabulous day. Mother Nature complied!" He waited for the applause to subside. "To present tonight's awards, I give you Beeno Powers. Our MCC PGA golf professional needs no other introduction."

Beeno sauntered to the microphone, enjoying recognition from Madison society's elite. "Hi there! Great day, wasn't it?" A few scattered claps trickled around the room. "Okay, then, let's get on with this. Tonight, I acknowledge some familiar names and some newcomers. I'll start with the winners in the new golfer division." Beeno smiled at Harriett. "Please help me congratulate Eddy and Harriett Kepler, with a round of 78. Both Keplers are new to golf, but not to sports. Eddy was a high school football phenom, and Harriett, well, she's just a tiny little dynamo!" He paused. "Eddy, Harriett, here is your first of many golfing trophies. You better build a big shelf."

More than several intermediate golfers grumbled. "Geez, they beat us."

Stan Kirk choked on his cognac at the announcement of Harriett's name. "When the hell did *she* join?" he asked.

A tablemate, Bill, offered, "I think in December. Quite a coup for MCC to get her. Westmoreland Country Club was hot on her trail."

Stan sputtered. "If I'd known she was up for membership, I'd have blackballed her."

"Why on earth for?" asked Bill as the others looked on with confusion.

"She's a bitch."

Bill cocked his head. "Not the story I got. She's a real smart cookie. CFO at Dugan & Co., respected member of the Madison community—"

This time Stan spit out his drink. "CFO!"

"Yep. From what I hear, she's not even 30, not to mention the female part." Bill slapped Stan on the arm. "Working on her master's degree, too. I'd watch out, buddy. I don't think she's to be tangled with. You try, and she may just blackball *you*."

Stan swallowed the lump in his throat. "I'll take it on advisement." He failed to mention that he had already unsuccessfully tried to tangle with Harriett several years earlier, and that it had cost him his job.

∞ ∞ ∞

Eddy carried the first-place trophy into the house. "Where are we going to display this?"

Harriett thought for a moment. "I guess in the office. Plenty of shelves, even if we win a few more." She grinned at Eddy. "I had fun today. Reminded me of when we were dating."

"Yeah, me too." He nuzzled her neck. "You were amazing."

Harriett pulled away from his breath and made a dash for the powder room.

"What's wrong with you today? You were okay out on the course." He herded her into the office. "Sit, I'll make us a drink."

"No Eddy. The thought of alcohol turns my stomach." She bit her bottom lip. "It was the smell of dinner that brought this on. Ugh. I think I'm going to bed."

Eddy kissed her cheek. "Sure you can't stay up a little longer?"

"Well...maybe," she purred as he led her up the stairs.

24

DIAGNOSIS 102

AUGUST 1954

*H*arriett's hair blew in the wind as she drove home, car windows down, on a hot, humid August evening. Happy to avoid the temptation, Harriett was glad that the car was not equipped with air conditioning. She was getting only seven-and-a-half miles per gallon and paying 29 cents a gallon for gasoline. It simply cost too much money to fill the tank twice weekly.

Her left foot tapped excitedly to the music playing on the radio. She was on her way to visit Alice and her three-month-old nephew, little Tony. Anthony Theodore Jenson joined the family in May. Already causing a stir in Campbellsville when he was named, little Tony unknowingly became the subject of town gossip at his Christening. A precious gift to Alice and his grocery business neighbors, the Lupinettis, Teddy Jenson chose to honor Antonio "Lupi" Lupinetti, Alice's first husband, who was killed in the Battle of the Bulge. Consequently, Dante Lupinetti, surrogate father-in-law, appeared every morning, delivering fresh produce, homemade pasta and sauces, or an assortment of Italian sweets. Every day since Tony's baptism, Teddy unlocked the pharmacy while carrying armloads of delicious food.

Harriett phoned the night before, requesting the odd meeting. Alice met her with a glass of iced tea.

"Where's the little man?" Harriett asked after taking a big gulp.

"He's down for a nap. Don't worry, he eats every 60 minutes. You'll see him." Alice motioned for Harriett to join her on the patio.

"They eat that frequently? Are you kidding me? How do you ever get any rest?" Harriett looked perplexed.

"Usually after three months, they go a little longer between feedings. Tony hasn't gotten that memo yet." Alice chuckled, then added, "Why all the sudden interest in babies?" Alice grabbed both of her sister's hands. "Harriett, are you…"

Harriett could no longer contain her delight. "Yes!" She jumped up and down. "I'm pregnant!"

Their celebration was interrupted by the sound of crying. "I told you he'd be up soon. Hold onto that thought!"

Alice returned with the baby, who was happily suckling his mother. Harriett's eyes grew large and dark.

"What's wrong sweetie? Does Eddy know yet? I bet he's ready to burst."

"No, he doesn't know. I found out this afternoon." Her face sobered. "But…I never gave breastfeeding a thought. How long do they eat that way?"

Alice broke into rolling laughter. "Don't worry about all those details yet. Things have a way of working themselves out."

Harriett shook her head. "Not for me, they don't. I need to plan! Geez, Louise, I need to go buy some books on pregnancy and childcare." With a sigh, she asked, "How do *ordinary* women manage this with such ease?"

Tony wailed; his feeding disturbed by Alice's giggling. "Hush, hush. Momma's sorry." The baby quieted. "Harriett, it's not that hard. As an *ordinary* woman, I manage just fine. So did June and Esther. How long is your maternity leave?"

She gasped, then buried her head in her hands. "I have no idea. The baby is due in March." Her brow creased. "I'm an idiot. What have I done?" She stood suddenly and began pacing. "Good grief, that's right before fiscal yearend. And I'm supposed to finish my master's next spring, summer at the latest." She ran her fingers frantically through her hair.

Alice covered herself and handed the satisfied baby to Harriett. "Here, hold him."

Harriett hesitated but took the cooing infant. Her heart melted when he looked up with little blue eyes and smiled. His tiny hand reached for her earring. "Oh, no you don't," she said as she grabbed the teeny fingers.

Alice cradled her sister's shoulders, smiling.

"Alice, he's precious." Tears began to flow down her cheeks, staining her tailored linen blouse. She wiped her hand across her face.

"Don't be afraid, Harriett. You're going to be a wonderful mother. All those other things in life can wait. Right now, it's time for you to be a Mommy." She took the baby from Harriett. "Now, go home, and tell your husband he's going to be a daddy."

Harriett stopped to blow her nose, then hugged her sister. "Will you babysit for me? Like you did for Esther and June? Can you manage another one?"

"Yes, darling. You have as many babies as you want. I'll help you. Now, scoot." Harriett headed toward the car, but stopped when she heard, "Wait! Momma Lupi constantly sends us food. Take some lasagna home. Please!"

∞ ∞ ∞

The kitchen reeked of garlic when Harriett arrived. Eddy was busy stirring something on the stove. She gagged. "What are you cooking? Alice sent over lasagna."

"Hi, tiger. When did you see Alice?" Eddy leaned over to kiss his wife, who was peeking at the contents of the skillet. The sight of the food caused a chain reaction. As Harriett grabbed her mouth to run, she hooked the handle of the pan, causing it and the contents to tip. Eddy caught the skillet mid-air to prevent the fall. He burned his hand, dropped the skillet, then burned his leg. He slid to the floor, holding both leg and hand in agony.

When she returned, Harriett's face drained of all color. "Oh, Eddy. What happened?"

Eddy moaned.

"Did I trigger this? I'll get some ice to put on the burns, then I'll call Ralph Paulson to tell him we're on our way." She emptied two trays of cubes into a dish towel, handed it to Eddy, then grabbed the phone.

"Doctor Paulson's office," the female voice said.

"Arlie, it's Harriett Kepler. Is Ralph in tonight? Eddy was burned."

"Hi Harriett; yes, the doctor is here. Normal evening hours." Arlie turned her head and covered the phone before saying, "Harriett Kepler's on the phone."

A male voice responded, "Tell her to come right in."

"Harriett, the doctor says to come in."

"Thanks, Arlie. We'll be there shortly." She hung up the phone, then helped Eddy to the car.

Eddy used Harriett as a human crutch as he hobbled into the waiting room of Dr. Ralph Paulson Jr., a second-generation Campbellsville physician. Arlie grabbed a wheelchair for him to sit.

"What happened to you?" asked Dr. Paulson as he removed the ice pack from Eddy's hand.

"Stupid accident," Eddy grumbled. "I played catch with a hot skillet."

Harriett reached for her mouth at the sight of his reddened skin. "Oh, I think I need to use the bathroom." She looked at Arlie for directions, then bolted.

Dr. Paulson and Eddy stared at each other.

"Is that out of character?" asked the doctor. "I pegged Harriett as being more stoic."

"She's been awfully squeamish lately." Eddy watched as Dr. Paulson treated his hand with salve and wrapped it in bandages. "Tipped over the skillet running out of the kitchen, holding her mouth."

Dr. Paulson's face lit up. "I think you'll get two diagnoses tonight. Let me look at that leg."

"What the hell are you talking about?" Eddy winced as Dr. Paulson cut away his pant leg. "Was it necessary to ruin my trousers?"

Harriett returned. Her white, clammy complexion shared the secrets of the bathroom visit.

"Arlie, please get Mrs. Kepler a chair."

Harriett turned her head, not wanting to watch.

After five minutes of cleaning and wrapping, Dr. Paulson spoke. "Okay folks, I have both diagnoses for you." He smiled before continuing. "Eddy, these are only first-degree burns. No nerve damage. All you'll need is to keep them clean and wrapped for a couple of days, then leave them open to the air." Dr. Paulson handed him a jar of ointment, then winked at Harriett before continuing. She nodded, with a knowing smile. "However, this second diagnosis is more serious, with life-long consequences. Are you ready to hear what must be said?"

Eddy gawked at the doctor. "It's just a burn! How will that affect me the rest of my life? What the...?"

Dr. Paulson looked at Harriett. "Mrs. Kepler, why don't you disclose the second diagnosis?"

Harriett smiled. Walking to Eddy, she grasped his good hand and gazed into his eyes. "Eddy, I'm so sorry I caused the burns." She kissed his knuckles. "You..." She giggled.

"Come on, Harriett, out with it! I'm dying here!"

"No, not even close to death. More like, life!" She paused. "Eddy, you're going to be a daddy."

It was Eddy's turn to go pale. "What?"

"I'm having a baby," she whispered.

Eddy jumped into the air. Forgetting the pain in his leg and hand, he grabbed Harriett around the waist and twirled her in circles.

"A daddy! I love being a daddy!"

Harriett cocked her head at that comment but overlooked it. *Just excitement,* she thought. "Isn't it wonderful?"

"Yes, yes, yes! When are you due?"

"Spring. March, if I calculated correctly."

He kissed her passionately, ignoring the medical staff onlookers.

My life is perfect. A thought she shared with Eddy.

25

WELCOME TO THE WORLD

MARCH 15, 1955

*T*he nurse reached for the infant cradled in Harriett's arms. "Mrs. Kepler, it's bath time. Are you strong enough to help me?"

Harriett groaned. "So soon? I just gave birth."

"Yes, we know." The nurse smiled at the new mother, reluctant to release her baby. "Why don't you take a nap? You've had a busy night. I'll teach you how to bathe a baby tomorrow."

Harriett smiled as she liberated her child. "Okay," she said drowsily. Within minutes, she was sound asleep.

Eddy paced back and forth in the waiting area, anxiously anticipating news of the birth. It seemed like days since Harriett went into labor the previous night. Her water broke mid-afternoon, with labor beginning around five. The pain intensified, which prompted the trip to the hospital around midnight. He looked at his watch. *Eight o'clock. I better call my boss*, he thought. He turned to look for a phone as the nurse entered the room. Four men stood, all expecting news.

"Mr. Kepler?" She waited.

"That's me. Here! I'm Eddy Kepler."

"Congratulations, Mr. Kepler."

Eddy couldn't wait. "Son or daughter?"

"Your wife is fine. You have a beautiful baby girl." She motioned toward the door. "Would you like to meet her? She just had her first bath. She's sound asleep, waiting to meet her daddy."

Eddy dropped to his knees. "I have a baby girl." Tears streaked his face as he accepted congratulations from the other three men. "A darling little daughter!"

He made a mad dash to view the tiny body, wrapped from head to toe in pink, lying in the bassinette. Eddy stared through the nursery window at the sign labeled "Kepler Girl." He marveled at how tiny she was. Harriett would beg to differ, after squeezing a seven-pound, twelve-ounce person from her petite hundred-pound body. The baby was seven and three-quarters percent of Harriett's entire being.

Eddy lost all track of time as he gazed at the infant. After 30 minutes, he searched for a phone to call work.

"Hi, Mr. Mack?" he said, when the head of human relations answered the phone. "Eddy Kepler here. I won't be in today. My wife just had her baby." He reached to replace the receiver, only stopping as he heard.

"Kepler. Kepler! Don't hang up. Girl? Boy? Wife okay?"

"Ah, yes. Baby girl."

"Kepler, you're going to have to give more details than that. Weight? Length? Wife's status?" Mack chuckled as he schooled his employee.

"Sorry. Baby girl, seven pounds-twelve-ounces. I guess Harriett is fine. No one said otherwise."

Mack laughed. "Okay Kepler, go see your family. We'll see you tomorrow." The phone went dead as the operator requested 10 cents to continue the call.

Eddy peeked into Harriett's room to find her sleeping angelically. Her brown, wavy hair was combed off her forehead and face. She glowed, as if her entire body were illuminated from within.

"Harriett," he whispered. "Are you awake?"

A groggy smile crossed her face. "Hi." She reached for his hand. "We have a little girl."

Eddy kissed her forehead, then sat on the edge of the bed, holding her fingers tightly. "I saw her. She looks perfect."

"She is perfect. Ten fingers. Ten toes. Strong lungs." Harriett yawned. "I am so happy."

Eddy stroked her hair. "Me too, darling. Me too." He sat holding her hand in silence. Before breaking the spell, he memorized how beautiful she looked. "Have you considered any names?" He ticked his tongue. "Stupid question. Of course, you've thought of names."

"I like Abigail for a middle name. After your mother." She blushed. "Okay with you?"

Eddy fought the tears welling in his eyes. "Yes. After Mother." His voice trailed off. "And for her first name?"

Harriett thought for a minute. "I can't decide. Sherri, Deborah, Heidi, Claudia. Something modern. What do you think?"

Eddy hesitated. A ring of sweat wet his forehead. "What about Rosa, or Josephine?"

She shook her head immediately. "No. Too Old World. Sounds like stuffy old grandmothers. I also like Shelby and Cynthia."

Eddy decided not to press his luck or the issue. His wife may be in a post-birth state of euphoria, but she was still sharp, too clever.

"I choose Shelby Abigail Kepler." He grinned as he removed a box from his pocket. "This is for you."

Hinges squeaked as Harriett snapped open the lid. Inside was a strand of matching cultured pearls.

"Eddy," she gasped then broke into uncontrollable sobs.

"I don't deserve these. I lost the last set you gave me. Please!" She handed the box back to her husband. "I'm not worthy."

Eddy's eyes popped open wide. "Yes, you are." He hid his face and guilt from her by turning toward the window.

∞ ∞ ∞

Harriett and baby Shelby arrived home a week later to find her two sisters and sister-in-law waiting for them. Her nose was greeted by a blast of light floral scents, remnants from the bouquets sent to the hospital, now relocated to the entryway.

Alice rushed over. "Give her to me. I want to hold my niece." She cradled the baby in her arms.

Esther cautioned her. "Don't be getting too comfortable. You'll want another one of your own."

"Hush! I'll have as many as the Good Lord will give me." She leaned toward Harriett. "The nursery is ready. Want to see it?"

Laurie looked on wistfully, wanting a brother or sister for daughter Deidra. "No more babies" was her obstetrician's recommendation. A rough pregnancy, gestational diabetes, and eclampsia had resulted in a Cesarian delivery.

Shelby's nursery was about 90 percent finished when labor began. The only thing left to do was hang a mobile above the crib, make up the bed, and hang a few wall adornments. Painted in bright colors, the room boasted a circus theme, minus all clowns. Esther and June voted against their inclusion.

Harriett entered the room, expecting minimal changes. She gasped as she walked through the door. "Who repainted this?"

The once bright room was now decorated in soft pastels

of pink, purple, peach, coral, blush, and salmon, garnished with pale greens and yellows. The longest wall was covered with a mural of flowers, birds, and friendly forest animals. Butterflies flitted midair amid puffy white clouds in a blue sky. Fluffy, flower-shaped pillows cushioned a large wooden rocker that was decorated with a massive pink bow. The chair matched the bassinette, crib, changing table, and chest of drawers, new purchases filled with all necessary accessories and clothing for an already spoiled child.

Harriett collapsed into the rocker. "How did you do this in just one week? Who did this? Goodness." Her mouth hung open. She tugged at her hair.

"Oh no. You don't like it!" Alice handed the baby to Esther before comforting her sister. "I'm sorry. It was my idea. Although gender-neutral, I thought bright red, green, and blue was too harsh for your little girl." She hugged Harriett. "Shall we change it back to your original colors?"

Laurie hung her head. "Harriett, I painted the mural. I brought Dee Dee along." She giggled. "Now I want to repaint Dee Dee's room, but Alfred forbids it."

"I love it. I never dreamed all this could be done in just one week." She hugged Laurie. "You are so talented. She'll be a real girly girl, like her Aunt Alice and Aunt Laurie."

"What? Not her Aunt Esther?" The eldest Bailey sibling scowled in jest as she tossed a clean diaper across the room.

"One thing's for sure, she'll be pretty. Look at that precious face!" The baby gurgled on demand as the women sighed.

The chubby-cheeked infant had bright blue eyes, like every other baby. But Shelby's eyes were piercing, latching onto everything with intense curiosity. A wisp of blonde curl poked out from under her bonnet, embellishing her otherwise fuzzy bald head. Long, slender fingers teased the potential of a future pianist.

"Shelby, this is your new room," Harriett whispered as she gazed at her child. "I promise you'll never wear hand-me-downs as long as you live!"

Esther and Alice burst into laughter. "Thirty minutes before an attack on Mother. That just might be a record," Esther teased.

Color rushed up Harriett's neck. "Stop it. I just mean I'll give her everything and anything she needs and wants."

"We know exactly what you mean." Alice giggled. "You mean that you've learned the kind of mother *not to be*. Our mother taught this lesson well!"

Esther changed the subject. "Harriett, come see how your supplies are organized. We have all your diaper products stored here." She pointed to a shelf inside the cabinet. "Her clothes are in the chest, folded according to item type."

Alice swung open the closet door. "And look at all these cute, tiny dresses."

Harriett swooned. "What happened to the boys' clothing that I got for shower gifts?"

"We exchanged them for these." Esther motioned to the rack filled with ruffles, frills, and lace.

"Shelby, you are such a lucky little girl. You have the best aunts alive." Harriett extended her arms beckoning to her sisters.

They embraced. "And a very special Mommy," said Alice.

∞ ∞ ∞

The next day, Harriett puffed as she climbed the basement stairs to the kitchen. A sedentary week in the hospital and childbirth left her winded.

I need exercise, she thought. *Or else we need to get on with the kitchen remodel!*

She dropped her laundry basket at the sound of the front

doorbell. The shadow of a woman's blowing headscarf was visible from inside. Harriett opened the door.

"Mother! What are you doing here?" Harriett's face went pale, her hand twitched. "You're not welcome." She swung the door, but Olive stopped it with her foot.

"I'm here to see my new granddaughter. Eddy invited me."

"Well, *Eddy* can entertain you, then. I'm busy." Harriett stomped down the hallway screaming at the top of her lungs. "Eddy, your visitor is here."

The sounds of a crying baby drifted from the second floor.

Harriett glared at Olive. "Now look what you made me do!"

"I didn't tell you to yell. You did that on your own accord, Missy. Blame no one but yourself. Now, maybe if I rock her, she'll go back to sleep." Olive started up the stairs toward the noise.

Harriett ran into the kitchen. Eddy was busy cooking. "How dare you invite her here?!" Harriett stood on tiptoes glaring into his face. "You know how I feel about her."

"Settle down, Harriett. She has the right to know her granddaughter. Where is she?"

"She's on her way upstairs. Go! Go up the back steps and intercede before she gets to Shelby."

Eddy shook his head. "You're as stubborn as her!" Taking the stairs two at a time, he reached Shelby's nursery at the same time as Olive.

"Olive," he wheezed in greeting as he caught his breath. "I'm glad you came."

"Harrumph. Unlike my daughter! Now, let me see the little one." Olive slowly stepped into the nursery. "Shh, shh. There, there." She lifted the infant, sat down, and rocked as she hummed a lullaby. "Aren't you a pretty little thing! But you should be. You come from good stock." Olive smiled at Eddy who looked on.

Shelby fell back to sleep immediately. Olive rocked and cradled her, gently and lovingly. The visit lasted 30 minutes. Finally, she looked at Eddy.

"Thank you. I better go. Can you sneak me out without getting Miss Priss all riled up again?"

"Come on. We'll go out the front. Can I drive you home?"

"No, I'll walk." She turned to look at the baby. Handing Eddy an envelope she said, "Here, for her education. Don't show Harriett."

∞ ∞ ∞

Eddy ushered Olive out, then found Harriett folding laundry in the kitchen. "She's gone. You were rather rude, don't you think?"

"Don't you dare lecture me." She turned to leave.

Eddy tossed the envelope at her, hitting her between the shoulder blades. "For Shelby, from Olive. She asked I keep it a secret, but you need to know."

"What?"

"A gift for her education. Open it." Eddy picked the card off the floor. This time he handed it to his wife. "She asked me not to show you, but you should know about her kindness."

Harriett opened the seal to find a card offering congratulations on the birth. Inside was a check. "Geez Louise. She gave Shelby one thousand dollars!" Harriett's pulse increased. She sank into a chair and stared at the check. "It will probably bounce!"

Eddy turned in disgust. "You're worse than her," he mumbled as he resumed preparing supper.

26

HATCHING DUCKLING

The Kepler family slowly adjusted to its newest member. Two weeks passed before Kimberly Coil began sending Harriett work via courier. Her six-week maternity leave sped by quickly. Overwhelmed for the first time in her life, Harriett suspended all classwork. She was perplexed that one tiny baby required the same amount of time and energy as six or nine credits of coursework; her master's degree was reluctantly placed on hold.

At her one-month postpartum appointment, Harriett requested an alternative to breastfeeding. Inadequate milk production coupled with pending long workdays justified the switch to an evaporated milk, water, and Karo syrup recipe.

By the second week of May, the newly adopted daily routine was as follows: Harriett read to Shelby each morning, fed her, dressed her, then dropped her off at Alice's before work. Eddy arrived home at 4:30, picked Shelby up, fed her, bathed her, read her a book, and put her to bed before making supper. Harriett arrived home around 6:30, ate supper, then prepared bottles for the next day while Eddy cleaned up the dishes. Eddy retired at 10, falling immediately to sleep. Harriett reviewed paperwork and covered feeding duties until one in the morning, when Eddy took over. Every day was like Ground Hog's Day, a repeat of the day before, and both adults were exhausted.

Shelby thrived on structure. By mid-June, her sleeping intervals increased. The dark bags under Harriett's eyes faded. Suffering less sleep deprivation, Eddy and Harriett delighted in the baby's development. A daily new discovery was realized as parenting became entertaining and fulfilling.

Summer, fall, and the holidays whizzed by as Shelby grew and Harriett and Eddy juggled sleep, work, and childcare.

∞ ∞ ∞

Christmas 1955 came and went. One early January evening, Shelby sat in her playpen, watching Harriett and Eddy wrap the candoliers in paper as they packed Christmas decorations to be stored in the attic.

"I'll take the next load up. Will you sort and organize the boxes once they are upstairs?" Eddy asked as Harriett labeled and sealed the last box.

Both adults stopped abruptly to the sound of Shelby repeating da da da da da as she slapped her hands against the bottom of the playpen.

"Harriett! Did you hear that? She's saying da da." Eddy rushed over to the baby. "Say 'da da.' I'm 'Da Da!'"

Shelby complied by giggling as she repeated da da da da.

"Eddy, I don't want to burst your bubble, but she's too young to understand that *you* are Da Da. She's just trying out her voice. Dr. Spock says she won't truly understand until she's at least one."

"Spock, Schmock! I don't care what he says. She's calling me!" Eddy lifted the child and carried her to the sofa. "Yes, you're Daddy's little girl!" He sat down, holding a squirming Shelby on his lap. "Sit still. You'll wiggle out of my arms."

"She wants down." Harriett sat on the floor in front of the couch. Extending her arms toward the baby, she said. "Walk to Mommy."

Shelby bounced up and down then squatted holding tightly to Eddy's fingers. Without warning, her knees pushed upwards as her legs moved forward one at a time. With her toes pointed outwards, Shelby placed her right heel onto the floor and rolled onto her toes. The process was repeated with the left heel.

"Eddy, hold her while she tries to walk." Harriett wiggled her fingers at the baby.

Eddy stood with Shelby holding on tightly to both hands. She released her left hand, squatted, then stood, tottering to keep her balance before stepping forward.

Eddy burst out laughing. "Oh my God! She waddles like a duck. Shelby, you're Daddy's little duck. Quack quack!"

The baby tilted her head upward and wobbled. She paused to regain balance, then, looking at Harriett, shook her right hand free and walked two steps, heel to toe, without aid.

"Come to Mommy!" Harriett grabbed Shelby under the arms, steadying her. "You can walk! I'm in trouble now." She squeezed the infant. Looking at Eddy, she bit her lower lip. "We better make sure this house is Shelby-proof. Nothing is sacred once she's mobile!"

∞ ∞ ∞

The house remained intact for the next two months. Shelby, walking duck-style, limited her excursions to a maximum of ten steps. She gained confidence daily, but remained content to hold onto objects for support or to stay in her playpen unless Harriett and Eddy were both in the room. She loved books and stories, listening intently to Harriett reading to her every morning and Eddy every afternoon.

According to Dr. Spock, she was learning to form different letter sounds, but despite his explanation of a baby's language development and timeframe, Harriett worried that her vocal skills were limited to ma ma, da da, ka ka, wa wa, and ta ta.

Shelby's first birthday fell on a Thursday, so Harriett planned a family celebration for Sunday, March 18th. On Saturday, she worked busily in the kitchen, baking a cake large enough for the entire family. Shelby sat in her playpen that was pushed into the corner out of traffic.

Harriett hummed softly under the sound of the electric mixer. As she clicked the appliance off, she was greeted with, "Mum-me. Bot-tell." Harriett looked around to see Shelby standing in the playpen, hands held high reaching for her.

"Shelby, did you just ask for a bottle?"

The baby shook her head yes and repeated, "Fee. Da. Bot-tell".

Harriett rushed to the child. "Oh, my goodness. Life will never be the same. My little girl is talking." She lifted the baby in her arms.

"Shaw-be. Bot-tell."

Harriett burst into tears. "*Shel*by. Can you say *Shel*by? Make an L sound."

"Shaw-be. Duck."

Harriett raced into the living room where Eddy was hanging crepe paper and balloons.

"Shelby, tell Daddy what you said," Harriett encouraged.

The baby smiled and reached for Eddy. "Dada. Shaw-be. Duck."

Eddy stared at Harriett, dumbfounded, then back to the

grinning baby. "You're going to be just as smart as your mommy, aren't you?" He swooped Shelby into his arms, swinging her in circles. "I think we have a new theme for tomorrow's party. I'll run down to the five and dime to see if I can find some decorations."

"Okay. And I'll ice the cake accordingly and make a couple of phone calls."

∞ ∞ ∞

The next day, the family gathered to find Donald Duck pictures taped to the walls, Donald Duck party beaks and hats, and a Donald Duck–shaped cake. Among her many gifts, Shelby received more than one sailor-style dress. Everyone donated a Donald Duck book to her growing collection of Little Golden Books.

The baby tore off the wrapping paper as she sat on Harriett's lap. "Look Shelby, *Donald Duck Finds Pirate Gold*. And this one is *Donald's Toy Train*. Goodness, here's *Donald Duck's Toy Sailboat*."

To each guest's delight, Shelby repeated the word "duck," every time it was spoken by her mother.

"I think I need to add some ducks to the mural," Laurie said as Harriett passed plates of cake.

Shelby answered for her mother by bouncing as she repeated, "Duck, duck, duck."

27

MASTER DUCK

JUNE 1957

Harriett resumed her classwork the summer after Shelby's first birthday. By the conclusion of the fall term in December 1956, she met the scheduled course requirements. The only thing left was to write her thesis, then graduate.

Twenty-seven-month-old Shelby was speaking in complete sentences and racing from room to room. Although she demonstrated acute agility and balance climbing steps, Eddy installed baby gates at the top and bottom of each staircase, just in case. It was a feeble attempt to corral the inquisitive toddler, who quickly learned how to unlatch the gate. While Harriett occupied her time studying and writing, Eddy filled his day with child chasing.

Madison College graduation was scheduled for Saturday, June 15th, 1957, at one in the afternoon. Harriett stood in the auditorium dressed in cap and gown, holding Shelby's hand as the toddler tried to pull loose.

"Eddy, I don't know how you'll manage to keep her still during the ceremony." Harriett tightened her grip on the little fingers. "Duck, listen to Mommy, please. This is a very special day. I'm giving a speech to all these important people. I need you to be still and watch Mommy get her diploma."

Eddy chuckled. "You may be brilliant and getting yet another degree, but you still don't understand you can't reason with a two-year-old." Eddy lifted Shelby, who was outfitted in a white dress trimmed in navy blue. "I'll handle this one. Now go get 'em, tiger." He kissed his wife and found his reserved seat near the front of the audience, next to a waiting Earl, Teddy, and Alice.

"Shelby, Duck," Eddy whispered. "Daddy has lots for you to read today." He handed the child a cloth bag filled with books. She removed them one at a time and stacked them on the seat between her legs. As soon as the pile was completed, she placed each book back into the bag.

"Good girl. Let's play that game again." Eddy patted her head. "Earl," he whispered to his brother who sat on the other side of Shelby. "Are you up to helping me with her today?"

Earl nodded. "Hopefully we can keep her occupied until after Harriett's speech. Then, I'll take her out to the car if she's fussy."

Shelby stacked the books, looked through the pages, snacked on dry Cheerios, bagged her books, and repeated. By the time Harriett was to speak, Shelby had already skimmed three times through the entire collection of titles.

Harriett stepped onto a platform, adjusted the microphone, and cleared her throat. Eddy whispered to Shelby. "Look Duck, it's Mama." He pointed to the stage.

Shelby cocked her head to the side. Holding onto Eddy for support, she stood on her chair and yelled. "Hi Mama, Duck is listening to you." She waved her arm in the air. "I being good for Daddy."

The audience burst into laughter at the tiny, blonde,

curly-haired child in a sailor suit bold enough to interrupt such a solemn ceremony.

Harriett blushed. Without hesitation, she waved back. "Hi, Duck. Mommy loves you. Thank you for behaving."

"You welcome."

The crowd roared.

Harriett smiled. Taking a deep breath, she began. "Hello, distinguished guests, faculty, students, and dignitaries. You just met my daughter, Shelby."

A little voice from the audience corrected her. "I Duck."

More laughter.

Harriett smiled at the child. Putting her notes aside, she began. "Shelby, AKA 'Duck,' is my motivation. It is my prayer that someday, she'll be here giving a graduation speech as well. I have worked hard, not only to better my life but to afford my daughter every opportunity…"

∞ ∞ ∞

Shelby lay cradled in Eddy's arms, sound asleep, by the time the ceremony concluded. Her only outburst was to greet her mother. Her cheek, red with sleep, seeped drool from the corner of her mouth onto Eddy's suit.

Earl, Alice, Teddy, and Eddy waited for Harriett, who was busy accepting congratulations from her professors.

Alice reached for Shelby. "We'll take her home with us so that the three of you can go out to dinner."

Earl shook his head. "Nonsense. You have her every day. Uncle Earl wants an evening with his niece. I'll take her; the four of you go. Eat, enjoy an evening away from the kids."

Alice nodded. "You'll get no argument from me. It will be nice to talk to adults."

"Eddy?"

"Sure, Earl. That's fine." Eddy chuckled. "Fair warning!

She can be a handful, so call the club if you need us. We'll be in the main dining room." Eddy waved as Harriett approached. "Nice job, sweetheart. Ready?"

Harriett stroked Shelby's hair. "She is just the most precious thing ever!"

∞ ∞ ∞

Earl lifted a drowsy Shelby into the front seat of his new '57 Chevy Bel Air, then adjusted the lap strap to fit her tiny body. Still single at 43 years old, with minimal expenses, his one splurge was trading in his car every three to four years. A new, red-and-white, two-door hard-top was the latest purchase, replacing his '53 convertible, whose soft roof was too chilly in the winter for middle-aged, arthritic bones.

Shelby rubbed her eyes, yawned, and fell fast asleep before they were out of Madison. The radio softly played Frank Sinatra, Mel Tormé, and Nat King Cole ballads as Earl drove the winding country road back to Campbellsville.

He parked in front of his house, carried a sleeping Shelby inside, laid her on the couch, then went to collect her bag of books, and diaper bag. *Good grief! How does tiny Harriett schlepp all this stuff around?*

He returned inside to find Shelby wide awake, walking around the room, exploring everything at eye level.

She looked up when Earl entered. "Hello."

Earl grinned. "Hello, Duck. You're staying with me this evening while Mommy and Daddy go out to dinner. Is that okay?"

"Okay. I hungry." She walked past him into the dining room, pulled out a chair, and proceeded to climb.

"Woah, Duck. Let me help you. I can't send you home with a bruised forehead." Earl rushed after the toddler, lifted her, and set her on a chair. "What do ducks like to eat?"

Shelby tipped her head in thought. "Tapoles and grass."

Earl choked at her answer. "I didn't know that." He chuckled. "What does Shelby Duck like to eat?"

She smiled as she shook her head. "Not tapoles. Yuck."

He rolled his eyes, ruing his decision to babysit. "Do you like…sandwiches?"

A tiny voice offered. "I like peanut butter, chicken, and milk." She paused. "And onions."

Earl coughed. "Onions! Where did you learn to eat onions?" He regretted the question as soon as the words rolled off his lips.

"Auntie Alice garden." Shelby slapped her hands on the table in exclamation. "They pull out when I tug." She wagged her finger at him. "Only eat if you shake off dirt."

Earl turned his back on the child to hide his giggling. "Why don't we start with a glass of milk while I look for the peanut butter."

"Okay." She folded her hands as if in prayer and waited.

Earl placed a small glass of milk in front of the child. Shelby held it tightly in both hands, raised it to her mouth, and swallowed until all contents were drained.

"More please." She pushed the empty glass toward her uncle.

"Wow! You are hungry."

"Yes," she wiped her mouth with the back of her hand.

Earl poured another glass of milk but waited to give it to her until he finished making a peanut butter sandwich. He cut it into four pieces before serving his niece.

"Thank you." She said before grabbing her supper.

"You are very welcome. Now, can you sit here while I make my dinner?"

"Yes," she said without looking up, intent on eating.

Earl returned with his own PBJ sandwich and two

napkins. Shelby immediately wiped her mouth with the paper.

"Mommy and Daddy have you well trained!" he chuckled.

She finished eating and sat quietly at the table watching her uncle. After several minutes, a frown crossed her face.

"Uncle Earl. I need go poopy." She held her belly.

Earl sprayed milk across the table. "You're potty training? Already?"

Shelby bounced up and down on the chair. "Now. I need go poopy now."

Earl gathered her and raced to the bathroom. Shelby stood while he fumbled with the pins in her diaper, grumbling to himself. "They didn't tell me she was potty training."

"Hurry." She jiggled making the pins harder to undo. Then Shelby stopped moving. "I sorry." Tears streamed down her face. "I pooped."

The diaper pin finally gave way, exposing a dirty, smelly mess.

"Poo stinky." Shelby held her nose. "I sorry."

Earl hugged her. Stroking her hair, he comforted her. "It's not your fault. Uncle Earl was too slow." He sat her on the edge of the toilet. "You hold on while I get the diaper bag. Okay?"

Her lip quivered. "Okay." She clutched tightly to the sides of the toilet seat as gravity pulled her bottom down.

Earl returned to find Shelby slipping farther and farther into the toilet. Her fingers turned red from her grip, her knees bent over the front as her heels dug into the toilet bowl.

"Oh my God!" Earl lifted her. "Are you okay?"

Shelby gazed at her uncle. "My bum is wet. Will you dry it?"

Earl hugged her. "Honey!" He shook his head and exhaled. "Let's get you changed into your jammies."

"Okay."

Butt bare, she lifted her arms waiting for him to remove her dress. "Will you read me a book?"

Earl blinked to stop his eye from twitching. "Sure. After I figure out how to pin a diaper."

Shelby grabbed the item from his hand. Spreading a clean diaper out onto the floor, she sat on top of it, then looked at her uncle. "I help."

Earl laughed until he cried.

∞ ∞ ∞

It took 20 minutes to accomplish the task, but her bottom was clean and dry in a new diaper, the rest of her secure in her pajamas. She sat beside him on the couch, snuggled under his arm, following along with her eyes as Earl read aloud.

"Fluffy the cat curled in the corner sleeping."

Shelby tugged at his shirt sleeve. "No. The cat curled *up* in the corner."

Earl cocked his head. "That's what I said. The cat curled in the corner sleeping."

Shelby shook her head. "You miss word *up*." She pointed to the book.

Earl blinked. "You're correcting me? For God's sake!" He looked at Shelby. "You're barely two and you can read!"

She bit her lip. "Only little words."

"What?" Earl gasped. "If you can read, then read it yourself." He handed her the book.

Shelby pointed to words in the book. "The. Up. Cat. In."

Earl coughed. "Okay, Shelby Duck. Uncle Earl had a very stressful night. Let's finish this book, then it's time for bed."

"Okay." She snuggled closer under his arm and listened while Earl carefully and succinctly read the remaining story.

∞ ∞ ∞

Eddy and Harriett arrived shortly after 10 p.m. to find Shelby sleeping on the couch and Earl drinking a cocktail, hair disheveled, and eyes glazed over.

Eddy smiled at his brother, completely understanding his body language. "How'd it go? You look tired."

"She's exhausting. Did you know she can read?" Earl refreshed his drink. "Nightcap?"

Harriett scooped Shelby into her arms. "She recognizes small words. She can't read yet."

"Well, the little brat corrected me!"

Eddy guffawed. "She'll keep you on your toes. I learn more from her than I ever did in school." He glanced at Harriett. "She's growing up so quickly. Ready for another one?"

Her eyes widened. "Oh, Eddy! We need to wait." She stroked the sleeping child's head. "I'm finally catching up on sleep! After two years." She hesitated. "Ah…and I enrolled in the Ph.D. program."

"You what?" Earl and Eddy asked in unison.

"I'll take my time. But, I think I want to teach." She dipped her head, eyes remaining upcast.

Earl slapped his brother on the back. "Better continue this discussion at home. I'll tell you one thing—personally, I'm too old to keep up with more than one Duck! She's a handful."

"That she is." Harriett gazed at the child, filled with pride. "She's so smart! Smarter than I'll ever be." Harriett kissed her cheek. Shelby stirred momentarily, looked at her mother, smiled, then fell back to sleep.

"Thanks, Earl. It was an enjoyable evening."

"Glad someone had fun." Earl blushed, then gulped his drink.

"What happened?" Harriett pried, as she met his gaze, hoping her admiration for her brother-in-law was disguised.

"Someday, I'll tell you about this evening. Maybe? I have a graduation gift for you, but not tonight." Earl ushered them to the door. "Go home. I need sleep!"

28

MOMMA BEAR

Eddy lay Shelby in her bed. He stroked her hair, then kissed her forehead before joining Harriett in her office. She was reading over her diploma, not acknowledging him entering the room.

"Harriett, can we talk?" Ice cubes clinked together as he dropped them into a glass.

"Yes, we may." She closed the document. "Make me one too, please."

Eddy frowned as he sipped his drink. "Why didn't you discuss getting your Ph.D. with me before you enrolled? Don't you think that's something for both of us to consider together?"

She clenched her teeth curling her lips at the corners of her mouth. "No, I don't. It's my education and my decision."

Eddy exhaled then rubbed his temples. "Seriously? A marriage is supposed to be a partnership. If you're unhappy at Dugan & Co., then tell me about it. We can live off my salary if you want to quit. We'll need to tighten our belts, but it—"

"Why would I want to quit Dugan & Co.?" She sat her drink down and stood. "I love my job."

"You told Earl you wanted to teach."

"I do want to teach. But I want to remain CFO also." She thrust her diploma at Eddy. "Read that! I have my master's degree in finance. This is a big deal, Eddy! For me. For Campbellsville!" Her lip trembled. "No one else in this town, certainly not another woman, has their master's degree except for me! Well, except for the doctor."

Eddy took the document. Laying it on her desk without opening it he sat down in the leather chair. "Harriett, is education the only thing you want? Don't you want a family?"

"We have a family! Shelby is a beautiful, brilliant girl. I don't need another child."

"What about what I need? Look at your sisters; they love having big families. I want one too." He waved his arms in the air. "Why did you buy such a big house if you didn't want to fill it with children?"

Harriett ran her tongue over her teeth as she thought about her response. "I used to want a big family, at least three, maybe four children that could play with their cousins, form lasting family bonds. I am close to my sisters. But," she paused. "I spent three years alone, supporting myself—"

"Christ, Harriett! Here we go again!" Eddy jumped to his feet.

"Sit down," she said calmly. "I'm not chastising you. I'm trying to explain *when* and *why* my dreams changed."

His face burned bright red. "Then, go on." He gulped his drink and made another.

"Easy on the booze. You've had quite a bit already tonight."

Eddy tossed his glass at his wife. It whizzed past her

head, crashing onto the wall. "Don't treat me like a child." His voice was deep and guttural. "I'm not your underling. I'm your husband, your partner. I'm listening to my wife tell me why she doesn't want any more children. If I want to drink, I'll drink!"

Harriett turned her back. "This conversation is over. I'll not try to justify my decision with an irrational, immature, child." She moved to exit.

Eddy's body blocked the doorway. Shaking his head, he raised his hands for her to stop. She flinched. "I'd never harm you. I'm sorry I lost my temper."

"Famous last words." She moved to her left. With her back tight against the door frame and her chest pressed to his body, she squeezed through the door.

"Wow! You're in a real mood today." Eddy moved, allowing her to pass. "Somehow, I know you'll win this battle, but for the record, I love being a father. I want another baby."

Harriett did not respond. Eddy remained in the office, thinking. When he finally went up, Harriett lay with her back facing the middle of the bed.

"Harriett," Eddy whispered. His hand glanced across her shoulder.

She opened her eyes but remained quiet with the sheet tucked around her ear. Eddy silently undressed and climbed into bed. Sleep eluded both. Eddy tossed and turned, bouncing up and down continuously. Harriett pretended she was on a rocking boat.

∞ ∞ ∞

By morning, both dozed from sheer exhaustion.

Awakened by his own snoring, Eddy rolled over, swatting at something tickling his face.

"Daddy," the little voice said. "Daddy, I go potty."

His eyes bolted open. "What?" He rubbed his eyes. "Shelby, how did you get out of your crib?"

"I climb." She held the top of her diaper. "Daddy, go potty now."

Eddy jumped out of bed. Lifting the child, he rested her on his arm while his fingers drowsily but nimbly unpinned her diaper. "How did you get out of your pajamas? When did you start using the potty?"

"I big girl. Like Maggie and Polly." She wiggled in his arms. "Hurry."

Eddy laughed. "Hold on if you can, Duck." He rushed into the master bathroom.

"Oh, Daddy. I pee." Crying, she bit her lip as the warm liquid ran down his arm.

"Don't worry, sweetie," Eddy said, wiping her tears with his dry hand. "Holding it overnight takes a while to get used to. Let's get you washed before Mommy wakes up."

The sound of running water and a giggling toddler disturbed Harriett. She glanced at the clock before calling out. "Eddy, for goodness sake, it's five on a Sunday morning. Why are you running a bath?"

"Go kiss Mommy good morning." He whispered to Shelby.

The naked child ran to Harriett's side of the bed. Grabbing onto the blanket, she stepped onto the edge of the mattress and pulled herself up to sit beside her mother.

"Hi, Mommy." Shelby threw her arms around Harriett's neck. "Bath time."

"Where are your jammies?" Harriett snuggled Shelby in the sheet.

"I almost a big girl. I peed." The child giggled as Harriett tickled her stomach.

"You peed? Well, then I guess you need a bath. Go back to

Daddy." Harriett helped her off the bed. Her bare feet slapping the floor echoed in the room as she waddled back to her father.

∞ ∞ ∞

Harriett refilled coffee mugs as Eddy tended the skillet. Shelby salivated at the aroma of bacon.

"Daddy, I hungry. Cook faster." Her command prompted laughter from both adults.

"Duck. Don't be bossy like your mother," Eddy said as he distributed fluffy yellow scrambled eggs among three plates.

"I beg your pardon?" Harriett growled her objection.

"Mommy big boss!"

Shelby's assessment broke any remaining tension from the previous evening.

Eddy chortled in agreement. "She sure is!" He turned to his wife. "What would you like to do today, Mrs. CFO Kepler?"

Harriett scratched at her food before eating a spoonful of eggs. "I was hoping to go to the club today. Maybe hit a bucket of balls." She paused for a bite of food. "We didn't golf much the past two years. Geez, Louise, I was just getting the hang of things when this rascal showed up." Harriett tickled Shelby's belly.

"I here!" Shelby declared with her hands on her hips.

"Yes, you are, Duck. You are certainly here."

Eddy set a plate of bacon on the table. "Now that summer is here, I think weekends should be family time." He handed an eager Shelby a piece of the crispy meat. "She's with Alice all week. I see her weeknights, but…" He paused. "She's usually asleep when you get home, Harriett. Don't you want to spend time with her?"

Harriett frowned. "Can't we make the club family time? Most of the yard chores are covered, since Toby is cutting grass and Lloly is helping weed. Same for Mother. It's a good arrangement; I want to help the kids earn extra spending money."

"How do you golf with a toddler? With one that has decided to potty train herself?"

"I don't know." Harriett rolled her eyes.

"I don't want her with a babysitter every weekend. I want her to be with her parents." Eddy squinted at Harriett. "Both parents!"

Harriett sighed. "Maybe we can enroll her in a swimming class, or get a private teacher?"

"She's two-and-a-half. Is she ready to learn to swim?"

"I'm thinking out loud, Eddy. I don't even know if swim lessons are available for toddlers." She exhaled. "I do know that I must continue golfing. Too much business is done on the course, and I must be part of it."

"May I ask how you plan to attend school with all the other things you *must* do?"

Harriett clenched her jaw. "I don't want to argue, especially not in front of her." She motioned to Duck who was happily chewing her bacon. "I figure I can spread course work over two, at the most, three years, taking summers off. Then take a year to write my thesis. I'll be done by the time she starts school. If I want to teach, I'll have time to do that too."

Eddy sighed. "You have it all planned, don't you? But no time for another B-A-B-Y?"

Harriett groaned a low guttural grunt.

Shelby looked up from her breakfast. "Why Mommy making bear sounds?"

Eddy patted her head. "Mommy's grouchy like a Mama bear waking up from a long winter's nap."

Shelby cocked her head. Staring at her father, she thought for a moment, her brain processing his words. She turned to Harriett. "You have a long nap Mommy? Then you hungry. No more talk, eat breakfast."

29

JEROME

JULY 1957

*H*arriett creatively and successfully avoided pregnancy for the next two months, but hated placing her future in the hands of chance and good fortune. She needed to act. Picking up the phone, she dialed the number written on her steno pad.

"Dr. Gerald's office. How may I help you?" said the answering voice.

"Hello. I'd like to make an appointment." Harriett opened her calendar and flipped to July.

"Is this an emergency? Are you a new or existing patient?"

Harriett hesitated. Is this what she really wanted? "New patient. Non-emergency, but important."

"All appointments are important. I'm sorry. Dr. Gerald is not accepting new patients at this time. May I have your name and number? I'll place your name on a waiting list."

Harriett's mouth contorted. "Harriett Bailey Kepler. My number is 555-6767."

"Thank you, Mrs. Kepler. If you need immediate care,

please go to the Madison Hospital emergency room." The phone clicked dead.

Harriett frowned. "Maybe this is a sign," she said under her breath. Her thoughts were interrupted when Kimberly Coil buzzed the intercom.

"Mrs. Kepler. You have a phone call from a Dr. Gerald. Shall I send it through?"

Puzzled, Harriett replied, "Yes, thank you." *At least it's an incoming call for curious eyes to pry,* she thought.

The phone line lit up. "Harriett Bailey Kepler speaking."

"Harriett. Jerome Gerald. I just happened to notice that you called. How may I help?" The male voice wavered.

"Hello, Dr. Gerald."

"Please, call me Jerome; we belong to the same country club."

"I was hoping to make an appointment." Harriett decided not to address him.

"Can you stop over this afternoon? I'll free my schedule. Will 30 or 40 minutes give you enough time? Do I need to do a physical examination?"

Harriett chuckled. "Forty minutes is plenty of time."

"Then I shall see you at two? Can you adjust your day?"

"Thank you. Yes, two is fine." This time Harriett ended the call. *That was strange*, she thought.

∞ ∞ ∞

Harriett parked her car and walked up the two flights of stairs to Jerome Gerald's office suite. The nurse blushed as she greeted Harriett. "Mrs. Kepler, I am so sorry. I didn't recognize your name. Please have a seat; the doctor will be right with you."

"Thank you." She glanced at five women sitting in the waiting room as she chose a chair in the far corner. One looked at her watch impatiently while two pregnant women absentmindedly rubbed their bulging bellies. A stack of magazines was piled on the table beside her chair. She rifled through them quickly, chose a copy of *Look*, then turned to the index.

A second nurse popped her head through a side door. "Mrs. Kepler," she announced.

A cacophony of groans filled the room as a red-faced Harriett stood and followed her into the inner sanctum of the office.

Harriett was ushered into an examination room. "Please have a seat. The doctor shall be in directly."

Jerome Gerald, a handsome, middle-aged man with graying temples, charged through the door with his hand extended. "Mrs. Kepler—may I address you as Harriett? Thank you for choosing my practice. I've seen you and your husband at the club, but it's a pleasure to finally meet Madison's bright young superstar."

Harriett's face burned bright red. "Quite the accolades. I fear I fall short of your assessment. However, thank you for making time for me today."

"So, Harriett," he waited for her approval. "What brings you in?"

"Doctor, may I ask you for complete confidence?"

"Always! Doctor-patient relationships are sacred." He looked on curiously.

"I want to discuss...well, I'm interested in preventing pregnancy." She dropped her head and her voice simultaneously.

"I see. Birth control." He tilted his head. "Am I correct in assuming Mr. Kepler feels otherwise?"

Harriett stood. "This is a mistake." She moved toward the door.

"Please have a seat, Harriett." He motioned to the chair.

"I appreciate your needs. There is no shame in wanting to control if and when you become pregnant, especially for a corporate executive such as yourself." He reached for her hand. "You'll have no judgment from me. What were you thinking? Permanent or temporary?"

Harriett considered her choices. "Temporary. My daughter is a toddler. Eddy wants another child now, but…"

"You don't. I understand." Dr. Gerald dropped her hand and opened a drawer. He removed two objects.

"I just completed my master's degree and enrolled in the doctorate program. I need to guarantee no babies for at least three years." She hesitated. "Well, I can endure a pregnancy while writing the end of my thesis, but not before."

"You have more than enough to fill your day with a family, studies, and a corporate position. Hell, I know few men capable of tackling such demands." His voice softened. "I take it your husband is against using a sheath?"

"I must convince him that nature is uncooperative. I have two extremely fertile sisters, however, my sister June has only one child. Perhaps we can fool him for the short term that…I imitate her?"

Dr. Gerald slid his stool next to Harriett. "We have two options. The first is called a diaphragm." He opened a plastic case to expose a round, flexible, rubber-looking disc. "This is inserted and functions as a barrier to sperm."

Harriett inspected the item. "So, I need to insert prior to," she paused before saying the word, "sex?"

"Yes. That is exactly how it works. It is easily cleaned with warm water and stored in this case."

"Do I have another option?" She turned the case over in her hands. "I may not be afforded time to prepare."

Dr. Gerald smiled. "Ah, to be young! Yes, Harriett. This other item is called an intrauterine device, or IUD. I insert it into the uterus, and you're set for up to four, maybe five years."

"Will Eddy be able to detect it?" She bit her lip, clearly embarrassed by the whole conversation.

"Two thin strings used to retrieve it hang in the vagina, but he should not be able to feel them." He handed Harriett the device to inspect.

After several minutes, she spoke. "Is there any pain or discomfort? What does this cost?"

Dr. Gerald handed her a hand-typed pamphlet on IUD usage and side effects. "Read this. I wrote this specifically for my patients. It should answer all your questions. As for the cost, I won't lie, it's a new concept and it's expensive. It costs about one hundred dollars, but it will last four to five years."

Harriett only considered for a moment. "I can justify twenty-five dollars a year to ensure no babies until after my Ph.D. How soon can we insert it?"

"How about right now? I'll have the nurse give you an exam gown. I'll treat another patient before I have a waiting room mutiny, and then we'll do the implant."

Harriett extended her hand. "Thank you," she paused a moment, "Jerome. For your flexibility, accommodation, and confidence."

"My pleasure. I'll be back shortly."

30

CONTRACTIONS

SEPTEMBER 1957

The leaves on the trees glowed with tints of red and yellow in the late afternoon sun. Eddy and Shelby played a modified game of ball. It was more "chase and giggle" than "toss and catch." Harriett sequestered herself in her office with a stack of library books, having started working on her Ph.D.

"Duck, Daddy's going to get us each a drink of water. Will you sit still for a couple minutes?" Eddy pointed to a lawn chair, indicating where she was to sit.

"Sure, Daddy." Shelby climbed up and let her legs swing freely in the air.

Inside, Eddy peeked into the office. "Harriett, bring your books outside. It's too beautiful a day to waste cooped up in your office."

"I have too much to read. I need quiet. Maybe tomorrow." Harriett's attention remained on her open book.

Eddy grumbled to himself then retreated to the back of the house. The newly renovated kitchen, with French doors leading to the terraced backyard, featured state-of-the-art industrial appliances on which Eddy honed his cooking skills.

Harriett's baking center boasted two wall ovens and a marble slab countertop for rolling dough. Her creations dwindled, however, from a daily obsession to a weekly obligation.

A sitting Shelby greeted her father with a big smile. "Hi, Daddy. I tired playing ball."

Eddy handed her a plastic cup of water. "Okay then. What do you want to do, Duck? Do you want to play a different game?"

Shelby considered the question as she drank her water, then, wiping her mouth with her hand, she said, "Go visit Grandma Olive."

Her answer bewildered Eddy. "Do you remember her? You've only seen her a couple of times."

"Yes. She scary, but I like her."

Eddy coughed. "Okay, but you have to promise not to tell Mommy."

"Why?" Shelby scrunched her nose. "She Mommy's Mommy."

"Yes, but Mommy isn't fond of her," Eddy blurted without giving his word choice much thought.

Shelby jumped to her feet. "No be silly, Daddy. Everyone loves a Mommy!" Her hands flew to her waist in exclamation.

"I agree, Duck. That's the way life should be, but…it doesn't always happen that way."

"If Mommy no love Grandma Olive, I need love her for two! We visit her today?"

Eddy shook his head. "How old are you?"

"I two-and-half." Shelby frowned. "You know that!"

"Yes, Duck, I know that." Eddy laughed until his belly ached. "Finish your drink and we'll go visiting."

∞ ∞ ∞

Olive stared at the pair standing on her back porch. "Eddy Kepler, Shelby, to what do I owe the pleasure of your company?" The permanent frowning wrinkles beside her mouth softened as her eyes twinkled.

Shelby, hiding slightly behind Eddy's leg, edged forward. Looking up at Olive, she grinned. "I come visit for Mommy and me."

Olive glanced at Shelby and then at Eddy.

"She asked to come." Eddy shrugged his shoulders. "So, we're here."

Olive reached down and lifted the toddler. "Did you walk all the way by yourself?"

Shelby squirmed but remained in Olive's arms. "Yes. I big girl."

Olive sat her in one of the ancient Adirondack chairs sitting on flagstones under the grapevines. "Why don't I get us each a glass of iced tea?"

Shelby looked at Eddy for permission. When he nodded his head, she added, "And cookie?"

Olive chuckled. "Eddy Kepler, you have a little spitfire on your hands, don't you?"

"That I do!" He ran his finger through Shelby's blonde curls. "She's a hoot."

After returning with glasses and a plate of cookies, Olive balanced her tray on the large chair arm.

"I hungry," Shelby said, eagerly reaching for a snack.

Olive scanned Eddy's face. "She doesn't understand contractions?"

"What?"

Olive laughed. "Contractions. 'I'm,' 'don't,' 'isn't,' 'can't.' Shortening two words into one."

"Oh, those. No, she doesn't use them." Color crept up Eddy's neck.

"Then it's high time she learns. Shelby, how old are you?"

Shelby looked at her father as if to say, *what's with the age question today?* "I two-and-half."

Olive smiled. "No. The answer is '*I'm* two-and-*a*-half.' Can you hear the difference?"

"I answer okay. I two-and-half," Shelby insisted.

Olive patiently explained, giving examples, and playing word games, until the afternoon sped by, and Shelby finally caught on.

"She's got it!" Olive winked at Shelby.

"She's," Shelby said, grinning with delight. "*I'm a* big girl for sure."

The sun was inching its way behind the opposite hillside. Eddy latched onto Shelby's hand. "We better head home to make supper. Did you have a nice visit, Duck?"

"Yes." Shelby slid off the chair. She threw her arms around Olive's neck. "Thank you for my lesson, Grandma Olive. But I go pee first."

"She's potty trained, too?"

"Yes ma'am. Did it all on her own. Wanted to be a big girl like Polly and Maggie."

Shelby wiggled back and forth. "Daddy!"

"May I?" Eddy asked. "She still waits until the last minute."

"Go." Olive was still chuckling when they returned.

"Thank you for a lovely afternoon, Miss Shelby." Olive kissed the child on the cheek.

Shelby wrapped her arms around Olive's leg. "I love you, Grandma Olive."

"Be off. Get out of here." Olive waved her arm toward the street as she turned her back to hide the tears slipping down her face.

31

AWOL TAKE TWO

MAY 1960

Life for the Keplers settled into an easy routine of Harriett working, and studying, Alice babysitting, and Eddy working, cooking, and parenting. Eddy and Shelby regularly visited Olive, who welcomed both into her inner sanctuary, sharing her many photos and their corresponding stories. Shelby absorbed information like a sponge soaking up water. She listened to tales of fall canning seasons, of her great Uncle Fred who fought in the First World War, of Great-Grandfather Henderson's prosperous farm, and of his joyful Christmas celebrations. Olive relayed, to Shelby's delight, how and why she was expelled from school. Olive even shared stories of Grandpa Tabs' adventures during the flood.

Harriett, aware, neither approved nor condoned the visits. Shelby had a right to know her grandmother, didn't she? That was something Harriett never had the privilege to do.

Shelby couldn't wait to start school that fall. Maggie and Polly filled her head with reports of school adventures. Tony ignored her, but secretly had a crush on his cousin. Alice was thrilled at having one additional year of daytime company, with all her children now in school.

Shelby watched out the front screen door for Eddy's car. "Aunt Alice, he's here. See you tomorrow." The child grabbed her lunch bucket, raced down the stairs, and jumped into the car. She slid across the bench seat to kiss her father.

"Daddy, how was your day?" Shelby wrapped her arms around his neck

Eddy ruffled her curly blond hair. Only five-years-old, she was already tall, resembling Olive, Alice, and Polly. But her square jawline and twinkling eyes were her father's, and her craving for knowledge, her mother's.

"Hey, Duck. My day was okay. What about yours?" He gently pushed her to the side for the two-block drive home. Eddy parked on the street, and carried Shelby to the door, while she protested, wanting to walk. Once inside, he began assembling ingredients for an easy dinner casserole.

Shelby tugged at his shirt. "Daddy, don't tell Mommy, but you're a really good cook, so much better than her. You're almost as good as Aunt Alice."

Eddy chuckled. "I won't tell her. You don't tell her either, okay?"

"Pinky swear." She held out her little finger to link with her father.

The task of slicing onions and celery was interrupted by a knock at the front door. Eddy dried his hands on a dishtowel. "Stay here, Duck. I need to see who that is."

Shelby climbed up onto a wooden kitchen chair to play with her cut-out doll. The visitor rapped again.

"Coming. Hold your horses." Eddy opened the outer set of double doors. "Holy hell! Wally Stuart. What are you doing here?"

Eddy took the man's hand. Wally returned the shake with a hug.

"Go-to-Guy Kepler. In the flesh. I was hoping to find you." Wally whistled through the gap in his front teeth.

"Come in. Please, here." Eddy motioned toward Harriett's office. "Take a seat. I'll be right with you."

Shelby peeked around the corner of the butler's pantry, witnessing the stranger's entry.

"Duck, sweetie, come meet one of Daddy's old army buddies." Eddy ushered the child into the office where Wally stood, observing the book titles on the shelf.

"When did you start reading literature? I never pictured you as a Shakespeare, Hemingway kind of guy."

Shelby looked at the man. "These are Mommy's books." Her hands flew to her hips. "This is Mommy's office," she said, then stomped her foot.

Wally laughed. "Pardon me. Easy mistake. I figured they belonged to your Daddy, you know. Because he's the man."

Shelby tilted her head. "What does being a boy or a girl have to do with owning books?"

Wally gaped. "Obviously, nothing."

Eddy smiled as Shelby schooled Wally on gender equality. "Wally, this is our daughter Shelby, or as we call her, Duck. Shelby, meet Wally Stuart."

Shelby thrust her hand forward. "Pleased to meet you, Mr. Stuart." Her tiny fingers gripped his palm and squeezed.

Wally guffawed. "Hell of a handshake, little Duck."

"I am Shelby. Only my friends call me Duck." She turned to her father and threw her hands in the air.

Eddy rested his back against the doorway, knee bent. Chuckling, he said, "Duck, play nice. Mr. Stuart is Daddy's friend. That's why he thinks he can call you Duck."

Shelby frowned, then climbed up onto Harriett's desk chair. "Daddy, you have raw chicken in the kitchen."

"My darling Duck." Eddy walked to the desk, tousled her hair, then faced Wally. "She's correct. I was making dinner. Let's move this conversation. Will you stay for supper?"

"I was hoping for an invitation."

∞ ∞ ∞

Harriett checked her calendar, straightened the papers on her desk, then depressed the button on her intercom. "Miss Coil," she said, summoning her assistant. "Do you have a minute?"

"Certainly."

Within seconds, Kimberly stood in the doorway to Harriett's office waiting for an invitation to enter.

"I'm leaving early today. I have some research to complete for my thesis. If anything needs immediate attention, please call my home office number to forward the message." She grinned. "I splurged and bought a new Ansafone machine."

Kimberly's eyes grew wide. "Impressive. That gives you the freedom to be away from your desk without missing important calls. Enjoy your research. Things are pretty quiet around here. See you in the morning."

Harriett jumped into her new, aqua blue, Cadillac Eldorado. The car was her gift to herself for her 30th birthday. Although well over 10 years old, her Buick only registered 60,000 miles. Unlike Thomas Roland, Glen Vincent, and Earl, who traded in vehicles every three years, Harriett could not part with her first car. She fingered the dashboard of the Cadillac then threw it in gear, to head to the university library. She hoped to finish her thesis—The *Financial Effect of Korea's Undeclared War on the US Economy*—and publish it by December.

Lily, the librarian, greeted Harriett, motioning to a stack of books and papers waiting for her perusal. After an hour of reading and notetaking, Harriett approached the front desk.

"Lily, do you have access to the records of local men who served? Where they were stationed, dates of service, and such?"

"Yes, Mrs. Kepler. That is on microfiche. I'll load it for you."

Harriett sat behind a reader, waiting for Lily to finish. A total of 87 men from Madison and Campbell Counties served during Korea. *This shouldn't take too long,* she thought. *It's a nice diversion from my other research.* She scrolled alphabetically to the Ks. Then, staring at her, in fuzzy sepia and gray, was Eddy's army record.

Edgar Gregor Kepler. Campbellsville, Pennsylvania, USA
Rank: Corporal
Assignment: Supply, Trieste Italy
Immediate Supervisor: Sergeant John Williams, Toledo, Ohio, USA
Misconduct: Absent without leave.
Punishment: Jail time. Recommendation of dishonorable discharge. Tribunal review recommendation of reinstatement with the demotion of one rank.
Rank: Private
Reassigned: Seoul, South Korea
Injured in the line of duty: Gunshot wound to right calf, resulting in a broken bone.
Transferred: M.A.S.H. Unit 8076
Reassigned: M.A.S.H. Unit 8076, Supply
Immediate Supervisor: Corporal Anthony Zarnecky, Kansas City, Missouri, USA
Discharge: Honorable. April 1, 1953

Harriett slumped forward, resting her head on the projector. She had only wanted a diversion from all her rigorous research. Add some local facts to her paper. Instead, she managed to open Pandora's Box.

Over the past seven years, she had detected inconsistencies in Eddy's stories. This was not a discrepancy; it was an outright lie. *Why did Eddy go AWOL, and why wouldn't he tell me?*

Harriett copied the information, carefully noting every line. Her hands trembled as she straightened the edges of her papers before placing them in her attaché.

"Lily," she said, returning the stack of books to the front desk. "I am so sorry, but I must leave early today. I'll be back next Wednesday to continue. Will you have this same list ready for me?"

"Certainly, Mrs. Kepler. Happy to help." Lily glanced at Harriett's face. "Mrs. Kepler, you look quite pale. Are you feeling okay?"

Harriett forced a smile. "Yes, thanks, Lily. I'm fine."

∞ ∞ ∞

Eddy, Wally, and Shelby sat around the kitchen table talking. All heads looked up as the front door slammed shut and the sharp staccato of high heels on the hardwood floor grew louder.

Harriett entered the kitchen, face red, eyes dark and glaring. Shelby ran to hug her mother.

"Hi Duck." Harriett kissed the child, then whispered in her ear. "Please go either to your room or into Mommy's office and read a book. Mommy needs to talk to Daddy."

"Okay, Mommy. But I'm hungry. I waited to eat with company tonight."

Harriett glowered at Eddy, then opened the refrigerator. "Here, Duck. Eat an apple. Mommy will fix you supper in a couple minutes."

Shelby skipped down the hallway. Grabbing a book from a

lower shelf, she plopped into the large leather chair, hoping to stay within earshot of her parents.

"Who is our visitor?" Harriett forced her words through clenched teeth.

A smiling Eddy moved to pour her a glass of iced tea. "This is Wally Stuart, an army buddy."

She raised her hand rejecting the glass, then drew a long deep breath. "How convenient. Then maybe Mr. Stuart will confirm my findings."

Eddy wrinkled his forehead. "What are you talking about?"

Wally stood. "I think I better leave." He turned toward the hallway but was blocked by Harriett.

"Don't you dare! Sit back down. I need someone to substantiate my accusations."

Wally looked from Eddy to Harriett, rubbed his palms on his trousers, then retook his seat.

"Harriett, what's gotten into you? You are usually so cordial and polite. Wally is our guest and my friend." Eddy rested his hands on her shoulders as the oven timer chimed. He gave his wife a questioning look before removing the casserole and turning off the oven. "Let's have a cocktail before dinner. Darling, you sound like you need one."

Harriett poured a glass of milk, then took a salad plate from the cabinet. Scooping a serving from the dish, she said, "Neither of you move. I'm feeding Duck in my office." The men gazed at each other as her steps echoed down the hallway.

Harriett placed the food on her desk. "Duck, I know I always say we must eat at the table, but how would you like to eat in here tonight? While you read your book?"

"Sure, Mommy, that's a fun adventure." Shelby climbed behind the desk and hungrily shoveled a spoon of chicken into her mouth. "Yummy. Mommy, why are you mad at Daddy?"

"Eat, Duck. I'll explain later. Right now, Mommy is making herself a drink and talking to Daddy and his friend in the kitchen. You stay here. Thirty chews per forkful, okay?"

"Yes ma'am." Shelby chomped as ice cubes clinked into a glass.

∞ ∞ ∞

Wally stared wide-eyed. "What the hell, Eddy? Seven years, and you're still the drama king!"

Eddy shook his head. "I don't know what this is about. We've been getting along fabulously. By now, I was hoping for more children, but otherwise, things are really great. Shelby is such a blessing."

Wally smiled. "You always were a good father."

"Shh." Eddy placed his finger in front of his mouth.

"Why are you shushing me?" Wally gasped, then grabbed his mouth. "Oh my God. You haven't told her about Rosa, have you?"

"Wally, shut the fuck up!"

The voice came from the doorway. "No, Wally, please continue." Harriett stood, staring, shoes and papers in one hand, glass in the other. Her gaze turned toward her husband. "Eddy, why did you go AWOL? Why were you in Korea?" She threw her notes onto the table.

Eddy gulped before glancing at the writing. His entire army career was summarized and exposed for him to remember and Harriett to see. The buzzing in his ears prevented him from hearing Harriett's next breathy question.

"Eddy, *who is Rosa?*"

Wally rushed toward the entryway, only to be blocked again by Harriett's tiny frame. She thrust her hands into his chest. "Stay. Please." Turning toward her husband, she growled. "Eddy, I want an answer. Who is Rosa?" Harriett's eyes were slits of fire.

Eddy stammered. "Ah...I don't know what..."

Harriett's shoe clipped his ear. "Don't lie to me. Who is Rosa?" The second shoe bounced off his shoulder. "What secrets have you been keeping from me?" The veins of her beet-red neck throbbed visibly in and out. Screeching, she yelled at the top of her lungs. *"Who is Rosa?!"* Beads of sweat circled her brow. Pounding heartbeats reverberated in her ears. Her head spun, then all went blank.

The tiny woman crumpled onto the floor. The crystal tumbler crashed, scattering ice and shards in every direction.

"Harriett!" Glass crunched underfoot as Eddy scooped Harriett into his arms. "Wally, call the ambulance." His head motioned to the phone hanging on the kitchen wall.

Shelby peeked around the corner. "Mommy!" She ran toward Harriett but was blocked by a faster Wally as he reached for the phone. "Shelby, honey, stay here. There is broken glass."

"Mommy!" Her arms reached toward her mother.

"Wally, help her!" Eddy rushed past the child. "Shelby, walk down to Aunt Alice's and tell her you need to stay the night. Okay, Duck? Go now."

He took the front steps two at a time, reaching the bottom as the ambulance, housed just down the street, arrived. Eddy placed Harriett onto a stretcher.

"Hurry, she collapsed." He jumped into the back of the ambulance, then called to a waiting Wally and Shelby, "We'll be at Madison hospital."

Without crying, Shelby watched the vehicle speed away, sirens blaring, and lights flashing.

Wally shook his head in dismay. "Don't worry, Shelby. She'll be okay.

"I know. Daddy will take care of her." She looked at Wally, waiting for his next move.

Wally glanced up and down the street, at his car, then finally, after staring at the child for several moments he said, "What do you say we lock up this house, then walk you down to your aunt's? Do you know the way?"

Shelby reached for Wally's hand. "Of course, Mr. Stuart. It's just down the street. The house will be okay unlocked." Tugging at his arm, she started down the front steps. Stopping, she grabbed her hip with her left hand, then standing on tip-toes to shake her right index finger in Wally's face, she said, "If you stay here, don't you steal anything!"

Laughter bellowed from Wally's bouncing belly. "Goodness, Shelby. I hope someday I have the privilege of calling you Duck!"

32

FATHER-TWO; HUSBAND-ZERO

Teddy opened the front door as Shelby barged in. "Come on in, Mr. Stuart. You may sit on the couch." She pointed to the sofa.

Wally blushed. Extending his hand in greeting, he said, "Pardon us. I'm Wally Stuart. Are you Shelby's uncle?" His sentence stopped but his arm continued pumping.

"Yes." Teddy pulled his hand free. "And why are you with Shelby this evening?" He faced the kitchen and the sound of clattering dishes and chattering children. "Alice, I think you need to come here."

"I'm an army buddy of Eddy's. Visiting today." Wally stopped to slow his breathing. "Harriett was rushed to the hospital. Eddy is with her." Looking at Shelby sitting quietly on the couch, he continued, "I was left with Shelby."

Alice entered the room to hear, "Harriett" and "hospital." "Is my sister okay? What happened? Was she in a car wreck? Why is the hospital—?"

"Slow down, Alice. Allow Mr. Stuart a moment to gather his thoughts. It sounds like he was thrust into an unusually awkward situation." Teddy motioned to the couch. "Please have a seat. May I offer you a drink, perhaps a whiskey?"

Wally sat down beside Shelby, who patted his knee. "It's okay. Mommy will be fine."

Teddy smiled at his niece comforting a grown man. "Mr. Stuart, our Shelby is an unpredictable, somewhat precocious child."

"I'm quickly realizing that." He accepted the glass and gulped. "I'm sorry if we interrupted your evening meal. If Shelby is safe with you, I'll finish my drink and be off."

"Alice will tend to the children." Jerking his head toward the kitchen, he sat down across from Wally. "Relax a moment until she returns."

The men overheard Alice barking orders. "Polly, make sure Tony eats his vegetables…make a plate of food for our guest…Maggie, help your sister clear the table." She was only gone a minute before rejoining her visitors.

"The children are settled. Now, Mr. Stuart, is it? Please explain yourself."

Wally swallowed a mouthful of whiskey before speaking. "I don't know many details. Eddy and I were best friends in Italy, but I haven't seen him in seven or eight years, not since he was transferred to Korea."

"What—Eddy was in Korea?" Teddy coughed the question.

"Hmm. Harriett isn't the only person surprised by this information." Taking a deep breath, Wally continued, "Yes, but that's another story for another day. How shall I put this…Eddy didn't make the *wisest* choices in the service."

Alice held up a hand. "Duck, did you have supper yet? Will you go into the kitchen with your cousins?"

Shelby stood, then paused. She twisted her mouth in objection but obeyed her aunt by leaving the room.

Alice waited until the children greeted Shelby. "Okay, please continue, Mr. Stuart."

"As I was saying, Eddy didn't use discretion, got into several binds. Somehow, Harriett uncovered his past record and confronted him this evening."

Alice bit her lower lip. "Harriett is brilliant. She's working on her Ph.D., so she'd know how to access information. What happened that she was taken to the hospital?" She wrung her hands together nervously.

"She fainted after confronting Eddy. Some sort of spell. Eddy went with the ambulance, and they were off, leaving me with Shelby." Wally tilted his head to the kitchen. "That child may be young, but she's self-sufficient!"

Teddy grinned. "That she is. Okay, here's what I think we should do tonight. Alice, get Shelby settled in for the night. I'm sure she has plenty of clothing here. I'll call the hospital to check on Harriett. They'll give me an update." He addressed Wally specifically. "I'm the town's pharmacist." Turning back to Alice, he continued, "if it's necessary for me to drive to Madison—for Harriett, or to pick up Eddy—I'll do so. Mr. Stuart, do you have plans for this evening?"

"I had intended to dine with the Keplers and stay overnight. But, just tell me where I can rent a motel room."

"There's one on the road to Madison, but no need for that. If you are to be Harriett's guest, then please feel free to make yourself comfortable in their home."

Wally laughed. "Shelby already warned me not to steal anything. Thank you, but I have a better idea. Why don't you stay with your family? I'll go to the hospital to be with Eddy. If he needs a ride home, I'll bring him and sleep overnight. Otherwise, I'll check out that motel."

Teddy nodded in agreement. "Alice, please feed Mr. Stuart while I make the phone call."

∞ ∞ ∞

Wally located Eddy pacing back and forth in the emergency waiting room. Approaching from behind, he slapped Eddy on the back.

Eddy jumped. "What the hell?" Exhaling a deep sigh, he said. "Wally, where's Shelby?"

"Yep—great father, terrible husband! She's safe with Teddy and Alice. Nice folks." Wally tugged on Eddy's arm. "Sit. How's Harriett?"

"She seems to be okay. The doctors are running some tests. I should know more in half an hour." Eddy sat beside his friend. "Wally, I really screwed up not telling her."

"How did you explain three years of silence?" Wally jerked his head with short rapid movements. "Why would you risk it?"

"I don't know! She took me back, life was good, she got pregnant, life was even better with Shelby. I hid it all these years. I didn't want to rock the boat." Eddy began pacing again. "Wally, I really do love her. Maybe not the crazy, hot-blooded, obsessive love I had for Rosa, but I care deeply for her. She's an extraordinary woman and we have a wonderful life."

"I don't know what to tell you." Wally stared blankly at Eddy. "Whatever happened to Rosa and Joey? Do you know?"

Eddy dropped his head. "I have no idea. They vanished. My first five years home, I sent money every week. At least enough to buy food. I felt obligated, but heard nothing."

"Where did you send it, if they 'disappeared?'" Wally's eyes narrowed.

"I mailed it to her mother. God knows if she gave it to her." Eddy paused to blow his nose. "I didn't know what else to do. I even sent back the strand of pearls, figured she could keep them or sell them if she needed money."

Wally glanced around the room. Spotting a coffee pot and vending machine in the corner, he stood. "Eddy, I'm pouring you a cup of coffee and getting you some chips. Sit, relax a little, or you're going to have a stroke."

"Stroke? Oh my God! What if that's what happened to Harriett? What if I caused her to have a stroke?"

Eddy's rant was interrupted when a man in a white coat opened the double doors leading to the room. All eyes peered in his direction, seeking news. "Mr. Kepler? Is there a Mr. Kepler?"

Eddy sprang to his feet. "Here!" He rushed to the doctor. "Is my wife okay?"

The doctor smiled and calmly tapped his back. "Yes, Mr. Kepler. Your wife is stable. She had a hypertensive episode, causing her to black out. We finally have her blood pressure under control, but she may need to continue taking antihypertensive medication for the rest of her life."

The doctor guided Eddy to a room where Harriett was resting. Eddy gasped at his wife...the force named Harriett... who was connected to medical machinery and an IV drip. She looked so frail and helpless.

"I'm going to keep her here for a couple days, monitor her. Has she been under extra stress or strain lately?"

Eddy sighed. "Her life is constant stress. I don't know how she copes. She's the CFO for Dugan & Co. and is working on her doctorate in finance. Plus, we have a five-and-a-half-year-old daughter that takes after her mother."

The doctor pursed his lips. "I suppose that is enough to trigger this episode, the accumulating effect. But, I've heard of your wife. Sorry, I didn't make the connection. From what I'm told, she has always managed to balance work, school, and life quite efficiently." His gaze latched onto Eddy's eyes. "Is there anything else happening?"

Eddy collapsed into a ball. He hid his face in his hands. "I did this. She found me out in a lie. It sent her over the edge. Oh God, Harriett, what have I done?"

The doctor stooped. "Son, she's going to be fine. Why don't you sit with her for a minute, then go home and get some rest." Shaking his finger in Eddy's face, he added, before leaving to treat his next patient, "Mind you, don't upset her again. Not tonight!"

33

BATTLE OF THE BROTHERS

Eddy was awake, showered, and—after dragging Wally out of bed before the sun peeked over the eastern hills of Campbell County—was on the road to Madison. Colorful pink-and-white spring blossoms were beginning to transform into the broad, green leaves of summer. He vigorously sucked in the fresh morning air hoping to gain confidence.

Used to being the driver, Wally slept as Eddy drove. They stopped at the gift shop on the way to the room. Wally waited in the lobby while Eddy selected a bouquet of flowers and a greeting card.

"You're open early," he said, pulling several bills from his wallet.

The middle-aged cashier sulked, wanting the comfort of her bed. She took his money, then returned his change without speaking.

Hospital information directed Eddy to the fourth floor, general population, where Harriett was moved overnight. Eddy entered the room to find Harriett awake, fully dressed in yesterday's work clothes, sitting on the bed while still connected to several monitoring machines.

"Hi, babe. How are you feeling?" He placed the flowers, already in a glass vase, on the nightstand. "These are for you. I brought you a nightgown and a change of clothing." He set a small case on the floor in the corner, then sat in a chair. "How did you manage to put on your clothes?"

Harriett glared at him. "I want you out of here!" A machine began to beep louder and more frequently. "Go back to Rosa, but leave me alone!"

Eddy winced. "Harriett, don't work yourself up. You need to stay calm." He moved toward the bed.

"Stop right there. Don't come any closer to me."

The rapid beeping summoned the nurse. "Mrs. Kepler! Why are you dressed? Is this man bothering you?"

"I want him gone!" Her head began to spin. Her eyes rolled in their sockets.

"Sir, you need to leave now!"

Eddy stumbled out of the room as the nurse rushed to Harriett's side.

"Mrs. Kepler, take a deep breath. That's it. Slowly, in and out. The man is gone." She reached unnecessarily for smelling salts. "There, that's better."

Harriett refocused. "He is not to have access to this room. Am I understood?"

"Yes, Mrs. Kepler." The nurse backed away from Harriett's bed. "But, he is your husband, correct?"

"Yes, he is. Why does that matter?"

"It's just…"

"Just what? I am the main breadwinner in my family. I am responsible for paying this bill, if that's your worry." Harriett hissed through closed teeth. "In fact, if this hospital wants to be paid at all, then I suggest you keep him away. Am I clear?"

The nurse backed out of the room as she acknowledged

Harriett's request. She found Eddy waiting in the hallway. "Mr. Kepler, your wife refuses to see you. I'm afraid I must ask you to leave."

Eddy rubbed his forehead. "I'll be in the waiting area, should she change her mind." He sulked away to join his waiting friend.

∞ ∞ ∞

"God, Wally. I'm damned to hell!" Eddy said as they sat in the fourth-floor waiting room. A fluorescent ceiling light buzzed and flickered. "What if I'm banned for life?"

"Eddy, I'm speechless, as usual." He shook his head. "The only part of you that's changed is your waistline." He laughed, then handed Eddy a cup of coffee.

"Don't joke! What if she wants a divorce? Or worse!" Eddy tugged at his hair. The stark aseptic room looked as bleak as his future.

"What's worse than a divorce?" Wally grappled with hiding a smirk.

"She could take Shelby away from me." Eddy buckled over as if in pain. "That would kill me, for sure. I can't lose both of my children."

"You need to start thinking before acting…"

Wally's words were interrupted by a male voice mimicking him. "Start thinking before acting! Not possible for this son-of-a-bitch. Eddy, what did you do to her?" Earl stomped into the waiting room. He grabbed Eddy by the collar and pulled him from his chair. "Stand up, coward. I want you to face me like a man."

"Earl, what the hell? Let me alone." Eddy swatted at Earl's grip. "Who told you she's here?"

Earl spit the words in Eddy's face. "Alice called me last night."

"Traitor!" Eddy dug his thumbs into Earl's wrists.

Earl tightened his grip. "Harriett deserves more than a self-loathing, despicable, lying, deceiving, *bastard* for a husband!"

"Shut up Earl. You're pissing me off." Eddy finally pulled away. He turned his back to walk out of the room.

Earl lunged at him from behind, pushing him into the wall.

"That's it, Earl. Now I'm really mad!" Eddy raised his hand in front of his face, rolling his fingers into a fist, he swung. Knuckles connected with soft flesh, cutting Earl under the eye.

Blood dripped down Earl's cheek. As the stream of red trickled down his face, years of contempt erupted. He no longer contained his angst of caring for his brother, while loving his brother's wife. Earl pummeled Eddy with his left fist, then his right, and repeated. Both men fell to the white-and-gray, checkered tile floor. As they rolled over, he located Eddy's nose. Red blood splattered the drab gray walls.

"You son-of-a-bitch, you broke my nose!" Eddy grabbed his face, leaving his body defenseless. Earl wound his arm high in the air. Channeling all his pent-up anxiety, Earl slammed Eddy in the ribs.

Wally heard the cracking noise. Thinking the fight was none of his business, Wally had sat back and watched—however, Earl's beating became so intense that he knew he must act either before the hospital called the police...or before it became a murder.

Wally heaved a struggling Earl from atop Eddy as the noise of the commotion filtered out the door, around the corner, and to the nursing staff. A nurse and an orderly rushed down the hallway, their rubber soles squeaking with each step. The orderly called for staff to call security.

"Let me go!" Earl twisted in Wally's grip.

"You need to stand down or you'll be in jail soon. Listen, someone is coming," Wally whispered to Earl, then pointed in the direction of the approaching footsteps. "You're lucky no one was in the room to witness you breaking his nose and his ribs."

"He deserves every punch." Earl complied and sat, watching Eddy gasp for breath and writhe in pain.

"I'm sure he does. I'm not defending him." Wally slid into a chair beside Earl. "I don't know you, Buddy, but it looks like you're a friend of Harriett's, and she needs all the friends she can get right now."

Earl slouched, bracing his back for support. He gazed at Wally. "Who the hell are you anyway?" he asked as the nurse bent over Eddy who was still curled on the floor.

Wally chuckled. "An old army chum. We served in Trieste together."

"This man has a broken nose," The nurse barked to the orderly. "Get me a wheelchair and get him down to emergency." She dabbed up blood as the orderly retreated.

Eddy wheezed as she treated him, "Check my ribs."

She touched his right side. "Probably broken." The nurse snapped at Wally and Earl, "No more fighting! Do you understand?"

"Yes ma'am," said Wally as he elbowed Earl into agreement.

"I need to tend to this man. I'll be back for you two later."

A big, burly, middle-aged man, with belly fat lapping over his belt and badge labeled "Security" on his chest, wheezed his way through the doorway. Finding three men covered in blood, he asked, puffing with each word, "Ma'am, what happened here? Do I need to call the police?"

The nurse rolled her eyes. "No, Bill. Everything is under control." She looked at Wally and Earl to confirm. "On your way out, tell my aide to bring me some water and clean towels. Oh, and Bill, you really should lay off the jelly doughnuts."

The orderly came back with the wheelchair, and he and the nurse helped Eddy sit in it.

"Mr. Kepler, we're going to have to wait for an x-ray. In the meantime, I need to know—would you like to press charges against the man who attacked you?"

Eddy sat in the wheelchair with two black eyes and a crooked nose, holding his side. He smirked, then grimaced in pain. He glanced toward Earl, paused, then said, "No. That's my brother."

Wally choked. "Your brother?"

"Yes!" Eddy clenched his teeth. "Oh! God, I hurt." He exhaled. "Bastard's in love with my wife!"

"Stop right there!" Earl stood momentarily, but sat down when the nurse grumbled a warning. "I care deeply for Harriett, but I don't…" He sighed. "No, dammit. I do love her. You abandoned her for three years. Someone needed to take care of her."

"Harriett is more than capable of caring for herself!" Eddy winced again.

"Maybe now, but not in the beginning. She was just a young girl when you left her." Earl glared at his brother. "She endured too much to become the amazing woman she is now. And all the while, she remained faithful and loyal to you. While you're in Italy siring a son—a son you never told her about." Every sentence was louder than the previous one. "You don't deserve her."

"Guys. Keep your voices down," Wally urged. "This is a hospital." He shook his head. "Unbelievable! Only another Kepler would fall in love with his brother's wife! I should have known to stay away. Everything 'Kepler' is complicated."

An aide grabbed the handles of the wheelchair and

pushed. Eddy was heard moaning the entire way to the elevator.

∞ ∞ ∞

Alice and Shelby arrived to find Wally and Earl being treated for their light injuries as a custodian wiped blood from the wall.

"Shelby darling. Stay behind me and don't look." She guided Shelby behind her dress skirt. "Earl, what happened?"

Shelby poked her head from behind Alice. Running to Earl, she threw her arms around his neck. "Uncle Earl! Are you okay?" The nurse backed off to make room for the child.

Earl smiled. "Yes, sweetie. I'm fine." He embraced his niece.

"Is Daddy with Mommy? Can I see her too?"

"Are you Shelby?" asked the nurse. "Your mother has been waiting for you all morning."

Shelby tugged at Alice's arm. "Come on, Aunt Alice. I need to see Mommy!"

A bewildered Alice looked at Earl and then Wally. "Why are *you* here, Mr. Stuart? Is Eddy with Harriett?"

Earl and Wally exchanged glances. "Eddy getting an x-ray." Earl cleared his throat. "We had a...how shall I put it in front of Duck...an *altercation*."

"What's an x-ray?" asked Shelby.

Alice's eyes grew large and round. She thought for a minute without answering. Finally, Wally answered. "Shelby, an x-ray is a machine that can take pictures of your bones right through your skin."

"Can I see one?" She touched the nurse's skirt. "After I see Mommy. I want to see Mommy first. Now, please!"

∞ ∞ ∞

"I better check on Eddy," Wally mumbled before exiting.

Earl sat alone in the waiting room, listening to Wally's footsteps fade and watching for Alice and Shelby to walk back down the hallway, and for his turn to visit Harriett. After about 45 minutes, a high vocal timbre accompanied by the swishing of squeaking sneakers indicated his wait was over.

The door to Harriett's room was partially closed. Earl meandered over and peeked inside. The form on the bed faced the window, back to the door.

Earl knocked. "Harriett, are you awake? May I come in?" He stood outside the threshold, staring at the tiny woman, as his heart throbbed anxiously. "Harriett?"

She rolled over to face her visitor. Red, puffy, wet eyes implored for comfort and relief from pain. "Hi Earl," she said as she wiped her face with the edge of the sheet. "Come in. Please, sit down."

He resisted the urge to rush to her side. Instead, he placed a vase of flowers on her dresser and took a seat. "For you. I hope you like daffodils. Harriett, how do you feel? You sure gave us a scare."

"I'm okay, I guess." She wiped her face again. "Thanks for coming over. Shelby said you were here." She gasped when she spied his blackened eye. "What happened to you? Wait, I don't think I want to know. Eddy, right?"

Earl nodded. "I'm fine. Harriett, what did he do to you? What caused this?" He cleared his throat. "I swear, if he hurt you, I'll..."

She interrupted, not wanting to hear the extent of Earl's intentions. "I discovered some truths about Eddy's past. Truths named Rosa and Korea."

"Oh." Earl ran his fingers through his hair. "I thought he might come to his senses and recant the gambling farce. I figured he'd tell you after you took him back." He looked away, trying to hide his guilt as an accomplice.

She inhaled slowly and exhaled with a long sigh. "You knew?" Her face sagged.

"I got the story on the ride home from Indian Town Gap." He stuttered. "But, but, I was sworn to secrecy. He... he promised to tell you." Earl blushed in shame.

"He told me he had a gambling problem, that's all." Newly formed tears flowed from her eyes. "Oh, I am so tired of crying. It hurts so badly!"

Earl's heart ached equally for the woman he loved and for his long-missed opportunity. "I have to ask. If he'd told you, seven years ago, would you have forgiven him?"

"I considered the same question repeatedly, all night. I think, yes." Rubbing her mouth, she continued, "Maybe not immediately, but given time, yes."

"And...what about now?"

Tightly clenched teeth triggered jaw spasms. Shaking her head, she turned away. "No. I can't. He deliberately perpetrated this lie. He's deceived me for *ten years*." Her voice cracked, giving way to uncontrollable sobs. "How could he? My heart is broken."

"Harriett, I'll always be here for you and Shelby. Do you understand?"

From under the covers, her hand reached for his. "Yes Earl, I know. You are a dear, dear brother. I am so glad you are part of my family."

34

EXPELLED

JUNE 1960

A week later, Harriett walked down the hospital steps, a prescription for Hydrodiuril in one hand and her overnight case in the other. Her gait was strong and steady, but her spirit was broken. The bus from Madison to Campbellsville was sparsely dotted with riders. She plopped her bag on the seat next to her, pulled down the top window, and tried unsuccessfully to nap. It was a bright, warm day. She marveled at how one week had yielded trees in full leaf. Gazing out the window, the scenery reminded her of youthful days spent roaming the woods with her father. She was only 30, but those moments seemed like several lifetimes ago.

The bus parked on Pine Street, the business street of town, in front of Lupinetti's grocery. The pharmacy was next door. She stopped to fill her prescription.

The bell tinkled when the door opened, the same as when she was a child. The same as when Olive was a girl. Harriett spotted Teddy and waved as she walked to the back of the store.

"Teddy, I assume this is for my blood pressure?" She handed the paper to her brother-in-law.

Teddy pushed aside his mortar and pestle to rush from behind the counter to hug Harriett. "It surely is good to see you. How did you get home?"

"I took the bus." Her voice sounded strained. Glancing around the pharmacy to ensure privacy, she continued. "I didn't want to bother anyone."

Teddy wagged his finger in Harriett's face. "Don't be silly. Alice would have made the drive! Her driving is improving."

Harriett tried to smile but bit her lip instead. "I love her, but I'm safer on the bus."

"Perhaps." Giving Harriett the once over, Teddy said, "You're looking well."

It was a lie. Her eyes were swollen and red from continuous bouts of crying and a week of sleepless nights filled with infelicitous thoughts.

"Thanks." She rolled her eyes. The whites of her eyeballs enhanced the contrast of dark, droopy, under-eye skin. "Did Shelby behave herself?"

Teddy chuckled. "Shelby is always good. But it takes some energy to stay a step ahead of her. Eddy picks her up every day after work. Our routine has been status quo." He walked to his workspace and continued grinding his preparation.

"I need to have a conversation with my husband. Can Shelby stay overnight?" Harriett sighed. She rubbed her weary eyes. "I'm afraid I might work myself into a frenzy again tonight. I can't afford another week in the hospital. Any suggestions?"

Teddy studied Harriett for a minute then handed her a green vial containing two capsules. "Take one of these if it's absolutely necessary. Do not drink alcohol at the same time. Then I suggest you talk to Doc Paulson about getting a sleeping aid. Looks like you need one."

"Thanks, Teddy. Yes, I desperately need some sleep. At least I've had time to think through what I want." She neglected to share her decision; rather, she waited quietly while Teddy typed her prescription directions and placed a label on an envelope containing small, peach-colored tablets.

"Be sure to take one every day, even if you're feeling good. Blood pressure is a silent killer. You should drink orange juice or eat a daily banana." He handed her the envelope. "Any questions, call me at home." He then leaned over and whispered in her ear, "Don't be alarmed, but this drug will make you pee more. So, take it in the morning, not at bedtime."

Harriett laughed for the first time in a week. "Thanks for the heads up." She started to leave, then turned around and went back. Hugging him, she mumbled as the tears welled in her eyes, "Thanks for all your support. I'm afraid I'm going to need it even more."

∞ ∞ ∞

The walk up the hill was usually considered modest exercise. Today, her breath labored while her leg muscles cramped. *How could one week make such a difference?* She unlocked the front door and collapsed into a corner chair in the foyer to catch her breath. Tears formed in her eyes.

"Stop it, Harriett," she chastised herself aloud. "You need to get a grip."

After fifteen minutes of staring into space, she dragged herself upstairs to unpack her case. Her suit jacket landed on the bed with a toss. She tugged at her skirt zipper that caught on a thread.

"In through the nose and out through the mouth," she repeated the mantra. Calming breaths allowed her thoughts time to settle and her eye to stop twitching. A week without sleep was ample time to assess her feelings, format a plan of action, remove all doubts, and confirm her resolve to move forward. However, she anticipated difficulties with tonight's conversation. Eddy had too much to lose not to object.

Due home within the half-hour, she neglected to call Eddy to cancel Shelby's pick-up. A small inconvenience for the three years of angst suffered during his silence. She reconsidered retreating to the office to reach for the whiskey bottle. Teddy warned her not to drink with the anti-anxiety capsules. Besides, she wanted to be clear-headed. Instead, she remained upstairs to pack Eddy's toiletries and a few items of clothing in an overnight case.

Eddy arrived home, his nose still bandaged, to find her sitting in her office sipping on a glass of water. "Harriett! What a wonderful surprise." He rushed over to embrace her, but slowed his pace when his ribs reminded him of his injury. "Why didn't you call me to pick you up? I missed you, darling."

Harriett held her breath. The moment of truth had arrived. "Sit down Eddy, we need to talk, and I don't want to fight." Her facial expression hid her pain, but her hands were sweaty, nonetheless. She wiped her palms on her slacks.

Eddy smiled, then moved to the bar cart. "Want a cocktail?" The ice bucket was empty. "Hold on while I get us some ice."

"No. I'm not drinking tonight. I'll wait for your return." Eddy returned, filled his glass then sat across from Harriett. She opened a steno pad and glanced at her notes. "I don't need details about Rosa. I can fill in the blanks with my imagination. The only thing I want to know is...did you love her?"

Eddy hung his head. "I'm sorry Harriett." He sipped; the whiskey went down smoothly. "I really am sorry." He exhaled, then sat silently looking at the floor. After waiting several minutes, he looked up before finally continuing. "You deserve the truth." His forehead wrinkled in pain. "Yes, I loved her very much. Joey too. But Harriett—"

Harriett's head jerked up. "Joey?" She felt heat flowing up her neck. Beads of sweat circled her brow. "A son?"

"Yes." Eddy kneeled in front of her and grabbed her hands. "Harriett, I love you, and Shelby too. We have a wonderful family. Please, understand. I was younger—"

Harriett shook her hands free. Steely eyes met Eddy's. "Past tense, Eddy. We *had* a wonderful family. This marriage clearly is not working. I detected inconsistencies in your stories, but I never suspected the depth of your lies and betrayal. A son, Eddy!"

Eddy leaned forward. "No, Harriett. Please. I can't lose you both."

"You should have considered that before you engaged in an affair." She gulped her water, then deepened her breathing to calm her nerves before asking, "Is Rosa the reason you never wrote? Never sent money?"

"...Yes. Oh God, Harriett." The tears flowed freely down Eddy's face. He sat back on his haunches. "I was building a new life in Italy. I never planned on returning home."

Harriett gasped. "You were going to stay abroad? I'm such a fool...You married me! Why, if you didn't love me?"

Eddy rubbed his face. "I was very fond of you. We had fun together, but the truth is...that I was hoping to avoid the draft by being married."

All color drained from Harriett's face. "I see." She paused. "I worked my butt off getting an education, while you continued the playboy routine. I faithfully wrote, remained loyal...and *celibate*, while you practiced adultery." She slapped the steno pad on the desk. "That makes this a little easier. I want you out. I refuse to be your second choice."

"You want a divorce?" The pitch of his voice rose. "Isn't

that too scandalous for a CFO?" The alarm of his voice was, for the second question, sprinkled with a bit of sarcasm.

"No divorce." She laughed nervously. "We remain married in name only. You leave my house but you are still my husband. If you ever decide to remarry, I want you *begging* me to set you free."

Eddy shut his eyes. When he opened them, he gazed directly at Harriett, then licked his lips. All cynicism dispelled, he asked, "What about Shelby? Are you taking her away from me?"

Harriett shook her head with the realization of Shelby's magnitude on their relationship. "No! It took two parents to make her, and it will take two parents to raise her. She loves her Daddy and should be part of his life. You may continue to pick her up after work, bring her home, feed her, and do whatever you do before I get home. But weekends and holidays are completely mine. I want her life to be as normal as possible, considering." Harriett rested her head in her hands. Her head throbbed with shooting bolts of anguish. "Eddy, you're breaking my heart. I gave it to you completely. Our vows were sacred to me, but obviously not to you." She allowed her pooling tears to flow. "How could you? "

Eddy laid his head on Harriett's lap. "I...I'm sorry, so sorry. Will you reconsider?" No trace of the infamous Kepler grin remained. He resigned to pleading. Folding his hands in prayer he said, "Darling, I do love you. More than you'll ever know. I'll make it up to you. Let me stay. Allow me to prove myself."

Her icy gaze met his wet eyes. "Too little, too late." She stood. The tiny woman towered over her prostrate husband.

"Where will I go? Earl won't take me. Hell, he's in love with you too."

Her body shuddered at the declaration of Earl's admiration. "Earl is my dear friend. He cared for me while you were gone. But, I'm offended you think there could be more than a platonic relationship. How dare you accuse me of imitating your behavior!" Fire blazed from her eyes. Her hands flew to her hips.

Eddy stammered. "Not accusing you. But...I just mean...I don't have any place to live!" He collapsed into a lump of tanned muscles. "But Harriett!"

"I don't care where you live, Eddy. That's your issue. Be a big boy and grow up. You no longer have me to solve your problems."

"God, Harriett! No! Please!" Eddy reached for her hands. She pulled away. "Harriett, I need you. I love you!"

"No. I am resolute. We'll tell Shelby together, tomorrow, without disparaging one another. Understood?" She left the office; Eddy followed. "Collect your clothes later this week. But as of this moment, you live elsewhere." She handed him the suitcase while motioning toward the door to usher him out of her life.

35

DOUBLE DOOZY

JUNE 1960

The early morning sun shone through the lace curtains of Olive's bedroom window, leaving a dappled pattern on the wall. She rolled onto her side with her back facing the light. Her alarm said 6 a.m. She scratched her leg, in nervous agitation, until it was red.

"Crap! Blasted itching." After ten minutes, she surrendered to the new day.

The treads of the center staircase creaked as she lumbered down them on the way to her kitchen and tea kettle. *I think I'll try some of that fancy English blend from Eddy this morning,* she thought as she scanned several flavors. Although June, the morning was chilly with the sun still low in the sky. She wrapped a sweater around her housedress. Carrying a tray loaded with teapot and toast, she headed outside to the Adirondack chairs for breakfast al fresco.

A flash of light coming from the alley caught her attention. She set down her load on the chair arm and decided to investigate. A champagne-colored Oldsmobile was parked off the street in the alleyway.

Is that Eddy's car?

Olive rapped on the window once, then again. On the third tap, a man, curled into a contorted configuration in the front seat, opened his eyes and looked up.

"Eddy Kepler, what the hell are you doing?" The answer escaped the clever woman's imagination.

A mist caused by the temperature variant fogged the inside of the car windows. Eddy wiped the side window with his sleeve to see his visitor.

With a big yawn, he greeted her. "Hi Olive," he said, his voice muffled through the glass. "Mind if I use your bathroom?"

"First tell me why the hell you're sleeping in your car." The wrinkles of her jowls deepened as she frowned. "Then, yes. I'll make you some tea."

Eddy unlocked the door, unwound his long body, and moaned as his knee cracked into position. "That was uncomfortable!"

"Explanation, please."

He bounced from one leg to the other. "I think you better allow me inside first. But I promise to tell you the whole story." He dashed down through the yard and into the house.

A second cup and saucer waited on the tray when Eddy finally joined Olive outside. She handed him some tea with the demand, "Time to spill—and I don't mean the tea!"

Eddy sighed as he combed his wavy hair with his fingers. "I'm homeless. Harriett kicked me out."

"I'll be damned. What did you do to deserve that?" She smirked. "It must be a real doozy for her to banish you."

Eddy's hands stopped midway across his head. He scratched, then covered his face. "It was. I screwed up big time. I don't think she'll ever forgive me."

Olive slowly crunched on a piece of toast, trying to hide her curiosity. "Go on."

Eddy, resigned to his fate, retold his indiscretions,

betrayal, lies, and abandonment. Olive didn't move, drink, or eat for 20 minutes until Eddy finished speaking.

"I'll be damned!" She sipped her cold tea. "I'll be damned," she repeated. "I always said you were a scoundrel, just like your daddy."

"I suppose I am." Eddy scrutinized the scenery, the valley, and the center of town, then continued searching the opposite hillside for his parents' house, now Earl's. "Olive, I really love Harriett. I admit that I didn't when we first married. Don't get me wrong—I enjoyed her company, and I was fond of her. But she didn't…set my loins on fire, if you know what I mean."

Olive laughed. "Yes, Eddy Kepler. I'm old, but not dead. I still remember young lust." She weighed her thoughts for several minutes. "Where do you intend to live?"

"I have no fu….sorry, I have no idea. I won't swear in front of you." His face colored.

A loud guffaw escaped Olive's lips. "I've heard the word before, but thank you for your consideration." She raised her finger in exclamation. Pointing it at Eddy's chest, she said, "I have an idea."

Eddy's stomach growled. "What's your idea," he asked before gobbling down two pieces of toast.

"Why don't you move in with me?" She looked directly into his eyes as the corners of her lips turned upwards.

"What? Are you serious?"

"Yes. You'll pay rent, of course." She glanced at the second-floor window. "You can have Harriett's old bedroom. You'll need to buy furniture, since she took her old suite." She paused. "Yes, that will work," she said, nodding. "I'd enjoy the company. You already help with maintenance. It's a good fit."

Eddy stared at Olive. He knew that time had mellowed

the crotchety old bat, but this offer bordered on the realm of fantasy.

"Really? You'll let me move in with you?"

"Did she render you deaf along with dumb?" Olive scoffed. "I choose my words carefully. You have until tomorrow night to give me a decision. Now, don't you need to go to work?"

Eddy checked his watch. "Shit! Yes." He leaned over to kiss her cheek. She jerked away.

"Cut the feigned love." She held up her hand to hinder his advancement. "This arrangement has mutual benefits."

∞ ∞ ∞

The workday sped by quickly, probably because Eddy hoped to postpone their discussion with Shelby. Perhaps if Harriett had more time to think, she'd change her mind.

Shelby waited at the door, bade Alice goodbye, and ran to her father.

"Daddy, what's for dinner? Aunt Alice gave me a snack, but I'm starving." The five-year-old kissed his cheek.

"Hello to you also."

Shelby giggled. "Sorry, Daddy. Hi, how was your day?"

"My day was okay. Are you a growing duck?" Eddy smiled lovingly at his daughter. "You'll soon be eating me out of house and home."

"Oh, Daddy! Quit it."

Shelby rolled on the seat, her feet kicking the dash, while Eddy tickled her tummy. "Let's get you home and fed before you starve to death!"

He parked the car on the street in his usual space, across from the house. Shelby jumped out of the front seat and skipped up the steps as Eddy watched. *I can't lose this child*, he thought. *She means the world to me*. He dreaded tonight's conversation. How does one explain a marriage gone wrong to a child? Especially when all her friends have two married parents.

Shelby waited at the door for Eddy to catch up and unlock it. "Come on, slow poke!" she teased him.

Eddy resolved to ensure her life was as normal as it possibly could be. He vowed to attend every play, recital, or sporting event in which she participated. He'd even man up and sit with Harriett if it meant Shelby feeling safe and secure.

Once inside, Shelby raced to the kitchen, pulled out a chair, and read a book while waiting to be fed. Eddy poured her a glass of milk and made her a PBJ sandwich. He served it cut on the diagonal, crusts removed, as a special treat.

"Oh, I get a tea sandwich tonight! What's the special occasion?" she asked approvingly.

"No special occasion. I simply wanted to cut it that way for you." Eddy sat at the table next to her.

She slid off her chair and jumped up on Eddy's lap to reach his cheek. "Thanks, Daddy. You're the best."

He gently swatted her butt. "I appreciate that, Duck. Now get down, eat your dinner while I cook for Mommy and me."

Eddy opened the refrigerator and removed a head of broccoli, three chicken breasts, butter, and heavy cream. He pushed on the lazy-susan and removed the flour canister. Next, he reached for a bottle of dry sherry from the upper cabinet.

Shelby inventoried the ingredients. "Oh, yummy. I like that casserole."

Eddy laughed. "You intend to eat a third time tonight?"

"Yes, Daddy! This is just a snack." She giggled. "You know that."

"Yes, I do, you silly goose." Eddy's heart almost burst with love for his daughter. At that moment, he imagined applauding her speech at her high school graduation or walking her down the aisle to be wed. He fought back pooling tears. *Please, Harriett, permit me the honor of the father of the bride.*

"I'm not a big goose. I'm a little duck." She emphasized the 'k' in duck.

"I will always be your best buddy, Duck. You believe that, don't you?" His eyes pleaded.

"Now who's the silly goose? Of course, I know that." Shelby slapped the table in affirmation.

∞ ∞ ∞

Harriett greeted Eddy in the foyer with a peck on the cheek, while Shelby got a bear hug.

"Hi, Mommy. How was your day?" she asked dutifully.

"It was long, Duck. Too long." She tossed her attaché into her office. "Do I have time to change?" She hesitated. "Oh, I just assumed…"

"Yes, I made dinner," Eddy said as he nodded. "And yes, you have time to change. Duck helped me set the table. We'll eat as soon as you are ready."

"Thanks."

Conversation flowed as Shelby relayed tales of her day playing chase and hide and seek. She rattled on about meeting a new girl that was Maggie's friend. Harriett marveled at how easily she made friends. So much like her father.

When they finished eating Harriett looked at Eddy. He tipped his head. "Shelby. Duck. Daddy and I want to talk to you tonight about something very serious."

Shelby pushed her plate forward and folded her hands on the table. "Sure, Mommy."

"If there is something we say that you don't understand,

you are to interrupt and ask a question. Okay? Don't wait. And if something scares you, then you need to tell us."

Shelby tilted her head. "Mommy, the suspense is killing me!"

Eddy snorted beer up his nose. "Good god, Duck. You're a trip."

Harriett smiled and rolled her eyes. "Okay, Duck, here goes. Your Daddy and I are not going to live together anymore."

Shelby followed orders by speaking up. "Who is living in this house?"

Eddy grinned. "That would be you and Mommy. You'll stay here. Nothing changes for you, Duck."

"Where are you living, Daddy?"

Knowing his answer would send Harriett into a tailspin, he hesitated. "Duck, before I answer you, I need to talk with Mommy in the office." His head bobbed to the front of the house. Shelby crossed her arms in front of her chest and with a scowl, waited for them to return.

"What's so important that you needed to stop the flow of that conversation? It was going pretty smoothly," Harriett chastised Eddy.

"Ah. I didn't want to blindside you. I'm moving in with Olive." He dried his palms on his trousers.

"You're what?!" she screamed as the blood rushed to her face. "When? Why?!"

"Shh."

"You're moving in with my mother? Have you lost your mind?" The furrows on her brow looked like a field freshly plowed for planting.

"No. I'm paying her rent. But it makes perfect sense. I already maintain her house. I need a place to live, and she is lonely. And she has extra bedrooms. Why not?" His hands, palms up flanked his ears.

Harriett paused for a moment, then began to laugh. "If you think you can tolerate her, then, by all means, go for it." Her laughter intensified to a boisterous roar by the time she reached the kitchen.

"Mommy, what's so funny?" Shelby scrunched her lips. "Tell me the joke."

"The joke is on Mommy. It seems your Daddy is moving in with Grandma Olive."

"That's not funny. I like Grandma Olive." Shelby glanced at her father. "So does Daddy."

"It seems so, Duck."

"I don't want to laugh right now." Shelby slapped the table. "Why is Daddy moving out?"

Eddy rested his elbows on the table, cradled his face in his hands, then leaned close to Shelby. "Duck, Daddy did a bad thing. It was a long time before you were born, but it was a really bad thing. I hurt your Mommy's feelings."

Harriett added, "Both Mommy and Daddy love you very much. We are…mad at each other, not at you."

"You don't look mad." Shelby concentrated on their every word, trying to understand newly introduced adult emotions.

Eddy smiled. "Sometimes you can be mad without looking it."

"Are you ever mad at me, without looking mad?" Shelby scowled, concerned by this confusing dynamic.

"Never, Duck," Harriett assured her. "Trust me, you'll know if I'm mad at you." She moved to embrace the child.

Eddy's eyes latched onto Harriett's as he nodded. "I can vouch for that!" He paused to give Harriett a chance to respond. When she was silent, he added, "Shelby, adults sometimes play games with each other…"

"I like playing games."

Eddy sighed. "These games are not the fun kind. They're

mean, spiteful, and can be dangerous." He paused to give Shelby time to consider his words.

Shelby cocked her head. Scrunching her nose, she wagged her index finger at both parents. "You shouldn't be nasty! Why do you play games that can hurt you? You say to always be careful. Why aren't you careful too?"

Harriett's voice cracked as she tried to answer. "Grownups can be silly, sometimes. They know what is right, and tell children how to act, but they don't always listen to themselves."

"That's not silly! That's being bad!" She stared down both adults. "You should get a spanking!"

"You're absolutely correct, Duck." Eddy pulled at his brows to relieve his intensifying headache. The longer this conversation lasted, the more ridiculous his behavior became. He was getting tired of listening to a child simplifying gray into black and white. "Our new living arrangement is like a butt whipping for grownups."

Shelby's mouth contorted. She jumped down off her chair mumbling as she stomped out of the room. "I'm going upstairs. You may not be mad at me, but I'm mad at both of you!" She turned to face them. Shaking her finger, she yelled, "Bad Mommy! Bad Daddy!"

36

NEW RINGER

SUMMER 1960

The news of Eddy Kepler moving into Olive Bailey's house spread through Campbellsville like a wildfire out of control. Olive's walks to Lupinetti's grocery were met with snickers and smirks which she waved off by extending three fingers high in the air and mumbling, "Read between the lines."

Determined to minimize the impact on her daughter, and to be home before 6:30 each evening, Harriett began every workday at 5 a.m. After a quick shower, she carried the still sleeping child to an awaiting, yawning Alice, dressed in nightgown and robe, with hair rolled in curlers.

Harriett usually switched on her office lights between 6 and 6:30 every morning. The cafeteria manager delivered a carafe of coffee, a bowl of fresh fruit, a buttered biscuit, and one slice of crisply fried bacon promptly at 7:15 each morning: a benefit of executive life.

Eddy continued workday hours of 7 to 3 p.m., which permitted time to shop for a few groceries, retrieve Shelby at 4 p.m., feed her an afternoon snack, and finish cooking dinner before heading to Olive's every evening. He enjoyed his kitchen time with his chattering daughter. With Harriett's blessing, Eddy prepared enough food for Harriett and Shelby to enjoy together and still take home evening fare for Olive and himself. To Olive's delight, her tenant not only supplied extra cash from rent but also extra savings from food, funded by her disgruntled daughter.

Shelby proved to be resilient and flexible. Her routine remained unchanged, except for weekends, which were split between her parents but always at the club. Saturdays were spent at the pool, while Eddy golfed and Harriett played tennis. A late morning group swim class, followed by an hour of a private individual stroke lesson, concluded with Eddy's arrival. Harriett carefully synchronized the timing. Eddy managed 18 holes with an early Saturday tee time, a shower, then a quick trip to the pool. Shelby and Eddy enjoyed lunch in the grill room while Harriett jogged from the courts to the course for an afternoon round of nine holes. The adults continued their exercise and play, just not together. The passing of one summer resulted in most club members' familiarity with the precocious Duck.

Sundays were usually reserved just for Harriett, but still spent at the club. Harriett's standing golf lesson with Beeno Powers helped hone her swing to maintain a spot on the club's Top Ten Women's ranking. Shelby spent the hour watching her mother or reading a book. Her reward for her patience was brunch ending with an ice cream sundae.

The brothers, both lonely bachelors, called a truce. Earl, a newly admitted club member, frequently ate Sunday dinner with Eddy while the women ate at home.

Rarely did the schedule deviate as the Keplers adjusted to a new family structure. On one such Sunday, late in August, Shelby sat quietly reading while Beeno instructed Harriett on the replication of her lob shot, the only weakness in her short game. Harriett suddenly dropped her club and ran toward the restroom, muttering to herself about *waiting too long*.

Shelby watched her mother exit, then stood and approached the club pro. "Mr. Beeno, may I swing a club?"

Beeno chuckled. The four-foot-eight-inch child was only four inches shorter than her mother. Harriett's clubs were the correct length. "Sure, Shelby." He reached inside Harriett's bag and handed her a nine iron. "Do you know how to hold a club?"

"Yes." She circled the club with her hands. "Is this right?"

Beeno's eyes popped open wide. "Yes. That is a good grip. Let's make one small correction." He strengthened the grip by repositioning her left hand. "There, you're set."

For anyone observing from behind, Shelby passed as an adolescent. Her blonde hair, gathered in a ponytail, swayed as she moved. Loose-fitting clothing disguised a shapeless body. Her exposed, long, lean limbs were tanned golden brown. Although void of muscular definition, her solid legs hinted at the shape to come, with the addition of puberty and hormones. No boney knees resembling a newly foaled colt on this child. She was solid. Only her face betrayed her youthful innocence, with its petite features, and peach fuzz covering of fine hair.

Beeno began, "Now, take the club back slowly…"

Shelby didn't wait for him to finish. Slowly, she rotated her hips to the right, keeping her arms straight. At the top of her backswing, she cocked her wrists, paused, then began her downswing. The nine iron and ball contacted in the sweet spot with a crack, as Shelby transferred her weight and swept the grass with the club. Extending her arms out and up, she completed the arc by finally relaxing her wrists. Her head remained level as she watched for impact, without following the ball flight.

The trajectory was pure. Straight down the middle

landing about fifty yards out. Shelby smiled as she ultimately looked up. "How was that?"

Beeno gasped. "Where the hell did you learn to swing a golf club?"

Shelby scrunched her brow. "From you, silly. I've been sitting here all summer listening to you explain things to Mommy."

"What have you been doing all summer?" Harriett returned, surprised to see Beeno and Shelby engaged in conversation.

"I hit a ball." Shelby pointed to the landing area. "Out there."

Harriett glanced at Beeno, then back to Shelby.

"Fifty yards," Beeno confirmed. "First try. Shocked the hell out of me." Beeno turned to Shelby. "Do you think you can do that again?"

"I better, or you're a lousy teacher. All you talked about today was swing relocation. Is that the right word?" Without waiting for a response, Shelby addressed another ball and repeated her swing. The result was the same.

Harriett's hand flew to cover her mouth. "Goodness, Shelby. I think you need to add golf lessons to your schedule." Looking at Beeno, she asked, "Beeno, do you teach children?"

His large round eyes grew into saucer-sized orbs. He sighed. "I don't teach kids; my assistant heads up the junior's program…but she's not your typical kid. She's going places, and I want to be along for that ride."

Both Harriett and Shelby giggled.

"Mommy, I think I'd like to play golf. Can I please?" Shelby bit her lower lip.

Harriett answered before Beeno. "Absolutely! If Mr. Powers agrees to teach you, then yes. We'll both have Sunday golf lessons." Her eyes beseeched Beeno. "Can you arrange your schedule to accommodate us back-to-back on Sundays?"

He glanced at his schedule book. "Whatever you need, Mrs. Kepler. You're my first client on Sunday. Let's start an hour earlier." He turned to Shelby, who groaned at the thought of leaving her bed sooner. "Miss Shelby, I think we may have the makings of a club champion in you."

Harriett blushed. "I'll admit, I was hoping to personally hold that title." With a smile, she hugged Shelby. "Perhaps both mother and daughter can boast of having their names on the same trophy. What do you say, Duck? I'll take top slot next year, and you can follow in a couple years."

Shelby reciprocated the embrace. "Sounds good to me, Mommy. I think I better wait until I'm at least 10."

37

TREATY

NOVEMBER 1960

The warm rays of summer became a distant memory as cold Canadian air on the jet stream swooped over the hills and into the Conemaugh valley. Silver-crusted blades of grass crunched underfoot.

Harriett wrapped a dangling wool scarf around Shelby, covering all bare skin.

"Mommy, not so tight. You're choking me." Her nostrils tingled as her warm breath froze. Mittened paws tugged at her neck.

"Shelby, don't pull. You need to stay warm." Harriett looked at the graying sky. "Brrr. I think we may get some snow today."

"Snow?" The child stopped fussing. Looking directly skyward, she asked, "Can we make a snowman?"

Harriett smiled. "I don't think it will snow that much. Only flakes, today." She ushered her daughter through the open garage. "We'll make one later in the year."

"Can Daddy help us?"

Harriett's smile drooped. The choice to live life as a single parent was forced on her by Eddy's careless decisions, but she vowed to be in control of any resulting changes. Still much in love with her husband, the sting of his betrayal triggered daily sadness. She doubted she'd ever recover and return to the bliss of ignorance, although she was determined to endure for the sake of her daughter.

"I'll think about it, okay?" Harriett opened the car door, then strapped Shelby into the front seat, before quickly jumping into the driver's side; she hoped the interruption would distract Shelby enough that she could change the subject. "Brrrrrr," rolled off her lips as she flipped up her collar.

The engine coughed into a purr as she cranked up the heater. Within minutes, a fog spread across the windshield, causing her to divert airflow from heat to defrost.

Shelby rubbed her window. "Mommy, do we have to go to the Club today?" She mimicked the other members by shortening "Madison Country Club" to the title of "*Club*." "I don't want to swim. The inside pool gets too steamy when it's cold outside, and today is *cold!*"

Harriett looked dumbfounded at her daughter. The pair traipsed to the club religiously every Saturday and Sunday throughout the summer and fall. The child excelled in swimming and golf in her age group—she assumed Shelby enjoyed her trips.

She stared at her daughter. "You don't want to swim today?"

"No, Mommy. I really don't. Can we do something different for a change?" Shelby slapped her hands on her knees for emphasis. "I need a break!"

Harriett suppressed a giggle. "A break?" She slowed the car, and flipped on the turn signal, before pulling off the road. "From what do you need a break? I thought you liked your classes?" she asked, giving Shelby her full attention.

"I do, Mommy. But I just want a day off." The child

exhaled an exasperated sigh. "Please, can I have a day off? This duck is waterlogged."

Harriett shook with laughter. "Yes, Duck, you may have the day off. What would you like to do?" She shifted into drive, her wide grin crinkling the edges of her eyes as she headed back into town.

The car stopped at the intersection of the main street leading through town to the bridge and the road leading up to their house. As Harriett turned the wheel, Shelby blurted out. "Wait—go straight. Then across the bridge. Let's visit Uncle Earl this morning."

A tingle traveled up Harriett's spine. All interaction with Earl dwindled to a minimum after her separation from Eddy. She felt uncomfortable in his company, knowing his feelings but not being capable of reciprocation.

Sucking her lips together, she drove straight ahead, then parked in front of the bakery.

"Why are we stopping here?"

"I can't very well go barging in unannounced and empty-handed. If I had known, I'd have baked. Or at least pulled something from the freezer." Harriett left the car running. "Stay here. I'll only be a minute."

She returned with three boxes stacked high in her arms, opened the back door, and placed them on the floor. The scent of cinnamon and nutmeg perfumed the air.

"Yum. That smells like Christmas morning." Shelby leaned over the seat to peek at the edible treasures. "What did you buy?"

"Something for Uncle Earl, something for us, and…" she hesitated, then added, "something for Daddy."

∞ ∞ ∞

Shelby trudged up the porch steps. Standing beside Harriett, their shoulders were nearly parallel. The fluffy ball on Shelby's hat waggled above the top of Harriett's bare head. She knocked and waited.

"Harriett! Shelby! To what do I owe this surprise?" Earl stood inside the open door, his wavy hair slightly tousled, wearing a baggy, cable knit cardigan sweater and cuffed corduroy trousers. The look was casual, comfortable, and confident. It met Harriett's approval.

"Hi, Uncle Earl." Shelby charged forward into the warm house, not waiting for an invitation.

Harriett inhaled. "Ah, I hope you don't mind." She exhaled too loudly before continuing, "Shelby convinced me to ditch the club today. Care for breakfast?" She thrust the box in his face.

Earl followed Shelby with his eyes then turned to Harriett. Sweeping his free arm backward he asked, "Please come in."

Harriett hesitated for a moment before joining her daughter. "We usually swim on Saturdays." She slid off her coat and tossed it over a chair. "Shelby is…"

"I'm bored with swimming, and I miss you." Standing on her tiptoes, she reached up to kiss Earl on the cheek.

"I miss you too," he said as he embraced his niece. "Goodness, you're growing like a weed."

Shelby relaxed into the bear hug. "Now, can we eat? I'm starving!" She plopped into a dining room chair.

"I think someone's feeling at home. Shall I make us a pot of coffee?" Earl patted Shelby's head before moving into the kitchen. "Harriett, will you help with the dishes?"

"Mommy, why are you making funny faces?" Harriett's camouflaged grimace looked comical.

"Goodness, Duck. I think we need to spend some time on filtering thoughts before they become words!"

"But Mommy! You and Daddy told me to not wait, say

what's on my mind!" Her hands flew to her hips in an exaggerated objection.

"We'll talk about this at home. Now, since this is your idea, please sit quietly and give Uncle Earl and me a minute. Okay?" Her speech was more staccato than intended.

Shelby didn't reply. She sat scratching her head, looking toward the kitchen with her nose scrunched, and head cocked to the side.

Harriett opened the cabinet door. She marveled that a man kept his kitchen neat and organized. Reaching for three salad plates and forks, she paused to find Earl watching her.

"Harriett," he began, "have you been avoiding me?" He tore three paper towels from the roll and folded them for napkins.

Her chin dropped. "Yes. I'm sorry." As she turned to go, Earl touched her shoulder. She flinched but halted. "Earl, it's awkward."

Twisting her shoulders gently, he turned her to face him. "Why would I make you feel that way?" His sorrowful eyes met hers.

She wet her lips. "Eddy said that…" she paused. "You said that…you have certain feelings for me."

Seizing a chance for affirmation, Earl said, "It's true. I do love you, Harriett."

She raised her hand to his mouth. "Shh, not in front of Shelby."

"I'll say it again. I love both you and Shelby." He locked onto Harriett's gaze. The portal to her soul revealed conflict and sorrow. At that moment, he finally acknowledged his fate. "But, you are my brother's wife even if you don't live together and that requires boundaries." Ushering her to the far corner of the room, away from little ears, he continued. "If that means I can only love you as a brother, so be it." He paused. "But I want to spend time with you, on *your* terms. I promise to always take care of you and Shelby. And by God Harriett, if you ever divorce him, I want to be first in line."

Harriett relaxed. "Thank you, Earl. I do love you too, just not romantically." She stretched to kiss his cheek. "I promise to allow you an active role in our lives if it's on brotherly terms."

"Agreed. I can live with that if I must." He pulled her close for a brief hug.

Harriett permitted the embrace that imparted security and stability. "I want to ensure that you understand that you are family. Will you join us for holiday dinners, plural?"

Earl bit his lip before removing the fresh Danish from the box. "Okay. Well, shall we feed the Duck, before she starts quacking?"

"Yes. That's an excellent idea." She took his hand momentarily and squeezed, then walked out of the kitchen, smiling.

∞ ∞ ∞

Two weeks later, Eddy wandered the sidewalks as he visited Madison College for the first time. He raised the collar of his jacket as the wind bombarded the back of his neck. His footsteps left imprints where he trod, although the earth, still warm from autumn, prevented light flurries from freezing the walkway.

Stopping an oncoming student, he asked, "Where's Webster Hall?"

The boy's head remained lowered as he trudged into the wind. "In front of you," he said without looking up.

Fluorescent lights buzzed as Eddy burst through the double doors and into the main hallway. Astonished by the Saturday afternoon throngs of bustling students, he looked for a sign directing him to classroom "A." The largest lecture hall on Madison's campus, the room accommodated two hundred people. It was easy enough to find, being only one door to the right; Eddy quietly slipped into the room.

He spotted Harriett standing with Alice, Teddy, Esther, and Earl. Fighting the urge to descend to join them, he grumbled to himself and slipped unnoticed into a seat in the back.

About 15 students and their accompanying families gathered in the lower space next to the podium. Today's celebration was void of all the fanfare and heraldry of its two predecessors. Within a matter of minutes, the title of Doctor of Philosophy would be bestowed upon his wife. Without him!

A few informal speeches, more like casual conversation, were followed by the presentation of students and their degrees. Tonight, two men and one woman would receive their Ph.Ds.: Harriett's in finance, one in music, and one in teaching. A round of applause was followed by multiple handshakes as the graduates made their way to the exits for home, restaurants, or—in Dr. Harriett Bailey Kepler's case—the club for dinner.

Eddy slipped out undetected.

38

THE RUBICON

DECEMBER 1960

The following week's holiday preparation managed to exaggerate Eddy's morose mood, which oscillated from depression to self-loathing. He was angry about missing another of Harriett's graduations, and about being separated from both his families, especially over Christmas. He contemplated Italy, that first and only Christmas with Rosa. Joey would have celebrated his ninth birthday in November. Rosa would now be 26. He wondered if they received the packages and letters that he resumed sending. He missed them, and prayed they were well.

Thoughts of Joey always led to those of Shelby, his precious daughter. So curious, bright, and creative. A spitting image of himself. But unlike the younger Eddy, she was confident and secure, without his false bravado.

Ascending the front steps, garland in hand, he tossed yards of pine roping onto Harriett's porch, grumbling as he unfolded a waiting step ladder. "Where the hell are those hooks?" he growled as he shoved his hand into his trouser pocket.

A tiny hand reached up. "Here, Daddy."

"Duck! How'd you get here?" He looked at his watch then looked around for Alice or Harriett.

"I walked from Aunt Alice's. It's only two blocks down the road. Aunt Alice always watches. I'm home," she yelled back to Alice as Alice waved from her front step.

The sight of his daughter cheered his spirits. "Want to help me decorate for Mommy?"

"Yes! I love Christmas." She opened the door and threw her book bag inside. "We only have one more week of school. Christmas is really soon!"

"Then I guess we better get busy." He hugged the child. Whispering in her ear, he said, "I love you, Duck."

Shelby knit her brow. "You silly goose, I love you too." She handed him a hammer. "Let's get to work and surprise Mommy."

"At your service." Eddy saluted.

∞ ∞ ∞

Roping, wreaths, and candles in place, the duo moved inside to erect the Christmas tree. As usual, Eddy placed it in the middle of the front living room window for everyone in the valley and adjacent hillside to view.

Stacks of ornament boxes filled the entryway. Eddy removed the lid and began inserting wire hooks.

"Daddy. Wait." She grabbed his arm. "We can't decorate the tree without Mommy."

Tears filled Eddy's eyes. He knew she was correct. This was Harriett's house, after all. Hanging garland was one thing; decorating the main tree was trespassing.

He turned his head. "Why don't I make supper? Will you put hooks on the balls?"

"Yep." She sat down to take over Eddy's task.

In the kitchen, Eddy chopped mushrooms as tears flowed

down his cheeks. The assembly of an easy recipe was clouded. Hearing the front door open and close, he splashed his face with water and dried it on a tea towel. The oven door closed as Harriett entered the kitchen.

"Eddy, thanks! The decorations look great." She walked toward the back staircase. "Will you stay for dinner? Then we can trim the tree after we eat."

His heart leaped with excitement. "I'd love to, but are you sure it's okay?"

Harriett stared longingly into his eyes. "This situation is far from perfect. However, we have Shelby to consider." She sucked in her lower lip. "This first year, it's best to keep traditions alive." Before turning to leave, she added, "And we need to discuss the holiday eating schedule. Tonight's as good as any other night."

She left him alone, setting the table and hoping for an amicable solution, for life with his family, and possibly for forgiveness.

As he took the food out of the oven, Shelby plopped onto the kitchen chair. Folding her hands, she counted plates. "Daddy? Are you staying for dinner tonight? What about Grandma Olive?"

"I'll call her and take home some leftovers. We're going to trim the tree tonight!"

"Yippie! I love Christmas!" Shelby squealed as she unfolded her napkin and placed it on her lap.

Eddy forced a smile. They ate, discussing the town's upcoming events and Shelby's school work, while filling in with small talk. The meal ended with Eddy plating Olive's food and wrapping it with foil, and Harriett storing leftovers in the refrigerator.

Shelby anxiously paced up and down the hallway as she fingered the arched garland of received Christmas cards that surrounded each room. "Come on, hurry up, you guys!"

Harriett lingered in the kitchen. "Eddy, have you thought about Christmas dinner? I know you are Shelby's father, but I think I want to celebrate with my family. Alone. Do you mind?"

The muscles of his face drooped resembling that of a basset hound. "Oh, I see. Will I see you, or her, at all over the holiday?"

"Of course. I thought from now on, Christmas Eve could be just for us. Maybe go to the club? Keep it neutral? No one cooks." She looked to ensure Shelby was out of earshot. "You're welcome to come over Christmas morning to unwrap Santa's gifts. But..." She paused. "The rest of the day, I'd like to be mine."

Eddy fidgeted with his trousers.

"It's more than I said initially," Harriett said." If you remember, holidays and weekends were to be mine." She moved to take his hand. "But Eddy, she needs you. And...you need her too."

"Thank you, Harriett." He hung his head. "Any chance I might be granted amnesty? A Christmas gift?" he whispered, holding his breath as he waited for an answer.

Her hand flew from his hand to her mouth to cover her shock. "As in total forgiveness? No, Eddy. Please don't push your luck with my generosity."

∞ ∞ ∞

Eddy queued a stack of Christmas 78 LPs while Harriett tightened bulbs on the light strands. Shelby danced and sang along with Bing Crosby's "White Christmas," and Gene Autry's "Sleigh Bells."

"Whew! Why does he sing so slow?" she asked as Perry Como completed "The Twelve Days of Christmas" with a full orchestra and an extended "partridge in a pear tree."

Harriett chuckled. "He sings metronome 60."

"What the heck does that mean?" asked Eddy.

"Shelby, do you know what a metronome is?" Harriett winked at her daughter.

"Something to keep time with, instead of tapping your foot." She grinned proudly.

"Duck, how do you know that?" Eddy gawked at Shelby. "She's bright, but where did she come up with that?"

"I'm going to take piano lessons this winter, since I can't golf." She pointed to an open corner in the room. "Mommy's putting it over there. The piano. It's my Christmas gift from her."

Eddy whistled as he sucked his lips together. "Very generous gift, Harriett. Are you intending to upstage Santa?"

Shelby's hands flew forward. "Don't be silly, Daddy. No one can outdo Santa!"

Harriett blushed. "We'll discuss it later, okay?"

"No need. I think I understand the rules now." Clicking his tongue, Eddy turned to the boxes of trimmings. "Figured it out myself, without a fancy title." Reaching for Shelby, he said, "Come on, Duck. Help me? I have to go home soon, okay?"

Harriett turned away. "That quip was unnecessary," she whispered to herself.

"Yep!" She skipped to her father's side, and they began adorning the upper branches of a tall blue spruce. Eddy left before they finished.

∞ ∞ ∞

Eddy carried a plate of cold food and placed it on the table. "Olive," he called to the light in the front parlor. "I'm home. Sorry, your food is cold."

The television clicked off, and Olive sauntered into the kitchen. "No worries. What's for dinner?"

"I made beef stroganoff. If you don't mind it all mixed together, I'll heat it in a saucepan for you." He removed the foil and dumped it before she answered. "Tell me, Olive, are you still banned from holiday dinners? Or has public opinion softened?"

She guffawed as she filled the tea kettle. "What do you think? Is my daughter, Dr. Kepler, the forgiving type?"

The obvious answer remained unspoken. "I have an idea," he said as he scooped the beef onto a plate.

"Yeah, what's that? I hope it's better than some of your previous ideas."

"Touché." He grinned at her playful jab. "Why don't you and I eat Christmas dinner at the country club? I'll take you shopping, buy you a nice dress, and we can do it up right."

Olive steeped her teabag. "Oh, so you're out, too. Will you get to spend any holiday time with Duck?"

"Christmas Eve will be the three of us at the club. And an hour on Christmas morning for Santa, but that's it." He handed Olive her food. "Here, all heated. What do you say? Club?"

"I say 'aye,' and 'thank you.' I would enjoy a shopping trip, although I'll buy my own outfit." She shoveled a forkful of food into her mouth. Her eyes sparkled. "I'll wear my fur!" Musing, she added, "I used to get dressed up in my day. Did I ever tell you the story of my trip to New York City? For Fred's graduation?"

Eddy listened patiently despite hearing the tale a dozen times. Olive often recanted memories, pleasant and otherwise. *I'll drive her to Madison on Saturday*, he thought.

Per Harriett's design, a new Kepler tradition was established, like it or not.

39

COFFIN DEUX

CHRISTMAS EVENING, 1960

*E*ddy steadied her elbow as they entered the house, then helped remove Olive's fur coat before hanging it on the back of a kitchen chair.

"That was enjoyable. Nice tasting piece of beef! Reminds me of the old farm." Olive filled the kettle with water. "You belong to a swanky club, Eddy Kepler. Care for a cup?" she called over her shoulder.

"No thanks. I think I'll have a bourbon. Want some in your tea?" Eddy moved toward the front parlor.

"Sure."

"You got it. I'll plug in the tree," he called back to the kitchen.

Olive carried a tray with a teapot, a cup, and a plate of cookies. "A treat for Santa." She grinned as she sat down on the ancient chaise covered by an old blanket.

Removing the lid to the teapot, Eddy spiked Olive's nightcap, then poured. "You know Olive, you're welcome to a drink anytime. That's why I set up the bar cart."

She slipped off her shoes. Rubbing her feet, she snuggled

back into the chaise and sipped. "I hate to admit it, but it was a pleasant holiday. Best in, hell, quite a few years. I enjoy having company, Eddy Kepler!"

"It went better than expected." Eddy collected a package from under the tree before sitting across from Olive. "I thought this separation would impact the holidays more but, thank goodness it didn't. Shelby is such a joy, but she's a trip. You should have seen her this morning. All those expensive toys. Two blonde Barbie dolls with complete wardrobes, a piano, and she spent the entire morning walking a Slinky down the front stairs."

Olive chuckled, remembering her own children's delight in simply shaking a cocoa can filled with marbles or pebbles during the Depression. All, except for Harriett. Her youngest was happy to sit on Tabs' lap and cuddle, with or without a story.

Reaching over, he passed her a gift. "I hope you like them," he said, feeling suddenly shy.

Olive ripped off the paper, opened the lid to the box, and pushed away the tissue paper to expose a pair of salt and pepper shakers in the form of newspapers.

Pointing to a curio cabinet shelf cluttered with others, he said, "To go with your collection."

Alligators, clowns, hot air balloons, champagne glasses, cookies, and of course her original set of cacti, covered the middle glass shelf.

"Since you read three different papers every day, I thought you might like them." Eddy blushed.

"I like them," she said, nodding approvingly. "And I like that club of yours. Reminds me of the old glory days." Her melancholy eyes closed as if ready for a nap.

"Why don't we make a standing monthly date? Dinner at the club. You and me. Give you a reason to wear that fancy fur coat!"

"How will the esteemed *doctor* feel about that?" Olive scoffed. "I can't imagine Miss Dr. Goody Two Shoes being overly happy about seeing me at her precious club."

"It's my club also. And you're my guest…" Eddy stopped mid-sentence. "Holy hell! I just got it. All these years, and I just got it."

"What did you get?"

"The rift between you and Harriett! It's really not just about Tabs' death, is it? The two of you are in competition! Have been all these years." He shook his head. "I must be stupid for not realizing sooner."

Olive burst out laughing. "Don't leave yourself wide open to slander. I usually jump at the chance, without a second thought." Suddenly, she sat up straight. "Eddy, follow me. I have something to show you."

He rose to follow her up the staircase.

She led him into her bedroom and motioned to the ornately carved chest at the foot of her bed. Hinges squeaked as she opened the lid. "Sounds like I need to get the oil can. This is getting old, just like me."

Eddy ran his fingers over the carved eagles, buffaloes, and deer. "Where did you get this?"

Olive sighed. "Fred sent it for Christmas. Hmm. It was 1916, I believe. The winter before he was sent off to France." She lovingly removed, caressed, and stacked the contents.

Eddy turned away from Olive and examined the pile of items. He touched a moth-eaten long, wool, women's skirt, as he watched the heap grow. Olive lay at his feet a lace-trimmed linen blouse, several wooden cigar boxes, a purple silk gown with matching gloves, and a velvet bag.

"Kepler, pay attention to what I'm showing you." Olive nudged his shoulder. "Here is the finger hole and here is the key."

"Key to what?" Eddy turned back to face Olive and the chest.

"Harrumph. Key to the secret compartment." Olive shook her head impatiently. "I'm showing you the false bottom. This is where I keep my stash."

Eddy's mouth dropped. "You have a stash? Stash of what, exactly?" He rolled off his knees to sit on his butt. Extending his arms, he leaned backward.

"Money, you dolt! I have something put away for a rainy day. How do you think we survived on Tabs' salary through a Great Depression and World War?" She removed the covering to expose at least 20 candy boxes about four inches wide and seven inches long.

"Tabs was a foreman. He made a good wage," Eddy argued. "What's all of that?" He pointed to the boxes.

"Eddy Kepler, try to keep up, please! I had a lovely day, but you *are* trying my patience," she scolded.

Opening the top box, Eddy spied bills bound in paper labeling one thousand dollars per bundle. Each box contained multiple bundles. Olive replaced the lid, locked the bottom, then turned to the velvet bag. She removed the pearls from around her neck and placed them in the soft fabric before restacking the items inside her chest.

"My father called this 'the coffin.'" Biting her lip, she continued. "Little did he know just how correct he was. One last gift from a doomed man." She wiped an escaping tear. "The pearls go to Alice's Polly. She looks just like her great-grandmother Polly, the original owner of the necklace. The chest itself goes to Shelby. The contents, well…" She paused. "I haven't decided that yet." Her eyes met Eddy's. "Will you make sure the girls get them?"

Eddy gasped at what he was witnessing. "Olive, who am I to tell your family? You should have that stipulation drawn up in a Will."

"Hmm. I guess you're right." Olive closed the lid to her treasure trove. "Now that's over, let's go back down and finish our drinks. Maybe I'll have your bourbon without the tea."

∞ ∞ ∞

Olive cranked the handle of her old Victrola. "Care if I play this?" she asked as Eddy refreshed his drink.

"I'd love to hear it. Was it your family's?" Dropping ice cubes splashed alcohol over the top of the crystal highballs.

Olive smiled wistfully. "No. It was mine. I bought it for my office." Holiday nostalgia washed over her. "I hid there to escape all the drama," she added as she lowered the needle.

Crackling noises escaped through the megaphone as the machine gained speed. A violin playing *Silent Night* followed.

"Seems like ancient times." Olive settled back into the chaise. She reached for the side table. Grabbing an envelope, she tossed it to Eddy. "Merry Christmas to you, Eddy Kepler."

"Should I open it?"

Olive cackled. "Yes. Today's Christmas, isn't it? Or do you want to wait 'till next year?"

Heat followed by color flushed Eddy's neck. He ripped at the seal and withdrew three folded papers. The first was a drawing, a hand-sketched blueprint. The second was a written description. A third was a schedule.

"Olive, is this what I think it is?" he questioned as he leafed through the paperwork.

"If you think it's a garage, then yes. It's what you think." The corners of her mouth turned upwards, contrary to its natural position. "I'm tearing out that old chicken coop. Hell, no one keeps chickens anymore." She sipped her drink before continuing. "It's a rat trap. Besides, that fancy car of yours needs a home. I'll make the garage big enough for a car plus tool storage. Construction is scheduled to begin late March."

Eddy bent over to kiss Olive's cheek. She flinched, stiffening. "Blasted. Why the hell not!" She relaxed, kissing him back. "Eddy Kepler, you bring out the worst in me!"

40

REDISTRICTING

JANUARY 1961

On Monday, January third, 1961, Harriett found herself back at the office. Tom Roland surprised her by having her door repainted "Dr. Harriett Bailey Kepler," reflecting her new title. Kimberly Coil, her assistant, arrived with a cake for an afternoon executive celebration. She spent the day acknowledging congratulations from her staff.

Thirteen short years resulted in the 31-year-old advancing to the role of CFO and the title of doctor. What more could the next 13 years offer? What did she want out of life? Afternoon daydreaming and contemplation were interrupted by a buzz on the intercom. Harriett jumped at the sound.

"Mrs. Kep—I mean, Dr. Kepler; you have a call from the superintendent of schools. Do you want to take it?" Kimberly asked.

"Hmmm." Harriett thought, *I must tell Kimberly to drop the "doctor."* "Yes, Miss Coil. Please put them through." Harriett waited for the click. "Harriett Kepler, speaking."

"Dr. Kepler, good afternoon." The speaker cleared his voice. "My name is Anderson Zufalls. I'm Madison's high school superintendent. Do you have a few minutes to spare?"

Curious, Harriett agreed to the conversation.

She was smiling as she placed the receiver in the cradle. "Miss Coil, I believe it's time to slice that cake."

∞ ∞ ∞

On Friday, Olive opened the morning *Madison Gazette* while her teabag steeped. She continued to purchase three different newspapers, more to help pass the time than to keep abreast of impending doom. She squandered her day immersed in reading material. Coughing, she read the second-page headline: *Schools merge, forming a new United Valley School District*. Her right eye began to twitch as she read on.

"Dr. Harriett Bailey Kepler, CFO of Dugan & Co. will assume the role of chairman of the board of the newly formed school district. Dr. Kepler, a resident of Campbellsville..."

Olive dropped the paper. *How does she do it? Manage to accomplish each of my dreams?* The news nearly sent Olive into a tailspin. Mustering every ounce of control, she decided to postpone her outburst until after she consulted her past. Olive walked to her bedroom dresser and removed a stack of letters bound by a faded ribbon. The stationery was brittle and yellow. Carefully, she removed them and read.

∞ ∞ ∞

Eddy returned home to find Olive sitting in her parlor, bourbon in hand. Her face was pale and her eyes red.

"Olive, are you okay?" he asked, as he poured his own drink. "Something upset you?"

Olive smiled at Eddy. "You know Eddy Kepler, you were right."

"Okay." Eddy sat across from his landlord and mother-in-law. "Good to know."

She cackled. "You have no idea what I'm talking about, do you?"

"Ah...no." He waited for her to continue.

"The competition. Between Harriett and me." Olive tossed the folded paper to Eddy. "Read page two. Your wife is the victor of new conquests."

Eddy read how the newly formed school district would result in the closure of the Campbellsville building to students in grades seven and higher. For the interim, Campbellsville students levels seven to 12 would be bussed to Madison high school, renamed United Valley. Construction would begin immediately on a new high school building, located mid-distance between both towns, that would open for the start of the 1963-1964 school year. Dr. Kepler would chair the board of directors overseeing the merger and restructuring.

She waited to continue only after Eddy whistled in response. "I was ready to hit the roof again," Olive said. "You know, 'anything you can do, I can do better!'"

"You have to admit, she's good at just about everything," Eddy defended Harriett. "I imagine her involvement is to dispel local objections."

"Possibly. She *is* brilliant. Most likely the best candidate to pull this off." Olive sighed. "Instead of jumping to conclusions, I revisited my letters from Fred. Eddy Kepler, I realized that she's not deliberately targeting *my* aspirations, *my* dreams. That's *my* mistake. She's pursuing the dreams of women all over this godforsaken man's world." Olive stared ahead as she sipped her drink. Reaching out her arm, she asked, "Will you give her this card? From me?"

Eddy nodded his head. "I won't see her until Monday afternoon. Can it wait?"

"Absolutely. It's waited 30 years. Depending on her reaction, it may be waiting 30 more."

∞ ∞ ∞

Monday evening, Harriett quietly slipped into her office, removed her suit jacket and hat, then placed her attaché on her desk. An envelope addressed "Harriett" in Olive's handwriting awaited her. Walking to the kitchen, she found Eddy and Shelby engaged in a game of Sorry!

"Did you bring this?" she asked, holding the card high in the air.

"Yes. Olive sent it for you."

"Well, I don't want it." She tossed it onto the game board.

"Mommy!" Shelby argued. "Don't be nasty."

Eddy chuckled. "You tell her, Duck." Turning to Harriett, he said, "Olive expected as much. Do with it what you wish. My job as delivery boy is done." Harriett took the card from his hand. His other hand tossed the pair of dice. "Hah! Doubles!"

Shelby groaned. "You win Daddy. Now that Mommy's home, I'm ready to eat!" Shelby folded the board and placed it back in the box.

"Duck, you're always hungry."

"I'm growing, Daddy!"

"Yes, you are. Into a beautiful young woman."

41

BACK TO THE FUTURE

LATE MARCH 1965

Shelby sat in her fifth-grade classroom looking out the window at the dark gray sky. Most likely the day would end wet and soggy.

"Earth to Shelby," repeated Mrs. Kirby, her teacher. "Shelby, will you approach the chalkboard?"

Shelby twisted in her desk. At five-feet-seven inches tall, she crammed her adult body into the child-size furniture. Stretching her arms, she walked forward and waited for the teacher to pull down a world map.

"Now, Shelby, please point out Vietnam on this map."

Shelby thought for a minute. *Vietnam? Sounds Asian to me.* She looked past India; scanning the map, she pointed.

"Thank you, Shelby. That is correct." Mrs. Kirby looked at the class. "Can anyone tell me why I asked Shelby to point out Vietnam?" The question was answered with complete silence. "That is your social studies assignment this evening. Write a short essay on the significance of Vietnam in today's headlines."

Several students groaned. Shelby grinned, no longer bored with the day's routine classwork.

∞ ∞ ∞

Alice's door opened and shut as the 10-year-old rushed in ahead of the rain. "Aunt Alice, may I use your phone?"

"Hi, Shelby. How was school? Is Tony with you?" Alice called from the kitchen. Polly and Maggie rode the bus to and from the new high school. Tony, five feet-four inches tall and one of the taller boys, was Shelby's diminutive classmate, despite being a year older.

"Tony is horsing around with some friends. Okay to use the phone?"

Alice strolled into the living room with a plate of cookies. "Hungry?"

"Always! Thanks." Shelby grabbed two.

"Who are you calling?" asked Alice.

"Grandma Olive. I may want to walk down for a visit if she has the answer to my question. Is that okay?" Shelby shoved a snickerdoodle into her mouth.

"Sure. Tell Mom we'll be down to visit over the weekend. And yes, you may call. If you leave, I want you home before dark, so you only have a couple hours."

Shelby lifted the receiver and dialed.

"What do you want?" the voice croaked on the line.

"Grandma, it's Shelby. I have a question. Do you know what's going on in Vietnam?"

"Hi, Duck." Olive chuckled aloud. "That's an odd question. School work?"

"Yep," she said as she munched the cookie.

"Does Alice allow you to visit?"

"Yep." She drummed her fingers on the table.

"Bring an umbrella. I'll see you soon." The line went dead.

Shelby giggled. "Aunt Alice, why does Grandma never say hello or goodbye?"

∞ ∞ ∞

Shelby and bookbag arrived at Olive's backdoor ten minutes later. Olive was steeping two cups of tea as Shelby barged in.

"Afternoon, Duck." Olive spooned a generous serving of sugar into each cup.

"Hi," she said before kissing Olive on the cheek. "You make the best tea."

She pulled out her notebook, then slurped the amber-colored liquid.

"You like my tea because it's weak and sweet. Now, Vietnam." Olive undid the clasp to a large envelope and removed newspaper clippings. Handwritten notes as to the source and date were recorded on each paper.

"This is the first one I saved." Olive handed Shelby an article from *The New York Times* dated April 18, 1961. "This isn't about Vietnam, per se, but it's relevant. Kennedy was pushing back at…"

Shelby interrupted. "President Kennedy, the one that died?"

"Yes, Shelby, the dead president. Bay of Pigs," she summarized. "A landing operation against Cuban dictator Fidel Castro and his communist party. It failed miserably. Stupid politicians. Dolts, every one of them!" She paused to collect her thoughts. "Okay, let me try to explain. This failed invasion of Cuba led Castro to align more strongly with Russia. Instead of Kennedy stopping communism, he actually strengthened it."

She looked at Shelby. "Do you know where Cuba is?"

"Yes!" Shelby stuck out her tongue. "Right off the edge of Florida."

"Right. Too close for comfort."

Olive opened another clipping dated October 1962.

"Cuban Missile Crisis. Here." She handed it to Shelby. "Because Cuba was buddy-buddy with Russia over the failed Bay of Pigs invasion, we were almost pulled into a nuclear war. This was a near catastrophe."

Shelby rolled her eyes. "They make us hide under our desks. What good is a desk going to do against a nuclear bomb? Besides, I'm too big to fit under it!"

Olive laughed. "Spot on, Duck! Now, on to Vietnam. Kennedy had a perception problem because of Cuba, and communism, which could be interpreted as policy weakness. He felt Vietnam was a good place to…ah…save face."

Shelby's brow wrinkled. "Is that a political thing?"

Olive's swallowed to avoid choking. "Again Duck, spot on!"

Olive opened a few more articles, one about the slaughter of protesting Buddhist monks, another titled "Vietnam president overthrown and murdered with brother," and a smaller envelope stuffed with articles about Kennedy's assassination. She refolded them and moved deeper into the stash.

"Grandma?"

"Yes, Shelby." Olive looked up from the envelope.

"How do you decide what to clip and save?"

Olive frowned. "Years of practice honey. Sadly, years of practice." Her fingers slid into the envelope. "Ah, here we go. Gulf of Tonkin. This is where *your* story should start."

"How do you spell that?" Shelby began writing as Olive recapped.

"T-O-N-K-I-N. Three boats from Vietnam approach one of our navy destroyers, the USS Maddox. The Maddox didn't like that, so they set off warning shots." Olive laughed. "Well, the Vietnamese liked that even less, so they fired torpedoes." She opened another clipping. "Then two days later, trigger-happy USS Maddox fired again."

"At more torpedoes?" Shelby asked as her fingers wrote frantically.

"No. Shadows." Olive guffawed. "Supposedly at sonar and radar images, but now the commander isn't so sure. We may never know. It's complicated, but for you, Duck, that little stunt was enough to cement LBJ into preventing the spread of communism in Southeast Asia."

"By 'LBJ,' you mean President Johnson?"

Olive smiled. "Yes. Now, your lame teacher probably has no knowledge of the background I just gave you. *This...*" She pointed to the top clipping. "*...is why she asked you about Vietnam.*" She held an article in the air. "We now have 'boots in country.' Do you know what that means?"

Shelby scratched her head.

"He sent troops to fight."

"Soldiers in Vietnam?"

"Yes. Johnson sent in the Marines to defend the Da Nang Air Base." Olive showed Shelby a clipping dated March 9, 1965, several weeks prior.

"In an invasion?" Shelby's eyes grew round. "Can he do that?"

Olive smiled again. "So, you listen in class, do you?" She rifled through more articles until finding another Gulf of Tonkin clipping. "Ah. This is what I was looking for. See this?" She pointed to an article outlining the Gulf of Tonkin Resolution. "This gives Johnson the power to do whatever he thinks is necessary to repel armed aggression against US forces. No declaration of war needed. He's using this as his 'get out of jail free' card. Now that we have soldiers on the ground, there's no telling how long this will last."

Olive exhaled a long sad sigh. "War is a very bad thing, Duck. Very bad. Hopefully, your cousins are too old to be caught up in this one." Olive paused, pondering how Tabs was drafted at age 29 during the Great War. "Someday I'll show you all the envelopes upstairs filled with clippings just like these. Geez, they go back to 1915!" She shook her head as her eyes narrowed. Icy blue dots showed through the slits, looking through Shelby and into the future. Or maybe into the past.

Shelby sat quietly, writing, allowing Olive time for reflection. "Wow. You are really smart, Grandma. Maybe smarter than Mommy."

Olive said nothing. After several minutes, Shelby looked out the window. "Grandma, I need to get home. It's raining and Daddy will be waiting for me." She closed her notebook and shoved it into her bookbag as she kissed Olive's cheek.

Olive accepted the embrace. "Thanks for stopping over, Duck. I fear I'll have many more clippings before this is over. Visit anytime. Now watch for cars on your way home."

Shelby bolted out the door, yelling, "I almost forgot. Aunt Alice and the girls are stopping in this weekend."

42

BUILD AN ARK

APRIL 1970

*E*ddy washed his breakfast dishes while watching puddles in Olive's backyard grow. *If this rain doesn't stop, I'm going to have to divert that water flow before it floods the basement*, he thought. Five straight days of continuous downpours, with no sign of it letting up. Even Albert, the meteorologist, was beginning to worry. A shiver ran up his spine as he remembered the flood, long ago, that killed his older brother.

Eddy quickly packed lunch before donning his hooded jacket. "Olive, I'm taking the bus today. See you tonight," he called as he shut the door.

He looked at the garage as he hurried down the street. Better to leave his new shiny blue Oldsmobile Delta 88 inside. This 1970 Olds had replaced his 1965 black Buick Riviera, a sleek-looking spy car with hidden headlamps. The gold Oldsmobile, for which Olive originally built the garage, was long gone.

Eddy had nothing better on which to spend his money, other than on Shelby or an occasional date. Harriett remained steadfast in refusing a divorce and Eddy refused to beg.

While it would have given her a potential court-mandated windfall, Harriett, dual assistant professor at Madison College and CFO at Dugan and Co., didn't need the money. Besides, Shelby would have scholarships—academic and athletic—enough to write her ticket into the Ivy Leagues if she so desired.

Happy to avoid headaches, Eddy dabbled by dating mostly discontented housewives on the sly, with whom there was no worry of commitment. His handsome face, wavy hair, and the guarantee of a good time rendered him a popular target.

The current living arrangement satisfied him. By attempting projects around the house, such as kitchen updates or refinishing the hardwood flooring, he felt needed. He belonged. And because he contributed to overall household expenses, Olive kept his rent to a minimum.

∞ ∞ ∞

Three o'clock arrived quickly without signs of the rain stopping. Eddy sprinted several blocks to the bus stop and quickly found a seat. He slid next to the window and stared out.

The door began to close when a woman, drenched to the bone, pounded on the glass. "Stop. Wait for me."

Several passengers and the bus driver grumbled, but the bus stopped. She climbed onboard and paid her fare. Eddy remained aloof until the woman sat next to him. Water dripped on his already wet arm. He scowled as she removed her rain bonnet, and snapped it shut, accordion style, spraying water on his face.

"Do you mind?" Eddy moaned. He wiped the excess with the back of his sleeve.

Bright blue eyes met his gaze as he turned to face his companion.

"Hello, Eddy Kepler."

"Olive? What the heck are you doing out today?" Immediately his tone softened. "If you wanted to come to town, I would have driven you. Why didn't you tell me?"

Olive repositioned her shopping bag on her lap to prevent spillage from the soggy bottom. "I had an appointment. A private appointment. No one's business where I go and what I do," she said, matter-of-factly. "What's for dinner tonight?"

Eddy no longer cooked for Shelby and Harriett. A high school freshman, Shelby was involved in golf, tennis, swimming, piano, debate and science clubs, student government, and chorus. Some days, Shelby arrived home later than Harriett. Eddy's after school involvement was shrunk down to only being an occasional carpool driver. Shelby, Harriett, and Eddy were all looking forward to next March and her birthday. A car was guaranteed for her sweet 16.

Eddy thought for a minute. "I feel like pasta topped with a lemon Alfredo. Maybe chicken breasts on the side?"

"I like the sound of that. I'll even make noodles." Olive watched Eddy's face contort.

"You know how to make homemade noodles? I love homemade noodles. Woman, you've been holding out on me!" he accused.

Olive grinned. "Only when it comes to noodles." She settled into her seat for the ride home. Quietly, she mused over today's secret and her visit with the esteemed Mr. Fazio.

43

FEASTING DUCK

SUMMER 1971

*S*ixteen-year-old Shelby Kepler stowed four clubs on the practice tee. Bending over, she stretched her back and taut hamstrings. The routine continued with shapely calves, shoulders, and finally arms and wrists. She looked out over the rolling Pennsylvania hills at a cerulean sky dotted with white, fluffy, cotton-candy bunnies, dragons, and eagles looking down from above.

She began her practice routine with her nine iron, moving on to the seven, then concluded with her three iron. After drying her palms on her shorts, she grabbed the last club, her driver, and swung. The sound was pure, crisp, and ringing as the ball launched forward, flying toward its target.

Harriett's head swiveled to watch. "Wow, Duck. You keep hitting them like that, we'll be looking for space on the trophy shelf."

Years earlier, Harriett had installed additional cabinets to frame out the office window seat for trophy display. The once-empty shelving of the massive room was now lined with awards, plaques, and prizes. Volumes of collections, first editions, references, novels, educational, and entertainment books crammed the stacks, scenting the room with musky, sweet leather. Couple that aroma with a woodburning fire, and both women were in heaven. Pure intoxication.

Shelby chuckled. "I just want to beat Daddy!"

"Not a competitive bone in your body!" Harriett attempted a lob shot, still the weakest part of her otherwise stellar short game. "Three-time club junior's champion and one overall women's champion trophies aren't enough for you?"

Shelby connected a second shot before answering. "Nope. I'm not competitive." She giggled. "At least I get it honestly. It was pretty cool beating you last year for women's champ! There should be a limit. Say, five consecutive years," she said, referring to Harriett's 10-year reign as the top woman golfer. "Fair warning, I'm going to do it this year too!"

"I don't doubt you, Duck. Geez, Louise, I'm 41 compared to your 16. You *should* be more flexible than me! Now, let's go take this trophy away from your father, shall we?"

"You look fabulous...for your age." She grinned at her mother. Before Harriett could object, she added, "And yes, ma'am. Daddy's going down! I can't believe they won last year by three strokes!"

The passing years had mellowed Harriett and Eddy's relationship. All Keplers, including Shelby and Earl, fell into a comfortable, friendly rhythm centering around the club and Shelby's many activities. Even Olive was acknowledged by club staff as belonging.

Teams for today's tournament consisted of one adult and one junior, mixed doubles. A way to engage younger and older golfers.

The voice of the starter over a loudspeaker interrupted their practice and banter.

"Attention: last group to the first tee."

"We're up." The two women hugged before climbing into their golf cart.

Eddy and his partner, Duane Musk—Shelby's nemesis in the junior division—awaited them on the first tee. To Eddy's dismay, his old partner, a semi-professional in his mid-20s, had moved to Pittsburgh at the beginning of the season to work as an assistant club pro and was therefore deemed ineligible to play. He picked the next best available player, Musk.

"Ladies," said Eddy as he extended his hand. "May the best man win."

Duane grinned as he looked on.

Shelby winked at her mother. "She will!" she said, as she shook her father's then Duane's hand.

"I won't be so easy on you this go around." Duane puffed his chest. "I *let* you win junior's."

Shelby smirked. "Yep. That's why I'm defending three years in a row. You *let* me win."

The starter joined the foursome, reviewed the tournament rules for alternate shot, then announced, "Our last group of the day for the championship trophy, and bragging rights of *Champion Club Alternate Shot* is ready. On the tee, we have Duane Musk, junior second-place winner and his partner, Eddy Kepler, two-time club men's champion. They are playing against Dr. Harriett Bailey Kepler, 10-time women's champion, and Shelby 'Duck' Kepler, current junior's champion *and* current women's champion. Should be a fabulous round. Ladies and gentlemen, players, enjoy."

The gallery burst into applause. Echoes of "Duck, Duck, Duck!" were heard coming from younger and older members alike. The men climbed the slight incline up to the blue tee box.

The starter extended a hat. "Ladies' choice." Shelby drew and presented a two. "Mr. Kepler," said the starter. "Men have the honors."

Eddy took two practice swings, then propelled the ball 250 yards down the fairway, leaving 110 yards to the front of the green on the par-four first hole.

Duane slapped him on the back. "Nice shot, for an old guy."

The women faced each other in a grimace.

"Hey, who are you calling old?" Eddy smiled. "Make sure you keep up. I don't want to be carrying your butt all day."

With the men safely off, the starter approached the group. "This tournament is designed without the advantage of a handicap. To compensate, the women shall hit from the red tees, giving them about 1000 yards."

Shelby flinched. Pulling her mother aside, she said, "Mom, I want to play from the whites. If we're forced to play the reds, we'll overdrive every hole. We always play white."

Harriett nodded. Approaching the starter, she asked. "May we choose to play from the whites?"

"Are you sure, Dr. Kepler? You'll lose 500 yards."

Shelby and Harriett nodded together. "Guys." Harriett called the men over. "The other women are using the reds, but Shelby and I want to play white today. Either of you have a problem with that?"

Duane immediately answered. "Hell no! I mean, *heck* no. The longer the better. I'm going duck hunting today."

Eddy eyed his daughter, then grinned, knowing she was most familiar with the course and club selection playing white. "Okay, fine with me."

"We want to win fair and square." She smiled. "Don't want you saying we won because of unfair yardage."

Duane eagerly bought the ruse; Eddy didn't, but he agreed to the change.

At the white tee box, the starter asked, "Who is going first?" Harriett pointed to Shelby. "Okay Miss Duck, the tee is yours."

With only a 15-yard advantage from the whites, Shelby slowly drew back the club, turning her hips into a tight coil that unwound on her downstroke. The ball sailed off the club's face, landing in the middle and rolling beside Eddy's ball.

Duane's eyes widened. "Oh no. The Duck is in good form."

Shelby winked. "The Duck shall feed on Musk-quitos tonight!" Looking at her mother, she asked, "Looks to be about 110, okay for you?"

Harriett sat in the cart. "One-ten is an easy eight iron. Let's show these men who's boss."

"Geez, Mom. You've been doing that your entire life!"

Caddies not participating, the two carts drove down the path. The remaining gallery, bringing up the rear, stopped midway down the fairway. Eddy had a slight advantage of about five yards, although Shelby left a more favorable approach angle. Harriett pulled out her eight iron. Keeping the ball right to avoid the sand guarding a left approach, she landed on the right edge of the green. Two putts needed for par.

Duane chose a nine iron. Pumped with adrenaline and bravado, the ball hit the back of the green and rolled into the rear trap. Eddy rolled his eyes at his partner.

"That's not an easy up and down! Stay calm, Duane. Don't let Shelby rattle you."

The youngster frowned. "How? She's brilliant, gorgeous, and too darn talented." He ogled Shelby in her pink-and-white Sears sucker shorts, pink logo shirt, and pink visor. "And she's a super jock!"

"Do I detect a crush?"

"A…what? No. Sheer admiration."

Eddy wrapped his arm around Duane's shoulder. "Believe me, I know firsthand how incredible both Shelby and her mother are. They are a hard act to follow." He jumped into the cart. "Keep breathing and concentrate on our game. Don't worry about them. Okay?"

"Sure, Eddy. Whatever you say." He dropped his head, dejected as if giving in already.

Eddy pulled at the boy's visor. "And don't you forget who her parents are! We both require shot cards."

∞ ∞ ∞

Both teams managed to par number one. At the turn, Harriett rushed to the ladies' room, while Shelby checked the scoreboard. As predicted, the tournament winner would most likely come from their foursome. The men finished the front at 37, the women at 39.

Harriett joined Shelby at the concession stand. "Here Mom, eat a hot dog. We'll need our strength for number ten. I always hate starting the back nine on the number one handicap hole!"

Harriett gulped down a glass of water and a dog. "I'm up, right?"

"Yes ma'am. Better you than me!"

Duane's drive flew down the fairway about 270 yards, landing in a poorly repaired divot next to the trap, leaving 170 to the back left hole. Harriett crunched her drive, thanks to the hot dog, sending the ball 220 yards and landing on the right of the trap, in the bump-out.

"Shelby, I calculate that shot at 180."

"Okay." She pulled her three iron, and swung, landing back left, pin high.

"Great shot, Duck!" Eddy complimented his daughter as he surveyed his ball. "Shit," he grumbled to himself. "This isn't going to be easy to pick clean."

He hit it fat, shanking the ball and landing in the front left sand trap. Both men grumbled as they motored forward. The women waited on the green, Shelby ready to tend the pin for her mother's putt. Duane skidded down the lip of the trap. As he addressed the ball, he grounded his club. One stroke penalty in a hazard. He looked around to see if anyone was watching. Thinking everyone was busy preparing for their own shot, he twisted his ankles to dig in his feet.

"Duane!" Eddy yelled. "Don't you dare swing! It's not your shot."

The women looked at each other, puzzled. Shelby whispered to Harriett, "What did I miss?"

"Not sure. I missed it too."

Duane's eyes flashed daggers. "Eddy, what's the big deal? I was ready to swing."

Eddy clenched his teeth. "From now on, I'm 'Mr. Kepler' to you. And the big deal is following the rules. You grounded your club in the hazard, costing us a stroke."

Color crept up Duane's neck. His face glowed red. "The girls have no idea what you're talking about. Look at them. You may have cost us the match, old man!"

"Golf is a sport of integrity and honesty. You lost us the stroke, not me." Eddy pulled his sand wedge from his bag. "If I've learned anything in life, it's that you can't cheat the devil. It took too long for that lesson to sink through my thick skull. I'm doing you a favor, son." Eddy planted his feet in the sand. "Now, if you don't mind, it's my shot."

Duane mumbled, "Yes, sir." With his head hung, he walked back to the cart to get his putter.

Eddy envisioned the ball as the face on a dollar bill. His club entered the sand on the right side of the bill and exited on the left side. The ball popped up, landed, and rolled pin high three feet to the left, leaving Duane a short putt for par.

Shelby and Harriett watched, trying to curb their excitement while knowing they had a chance to pick up a stroke.

"Mom, you ready?" Shelby asked as she removed the pin. Harriett spotted her ball, cleaned it, lined the logo with the break, and stroked the entire cat, just like Beeno taught. The 30-foot putt broke slightly left, the ball circled the cup, then dropped, giving the women a birdie.

Shelby whooped as she replaced the flag. "Way to go, Dr. Kepler!" Turning to her opponents she asked, "Duane, have your line?"

He grumbled, "Pull it," under his breath.

She backed away holding the flagstick. "What was that all about?" Shelby asked Eddy as Duane lined his putt.

"You'll find out soon enough."

Duane struck the ball firmly, too firmly. It circled the hole before spinning out. Four players, four sighs.

Eddy sank the remaining putt to finish the hole.

"Geez. I was hoping to tie you, after Mom's great tee shot." Shelby replaced the flag. She looped her arm through her father's as they headed off the green to the carts.

"You did."

"I did what?"

"You tied us. Didn't they Duane?" Eddy looked at the Madison High School senior, daring him to back down.

"Yes. You tied us." He sighed and turned to face away as he mumbled, "I grounded my club in the sand. Card a five."

∞ ∞ ∞

Members cheered Harriett and Shelby as they shook hands with Eddy and Duane, then walked off the 18th green, back to the clubhouse, waving to the crowd. Both groups signed, then relinquished their cards to the tournament referee, who checked and posted scores, hole by hole, on the leaderboard.

Fifteen minutes passed before the microphone crackled,

"Ladies and gentlemen, it is official: our runners-up are Duane Musk and Eddy Kepler with a three-over, 74. Dr. Harriett Kepler and Shelby 'Duck' Kepler, are this year's Alternate Ball tournament champions. Ladies, step forward, please, to receive your trophy."

Shelby grinned ear to ear. "Way to go, Dr. Kepler."

Harriett smiled with pride at her offspring. "Your tee shot on number 13 setting up that birdie gave us the match."

"I almost peed my pants when they went in the water. Another two-shot swing." Shelby strutted forward, making club history as the youngest member and only female member to sweep all three major tournaments consecutively. If she took the women's next week, she'd complete a season grand slam.

"Ladies and gentlemen, your winners." Beeno handed the large, silver-plated trophy to Shelby. "With a final score of 70, one under par."

The crowd burst into applause and chants of "Duck" as Shelby hoisted the metal above her head. Someone yelled out, "Duck, I'll take that if you're out of space." Chuckles and replies of, "Me too," followed.

"You'll have your chance to take it home next year."

She viewed the line dated "August 1971," where their names would be engraved to join past winners dating back to 1943. Per tradition, the trophy was on loan until May first of the following year, when it was returned to the club.

The women scurried into the locker room for quick showers before dinner, as members drank, mulling over the final scorecard and touting the prowess of the women as they enjoyed an August evening.

Shelby sighed, relaxing her muscles as warm water flowed over her long blonde hair. Despite natural waves, it reached her waist. She wanted to cut it into a short shag, but Harriett discouraged her. On nights like tonight, after a full day on the course in the summer heat and wet from a shower, she wished she hadn't listened.

Flipping her hair over her head, she waved the blow drier up and down as she tugged at a brush. The only thing visible beneath her hair were her legs. She looked like Cousin It from *The Addams Family*.

In keeping with the color scheme of the day, she slipped on a short, pink-and-white striped dress, donned a matching headband, then slipped her feet into pink, wedge, platform shoes.

Harriett smiled approvingly. "Duck, you have your father's good looks."

"And my mother's athletic skills! I am a lucky girl." She looped her arm through Harriett's. "Shall we?"

Eddy waited outside the locker room door. "Ladies, may I join you for dinner?"

Shelby kissed his cheek. "Absolutely. Uncle Earl is joining us, too."

Earl, with Harriett's sponsorship, had joined Madison Country Club nine years earlier. Shelby, Harriett, and Earl spent many enjoyable weekends together golfing, swimming, and playing tennis. At times, Eddy even joined them. To everyone's amusement, new caddies and parking valets often confused Mr. Earl Kepler as Dr. Harriett Kepler's husband. But, no one mistook Shelby as Eddy's daughter, two exact replicas of the other.

Eddy escorted Shelby to a front table, while Harriett linked arms with Earl. Members no longer gossiped; all involved had adjusted to the strange family arrangement long ago.

Eddy pulled out the chair for Shelby to sit. "Thanks, Daddy." She glanced around the room. "Did Duane really try to cheat?"

"He sure did."

"Are you going to report him to the board? They'll likely kick him out of the club." She fixed her gaze on a laughing Musk family. Duane seemed to garner all the attention.

"I think I'll have a quiet chat with the boy. See if he comprehends the severity of his action." Eddy shook his head. "God knows, if someone had held me accountable in high school, my life may have been different."

"Really, Daddy? I think otherwise." Eddy met her stare. "A chat isn't being held accountable. Real consequences need to be suffered for lasting behavioral changes."

Eddy's shoulders rolled in laughter. "What is your recommendation?"

She looked from Eddy to Duane and back. "Report him to the board," she said. "Who knows how often he's tried to cheat or succeeded in cheating in the past? Make this lesson meaningful."

"Ouch!" Eddy grimaced. "Like mother, like daughter."

44

SPOILS OF CONQUEST

LABOR DAY, SEPTEMBER 1971

Shelby pulled her shiny, midnight blue Camaro into the enlarged garage. She leaned over the seat to the back before sliding the trophy toward the door.

"Well Mom, we knew this was coming home, one way or the other." She smiled at her mother. "Sure glad the garage is now attached to the house! I hated dragging stuff up the front stairs. Mind you, I don't object to winning, but this thing is heavy."

Harriett watched her daughter juggle the large, women's champion trophy with pride. "Well done, Duck! You are a fabulous ambassador for golf. What's on the agenda tonight?" Holding the door open for Shelby, Harriett followed her into the kitchen. "Getting clothes ready for the first day of school tomorrow?"

"No." Shelby walked to the office and placed the rewards of the day into the cleared space. "Mom, think we could talk? There's something I'd like to ask." She paused, then added, "It's sort of...personal."

The corner of Harriett's mouth dropped. "Oh. Sounds

serious." She pointed to an office chair. "Sit there. I'll be right back. You want a Coke?"

Shelby nodded yes and waited for Harriett to return.

Mother and daughter stared at each other for several moments before Harriett broke the silence. "What's on your mind?"

Shelby cleared her throat. "You always taught me to speak my mind. So, here goes." She licked her lips. "There was a certain guy that followed me today, hole by hole. Did you happen to notice him?"

Harriett grinned then frowned at the thought of her baby growing up. "Shelby, do you have a crush on this fellow?"

"Sort of. Well yes." Shelby sipped her drink. Carbonated bubbles caught in her throat. "O hear, goes! Mom, I understand how women get pregnant, but are there ways to prevent it?" Her voice dropped. "Other than…you know… not…?" Her leg bounced up and down. "I guess I really want to know why I am an only child? Your sisters seem to be rather…fertile."

Harriett sat on the couch. Her hands clutched the cushion as if she were clinging to a life vest. No one, not even Eddy, questioned her inability to bear another child. She swallowed hard, but her mouth remained dry.

"Ah…well." Harriett's knuckles turned white from her grip. "In the past, the only way to prevent was to use a condom, sheath." Her face turned beet red as her eyes darted away from Shelby. "The man was responsible." She coughed. "Now the woman has options."

"Yes. What kind of options did you use?"

"Shelby Kepler." Harriett struggled to regain control of her emotions. "That's personal. Wait! Are you thinking about having sex?"

Shelby laughed, "Not yet. That boy is off to college next week and I doubt he'll be interested in me once school starts.

Besides, I'm not ready for that kind of emotional commitment. Some of my friends... experiment. From what I can tell, I want a connection, to be more involved than just the physical." She hesitated, "but it doesn't hurt to be informed." She stammered. "Oh heck...I can't play dumb. I know about birth control options. What I really always wondered is why am I an only child?"

Harriett stood and paced. "I confess, I used a device called an IUD. I'm guilty of never telling your father. He wanted more children; I wanted my education."

Shelby smiled. She enjoyed catching her mother in a cover-up. Both women tensed slightly, as Shelby continued. "While we're on the subject, Mom, why did you and Uncle Earl never get together? After you kicked...after Daddy left?"

Harriett coughed. "Geez! Shelby! Thinking of my baby having sex is bad enough. I wasn't expecting an inquisition. Earl and I have an...an understanding." She studied her daughter. "Are you sure you're not interested in this boy, Shelby Kepler?"

The blood rushed up Shelby's neck. Her cheeks glowed red. "I'm mixed up, Mom. It's not this boy in particular. But...this whole love thing confuses me. I feel like I got conflicting signals my entire life." Her chin dropped. "Don't get me wrong, growing up the way I did...with you and Daddy separated, was fine. But, I learn from watching, and there wasn't much for me to observe. At least to learn from in home life." She hung her head. "It's obvious that Uncle Earl is in love with you, and you reciprocate fondness. Why not get married? Are you truly happy being alone?"

Harriett wrung her thumbs. Her lips formed a thin line across her face as if they could disappear. "Duck, I'm so sorry, but this is a private matter."

"Mom, I'm going into my junior year in high school. I'm

entering a new phase of my life and want some answers." She grinned at her mother. "I need to understand."

Harriett stood and mixed herself a cocktail, the all too familiar escape. "Duck, I'm very happy on my own. In fact, I prefer it. Yes, Earl and I care for each other...but we have an agreement. Strictly platonic. I'm still technically married, you know." Ice cubes clicked on the bottom of the glass, while words of self-denial spilled out of her mouth. "Living without a man is not for every woman. It takes fortitude and self-reliance. I'm fortunate. My education and career allow me the ability to support myself. Most women, even today, must depend on a man for daily sustenance." She sat across from Shelby and took her by the hand. "Darling, my goal for you is to follow in my footsteps. Be self-sufficient. No matter if you live with or without a man."

Shelby's lips pressed tightly together. "I agree that a woman should be able to support herself." Her eyes pierced Harriett's. "But, as to the other stuff, I don't believe you. I don't think it's about your self-reliance at all. I think you like controlling everyone, by not divorcing Daddy. You use it as a tool."

"What?" Harriett reflexively jumped to her feet.

Shelby hesitated, gathering her nerve, before continuing. "You torture poor Uncle Earl and Daddy. And I don't believe that you are happy being alone. Sure, it's okay right now, but what happens when I go off to college?" Shelby took a deep breath and held it for a moment. "Initially, I thought you had pure, unadulterated ambition. But now..." she paused. "I think working two jobs, excelling in sports, baking, all the other things you do—I think it is all just a front. To fill the void of being alone." Shelby bit her lip. "I think you want to be miserable and isolated because you don't know how to be otherwise. That life is not for me, Mom. I need people."

Shelby leveled the final blow. "I think you and Grandma Olive are more alike than you care to admit."

∞ ∞ ∞

The blood rushed up Harriett's neck. She clenched her teeth as she gazed at her daughter. *Is she right? Does she understand me better than I understand myself?* Without reply, Harriett rose and left the room, leaving Shelby alone in her office.

Harriett repeated *I'm not lonely, I'm not like my mother*, as she climbed the stairs to isolate herself securely in her bedroom. *Damn you, Shelby Kepler! How dare you?*

45

THE END OF A LEGEND

SUMMER 1980

*T*he sun slowly peeked over the hills, welcoming Campbellsville to another glorious summer day. Alice unlocked the front door of the Maple Street house, linking arms with Polly and Maggie, who braved forward.

"Come on, girls. We need to relieve Esther," she said, grateful that her adult children had remained in town.

They climbed the central staircase and entered the large front bedroom. Esther and Heddy sat quietly, watching a sleeping Olive.

"How was she last night?" Alice handed an eager Esther a thermos of coffee.

"Thank you! We already drank the pot Eddy made this morning." Esther swallowed a big swig of the aromatic beverage. "You are the best sister!"

Polly smiled. "Don't let Aunt June hear you say that."

Hands on her hips, Esther tossed her head. "Aunt June isn't the one helping me with Mother. She's hiding in Georgia."

"In all fairness, June can't jump on a plane every time Mother has a spell. With or without Dave's pilot benefits,"

Alice defended their sister. "Just like Violet, who can't always be driving in from Pittsburgh."

"You're right, but—"

Olive groaned. Bolting upright she clutched at her stomach. Heddy thrust a bucket under her mouth in time to prevent soiled bed linens.

Esther wiped her mother's forehead with a damp cloth. "She's gone gray. Look at her eyes."

"Teddy said that we are probably near the end. Have you phoned June? Albert?" Alice tied apron strings around her waist before nudging Esther aside. "I think we should assemble the family, just in case."

"Agreed. I'll do that when I get home. I need some sleep. Thank goodness for Eddy. Poor man helps like a doting son, despite having to work in the morning."

Alice nodded. "He cares for her. Loves her like a mother."

Esther rolled her eyes. "A caring son to replace an uncaring Albert."

The sisters and cousins hugged and kissed, saying goodbye.

∞ ∞ ∞

Two evenings later, at Dr. Paulson's suggestion, the entire family gathered. Her offspring and the adult grandchildren, of which Shelby was the youngest at age 25, squeezed into Olive's bedroom. They left the great-grandchildren hiding in the front parlor, too terrified to make a sound.

Alice, scheduled for night duty, sat in the chair beside the bed with Polly and Maggie at the ready. June and Esther observed from the foot of the bed, once again with their arms entwined, inseparable as in their youth. Dave and Susie wiggled together in the bay window with Darrell, Toby, Heddy, Lloly, and Violet. Teddy and Tony Jenson stood guard in the hallway. Albert leaned against the far wall, arms crossed in front of his body while Laurie rested her head on his shoulder. Their daughter Dee Dee was absent, in California, pregnant with her second child.

Their soft murmuring ceased as Olive lifted her head. "Eddy? Shelby?" she asked.

Eddy laid his hand on top of her cold, bony fingers. "We're here Olive. Don't strain yourself."

"Eddy, listen closely." Her finger motioned to Eddy. He moved his ear beside Olive's mouth. She tried lifting her head from the pillow. Olive's glazed eyes searched the room. "There's an envelope and instructions, in the top drawer." She pointed to the dresser before she asked, "Is *she* here?"

Eddy's silence answered the question.

"Hmm." Olive sighed. "She's no different than me. Hating to the very end." She licked her lips, head thumping back into the pillow. "It won't be long before I can forgive Father to his face. Should have done it years ago."

Polly whimpered. "Don't talk like that, Grandma. You'll get better." The fourth-generation Westchester beauty pushed her blonde curls from her face.

Olive paused. "She's so much like me. Forgiveness will wait for her, too."

A voice from the doorway interrupted. "Actually, I'll reconcile today, if you don't mind."

"Mom?" Shelby ran to Harriett.

"Hi, Duck. Good to see you." Harriett looked at her siblings. "I got here as soon as my lecture ended. Eddy called me at the university." Harriett kissed Shelby's head. Walking to the bed she brushed her hand against Eddy's free arm. "Mother, I'm not like you."

Olive's laugh morphed into coughing. She covered her mouth. "Harriett Jane Bailey, you most certainly are! Like it or not, you are."

"Hush, Mother…whatever you say."

Albert and Alice glanced at each other, both smirking.

"Harriett, before I go, you have to know it was an accident." She choked on her words.

Albert rolled his eyes.

Blood rushed up Harriett's neck, flushing her face. "Don't!" Harriett covered her ears with her hands.

"The night before, Tabs and I were up all night, hashing over all my grievances. It was a good talk, the most honest one of our marriage. We spent the early morning together, in my bed, just snoozing and cuddling." Olive exhaled as she slumped into her mattress. "It was a playful day. I nudged the ladder to get his attention but caught him unaware." Tears filled Olive's eyes. "He twisted too quickly. The ladder fell."

Ears strained to hear. As she finished, the group gasped a collective sigh. The coughing continued.

Harriett's face drained as quickly as it colored. "Why did you wait to tell us? Mom?"

"Would you have listened?"

Harriett stood in a trance, silently gazing at Olive. Her ears buzzed as her wide eyes darted away only to glance at Dr. Paulson who elbowed his way to the bed.

"I think we better give her some space."

"Nonsense." Olive continued to cough and hack. The sputum on her handkerchief was laced with blood. "I want my family here."

Olive clawed the air, gurgled, smiled in recognition and greeting, then her eyes rolled back into her head.

Dr. Paulson felt her neck. "She's gone."

Seventy-eight years after her birth, Olive Westchester Bailey finally authenticated her place within the family. All Westchesters, by name or association, welcomed her into the cemetery, atop the knoll overlooking the old homestead. She rested eternally beside her husband, Tabs, and across from her brother, Fred, both of whom loved her dearly.

∞ ∞ ∞

Three days after her internment, the family was summoned to the office of Fazio and Fazio, attorneys at law in Madison. The entire crew crowded around a large conference table, faces blank, as they waited for Mr. Francis Fazio to join them.

Fazio entered the room carrying a folder followed by a secretary carrying a stack of papers and a steno pad. Fazio took his seat at the head of the table before beginning.

"Thank you for assembling today. I tried to schedule this as quickly as possible. I realize many of you are out-of-towners only in for the funeral." He paused, waiting for a familiar head bob. "Olive Westchester Bailey, my client, engaged me several years ago to write her Last Will and Testament." He opened the file folder. "Olive was a peculiar woman…"

Albert burst out, "That's one way of saying it!"

Several others chuckled.

Fazio continued, "Peculiar in that her final wishes are, shall we say, unconventional?" He cleared his throat. "Usually, I only gather those who are bequeathed. However, in this particular case, I wanted the entire family together to witness the reading of Mrs. Bailey's will."

Albert blurted again, "Get on with it. We all have places we need to be. She gave us little as children; I, for one, don't expect anything as an adult!"

Alice shook her head. Catching Albert's eye, she said, "Please, Albert, we all know there is little love lost between you and Mother. Be civilized, for the rest of us."

Fazio scanned the faces around the table. "Given your

outburst, this may be easier than I expected. It seems Olive bequeathed nothing to her children, listed as Esther Cline, June Ralston, Albert Bailey, Alice Jenson, and Harriett Kepler." The collective inhalation of air sounded as if the climax of a thrilling movie scene was achieved.

He continued, "However, her grandchildren, Tobias, Heddy, Lloyd, and Violet Cline; Susan Ralston; Polly, Margaret, and Anthony Jenson; Deidra Bailey; and Shelby Kepler, notwithstanding married names, are listed as beneficiaries, each of which shall inherit the sum of 5,000 dollars." He poured himself a glass of water as he allowed his words to settle.

The grandchildren looked at each other in shock. Toby whispered to Lloly, "That's enough for a down payment on a house!"

"So, Kepler, I guess this means you're looking for a new living arrangement! The house will have to be sold to meet a 50,000-dollar promise!" Albert laughed at his own joke. "You never should have been allowed to move in with her!"

"Albert, shut up!" This time, Harriett scolded her brother. "Eddy's been good to Mother. Look at all the improvements he's made since he moved in, most at his own expense." Her expression was set, firm. "He paid her rent, cooked, and did the chores. Cut him a break."

Albert clenched his jaw, showing his teeth. "God, Harriett. After all these years you still defend him. He's a no-good louse and you, of all people, should know it. Maybe Kepler will buy the house? God knows none of us want it!"

"Please keep the family feuding to yourselves?" Fazio regained control of the meeting. "The house and the remaining estate are bequeathed to Edgar Gregor Kepler Jr., relationship listed as son-in-law, and family friend." Fazio glanced at Eddy. "Is that you, sir?"

The color drained from Eddy's face; his mouth dropped to

his chin. "Yes." He gulped for air. "I am Edgar Gregor Kepler, Jr.

"Then the house and all of its contents are yours." He closed his folder. "The house and contents remain intact. That is the entirety of this Last Will and Testament. My secretary has a check addressed to each of the grandchildren. I ask you to sign signifying receipt of payment." Fazio stood. "Thank you all for coming."

∞ ∞ ∞

Fazio vacated the room, giving the family time alone. Teddy and Darrell congratulated Eddy on his good fortune. Albert signed for Deidra's check, then stormed out of the room, dragging Laurie behind him, as he grumbled the whole way to the car. Alice and Esther waited for Harriett to leave before approaching Eddy.

"Eddy, I hate to ask this, but there are a couple things of Mother's that really should stay in the family." Alice twisted her lips into a sideways frown. "When you go through her bedroom, may we assist you?"

Esther touched his hand. "At least to identify specific items of..." she hesitated, "...family significance?"

"Ladies, I have no intention of keeping Bailey or Westchester heirlooms for myself." He wiped his brow. "I'll gladly welcome help from any or all of you." Eddy walked to the head of the table and poured himself a glass of water. "I'm flabbergasted. I don't know what to say."

Alice kissed his cheek. "You don't need to say a thing. Mother was a difficult woman. You somehow managed to do what none of us could."

"What do you mean?" Eddy persistently rubbed his eyes.

"I mean you lived with her!" Esther laughed. "Peacefully,

for 20 years! God, she nudged me out at 16, pushed Albert out at 17."

Alice waved her hand in the air. "I moved in with June and Esther, at 16, during the war. My excuse was to babysit, but it was really to escape. Even Harriett bought her house at age, what?" Alice looked at Esther for confirmation.

"She somehow pulled together enough funds at 21," Esther said, "to buy the biggest house in Campbellsville. Just so she could evacuate and spite Mother. Double whammy!"

The sisters each linked one of Eddy's arms. "Come on," urged Alice. "Let's get out of here. You and Harriett may not be able to live together, but you're still family. We'll always love you as a brother."

Eddy squeezed their hands. "Thanks. You have no idea how much that means to me. Now, when do you want to go through your mother's bedroom?"

Esther giggled. "As soon as possible. I want this whole thing done and over. Alice, you free this afternoon?"

"I'm free if Eddy's free. One o'clock?"

Eddy grinned. A glint, reminiscent of the infamous Kepler grin, twinkled in his eye. "It's a date!"

∞ ∞ ∞

The three adults sat on the floor in Olive's bedroom, inspecting a pile of items pulled from the closet. Alice held a lamb-fur coat in the air. "I didn't know she owned this! I can see her strutting in it now." All three chuckled.

"She used to wear it to the club." Eddy's nostalgia caused him to blush. "We went at least once, usually twice a month for dinner. She was so proud walking into the lobby snuggled in fur. She always chided the coat-check girl to keep it safe."

"What do you think is in this chest?" Esther pointed to the carved trunk at the bottom of the bed.

Eddy exhaled. "Well…It may surprise you to see." He opened the lid and removed an envelope addressed to *Eddy Kepler*. He read aloud.

My dear son-in-law. Thank you for your years of kindness, for tolerating my moods and my tantrums. Remember long ago, when I showed you the items in this coffin? The contents of the candy boxes are yours, and yours alone! Don't share with the rest of them, or I'll haunt you.

Remember to give my beloved pearls to Polly. God, I was so happy the day my father gave them to me!

Alice whimpered her approval.

As discussed, the coffin itself goes to Shelby. Make sure she knows the story of my darling brother Fred. Next to Tabs and Fred, I have been closer to you than any other human being. You are a good man, Eddy Kepler.
I love you.
Olive.

Eddy leaned back on his heels as tears streamed down his face. "I must show you this," he said as he reached to remove the false bottom. Pulling out box after candy box, he opened the last. "They are all like this. Filled with money. She showed me over 10 years ago and I estimated there must be close to one hundred thousand dollars. God only knows how much she has now."

Alice maneuvered her fingers to physically close her mouth. "Wow!" was all she managed to say.

"How should I divide this?" asked Eddy.

Esther rubbed her eyes. "You don't. She just said the

money was yours! You don't want the ghost of Olive Westchester Bailey visiting you each night, do you?"

"Good God, no!" Eddy managed to laugh. "But I neither want nor need this money."

Recovering from her shock, Alice said, "I don't ever remember her saying 'I love you.' Eddy, the rest of us don't need the money either. We have all managed to make a comfortable life for ourselves. We all have wonderful children, loving spouses…well, you know what I mean." She blushed. "Secure jobs and homes. Geez, Eddy. I'm sure you'll find something to do with the dough."

Eddy thought for a moment. "Okay. If you are sure about it, then I'll make a plan for her stash… We better get busy. Lots more to go through—family pictures, clothes galore, all those salt and pepper shakers…and let's not forget the chest of drawers filled with newspaper clippings! Do you think the DAR might want them?"

∞ ∞ ∞

One street above the trio working to organize Olive's fortune, Harriett sauntered into her office. Although out of fashion, she removed the hat pin holding her 1960s-era chapeau. The round, black pillbox resembled the style of Jacqueline Kennedy. She slipped off her shoes. Rubbing her feet, she sat in the comfort of her desk chair.

Harriett gazed at the abundant shelves crammed with books and trophies. She inventoried the many titles—some rare first editions, many remnants of Shelby's childhood. They were the accumulation of her lifetime.

"Lifetime!" she mused. "What have I actually accomplished?" She slid open her desk drawer and removed a sealed envelope she had not touched or read since receiving her doctorate. Slicing the edge with a sword-like letter opener, she removed a greeting card.

"Congratulations Graduate," read the front. A folded paper fell to the floor as she scanned the inside verse. The print, mentioning something about hard work and reward, was blurred by tears streaming down her face.

She dried her eyes, then retrieved the note from the floor.

Dear Harriett,

Congratulations, Dr. Kepler. Quite the accomplishment!

I am proud of you, seriously. I know you don't believe that. I'm not sure you'll even read this, but if you do, I want you to know that you managed to achieve everything that I failed to do.

I'm no longer jealous of you. I used to be, but Eddy helped me see that the similarities in our personalities and goals are not a competition, but rather, genetic parallels.

Growing old has a funny way of changing your point of view. I can now overlook what I considered the faults of my father, brothers, sisters, children, and myself and see them not as personality flaws, but as quirks that gave them…us…uniqueness and charm.

Dear daughter, I wasn't the most caring mother. That was your father's job. You, on the other hand, are a wonderful mother. Shelby is blossoming into an amazing girl, just like you.

Although, in all honesty…I must divulge that despite the wisdom of advanced degrees, awards, and titles, you fail at forgiveness. I hope that you can learn to pardon others' transgressions. Find it in your heart to excuse an old woman's bias and a young man's impulsive ego. Eddy Kepler is a good man, and he loves you.

Enough of sentimentality. Well done, Harriett! Well done.
Olive

Harriett refolded the stationery. Placing it inside the card, she returned both to the envelope and desk drawer. She contemplated Olive's final words. Was Tabs' death truly an accident? Did her mother really learn to forgive? Maybe Olive deserved some slack, but Eddy? After what she suffered from his hand, did he qualify for clemency?

The veins of her temples visibly throbbed. She wet a washcloth and placed it on her pounding head, hoping to ease the pain. Resolving nothing, she downed three aspirins with a glass of cold water and went to bed before noon.

46

SCHOLARSHIP

On Saturday, Eddy took a break from purging the house of "all things Westchester" to drive Shelby back to the Pittsburgh airport. Although only traveling across the state, Shelby opted to fly, needing a quick return to Philadelphia. The third-year Penn medical student, enrolled in the exclusive MSTP combination program, would graduate in another five years with joint MD and Ph.D. degrees. She dared not take additional time away from her intense coursework.

As they travelled the rolling hills toward the city, Eddy glanced at his daughter, who was reading in the seat beside him. "Duck, I was hoping to at least play nine holes with you."

Shelby looked up from her papers and smiled. "Ah, Dad. Sorry. I rarely play now. But I promise as soon as I can manage, we'll play. Even without practice, I can still beat you!"

"I'm sure you can." As he spoke the radio began playing Harry Chapin's song *Cats in the Cradle*.

Eddy sadly watched Shelby board her plane. As he drove

back to Campbellsville, his thoughts turned to a pessimistic future of living alone without Harriett, Shelby, or Olive.

He worked tirelessly with Esther and Alice over the next week, sorting, stacking, and delivering the accumulation of Olive's life to worthy recipients and charities. Household, kitchen items, and furniture remained within. After 11 days, the presence of Olive's overpowering personality had diminished to neutral ground. The house was all his.

He had never felt so isolated.

On a whim, Eddy called Harriett. She answered on the first ring. "Harriett Bailey Kepler."

Eddy cleared his throat. "Harriett, are you free tonight? Any chance I can make dinner for you?" He waited. "I need to discuss something with you."

Her voice sounded like a groan as she said, "Ah...sure. Where?"

"Your place, if that's okay?"

"You still have a key?"

"Yes, I think so." He rummaged through a box containing a collection of keys. "Yep. Here it is."

"Good. How about seven?" She paused before asking, "Do I need to stop and pick anything up?"

"No. I got this. I feel like cooking, and I need a change of scenery. See you later."

∞ ∞ ∞

At the workday's conclusion, Eddy walked through Harriett's kitchen to thumb through his old copy of Julia Child's *Mastery of French Cooking*. Tonight needed to be memorable.

Eddy chose the classic Boeuf Bourguignon recipe. Glancing at the wall clock that seemed to shout "warning: 4:15," he began reading.

Ten minutes was all he needed to refresh his memory,

reconnoiter the pantry, and compose a shopping list. Before exiting the house, he dialed the phone number for Lupinetti's grocery.

"Mr. Lupinetti," he said. "I need..."

The bell jingled as he walked through the door to a waving clerk.

"Mr. Kepler, I have your order over here!"

Two bags awaited his arrival. Lupinetti no longer kept monthly customer tabs. With the introduction of the Visa and MasterCard credit card companies and the economy encountering a fifth economic recession since 1950, convenience for consumers was no longer a sound business practice. Unemployment was pushing eight percent. The risk was too large for the aging grocer.

Eddy placed three bills on the counter and waited for his change. Before driving back up the hill, he stopped at the florist. The "closed" sign was swaying back and forth. Eddy's rapping on the door was met with a grunt and frown, but the clerk turned the lock.

"We're closed," she said.

"I know. Sorry. I need a bouquet of cut flowers. Whatever is handy." He winked at the girl, who like so many before, fell prey to Eddy's sparkling eyes.

"Okay. But make it quick. I have supper to cook."

"So do I." Eddy quickly surveyed the cooler. "How about a dozen of those roses?"

The corners of the girl's mouth turned upwards. "That will be 20 dollars," she said as she arranged the stems and began wrapping.

"I suspect a little price gouging," Eddy grumbled as he opened his wallet.

"And yet, you are willing to pay it!"

Flowers in hand, Eddy threw his car in gear and sped past

Olive's house..._his_ house, to the large fortress on the hill, standing guard over the town.

∞ ∞ ∞

"Something smells terrific!" Harriett climbed the stairs from the garage. "I think I missed coming home to a waiting dinner." She smiled at Eddy.

"I can arrange that." Eddy quipped as she hurried down the hall to her office.

Passing the dining room, she glanced left to see the table set with her best china and crystal. Red roses filled an antique crystal vase, while a bottle of uncorked French Burgundy sat breathing, waiting to be admired.

Harriett stopped mid-hallway and dropped her monogrammed attaché. "What's the occasion? The table looks spectacular."

Sheepishly, Eddy approached her from behind. "I have an idea, but I'm not sure you'll approve."

"So, you intend to bribe me with food, wine, and roses? Thinking your..._proposal_ might be more palatable that way?" Her words were harsh, but her tone was gentle.

"We'll see."

Eddy jumped at the sound of the kitchen timer that signaled _dinner is ready_.

∞ ∞ ∞

Harriett poured more wine as Eddy relayed the contents of Olive's note and chest.

"So, you see..." he hesitated. "I neither need nor want the money. But your sisters insist that I keep it."

"How much again?"

"One hundred twenty thousand dollars, and change." Eddy scratched his head nervously. "What do you think? Can you oversee investing it and creating a scholarship endowment in Olive's name?"

Tears formed in Harriett's eyes. "You are willing to give up a small fortune, just to honor my mother?"

Eddy reached for her. Taking her hands in his, he locked eyes with his estranged wife. "I don't need the money. Neither do you." He shook his head. "And God knows Shelby will blaze her own trails." He cleared his throat. "Education was Olive's deepest desire. I think she'll smile down on us knowing that she enabled deserving women the opportunity to study on her nickel."

"Let me reiterate. This is to be established for only female recipients who enroll to study either literature or finance. Either undergrad or graduate. They must be financially deserving, meaning in need. And their permanent residence must be in Pennsylvania." She stopped to gather her thoughts. "This is offered exclusively at Madison University. Did I get it all?"

"That about sums it up. And I want it to be called 'The Olive Westchester Bailey and Frederick Westchester Scholarship in Finance or Literature.' Fred gave her the initial money to pursue her own education. Including his name and his love of books will make her so happy." Eddy scratched his forehead. "I know she wanted to study medicine, but Madison doesn't offer that degree, so...since she worked in finance on her father's farm, I picked finance alongside literature."

Harriett pushed a gush of air through her parted lips. "Nothing made Mother happy in life. Nothing! But I truly think this scholarship will." She squeezed his hand. "Very generous, Eddy. You've changed."

He withdrew his arm. His eyes turned dark with sadness. "You have no idea how much I've changed," he mumbled as he stood to clear the table.

47

RECONCILIATION

LATE AUGUST 1980

*H*arriett made quick work of establishing the endowment. The administrators of Madison University were more than ecstatic to add a well-funded scholarship to their coffers. Harriett's clever investing ensured a minimum five percent annual return to fund tuition, room, and board for a total of four students every year.

Within the month, guidelines were established, monies were invested, and applications were accepted and reviewed. By early autumn, one worthy woman would receive the inaugural Olive Westchester Bailey and Frederick Westchester Scholarship in Finance or Literature. A full ride, the duration of four years, provided they maintain a suitable QPA, whose range was disputed by Madison University, Dr. Kepler, and Eddy Kepler. Though Harriett wanted higher, and Madison wanted lower, after deliberation, it was decided to use Eddy's number—if the recipient maintained a 3.5 quality point average on a four-point scale, the scholarship money continued.

Harriett tapped the edge of her paperwork on her desktop, evening the edges, before dialing the phone. "Eddy," she said into the receiver, "are you available to review the scholarship finalists tonight?"

"Sure. But you're more qualified to choose than me."

"I've already narrowed it down to five girls." Her tone of voice reflected her smile. "This is your money, Eddy. You should have the final say."

"If you insist. Let's meet at the club."

"See you at 6:30," she said as she hung up the phone.

∞ ∞ ∞

The valet held the door. "Good evening, Dr. Kepler. Mr. Kepler is already here, waiting in the dining room."

Harriett searched the room to find Eddy sitting in the corner, waving his arm in the air. "Harriett! Over here."

Several club members interrupted her advance with a belated, "Dr. Kepler, so sorry to hear of your mother's passing." Or, "The club won't be the same without Olive's visits." Or, "Sorry for your loss. She was one spunky lady." Or, "We're going to miss that sassy mother of yours. My condolences."

Harriett smiled at the impact Olive had on *her* club. *Somehow, that woman managed to infiltrate every aspect of my life! Down to my subject of study.*

She stopped, mid-stride and mid-thought, to gaze at her surroundings with the eyes of a stranger. The room exhibited a haughty air, almost pretentious, with its dark-paneled woodwork, large windows, and heavy draperies. Harriett turned aimlessly, spinning in circles among the white-clothed tables, gawking without recognition. Time stood still.

Eddy watched anxiously as conversations ceased and other diners began to stare at her. After several moments, he strode to her side.

"Harriett." He took her elbow. "Come, dear, our table is there," he said, pointing to his right.

"Huh? Oh." She shook her head to clear her ringing ears, then, as if in a trance, she turned to face her husband. "Eddy, have I been wrong? All these years? Is it possible?" A furrowed brow added wrinkles and years to her face.

"Wrong about what?" Eddy guided her gently to the table, held her chair, then waved to their waiter. "Timmy, Dr. Kepler needs a drink."

"The usual?"

Eddy nodded his head as Harriett stared ahead, blankly.

Harriett leaned across the table to ask again, this time with the urgency of a deadline. "Eddy, am I wrong? Please tell me!"

Eddy shifted. "Darling, I don't know what you're talking about." The determination of her voice frightened him.

"Mother? You? Our life…" She bit her lip as one tear slid over her tiny cheek. "Oh my God!" replaced the usual "Geez, Louise." For the second time in her life, she swore. "This is Mother's deathbed prediction!"

Eddy handed her his handkerchief to wipe her freely flowing tears.

"Eddy! Am I too late? Please say I've not waited too long!" She grasped her thick brown hair with both hands, then, burying her face, she wept openly. The grief and pain of the past 50 years flooded her memory. Her father's untimely accident, Eddy's lies, and her mother's death compounded on one another. Her sobs echoed throughout the room. No conversations buffered the noise. Forty eyes peered in her direction.

Eddy stood to shield her from curious onlookers. "Harriett, dear. Allow me to usher you to the ladies' room." His still-muscular body engulfed her so that she was no longer distinguishable from his form.

As they walked toward the lobby, Harriett embraced him. "Oh Eddy, I don't want to regret my life," she said as she buried her head into his chest.

Concern flashed over Eddy's face. "What do you have to regret, darling? You have accomplished so much. Enough for *three* successful professionals." Eddy tipped her chin to study her face.

As their eyes met, Harriett stood on tip toes and kissed his mouth. A deep, passionate kiss, filled with 20 years of emotions. Love, hate, loathing, lust, desire, and despair were represented in one kiss. One kiss followed another. Fearful of causing a scene, Eddy backed away.

Gently, he caressed her face. "That was nice. Intense, but nice." He tilted his head to the side. "Why so distraught? Tell me what is bothering you."

"Oh, Eddy." She clasped his hands. "I want you to come home. Shelby was right all those years ago. She had the guts to call it outright—I am lonely!" Her eyes pleaded with his. "I want my husband back! Can you forgive me enough to try again?"

Eddy's knees buckled. He wobbled to a nearby settee and sat, as Harriett's outstretched arms continued to cling to his hands. "I've been praying every day for the past 20 years to hear those words. Of course, I'll come home." He hesitated. "But, darling, it doesn't change the past. I've done what I've done and can't undo it."

Harriett snuggled beside him. Resting her head on his shoulder, she looked into his eyes and batted her lashes. "We can't undo the past, but we can direct the future. Too many have suffered due to my stubborn, unforgiving streak." Sobbing again, she choked out, "You, Shelby, Mother, myself, Earl...poor, loving Earl." She collapsed into his arms. "Eddy, I love you. I need you. I'm so tired of being strong, always the one in charge." She paused. "A solitary figure."

Eddy kissed the top of her head. "Dry your eyes, Harriett. We have a scholarship candidate to select. Then, we have 20 years to make up for." He dabbed her eyes with his handkerchief and returned it to his pocket. Then he linked his fingers with hers. "Come, darling. Timmy is waiting with your drink."

48

THE END IS NEAR

MONDAY, OCTOBER 12, 2010

"I'll get it," yelled Shelby as she raced to get the ringing phone.

The old man sat staring without any attempt to answer.

"Walter Stuart! It's good to hear your voice." Shelby covered her mouth to muffle the sound. "How did you hear so quickly? I've only made a handful of calls," she said to the voice on the phone. "You're his trusted friend to the end... Daddy will be so happy to see you. Do you need a place to stay?"

"I'm in a hotel. You have enough to worry about." Wally cleared his throat. "How's he doing? How are you?"

"I'm fine, tired. Mom had been a handful the past couple of years. We never knew from day to day which personality we'd meet. Daddy did a fabulous job taking care of her." The tear rushed down her face. "It was hard on him, me living in California. I gave him an out, more than once, suggesting an institution or hospitalization."

"Hmm." At a loss for words, Eddy's army buddy and life-long friend hummed in response.

"Mother had qualified for nursing home care, and they

certainly could afford a luxury facility. Daddy refused, saying they had to stay together." She caught her breath. "Alzheimer's is a destructive disease. I'm not sure how Daddy managed it every day." Shelby sighed. "Geez, I'm a geriatric neurologist and Alzheimer's researcher, and even so, she was too much for me at times. The man deserves an award for patience."

Wally laughed. "Knowing Eddy, he was doing penance. Payback for past indiscretions."

"I can vouch that once reunited, they worshiped each other. Spent every waking hour together, traveling, golfing, and swimming. Enjoying the good life." Shelby chuckled as she reminisced. "That woman was diving late into her 60s." Her voice dropped. "Before she got sick."

Shelby recollected hearing the diagnosis, 10 years earlier. Harriett began forgetting names, then dates. As the disease progressed, Shelby elected to shift her neurological research from Parkinson's to Alzheimer's, in hopes of saving someone else's mother if she couldn't save her own. Eddy eventually hired a live-in nurse when Harriett's mood swings and incontinence became overwhelming. *Caring for a loved one exerted tremendous stress on the family*, thought Shelby. With Alzheimer's, unfortunately, the caregiver often died before the patient.

Of course, not in this case.

"So, what is Eddy's condition?"

"I'm not sure. He is just staring into space. Not crying, just looking at nothing. I think I need to have an unofficial... psych session tonight. I know he is toting tons of baggage." She peeked around the door to ensure her conversation was private.

"Your father was always a bit of a drama king."

"I have never pried, but I can read the signs. I may be a doctor, but I'm not a psychiatrist or his therapist...although I have suggested many times that he see one of my colleagues. He needs to unload. Nevertheless, I'm his daughter and I love him. So tonight, I think I must change roles from daughter to doctor. Especially considering the circumstances."

"Good luck, honey. He does not share readily. God, I am a lifelong witness to that behavior. Good luck tonight…" Before hanging up, Wally blurted out, "Shelby, before I forget, what time is the funeral service, and which church?"

Shelby dragged a stool over to the phone to sit. "I managed to get everything done today after she was pronounced." She chortled. "Even in death, she remains in control by preplanning. The viewing is Wednesday at Sinclair Memorial Funeral Home in Madison. Only two to four in the afternoon, then six to nine that evening."

"I'll attend both. What about the service?"

Suddenly weary, Shelby's fingers raked her wavy blonde hair. "Service is at Campbellsville Presbyterian, on Thursday morning at ten. Be early to get a seat. We're expecting a full congregation, considering everyone's social circles. Counting my colleagues, Richard's partners, her students, past associates at Dugan and Co., clients, club members, and family, we shall have several hundred in attendance."

"Will do. Shelby, do you need me to stop over this evening?"

"No, but thank you. We'll be fine. I need to talk with him tonight. If I'm not successful, he'll be a zombie the rest of the week."

"Call me if anything comes up. Promise me!"

"Thanks. Love you too." Shelby smiled, then hesitated before adding, "Wally…come by tomorrow night. I expect we'll still be talking, but he may need a break from me, and there's some things you need to hear. Goodnight, and thanks."

"Goodnight, Shelby...Duck. May I still call you that?" asked her father's long-time friend.

"Of course. I'd be hurt if you didn't. You've called me that since I was six years old."

Shelby hung up the phone and went into the office. She sat on the ottoman in front of her father and put her hand over his. Not recognizing her touch, Eddy continued to stare ahead. Thin gray hair, twisted into a curl, hung in his eyes, reminiscent of his once wavy locks. Clothes dropped off his sagging shoulders. No muscles held them upright. Shelby squeezed. Eddy finally looked toward his daughter. His eyes showed signs of welling tears, but no liquid fell.

"Daddy, we need to talk. You need to talk." She lovingly squeezed his hands again, hoping to evoke another response. "I hate to do this, but Richard and I are moving in two weeks. I need to get some things out in the open, face-to-face. Do you want a sedative first?"

Eddy looked at his daughter and sighed. "What about? Why do I need a sedative?"

"I want to talk about your past."

Eddy scowled. "It's no one's business but mine. It almost destroyed my life. Earl and Wally knew the story. That's two too many!"

"I truly am sorry. We need to talk about this, and unfortunately, it needs to be done tonight and tomorrow. Before the funeral and before I'm on a plane for Europe. I wish we had more time, but we don't."

The wrinkles around Eddy's eyes drooped. Dark lines from sinking jowls disguised his former square jaw.

"I know we are both tired, so the sooner you start, the sooner we sleep," commanded Shelby. Eddy looked at his daughter. He knew the look all too well. Like her mother, she was not going to budge until she got what she wanted. After deliberation, he capitulated.

"I suppose I should tell you now that she is gone. I don't know where to start."

"Just start anywhere. We can weave the story together if we need. The important thing is for you to talk about it. You need to purge your skeletons. Otherwise, you shall never find peace."

"Can I have a drink?"

"Your choice, drink or sedative," prescribed his daughter, the second family member to own the title of Dr. Kepler.

"Drink! Make it a double. This is a long story."

"Start talking," said Shelby as she poured two bourbons: doubles, on the rocks.

Eddy sighed. "We were only married a month before I was drafted and left your mother in October of 1950. I shipped out to Trieste, Italy in January of 1951. One warm evening, Wally and I went to the Piazza. There she stood, with long black hair, and emerald eyes, the most beautiful creature I'd ever seen. Her name was Rosa Romano…"

∞ ∞ ∞

Eddy rambled nonstop for nearly an hour, recanting past pleasures and sins. His never-wavering eyes locked onto the large carved desk, Harriett's desk, as if her ghost was standing listening to his confession.

The hand on his shoulder startled Eddy back to reality. His fingers ran through his thinning gray hair before reaching for the crystal tumbler. He sipped the diluted bourbon. The term "on-ice" no longer applied.

"Dad," Shelby repeated. "Dad, are you listening? I said it's okay. I already know the story of Rosa and Joey."

Eddy's sweaty palms tingled. "How could you possibly know? I'm only telling you now." He paused for several moments. "Is she alive?"

Shelby opened her briefcase and held an envelope stamped "airmail" with an Italian return address high above her head. "This is from Joey."

Eddy's eyes grew wide and dark. The blood drained from his face. He swooned, then, slumping back into his chair, he fainted.

"Daddy—Daddy!" Shelby reached for the smelling salts, which were preemptively placed in her pocket. Waving the bottle under his nose, she continued, "Daddy, time for bed. I think we've had enough for one night."

As the old man revived, Shelby slipped her arm around his waist. "Come on. Up we go. Wally's in town. I'll relate my part of the story tomorrow night after the three of us have dinner."

"Wally?" mumbled Eddy. "Dependable friend to the end."

49

THE REVEAL

TUESDAY, OCTOBER 13, 2010

"Dad, are you awake?" called Shelby as she entered the kitchen carrying a grocery bag from Lupinetti's.

"Yes, Duck, I got up about 30 minutes ago. Want a cup of coffee?" He replaced the K-pod and depressed the "brew" button, not waiting for her answer.

"Sure. I picked up our lunch. Are you ready to eat?"

Shelby unpacked the boxed salads from Lupinetti's Bistro and Deli. The refrigerator was already full of culinary creations donated by neighbors; however, most were delicious-looking, high-calorie selections. Shelby, naturally thin like her mother, held her weight easily. She was tall like her father and grandmother and cut a fashion model silhouette. However, at 55, she chose her food carefully.

"How did you sleep?" she asked, her voice serious and cautious.

"Not well at first. I'm still bothered that you knew about Rosa and never said anything."

"That bothers you? You chose not to talk about it. I was

trying to respect your privacy," answered the doctor, not the daughter.

"You weren't upset? She is the reason you grew up minus a father."

"I had a father growing up. The best father in the world." Shelby kissed Eddy on the cheek.

Eddy heaved an exasperated sigh. "Rosa was the wedge that split your mother and me. My greatest mistake—"

"My job, as a daughter, is to accept and love you, including *all* your faults. And to hear your side of the story, to listen, and help you heal. That's why I asked you to talk about it, why I've done what I've done." She waved *The Campbellsville Herald* in the air. "Let's talk about Rosa later. I picked up a couple of newspapers. I have Mom's obituary."

Father and daughter ate their salad and drank tall glasses of iced water while Shelby flipped to the obits.

> Our distinguished Dr. Harriett Bailey Kepler, Ph.D., went to her Savior Monday, October 12, 2010. Dr. Kepler, who died suddenly from a stroke, suffered severe memory loss over the last years of her life due to Alzheimer's disease. She had an illustrious 25-year career as the first female Vice President and CFO at Dugan & Co. She followed her corporate life with an eminent teaching career. Dr. Kepler was a tenured associate professor at Madison University, where she taught business and finance classes for over 30 years. The diminutive Grand Dame of Campbellsville was well-known for her endless energy, infinite enthusiasm, superior intelligence, athletic prowess, and delicious baking skills.
>
> Dr. Kepler was admired by all. She was a long-time member of the Campbellsville Presbyterian Church,

Chamber of Commerce, Daughters of the American Revolution, Madison Country Club, and Rotary Club. She is survived by her beloved husband Edgar Gregor Kepler, Jr., and daughter Dr. Shelby Abigail Kepler Patrick, son-in-law Richard Anthony Patrick, grandson Stephen Patrick, granddaughter Jennifer Patrick, sister Alice Bailey Jenson, brother Albert Bailey, brothers-in-law Theodore Jenson, Roy Kepler, and George Kepler, and many nieces and nephews.

Dr. Kepler was preceded in death by her loving father Tobias Bailey, mother Olive Westchester Bailey, mother-in-law Abigail Kepler, father-in-law Edgar Kepler Sr., sisters Esther Bailey Cline and June Bailey Ralston, brothers-in-law Earl Kepler, William Kepler, and sister-in-law Laurena Williams Bailey.

She was the granddaughter of the late Henderson and Polly Sinclair Westchester, whose area roots grow long, strong, and deep, tying her renowned maternal ancestors to Colin Westchester and her husband's ancestor Gregor Campbell, both original founders of Campbellsville.
Dr. Harriett Bailey Kepler was 80 years old.

Family shall receive visitors at Sinclair Memorial Funeral Home on Wednesday, October 13 from 2:00 to 4:00 p.m. and again from 6:00 to 9:00 p.m. Funeral services, including a DAR Celebration of Life is on Thursday, October 14, at the Campbellsville Presbyterian Church, ten o'clock in the morning. Husband and daughter invite friends and family to join them at Madison Country Club, for a luncheon celebration of

Dr. Kepler's remarkable life, immediately following burial in the family cemetery.

Shelby read the obituary to her father as he finished eating his lunch. "What do you think, Dad? Did I miss anything?"

"Nicely done, Duck. You are your mother's daughter." His bloodshot eyes lacked enthusiasm.

"Thanks, but not quite. I want to talk about Mom, this afternoon," she said, with a grin.

"Must we? Really? I'd rather talk about how you know about Rosa!" demanded Eddy. "And how you possess a letter from Joey! And Shelby, I must read that letter, I—"

"All in time, we'll do that tonight. After Wally arrives."

"Wally's here?"

Shelby smiled, understanding Eddy's distraction the previous evening. "He heard yesterday, shortly after her death. Arrived last night and stayed at a Madison hotel. I've invited him to join us for dinner and to stay the night."

"What about Richard and the kids?" Eddy scratched the back of his neck before resting his hand over his shoulders.

"Jenni and Steve are both coming in later today. They are staying at the hotel in Richard's suite."

"Wally! Damn. He's true blue!" Eddy shook his head. His lips turned up at the corners as his mind drifted to the past. "Yes, Duck. I would like him here tonight."

∞ ∞ ∞

At six that evening, Eddy answered the knock at the door.

"Wally, you son-of-a-bitch! Thanks for coming." The men embraced before walking into the familiar Kepler inner sanctum.

"We have tuna casserole, lasagna, cold cuts, mac and

cheese, spiral cut ham, potato salad, apple pie, chocolate cake, raisin cookies, three bottles of wine, a case of beer, bagels and cream cheese, and a broccoli quiche. Anything sound good?" Shelby shouted to the men who were already making themselves comfortable in the office with whiskies. "Whenever you decide, I'll make up trays so we can be more comfortable eating in the office."

"Ham and potato salad," chose Eddy over the growl of his stomach.

"Sounds good," laughed Wally. "Eddy's stomach agrees too."

Shelby pulled wooden TV trays out of the office closet and placed one in front of each of them. "Get comfortable. Dad, be sure you have plenty of whiskey ready. I guarantee this is going to be a long night."

The men looked at each other. "What can she possibly tell us?" asked Eddy as Shelby left to get the food.

"How the hell do I know?" conceded Wally. "I'm almost afraid!"

"She said she knows! I am terrified," professed Eddy.

Shelby returned with three plates of food. As a physician, she calmly consulted her patients. As a daughter, the pending conversation was a bit unsettling. She understood the importance of a face-to-face encounter, yet she felt angst. She inhaled several times to steady her nerves, then after setting a plate in front of each participant and a tray of cookies on the desk, she said, "Shall we begin?"

"You know, Duck, I am afraid to hear what you have to say," said Eddy as he wrung his hands together.

"I want you both to remember one thing: I am both a daughter and a doctor. As a doctor, I collect information, analyze, and process. As a daughter, I listen, accept, forgive (if necessary), and move on. I make no judgment. I love you both."

"Good God, Duck, this sounds like I am on trial for my life," stated an anxious Eddy.

"Not your life, perhaps your soul." She smiled lovingly at her father. "You may finally find self-forgiveness and peace of mind. God willing."

"Let's get on with it. I can't stand this waiting. I'll not be able to eat if you don't start talking," concluded a fearful Eddy. "Begin already!"

"Do you remember a few years ago—I think it was in 2008—when I was trying to prove the ancestry of an obscure patriot for DAR? I thought it might be helpful if I took a DNA test, so I did. I was able to justify the ancestor to earn another patriot pin, but the test had a second outcome." She paused, ensuring both men's attention. "This June, I got a call from a man living in Switzerland. He said that he'd taken the same test, and our DNA matched. Sibling DNA, having at least one common parent. We discussed age, basic history, and shared pictures via the internet. Dad, we could be twins. His name is Joey Novak."

Eddy's voice wavered as his body swayed. Wally reached to stabilize him. "My little Joey?"

"Yes, Dad. Joey," confirmed Shelby. "Joseph Earl Novak."

Eddy stopped breathing. Fearing a repeat of the previous night, Shelby was quick again with the smelling salts. Reviving her father, she reclined him slightly, propped him with pillows, and raised his legs on the ottoman. "Not again!" she groaned.

They allowed Eddy several minutes of silence. "Feel well enough to go on?" Shelby questioned.

"Yes," Eddy agreed weakly.

"I'm not sure I'm ready," braved Wally.

"Okay, take a few minutes. Let this sink in. I had contact with Joey. But, ready yourselves...there is more, and some of it may be disturbing."

The men drained their glasses. Wally poured more.

"Okay. Let's go," yielded Eddy.

Shelby walked to the desk and sat in her mother's chair. "Well, do you remember when Richard and I traveled to Italy in July?"

"Just this summer. Yes." Eddy's head jerked in rapid succession. "I thought Richard had some international business."

"He did. We went to investigate his firm's potential business in Switzerland, which is prompting our move next week. While we were there, we met Joey." She paused. "We both look so much like you. Here, I have a picture."

Shelby offered Eddy a picture of Joey and her standing together in front of the Trevi Fountain. Both exact replicas of Eddy. A very handsome pair.

Eddy fondly ran his fingers over the picture. "My tiny little Joey," he said softly. "I'm so sorry I left you. I love you very much." Looking at Shelby, Eddy braved the question. "What about Rosa?"

"Why don't I tell you the entire story? It will all come together. This is the story told to me by Joey."

50

ROSA'S ADVENTURE

FEBRUARY 1952

She fussed, straightening the tiny Alpine cabin in preparation for her husband's return.

"Joey." Rosa smiled at her baby boy. "Daddy is coming home today." The girl swooned, imagining their greeting after a week apart. The excited tone of her voice made the baby bounce on the bed.

"You sweet little man! You look just like him." The baby grunted and reached for his mother. Picking him up, Rosa took stock of supplies. "Good thing he's coming, too. We are low on just about everything. Why don't we make a stew from this salted beef bone and some wild onions?"

She nibbled the baby's neck. She was rewarded with a hug from tiny but strong hands. Rosa had no conversation other than with the baby, except for weekends. During the week, Eddy traveled to Godovic for work as a butcher's apprentice. The commute, too far and time-consuming to make on a daily basis, required the young couple to live apart on weekdays. The Sunday train, making stops in Godovic and other towns west of Ljubljana, carted him away for the week so that he may reverse course and return to Rosa every Friday night.

"If I'm going to cook, I need to stoke this fire," she said, tickling Joey. Walking over to the fireplace, she chose two appropriate cooking logs. Alarmed to realize she had little wood, she staved off panic.

"Eddy will be home tonight. It will be okay." Rosa sat the baby back on the bed.

He immediately began to play with a ragged cloth toy. His attention remained captured until it was his turn to eat; he let his mother know he was hungry by his screams. Rosa picked him up and bared her breast to let him feed. She hummed softly to the child, both mother and son content. Rosa's milk production was low due to malnutrition. At the same time, Joey was growing rapidly and required much more than she provided. Sadly, Mama and baby both went to bed hungry on most nights.

"Here, little man, try to eat some of Mama's noodles." She offered mashed pasta on a spoon. Joey gladly accepted extra food. Full belly, the baby compliantly fell asleep. Rosa continued her meal preparation for Eddy.

He usually arrived around 11 in the evening on Friday night, having to finish work, close the shop, take the train, and then walk 45 minutes to the cabin. Although meager, the aroma of the beef and onion stew was inviting; as inviting as the thoughts of having Eddy's strong arms around her waist. Rosa set the table and then lay down on the bed with Joey to wait for Eddy's arrival.

She awoke with a start to find she was alone. Without a timepiece, it was hard to know the exact time; however, Rosa knew it was close to midnight.

"Maybe Papa missed his train," she whispered to Joey. "We'll see him in the morning."

Eating only a spoonful of their dinner, she tightly covered

the pot. Outside the cabin door, she arranged it under a pile of rocks and packed it in the snow. Having so few provisions, the stew would be reheated for tomorrow's supper. Shivering, Rosa crawled under the quilt, snuggled Joey, and dreamt all night of her soldier.

Early morning light shone through the flour sacks on the window. Rosa donned her threadbare coat, wrapped herself with her shawl, and went searching for firewood. Joey would sleep for another hour before demanding his breakfast. Incapable of chopping trees—Eddy's job—Rosa gathered shrubs and twigs. Continued foraging, forcing her to go farther and farther from the cabin to scour; she filled a basket and headed back, trying to beat Joey's awakening.

She was met with the howl of a hungry, frightened baby. "There, there, Joey dear. Mama is here," Rosa said, lifting the child into her arms to hug him tightly.

Somewhat satisfied that he was no longer alone, Joey changed his demand to one of food. Joey suckled her exposed breast earnestly.

"Better, little guy? Feeling better?"

He ignored his mother. Feeding was the only thing on his mind this morning. *It's amazing how quickly a baby returns to sleep with a full belly*, she thought. As he slept, Rosa went about cleaning the cottage and taking stock. She had enough wood for probably four days. She was low on flour, sugar, bacon fat, and rice. Four jars of jelly remained in the pantry, along with an additional salted bone. Two potatoes, one apple, two carrots, three tea bags, one cup of ground coffee, and one bottle of cow's milk completed her food inventory. Checking her coin purse, she possessed a total of four US pennies, one US dime, and one Italian ten lira coin.

Eddy desperately needed to resupply her stocks. As the day lapsed, Rosa carried Joey, prancing anxiously around the cottage. "Let's sing songs," she suggested. The boy was open to all suggestions if Mama was involved. Rosa tried singing every song she knew. Soon, Joey was once again fast asleep.

She put him down and picked up her knitting as she tried to take her mind off Eddy. She needed a new pair of socks; this was a good time to make them.

Without a phone, it was impossible to relay a message. The nearest telegraph line was a 45-minute walk to the train station in Predmeja. That was also the nearest place to secure transport. Walking was difficult in the spring and summer, but during the cold winter with snow, it was laborious; being a woman toting a baby rendered it nearly impossible.

That night, she prayed. "Dear Jesus in heaven, please keep Eddy safe. Please bring him back to me. Watch over us, keeping Joey and me in your tender care. Protect Nonna and Nonno. I pray in the name of God the Father, God the Son, and God the Holy Spirit, Amen."

She needed to keep her strength up for Joey's sake. Rosa heated some of the beef stew and ate supper. There was enough left for tomorrow. After that, she would be down to the last of her provisions. Holding the baby tightly to her chest, she wept, rest eluding her. Shortly before dawn, exhausted, she surrendered to sleep.

Sunday morning, Rosa lit a candle and said all the prayers she could remember from Mass. She knew Eddy would not venture home today. Sunday's journey to Godovic required him to start out around one in the afternoon. Arriving at 10:00 a.m. and leaving at 1:00 p.m. was senseless. Wrapping Joey tightly in the bed blanket, Rosa tied him in the sled and went out in search of kindling. She took along the ax just in case she found a sapling small enough for her to cut.

"Come on, big boy," she encouraged Joey. He was not yet walking, but he was old enough to thoroughly enjoy a sled ride. Rosa sang as they trekked through the woods. Her choice of a different direction yielded a sled full of kindling and a few small branches.

"We can stay warm this week," she divulged to Joey. He appraised their situation by clapping his hands with a giggle.

The weekend and disappointment both dissipated, Rosa and Joey returned to their normal weekly routine. She rationed her foodstuffs, saving enough to make dinner for Eddy on Friday night. He would bring items to restock. Trying to disguise her hunger, Rosa chose physical activity to suppress belly grumbles. Joey ate plenty between his mother's milk and the bottle of cow's milk. Rosa cooked a potato and the apple for herself, sharing them with Joey as a nutritional supplement.

After a long, hungry week, Friday finally arrived. Elated, Rosa danced around the cottage all day, singing as she danced, "Papa's on his way. Yeah, Yeah! Papa's on his way!"

Midday, Joey looked at his mother, gurgled, and mouthed something like, "Papa" or "Paaa."

"Joey, you said your first word!" She kissed the baby all over, who giggled, loving the added attention.

"Wait until your papa arrives tonight and hears you call him by name. He's going to be so excited. What a smart little boy you are."

Joey continued to giggle. Using the last of her limited supplies, Rosa made a pot of broth. When Eddy arrived, he would have bits and pieces of meat from the butcher and vegetables to make a proper soup. She would add them later. She spent the afternoon knitting her new socks. With holes in the heel and toes, her old socks were no more than rags. She looked at her shoes, with their gaping separation between the soles and sides. Rosa made a mental note for Eddy to have them repaired in Godovic.

"When we save enough money, your daddy and I will buy a little house, and the three of us can live happily ever after—

with real shoes." Rosa smiled. "Where would you like to live? Italy, Yugoslavia, Switzerland, Germany, France? We can live anywhere we want, as long as we are a family!"

The baby cooed.

Evening approached, with no sign of Eddy. The pit of Rosa's stomach churned as she washed and dressed Joey for bed.

"Little man, something terrible may have happened to Papa," she admitted, talking aloud to the boy.

"Paaa," said Joey smiling.

"Oh yes, my sweet darling. Papa." Rosa burst into tears with the realization that she and Joey were on their own for yet another week. Her heart was heavy with the decision of whether to go for help or wait another day. She peeked out the window.

No snow, she thought. *I need to leave before the path becomes impassable.*

She tucked Joey into bed, then began the task of packing. One rucksack held all her worldly possessions.

"Where are my pearls?" she asked the sleeping child. "I need to trade them for our train tickets."

Low spirits sunk lower as she remembered. She wore them on Eddy's last weekend home. She held her breath as she also remembered putting them in Eddy's pants pocket to prevent Joey from reaching for them.

"Oh no. Jesus save us," she whimpered. "We have no money, and I have nothing to use as barter." She cuddled close to her son. "Baby boy, I will find a way. I will find a way."

She closed her eyes and fell asleep. The morning was cold and windy but without snow. She layered her clothing on her body. Most of her dresses were threadbare, but en masse, they offered some protection. She did the same with Joey, who fussed. He was used to having his limbs free. Then, she wrapped him in the bed blanket, tied him to the sled in front of the rucksack, and completely covered him with the checked tablecloth.

Glad to have new socks, she layered her old socks, new socks, and split shoes, then wrapped each foot tightly in one of the flour bag curtains from the kitchen window.

Through the bare window she scanned the icy scenery. The hillside was beautiful, even in the snow. It was the special home that she and Eddy shared. She loved it here, but they would die if she stayed.

"I must leave for my son!" she said aloud for encouragement.

Taking one last look at the blue sky dotted with white clouds and the mountains beyond, she threw her shawl over her head and shoulders. With a sigh, she lifted the strap to the sled and began pulling.

Out in the cold, Joey no longer fussed. He was quite happy to be bundled and warm. Rosa checked on him every 10 minutes. She plowed on, stopping once in a grove of trees to feed Joey. Rosa finally arrived at Predmeja three hours after their journey started. Now cold, hungry, and fussy, Joey demanded the attention of his mother. Rosa was exhausted and near frozen. Her feet were numb. She hobbled up the wooden step and across the train platform.

She struggled with the handle. After throwing all her body weight into her task, she pushed open the station entry door. The small, dark train station consisted of two long benches placed back-to-back. The tile floor was surprisingly warm due to the large stove in the corner. The walls were dirty gray plaster in need of a fresh coat of paint. It smelled of wet leather and fur. One lightbulb hung overhead. The station master's wooden desk with a locked drawer was the only space in which to do business. A time schedule hung on the wall behind the desk.

Three trains per day, she thought. This is certainly a secondary stop. She shuffled over to the Kachelofen—masonry stove—and sat down, as she tried to thaw her hands and feet by unwrapping each layer to allow them to dry.

The station master, watching with curiosity, issued no warning.

Thirty minutes after her arrival, she mustered the energy to speak. "How much for a ticket to Santa Croce for me and my baby?"

"The train to Santa Croce already left for the day," said the station master. "One ticket costs 75 lire," was added by the monotone tenor.

Gasping, Rosa opened her coin purse. "Is this enough?"

"I'm afraid not." His tenor voice rose an octave.

"Sir, I have no money. Is there a way for me to earn transport?" she asked. Fearing he may request sexual favors, she tightened her shawl around her shoulders.

"You are welcome to sit in that far corner and beg until you have enough for fare," he answered. "You may remain inside if the station is open for business. However, each night, you must leave the building." He frowned, knowing the night wind would end them both. "I am sorry. There is a small shack behind the station that will provide some shelter during the night. Feel free to huddle there."

Rosa burst into tears. She staggered to her feet. "Oh, thank you, sir," she said as she kissed his hand. "You are most generous."

Joey interrupted the awkward moment by letting both adults know that he was hungry.

"Forgive me, my son is hungry, I need to nurse," she said as she turned away. She encouraged Joey to suckle but her breasts produced little milk.

The station master noticed that the nursing finished sooner than the baby's need for food. Rosa took out a jar of jelly, ate a spoonful, and then fed some to Joey. The sugar satisfied his need for energy. Rosa hoped he would sleep soon.

"Are there any trains coming through today?" asked Rosa, wondering how long she would be destined to beg.

"One more train today, signora, then I close up to go home."

All pride aside, Rosa Romano, once the spoiled, prima donna daughter of a wealthy Trieste magistrate, sat in the station corner and begged for money. The world of being Miss Untouchable and wearing her 6 mm matching strand of pearls was long forgotten. She would do whatever was needed to keep her son safe.

∞ ∞ ∞

"Stop. Oh God, stop!" Eddy shouted. "I can't bear to hear this. My God, what did I do to them?"

Tears filled Shelby's eyes. "Daddy, I'm afraid you must hear this. This exchange needs to be made face to face. And I am leaving soon, and I'll be gone at least six months." She cradled her father's head in her arms. "Oh Daddy, I wish we weren't moving, but we are. We need to talk before I go."

"I can't. I can't listen to this." Eddy doubled over. He glared at Shelby. "I thought you loved me! How can you make me bear this now, as I bury my beloved Harriett?"

Eddy clenched his teeth. In a fit of anger or despair, he flung his crystal glass across the room. It shattered as it hit Harriett's desk.

Shelby pursed her lips tightly together as she narrowed her eyes. Her demeanor changed from loving daughter to therapeutic doctor. "Dad, I'm sorry. You need to sit down and calm yourself."

Eddy hissed. "I don't understand why you are torturing

me. Why wait until this moment to tell me your awful story?"

"This story is not my doing." She whistled through her teeth as she inhaled. "When was I to tell you? I've only been home once since July, to help with her. Yes, I call weekly, but she's always underfoot. What do you think would happen if she heard any of this?" Shelby paused for effect. "You remember what happened after Uncle Earl died, don't you?" Her voice broke. "His death didn't go over very well. For a woman with a failing memory, her reaction was rather violent to that news."

Eddy moaned, his fingers grasping his head. "I can't. No! Stop."

"You can do this, buddy," said Wally, embracing his old comrade. "You wanted to know about Rosa your entire life. Now you will. Think what a blessing that is. You don't want to die never knowing their fate, do you?"

"No! Oh God, I never wanted them to suffer."

"I'm afraid you are notorious for causing suffering to those who love you," Wally spoke again. "Look what you did to Harriett. Why is Rosa less immune to the curse of Eddy Kepler?"

Eddy clenched his fist as if to punch Wally. Shelby, ready to intercede, jumped over the broken glass. Grabbing Eddy's arm, she gripped tightly.

Before he could follow through, Eddy released his fist. Looking at Wally, he said, "I should thump you, but at 81, my whacking days are over."

"Lucky for you, I'll back down! I'm only 82. I can still whack."

The men relaxed. Eddy calmed himself and then agreed for Shelby to go on.

∞ ∞ ∞

The shed behind the station was more of a three-sided lean-to. Rosa and Joey crouched behind a one-wheeled garden cart as a windbreak. It provided some protection, but it was still very cold for an improperly dressed mother and child. The next morning, the station master appeared earlier than usual. He knew the two would be freezing outside. He let Rosa and Joey back into the station and lit the stove fire. Then he gave Rosa some milk for Joey and some stale bread for herself.

"Grazie!" Rosa gratefully accepted and hungrily ate. Although determined to save her child, she was mortified that someone would pass through who knew her and report to her father. She secretly prayed for minimal embarrassment and anonymity.

"Dear Jesus, please end this journey quickly." Those words were repeated in 15-minute intervals.

At the end of the day, she still hadn't earned enough for a ticket. The station master reluctantly ushered them back into the cold. The wind blew from the north, over the mountains, penetrating every crack and crevice. Rosa fed her son one last time, then cuddled him close to her body. She shivered with each brutal gust. *I don't remember it being this bitter last night*, she thought as she pulled her shawl around her neck and over her ears.

Sleep came in fits as she squirmed for warmth.

Past midnight, she bolted upright, as she realized the baby was no longer in her arms. She felt the floor around her. No Joey. Crawling on hands and knees, she searched. There he was, in a corner, exposed to the icy north wind. She gathered him in her arms, but the little body was cold. Lips and cheeks blue.

Frantically, she rubbed his face. "Joey, please, wake up. Please. Oh, Jesus, help us," she repeated as she blew into the infant's mouth.

Joey's scream awakened Rosa from her dream. The perceived freezing infant was snugly wrapped and secure in her arms, but clearly unhappy to be blown on and rubbed.

"Oh, baby...you are okay," she sobbed. Her tears froze as they trailed down her face. "Thank you, Jesus."

After rearranging some loose boards as additional windscreens, she propped her back against them and sat holding her baby, wide awake, waiting for first light.

Again, the generous station master arrived early, with milk for the baby. "I'm sorry miss, this is all I can spare. I have three children of my own." He frowned. "My wife and I ate the last of the moldy bread for supper. We saved the broth for the children."

"Sir, please don't apologize. You are kind." Rosa and Joey gratefully accepted the milk.

Around noon, the station master suggested he hold Joey for Rosa to visit the toilet. He handed her a sliver of soap. "I snuck this away from my wife. Here is a pail, heat some water on the stove. A bath may refresh you."

Rosa washed her body and her hair. The grime and humiliation of the past several days swirled counterclockwise down the drain. She returned with her hair piled on the top of her head, causing the station master to gasp.

"Miss, how old are you?"

Rosa blushed. "Eighteen. Well, almost."

He sighed without response.

∞ ∞ ∞

It took four days of passenger petitioning and three nights of wakeful, intolerable cold until finally, Rosa had enough five-lire coins for a ticket to Santa Croce. The ticket master contributed the last bit himself, by way of discounting the price.

The sled, donated as firewood, remained. Boarding the train, she blessed the gentle ticket master for his kindness, found a seat, and fell asleep. The train stopped six blocks from Isabella and Joseph Cortina's house—her grandparents.

Tired, cold, and hungry, Rosa carried Joey the last length of their excursion in search of safety, warmth, and food. She could barely hold herself up as she knocked on the door. Isabella opened the door and gasped as Rosa fell inwards.

"Joseph," she yelled, then she reached for Joey.

"Nonna," mouthed Rosa through parched lips. Isabella hoisted Joey onto her hip as she helped Rosa prop herself against the doorframe.

Rosa collapsed to her knees.

"Shh, little one," Isabella said to her fussing great-grandson. "Let me help your mama. Joseph! Come quickly. Rosa needs help!"

Her grandfather, although old, lifted the failing teen into his arms and carried her inside. Meanwhile, Isabella comforted Joey. She sought to nourish both by heating some milk and broth.

A change of diaper and full tummy was enough to comfort Joey. Isabella unwrapped him from his ragged layers, then rewrapped him in a cashmere blanket before cradling him in a stuffed chair.

Joseph carried Rosa to a plump, down-filled bed, unwrapped her feet, then tucked her in, completely clothed.

"She's sleeping. Still fully dressed." He looked at his wife for guidance. "Should we get her out of those rags?

"Let her sleep," said Isabella. "She can have a warm bath and change of clothes in the morning. Now, my husband, you must buy milk to feed this hungry boy!"

Isabella and Joseph welcomed their granddaughter and great-grandson again into their home. The next day, as

Isabella undressed Rosa, she asked, "Darling, what happened? Where is your young soldier?"

"Nonna, I don't know. He must be in some sort of trouble. He would never abandon us," she declared as her grandmother helped her into a warm bath.

To Isabella's dismay, her naked body was thin, barely skin over bones.

Rosa sighed. "Ahh. This feels wonderful. I had forgotten how wonderful it is to have a bath and be warm." Then she coughed.

Isabella helped her into a warm flannel nightgown, felt her forehead, and lifted the tiny girl into bed.

"Joseph, please fetch the doctor. I'm afraid the journey has made Rosa sick," she called with concern to her husband. "We better check Joey too."

After a full examination, the doctor determined both Rosa and Joey were sick due to overexposure. "Keep them warm and hydrated with plenty of broth and tea," he prescribed. "The boy should be weaned, and bottle-fed, adding cereal. His mother can no longer produce enough milk to nourish this brute."

Rosa remained in bed for a month. Isabella brought Joey to her daily for playtime, but not for feeding. Soon, Joey was rattling off several words. Along with "Papa," he added "Mama," "Bella," "Non," and "Lat." "Nonno" and "Latte" were to follow.

Rosa could wait no longer. Her strength regained, she insisted, "Nonna, I have to find Eddy. This is not like him. We have pledged our love. Please contact Mama and Papa. Surely, they will tell me if he's contacted them."

Agreeing with Rosa and sharing concern over Eddy's whereabouts, Isabella phoned her son-in-law.

"Giovanni, for god's sake, if you know the whereabouts of this young soldier, or if he has contacted you, you must tell her! They are in love. How can you be so cruel?" grilled Isabella.

Giovanni Romano made no response, just as he made no response to Eddy's letters. He shouted, "Stay out of my business, old woman!" then slammed down the phone.

It was spring before Rosa fully recovered, but her lungs were left weak and susceptible to infection. Joey grew into a handsome toddler; Rosa regained the beauty of her youth. By summertime, she was once again the envy of all her peers.

Rosa shied away from soldiers. In May, finally feeling well enough to venture out, Rosa visited the base, looking for Eddy.

"Sir," she asked the sentry at the base gate, "Do you know a soldier named Eddy Kepler?"

"Kepler, hmm, he was in prison, maybe transferred to Leavenworth?" offered an unknowing sentry. "Anyway, he's not here now."

Rosa gasped but kept trying. "What about a Walter? I don't know the last name."

"Don't know any Walter," he added, not realizing that "Wally" was short for "Walter."

Rosa, dejected, was sure Eddy would come for her, but if he was back in the USA in jail, her rescue became an impossibility.

Hoping beyond hope for Eddy to return, Rosa rejected all dating offers. By autumn, a handsome Yugoslavian businessman by the name of Anton Novak noticed her. Within a month, he fell in love.

Rosa consented to weekly Sunday afternoon strolls. Anton, fifteen years older than Rosa, counseled, "Rosa, I understand you wait for your son's father. But you must accept that he is not coming for you."

"Anton, I do have feelings for you," she admitted, "but yes, I love Joey's father."

"I know not why he would abandon a beautiful woman—he must have a very good reason. I promise to love you and little Joey. I can offer security, safety, stability, and love. Will you not consider marriage?" asked Anton Novak.

"Anton, please allow me to try one last time to find Eddy," pleaded Rosa.

"If that is what you please, then of course."

Shocked that her mother took her call, Rosa questioned, "Mother, I am desperate! Has Eddy contacted you in search of me?"

Sofia Romano lied. "He has never tried to find you," she said, denying any contact from Eddy, even though Sofia had a large stack of letters and money from him tied into a bundle with one of Rosa's silk hair ribbons.

∞ ∞ ∞

"Why, that no-good lying bitch!" blurted Eddy. "I wrote hundreds of letters and sent money every week!"

"Daddy, easy. Take a deep breath. Do you want another drink? Uncle Wally?"

Wally obediently mixed three more drinks.

"Just settle in and listen. I promise—through the pain, you will reap the reward," said Dr. Kepler.

∞ ∞ ∞

Convinced that she was abandoned, Rosa yielded later that winter, as she and Anton walked along the harbor.

"Anton, my grandfather's health is failing. I cannot leave him alone. I shall marry you on one condition—all four of us, me, my son, and my grandparents, come as a package."

"My darling Rosa—that is no condition. It is the duty of the man. Of course, your grandparents are welcome in my home. As for Joey, if you permit, I shall take him as my own son and even give him my own name."

Rosa leaned up to kiss Anton. As she did, he slipped a beautiful emerald ring on her finger.

"To match your eyes," he whispered. "Trust that I love you. And I have room for you to continue loving Eddy. As long as you love me too."

"I do not deserve such a kind man," confessed Rosa.

"My darling, you deserve much, much more." Rosa moved Eddy's faux wedding band to her right hand. She never moved it again.

Anton and Rosa married in December of 1952. The Novak family moved to Yugoslavia, Anton's native country, outside of the city of Split. The next fall, Joseph Cortina died and was buried in Anton's family plot in Split; Isabella, Rosa, and Joey remained under Anton's loving care.

∞ ∞ ∞

"Sheer madness! I searched for her, she searched for me, but we could not find each other," whispered Eddy.

"It does sound a bit like a Russian tragedy," chuckled Shelby, trying to lessen the tension in the room.

"Can't say I've ever read one, but I have to agree," replied Wally.

"Is that it?" asked Eddy. "Is she alive?"

"I don't want to prolong, but I think you need a break. Let's take a minute, go to the bathroom, mix another drink, take a short nap, whatever you want," offered Shelby. "We can start again in 20 minutes, if you want to hear more."

"Holy shit, Duck! Are you sadistic? If there is more to hear, we need to hear it," Wally answered for both men. "Now!"

A blushing Shelby agreed to finish the story without delay.

∞ ∞ ∞

Anton, Rosa, Isabella, and Joey lived happily in Split for several years—until Anton became suspicious of the direction of the communist government. The government threatened the nationalization of all industries, and Anton, a businessman in steel wire manufacturing, decided it better to relocate his business and family. In the summer of 1956, Anton, Rosa, and Joey Novak, taking Isabella Cortina and the wire mill with them, moved to Kilchberg, Switzerland, on the west banks of Lake Zurich. Anton, Rosa, and Joey lived a charmed life in the beautiful setting of an Alpine Lake. His factory, located just outside the idyllic town, prospered. Anton provided his family with a beautiful home and a wonderful water view.

Neither Joey nor Rosa wanted for anything. Anton was a generous, kind, and gentle man.

"Rosa, now that we are settled in Switzerland, my business is running successfully, and your health is improved, I would like to ask a favor of you."

"Why, Anton, anything. Whatever can I give you that you don't already possess?" replied Rosa.

"I want my own child. It is no matter whether girl or boy, but I want us to have a baby."

Rosa smiled tenderly at her husband, "I'm surprised it hasn't happened already." She giggled. "We shall try harder to make you a baby," she added, flirtingly. "It shall be a fun quest."

Rosa found herself pregnant by November. "Another summer to carry a baby through all the heat," she gently complained to Anton, who smothered his wife with kisses.

"My darling, I have a gift for you," Anton said as he handed Rosa an elongated jewelry case. "You have given me so much already; this is not necessary."

"I understand, from Nonna, that, as a teen, your father gave you a beautiful strand of matching 6mm pearls but absconded with them when he discovered you were pregnant with Joey. I know these will never replace the originals, however…"

Rosa opened the box and found a perfectly matching set of 8mm, rare, black pearls.

"Oh—" She gasped. "Wherever did you find such a beautiful rarity? This is too extravagant."

"Nothing is too extravagant for the mother of my child."

A seven-pound, 12-ounce, 20-inch baby boy was born to Rosa and Anton Novak on August 5, 1957. Rosa's hospital room was filled with flowers from Anton, his workers, their Swiss friends, family from Split, and Isabella, Rosa's only relative.

"My dearest darling," said Anton, kissing his wife. "What shall we name my perfect son?" Anton held six-year-old Joey in his arms.

"Mama, Mama, I want kisses too," asked Joey.

"Come here, my sweetie, and meet your brother," urged Rosa.

Anton placed Joey on the bed. "Do not bounce. It will make your brother sick," he warned.

Joey snuggled into his mother's arms as they held the new baby together.

"Shall we call him Anton, after his father?" Rosa smiled at her husband, hoping she pleased him with such an honor.

"Darling, you are so generous, but I can't. Look at our boys together. If I name him Anton, will Joey feel less like mine? That I cannot risk," stipulated Anton. "We shall name him Danis, after my father."

"Danis Anton Novak," sighed Rosa.

"No, Danis Edgar Novak," explained Anton. "We mix all parts of the family together to make it ours. This way, Joey and Danis shall be blood brothers for all times."

The family enjoyed the beauty of a lakeside home. Anton amply provided for his family. The boys grew under Rosa's and Isabella's supervision. In 1960, Isabella succumbed to a bout of influenza and died. Anton ensured that Isabella was transported back to Split, to be buried beside Joseph.

Joey was encouraged to excel at both academics and athletics. Having Eddy's gene pool and Anton's support, Joey played team sports of rugby, soccer, lacrosse, and polo. His father kept a boat on the lake, so Joey learned to sail and water ski. However, his best sport was downhill skiing. Switzerland was a wonderful place for a sportsman to grow up. It was a wonderful, endowed childhood.

Danis, six years behind his brother, attempted to keep stride. The parents deeply loved both boys; they were Anton's pride and joy. The boys loved each other. Rosa, although very fond and grateful of her husband's kindness and love, reserved a small place in her heart for Eddy. Anton understood and accepted Rosa's sense of hurt and abandonment.

In 1962, Rosa received word that her father died. She neither grieved nor attended the funeral. She felt nothing toward the man who disowned her for getting pregnant. She correctly blamed her father for Eddy's trouble and absence. If her father had accepted Eddy, he would not have gone AWOL, she would not have been destitute, and she and Eddy would have remained together and in love.

Shortly after her husband's death, Sofia Romano sent a package addressed to Isabella in Switzerland. Sofia, unaware of her mother's death, had kept the return address from one of Isabella's letters where she pleaded forgiveness for Rosa.

To Rosa's surprise, she opened Nonna's mail to find a large bundle of letters wrapped in a silk ribbon.

"Anton, My God, come here quickly," she called as she fell into a chair.

"What is it, darling?" he questioned, worried by Rosa's pale face.

"From Mother to Nonna. All letters from Eddy." She opened the oldest, on the top of the pile. "This was written three weeks after his disappearance."

Twenty American dollars fell out of the envelope. Her knees shook as she read aloud. Anton held her hand.

Dearest Rosa,

I have been arrested. I foolishly went skiing with Luigi and his family. I was recognized, and now I am in the stockade at the base. I love you so much. I pray you and Joey are surviving. I sent Wally to the cottage with food, firewood, and money, but you were gone?

Where did you go? How did you travel? What did you use for money? Please, dear God, please, not your body!
I am still in jail. Next week I can receive visitors. If you get this, will you visit? I will make this right. When I get out of the army, I intend to stay in Italy with you and Joey.

She opened the second envelope and continued reading.

Dear, dear, Rosa. You and Joey are my life. Please forgive my stupidity. I shall continue to search for you. Please visit at the brig next week.

With my everlasting love,
Eddy.

Rosa burst into tears. "He didn't abandon me. He tried..." She threw the collection of at least 400 letters in the air. "Look, Anton, he tried!"

Rosa fell into her husband's arms. He held her tightly, afraid that if he loosened his grip, he may lose her forever.

"Rosa," Anton asked gently, "Do you want to resume your search for Eddy? I have resources..." While he was secretly hoping she would say no, Anton was too much of a gentleman not to offer his wife her lifelong dream.

Rosa met his gaze. "No, my dearest Anton. No. I wish to live my life with you, Joey, and Danis, here in Switzerland, forever." She wiped her eyes. "Eddy was my past, that is over. You are my *now* and my future."

Anton scooped his wife into his arms and twirled her around. Hearing the commotion, the boys questioned the reason for an afternoon dance. Rosa answered them by grabbing their hands.

"We shall all dance together forever," she cried. "Mama and Daddy are so happy today. Let's have a decadent dinner, ending with cake tonight."

The next day, Rosa and Anton sat arm-in-arm while they read Eddy's letters. At times, Rosa cried, sometimes she laughed.

Stacking and counting the money, Anton figured they had enough to start a generous college fund for Joey.

"Although higher education in Switzerland is free," reminded Rosa with a smile.

"Then enough to set him up in business," Anton altered its use. "A legacy from his father."

While Rosa was glad to have the letters from her mother, she was beyond forgiveness. She neither responded to her mother nor told her of Joseph's and Isabella's death; their gravesite was eternally hidden from Sofia Cortina Romano.

51

LIKE THE PHOENIX

"Dad. These are for you," said Shelby, handing Eddy a large bulging envelope. "Open it. I think you will enjoy the contents." Eddy shook the objects from the package onto his lap. He inspected several photographs questioningly.

"That's Joey, his wife Claudia, son Anton, son Peter, and daughter Bella. It was taken five years ago," Shelby explained. "Here is Joey, Richard, and me. Don't we look alike? I think the similarity is astounding. This is Anton, he's in his nineties. Oh look, Rosa and Anton's wedding. Nonna Cortina is holding Joey—do you remember her?"

Eddy lovingly viewed each photo. "He's so handsome. She's so beautiful," was all he said.

She flipped to the next photograph. "Here is Joey and his brother Danis, 30 years ago. Here are the three of us together."

"Do you have any other pictures of Rosa?"

"Yes, but just one. Here. This was from 1976. Anton, Joey, Danis, and Rosa. Aren't they a beautiful family?" The group sat under a pergola beside a beautiful blue lake dotted with sail boats. A picnic lunch was spread on a colorful blanket. White clouds and darting birds filled the sunny sky. It was an idyllic scene, straight out of a fairy tale.

He touched her face in the photograph. "Shelby. I need to know. Is Rosa still alive?" demanded Eddy. "I can wait no longer, tell me now!"

"Dad, here's a letter to you from Rosa. It arrived just last week. Joey said he found it after our visit."

"So, she is still alive?" asked Eddy anxiously. He ripped open the envelope.

July 1975
My Dearest Eddy,

I have procrastinated for the past 13 years to write to you.

I have remarried. He is a loving, caring, decent man. We have two children—Joey, who Anton adopted as his own, and Danis, six years younger. Please do not be upset over Anton adopting Joey. He is a wonderful father and role model. You would approve. On Anton's request, our second son is named Danis Edgar, to unite the two families.

My despicable parents kept your letters from me. I know now that you did not abandon us and that you tried very hard to find us for several years. Anton and I have read and reread your letters many times. He held me as I cried and mourned the loss of our union.

We saved all the money for Joey to open his own business. Joey is finishing the last phase of his education and will graduate with the highest degree. His intention is to teach at the university level. He is a very smart lad. He looks just like you—a tall, blond, strapping example of manhood. The girls swoon around him. Just like I swooned around you.

Please know that my love for you was—is—very deep and true. Anton understands the fire of first love. With your package of letters, mother also sent mail from the USA. I have your home address. Don't be angry, my love, for not writing sooner. I have Anton and you have Harriett. I truly hope that you are happy and have children.

I only write now because I have little time left in this life. I suffer from tuberculosis. My case is advanced and not curable. Eddy dear, thank you for the beautiful gift of Joey, and for the wonder of first love. *You will always be in my heart.*

With unending devotion,
Rosa

Eddy handed the letter to Wally. "Hand me a cigarette."

"You silly old man, you quit 40 years ago!" declared Shelby, as she grabbed for the smoke.

Eddy sat speechless for several minutes. Trying to comprehend his loss, he said, "She's gone. I can't believe that Harriett's gone!"

Shelby put her arm around her father. "They are both gone. But Harriett and Rosa deeply loved you. And in their own way, they both forgave you."

She permitted her father a moment to grieve. When he dried his eyes, Eddy reached into the envelope for its last contents. He fingered the object stuck in the corner until it was free. With a tug, out popped the strand of pearls he had given Rosa. The ones that were to be used as barter for her escape. The ones that Harriett mistook for her anniversary gift. The ones he stole from Harriett to send back to Rosa.

"I'll be damned!" Eddy cupped the necklace in his hand. "Your mother loved these. This necklace was my ticket back into her house, at least the first time around. I allowed her to believe that she lost them to cover myself sending them to Rosa. God, I'm a sick bastard!"

Wally embraced his friend. "Eddy Kepler! You are a much different man today than you were in the '50s. Don't be so hard on yourself. You turned out okay."

Shelby studied their friendship. After several moments, she asked, "Dad, do you want to meet Joey? We can set it up for you if you like."

"He wants to meet me?" asked a surprised Eddy. "In person?"

"Yes, he does. Knowing your age, he is willing to fly his family to the USA for the occasion. Danis wants to come also."

"Yes. I would like that," murmured Eddy. "I'll send money, if he needs it, to buy tickets."

Shelby laughed. "Not necessary. He is quite wealthy on his own account. In fact, he saved all the money you sent. He was wondering if you wanted to use the money you sent Rosa to sponsor a Rosa Kepler Novak scholarship, at his university."

Eddy sat thinking. "Joey may do whatever Joey wishes as far as scholarships are concerned. I have already done a scholarship." Then, with a smile, Eddy changed his mind. "Wait! I'll use the money." A grin spread across his face. "What about a foundation to support single mothers? In both Rosa's and Harriett's names. It can be international, in Europe and the US. They both struggled to raise children alone. Maybe in some small way, I can make amends by helping other single mothers?"

"Look at you, Mr. Philanthropist! I'll contribute to that!" Wally slapped Eddy on the back. "In fact, I'll write a check tonight and spread the word tomorrow."

Shelby's eyes filled with tears. "Mother would love that. Of course, Richard and I shall contribute too. I'm sure Richard's firm will be generous. This is a great idea—a loving tribute to both single mothers, and to women who managed to love the infamous Eddy Kepler."

52

BETWEEN TWO DREAMS

THURSDAY, OCTOBER 14, 2010

*S*helby and Eddy sat holding hands on the wooden bench facing Tabs' and Olive's graves as they watched the throng of grievers descend the hill. A breeze from the west sent a chill over Shelby's body.

Although the stand of birch trees endured, the view from the tiny cemetery was altered by the passing of seasons. Three chimneys stood sentry over piles of bricks and assorted rubble. Rooflines swayed like the back of an old nag. Memories were all that remained of the Georgian mansion from Olive's youth. The original cottage, also in decay, joined the grand home as "past tense."

Gone were the meticulous rows of amber corn and wheat for which Westchester farm was once famous. Untended fields were overgrown by weeds and bramble. An occasional fruit tree—offspring of the once cultivated orchards—or a pine, or a maple tree stood sentry over each pasture. The distant rolling hills, blazing vibrant oranges, reds, or golds, would soon fade to gray. However, one constant of time remained: brown seed pods, swaying in the breeze, would soon be spread by the winter winds. Next year, the meadows would burst to life with yellow and white daisies in spring and golden sunflowers in summer; the pride of Polly Sinclair Westchester would once again be renewed.

"Mom was loved by so many people." Shelby's lips curled downward as she depressed a tear. "I thought I was all cried out, but…"

Eddy squeezed her hand. "Me too." He paused to catch his breath. "I really loved your mother; you know that, don't you?"

"Yes, Daddy. And she loved you. Enough to prevent her from marrying Uncle Earl." Shelby dabbed her eyes, then smiled at the cloth handkerchief. "This was Grandma Olive's. Mother pretended to hate her, but she kept all of them." Shelby coughed a laugh.

Eddy sniffled. "She requested them right after Olive's death." Reaching into his pocket, his hand brushed past an object. "What the heck?" He pulled out the strand of pearls. "God! Here they are again! I forgot that the funeral director gave these to me. I wanted your mother to wear them eternally. He refused to bury them."

He dangled the necklace above his head. The late afternoon sunlight glinted off the well-worn orbs. "Shelby, take these. They belonged to both women whom I loved dearly. You are the only other woman in that category. Except for my granddaughter." His chuckle was barely audible. "Honey, may I ask a question? Offer some advice?"

"Sure."

"Don't squander your happiness." His bloodshot eyes gazed directly into Shelby's. "Time passes too quickly!"

"Oh, Dad. I am happy." She paused. "Richard and I are happy, in our marriage, and our work." She inhaled deeply before continuing. "One thing I learned from you and Mom is that trust and truth are *essential* to a relationship. I didn't need a fancy Ph.D. or MD to learn that tidbit. Richard and I have that trust. And although we are both busy," she groaned, rolling her head. "So busy! We still manage to find balance and love." She watched as car doors opened and closed in the driveway below. "I wish we weren't moving so far away. I really do. But, Daddy, it is an adventure for us, and the kids. Jenni is more excited than Steve. A semester of touring and studying abroad!"

Eddy stood. Steadying himself with his cane, he hobbled over to the freshly dug grave. Warm, salty streaks ran down his cheeks, then dropped onto his chest. A waft of freshly manured fields drifting over the knoll reminded him of Olive's stories of Westchester Farm's glory days. Shelby hesitated, giving him a moment alone. She took his hand and rested her head on his shoulder.

"My darling daughter. I love you so much. Please learn from my mistakes. Make the most of every moment." He groaned. "I'm an idiot. I missed out on 20 years with that amazing woman. What a joke I am. I almost lost them both due to my stupid pride and arrogance."

Shelby kissed her father's cheek. "But you didn't lose her. You eventually salvaged a life with Mom, as Rosa salvaged a life with Anton." She gently brushed a gray curl of hair from his forehead. "I think everything turned out just fine."

"But I wasted so much time. Time, when we could have done things as a family. Time, when…when we were young enough to enjoy and explore." Eddy coughed. "Despite our reconciliation, I think she held back. As you said Rosa did with Anton. Just a tiny bit, but I'm sure I felt it."

Shelby flushed. "Stop it right now! First off, Mother never held out. She did everything full throttle. And that applies to your reunion." With a finger waving in his face, she scolded. "No more self-pity! You…we…made the best of the situation. We have albums filled with fabulous memories. One big unconventional, but happy family!"

Eddy's eyes, void of all twinkles, focused blankly on the mound of dirt. "Yes, but for too many years, I wasn't always an active participant, Duck." He squeezed her tightly in his arms. "My darling daughter, I concede. Nonetheless, I sadly missed too much of my fleeting life, living between two dreams."

EPILOGUE

Two weeks and two plane rides later, Shelby clicked her seat belt as the flight attendant recited pre-flight instructions. She slid her laptop into the seat pocket, smoothed her sweater, then sipped her champagne. Jenni occupied the window seat, while Richard and Stephen settled in across the aisle.

"Are you ready for a new adventure?" she asked Jenni, who was the spitting image of her Aunt Alice, and cousin Polly. Long lean shapely legs lounged comfortably in first class accommodations. Her blonde curls bounced as the plane taxied for take-off.

Jenni closed her eyes. "I wish we hadn't lived so far away from Campbellsville. I didn't have much time at Grandma Harriett's funeral to get to know everyone." Passing as older, the 20-year-old sipped her own flute of champagne. "Visiting once or twice a year, for a couple days, is not enough time."

"Oh darling, I know it's been hard living on the west coast and being so far away from the rest of the family." Shelby passed both glasses to the attendant as the plane's engines roared. "I'll make you a deal. When we return to the states, in six to eight months, I promise to take two weeks off. You and I will go back to Campbellsville for a proper holiday. I'll reintroduce you to all your cousins, try to help you make sense of your genealogy."

"And can we go back to the cemetery to study the graves? And explore that dilapidated old Westchester mansion? I bet it has tons of stories!"

Shelby's mind drifted back to days of sipping tea with Olive, and afternoons spent on the fairways of Madison Country Club. "I promise. In fact, let's make it a full month. Four weeks...even then, we'll only begin to scratch the surface of all the amazing women from Campbell County.

The End.

AUTHOR'S NOTES

- *The Adventures of Ozzie and Harriet* was a sitcom that first ran on radio in 1944 and then switched to television in 1952, running through 1966. It starred the real-life Nelson family, Ozzie, Harriet, David, and Ricky Nelson.
- "Crocodile shirt" refers to the Izod Lacoste company. An embroidered crocodile is the emblem of the shirt.
- "OS bonded eight" means Old Schenley brand, bonded and aged eight years.
- Beaune is a wine region in France known for its Burgundy wines. Côte-d'Or (literally golden slope) is a department in northeastern France of which Beaune is a sub-area.
- The inheritance of traits from one generation to the next was well documented and known throughout history. However, it wasn't until 1953, when James Watson and Francis Crick discovered the double helix of a DNA molecule, that the use of the word "gene" became common practice.
- A "one-eighty" refers to 180°angle, meaning the complete opposite.
- The average price of $0.29 per gallon of gasoline in 1954 was equivalent to paying $3.12 per gallon in 2022. Considering the Buick had a 19-gallon tank, that is the equivalent of paying just under $60 per fill-up in the 2022 market.

- One thousand dollars in 1956 (Olive's gift to Shelby) had the spending power of almost $10,000 in 2022.
- IUDs were not commonly used as birth control until the mid-1960s. However, the author takes artistic license to fit the story's timeline.
- The $100 price tag of an IUD in 1957 is the equivalent of over $1000 in 2022.
- The golf tournament between Eddy/Duane vs. Harriett/Shelby was based on the actual hole design and yardage of the Oglebay Speidel golf course in Wheeling, West Virginia.
- The 1980 inheritance of $5,000 is equivalent to about $18,000 in 2022.
- The $120,000 inherited by Eddy and designated to be used for scholarships is equivalent to about $431,300 in 2022.

ALSO BY S. LEE FISHER

A Mystery of Grace

Becoming Olive W., book 1, The Women of Campbell County
https://www.amazon.com/dp/B08Y5LC5BJ

Westchester Farm, a novella, The Women of Campbell County
https://www.amazon.com/dp/B09R67BJ4R

Under the Grapevine, book 2, The Women of Campbell County
https://www.amazon.com/dp/B0981M5QYN

Hill House Divided, book 3, The Women of Campbell County
https://www.amazon.com/dp/B09Q1KC29Y

ABOUT THE AUTHOR

Pharmacy to Fiction.
Award-winning writing as a second career.

S. Lee Fisher, aka Dr. "P.," a clinical pharmacist, was born and raised in "small town" Pennsylvania. After moving to Pittsburgh, she enjoyed a successful corporate career managing retrospective clinical programs for the PBM side of a Fortune 20 company.

Fisher began writing fiction as a means of channeling the pain and grief of her father's passing. In the process, she discovered that she enjoys the creativity of telling stories.

Now a full-time novelist, Fisher lives on Florida's gulf coast with her husband of 38 years, Ralph. When she's not writing or dodging hurricanes, she enjoys painting watercolors, ballroom dancing, and swimming.

Becoming Olive W., Book 1 in the Women of Campbell County Series, won four awards in 2021 and is awaiting outcomes on several other nominations.

www.sleefisher.com

Facebook: @SherriLeeFisherProgar
Twitter: @ProgarSherri
Amazon: @author/sleefisher

Made in the USA
Monee, IL
17 January 2023